ROBERT GRAVES
Complete Short Stories

ROBERT GRAVES 1895-

Complete
Short Stories

Edited by Lucia Graves

St. Martin's Press
New York

COMPLETE SHORT STORIES

St. Martin's Press, Scholarly and Reference Division,
175 Fifth Avenue, New York, N.Y. 10010

First published in the United States of America in 1996

Set in Ehrhardt by XL Publishing Services, Nairn
Printed and bound in England by SRP Ltd, Exeter

ISBN 0-312-16055-0

Library of Congress Cataloging-in-Publication Data

Graves, Robert, 1895–
    [Short stories]
    Complete short stories/Robert Graves: edited by Lucia Graves.
        p.   cm.
    Includes bibliographical references and index.
    ISBN 0-312-16055-0
    1. Manners and customs — Fiction.   I. Graves, Lucia.   II. Title.
PR6013.R35A6   1996
823'.912 — dc20   96–5343
                                                          CIP

Contents

Preface

Robert Graves first published his *Collected Stories* in 1964. Until then they had appeared in miscellanies which came out from time to time, bringing together his latest essays, poems, talks, reviews, stories and other loose material on his desk; or else they had only seen the light in magazines. Among the stories he left out of his 1964 collection are gems like 'Está en su Casa', 'Flesh-Coloured Net Tights' and 'Bins K to T', presumably due to limitations of space. This volume aims to bring together all the short stories written by Graves.

In the brief introduction to his *Collected Short Stories*, Graves claims that 'Pure fiction is beyond my imaginative range', and adds that most of the stories in the collection are true stories, 'though occasional names have been altered'. I can vouch for that, having myself lived through some of the experiences described in the pieces about our family life in Majorca during the 1950s – stories such as 'A Bicycle in Majorca', 'A Toast to Ava Gardner' and 'School Life in Majorca'. Indeed, most of his short stories are either strictly autobiographical, or else are based on events which he heard first-hand from friends or family. There are some exceptions, such as the three tales set in Roman times and 'The Shout' – although even in this imaginary setting Graves admits his presence: 'Richard in the story is a surrogate for myself: I was still living on the neurasthenic verge of a nightmare.'[1]

Among Graves's writings there are pieces of an autobiographical nature which cannot readily be classified as short stories. In compiling this book, the main problem has been to decide where the dividing line can be drawn between an autobiographical story and a piece of non-fiction containing elements of personal history. At all times I have been guided by Graves's own choice of material for his *Collected Short Stories*.

Historically speaking, the themes range from accounts of his Edwardian childhood and his schooldays – as in the early piece 'My New-Bug's Exam', 'The Abominable Mr Gunn' (1955), or 'My Best Christ-

---

[1] From the introduction to *Occupation: Writer*, New York: Creative Age Press, 1950; London: Cassell & Co. Ltd., 1951.

mas' (1962) – to a story set in New York in the late 1960s – 'No, Mac, It Just Wouldn't Work' – in which Graves writes about the contradictions of Western society and the development of inner-city violence.

It is interesting to relate that Graves did not always find it easy to publish his stories, as his correspondence with *The New Yorker* in the 1950s shows. 'You Win Houdini' was turned down for being 'so tough and unpleasant as to be cruel'. 'A Toast to Ava Gardner' met with all sorts of problems with the legal department, who were afraid of infringing the American libel laws and suggested endless changes of tone and wording – such as calling her Miss Gardner throughout, instead of Ava. 'The Viscountess and the Short-haired Girl' was found to have excessive 'under-cover sexual involvements'.

The stories are arranged in chronological order, and have all been previously published. The texts I have used belong to the last published version of each story in book-form, or in periodicals when they were not otherwise published. For my main source, the *Collected Short Stories*, I have used the original English edition, 1965. I have picked up some minor inconsistencies and typographical errors, some of which were corrected in the 1968 Penguin edition. I would have been inclined to leave Graves's Spanish misspellings untouched, but as the Penguin edition incorporated a number of corrections, I decided to make these consistent wherever appropriate. At the end of the volume there are publication details of each story.

Lucia Graves

Honey and Flowers

A leaf from the diary of a Carthusian in the Golden Age.

6.45 a.m. Awaked from my couch of rose-leaves by the trill of a lark and the bite of a mosquito. Shook off the flies and laved myself in a crystal fount. Water exceedingly cold. Think I prefer my weekly bath in the sulphur-spring. Donned my tunic of fair linen, and my sheepskin cloak. Placed on my crown a garland of crimson roses, flowers that cannot be worn save by those who have sojourned here two years and more, – so that I am the envy of the fags. Seized my crook and descended.

7.15 a.m. Assisted the School-band in delivering a series of hymns to our local Gods. I am a performer, a poor one, 'tis true, upon the Pan-pipes.

7.30 a.m. Headmaster arrives clad in a new scarlet robe and wearing a chaplet of mint and eglantine. He is borne on to Green in a litter supported by four stout school-monitors and preceded by the School Sergeant bearing a book of Notices.

7.35 a.m. He lectures on bee-keeping.

8.15 a.m. Breakfast off strawberries culled from the Wilderness, with honey, draughts of goat-milk and incidentally a brace of earwigs.

9.15 a.m. Slept.

12.15 p.m. Aroused from slumber by a cow who mistook me for a buttercup and began to chew my hair. Told her I was a daisy and she departed.

1.30 p.m. Lunched off Honey and Flowers. Honey ran out, so caught some in a jam-pot as it dripped from the oaks on Green. More fell on my head than in the jam-pot. One consolation is that I shall not have to anoint my locks for many a long day.

2.45 p.m. When to 'Crown'. Devoured an apple of the Hesperides and quaffed a crimson drink.

3.0 p.m.	Wended my way to Lessington. Game of 'Hunt the Sandal' terminated by theft of sandal by peripatetic Centaur. Played Hide and Seek with wasp. Wasp won.
4.15 p.m.	Goat races. My goat made for May-pole. I got entangled in the chains of roses.
5.30 p.m.	Went hunting the multi-coloured beasts on Under Green. Succeeded by strategy in capturing a little Green Bice lamb with *vieux rose* legs, one gambooge and puce ear, and an ultra-marine tail. It was so shy that I could not approach it save by planting my rose-garland firmly on my head, plucking a couple of branches from a melodiferous flowery arbute, and simulating a rose-bush. Received a shower of soapy water and a generous dose of weed-killer from a preceptor who professed gardening as a hobby, but I captured the lamb. Was carrying it back to the house when I met the School-bard muttering darkly to himself. He was clad in a long purple garb with a garland of rhubarb and tea-leaves. He addressed an ode to my lamb, who died in convulsions.
6.30 p.m.	More honey and flowers.
7.30 p.m.	Assumed a wreath of vine-leaves, grasped by thyrsus and joined the Bacchic revels in Founder's Court, where the fountain e'er runs with wine.
9.0 p.m.	Retired for the night to my couch of rose-leaves.

My New–Bug's Exam

WHEN LIGHTS WENT out at half-past nine in the evening of the second Friday in the Quarter, and the faint footfalls of the departing House-master were heard no more, the fun began.

The Head of Under Cubicles constituted himself examiner and executioner, and was ably assisted by a timekeeper, a question-recorder, and a staff of his disreputable friends. I was a timorous 'new-bug' then, and my pyjamas were damp with the perspiration of fear. Three of my fellows had been examined and sentenced before the inquisition was directed against me.

'It's Jones's turn now,' said a voice. 'He's the little hash-pro who hacked me in run-about today. We must set him some tight questions!'

'I say, Jones, what's the colour of the House-master – I mean what's the name of the House-master of the House whose colours are black and white? One, two, three…'

'Mr Girdlestone,' my voice quavered in the darkness.

'He evidently knows the simpler colours. We'll muddle him. What are the colours of the Clubs to which Block Houses belong? One, two, three, four…'

I had been slaving at getting up these questions for days, and just managed to blurt the answer before being counted out.

'Two questions. No misses. We must buck up,' said someone.

'I say, Jones, how do you get to Farncombe from Weekites? One, two, three…'

I had issued directions only as far as Bridge before being counted out.

'Three questions. One miss. You're allowed three misses out of ten.'

'Where is Charterhouse Magazine? One, two, three, four…'

'Do you mean *The Carthusian* office?' I asked.

Everyone laughed.

'Four questions. Two misses. I say, Robinson, he's answered far too many. We'll set him a couple of stingers.'

Much whispering.

'What is the age of the horse that rolls Under Green? One, two, three..'

'Six!' I said, at a venture.

'Wrong; thirty-eight. Five questions. Three misses! Think yourself lucky you weren't asked its pedigree.'

'What are canoeing colours? One, two, thr...'

'There aren't any!'

'You'll get cocked-up for festivity; but you can count it. Six questions. Three misses. Jones?

'Yes!'

'What was the name of the girl to whom rumour stated that last year's football secretary was violently attached? One, two, three, four...'

'Daisy!' (It sounded a likely name.)

'Oh, really! Well, I happen to know last year's football secretary; and he'll simply kill you for spreading scandal. You're wrong anyhow. Seven questions. Four misses! You'll come to my "cube" at seven tomorrow morning. See? Good night!'

Here he waved his hair-brush over the candle, and a colossal shadow appeared on the ceiling.

Thames-side Reverie

(Written while I was living in a converted Thames barge moored at Hammersmith.)

A SUDDEN HOARSE shouting woke me. I looked out of the window beside my bed. Nearly full tide on the river and no wind; a tug was neatly casting off one of its train of barges at the wharf next door. A consignment of glassware in crates. The early morning greetings of tugmaster and wharfman were of their usual mock-abusive friendliness. After all this hubbub there followed half an hour of calm, in which I half slept and half watched a pair of dabchicks bobbing about only a few yards from the window. The water was pink and grey in the dawn, the towpath on the opposite bank was deserted and there was no river traffic. The stage was well set for the five swans that floated up with the tide and swam about under my window for some time. They expected bread; they should have known that it was too early. I could distinguish the plebeian swans, with their nicked beaks, the property of the Vintners' and Dyers' Companies, from the royal swans with unnicked beaks which owe immediate allegiance to the Crown. But I could distinguish them only by their nicks, not by their carriage. They went off sulkily after a while.

The next event was the drifting past of a brown-paper parcel, accompanied by a flock of about twenty gulls. They screamed and wheeled and dived and tore at it; and fluttered and squabbled and grew very excited. Though it passed slowly, I could not make out what it contained. I was glad when it had gone, because I was still sleepy. The amount of things that drift by! Especially at high tide, when there has been heavy rain two days previously up the Thames Valley. Baskets, cabbages, chairs, fruit, hats, vegetables, bottles, tins, heaps of rushes or straw, dead things. Not so many dead things now as in the summer. Far fewer dogs. That is because in the winter they don't go in so much after sticks and get carried away by the current or murderously held under water by the swans, who are jealous of their river.

Twelve lemons have just gone past. Now there are several more. They look sound enough. An accident to a barrow? One learns to distinguish accidental flotsam from intentional flotsam. That hat over there, for instance, was accidental, blown off at Westminster or Kew, by the look of it; the one that went by a few minutes ago was surely intentional – a discard from Brentford or Rotherhithe?

The amount of drift-wood is extraordinary. I wonder that someone does not farm it for profit. But perhaps someone does. I do not count the old woman who walks along the narrow foreshore at low tide and puts a few pieces into a muddy sack; I mean somebody who collects it by the ton, dries it in front of huge furnaces, and sells it in bundles for firewood. Perhaps the supply would give out sooner than I suppose. A lot of the variety is repetitious. After all, certain pieces that I recognize when I see them again (for instance, that bit of 'Diving Girl' apple box) go up and down with the tide for a week or more before I lose sight of them.

Human corpses are rare. If one can catch a corpse and pull it out, one is paid seven shillings and sixpence. I wouldn't do it for that. And I suppose one also would have to give evidence at the inquest. No, I would leave the corpse for someone else to earn money with. There go the river police in their motor launch. They are watching suspiciously in case I throw my apple core out of the window. It is a prosecutable offence. I will wait until they have gone. Here comes the *Mary Blake*. I am getting to know the tugs well. I can distinguish the *Mary Blake*, the *Vixen* or the *Elsa* at half a mile. But every day something new of one sort or another goes by. One early morning last year was sensational. There went by an opera hat, a submarine, and a seal. Today I am content with the dabchicks and the lemons. At low tide I expect the old woman with the sack and the old man who pokes about under the stones and puts what he finds into jam jars. He would puzzle you, but I have been at this window long enough to find out what he is after. He is an anthology poem by William Wordsworth, 'The Leech Gatherer'. Plenty of leeches on these beaches. The demand, I hear, is steady. Whether from extremely old-fashioned doctors or from extremely modern ones I do not know. Or care much at the moment. I am busy being pleased with the river, which is now as still as a lake, at the exact balance of the tide. A child's ball floats motionless under the window. I am tempted to get up and rescue it. But it looks as though it mightn't bounce. I'll stay in bed a little longer.

The Shout

WHEN WE ARRIVED with our bags at the Asylum cricket ground, the chief medical officer, whom I had met at the house where I was staying, came up to shake hands. I told him that I was only scoring for the Lampton team today (I had broken a finger the week before, keeping wicket on a bumpy pitch). He said: 'Oh, then you'll have an interesting companion.'

'The other scoresman?' I asked.

'Crossley is the most intelligent man in the asylum,' answered the doctor, 'a wide reader, a first-class chess-player, and so on. He seems to have travelled all over the word. He's been sent here for delusions. His most serious delusion is that he's a murderer, and his story is that he killed two men and a woman at Sydney, Australia. The other delusion, which is more humorous, is that his soul is split in pieces – whatever that means. He edits our monthly magazine, he stage manages our Christmas theatricals, and he gave a most original conjuring performance the other day. You'll like him.'

He introduced me. Crossley, a big man of forty or fifty, had a queer, not unpleasant, face. But I felt a little uncomfortable, sitting next to him in the scoring box, his black-whiskered hands so close to mine. I had no fear of physical violence, only the sense of being in the presence of a man of unusual force, even perhaps, it somehow came to me, of occult powers.

It was hot in the scoring box in spite of the wide window. 'Thunderstorm weather,' said Crossley, who spoke in what country people call a 'college voice', though I could not identify the college. 'Thunderstorm weather makes us patients behave even more irregularly than usual.'

I asked whether any patients were playing.

'Two of them, this first wicket partnership. The tall one, B.C. Brown, played for Hants three years ago, and the other is a good club player. Pat Slingsby usually turns out for us too – the Australian fast bowler, you know – but we are dropping him today. In weather like this he is apt to bowl at the batsman's head. He is not insane in the usual sense, merely magnificently ill-tempered. The doctors can do nothing with him. He wants shooting, really.' Crossley began talking about the doctor. 'A good-hearted fellow and, for a mental-hospital physician, technically well advanced. He actually studies morbid psychology and is fairly well-read, up to about the day before yesterday. I have a good deal of fun with him. He reads neither German nor French, so I keep a stage or two ahead in psychological fashions; he has to wait for the English translations. I invent significant dreams for him to interpret; I find he likes me to put in snakes and apple pies, so I usually do. He is convinced that my mental trouble is due to the good old "antipaternal fixation" – I wish it were as simple as that.'

Then Crossley asked me whether I could score and listen to a story at the same time. I said that I could. It was slow cricket.

'My story is true,' he said, 'every word of it. Or, when I say that my story is "true", I mean at least that I am telling it in a new way. It is always the same story, but I sometimes vary the climax and even recast the characters. Variation keeps it fresh and therefore true. If I were always to use the same formula, it would soon drag and become false. I am interested in keeping it alive, and it is a true story, every word of it. I know the people in it personally. They are Lampton people.'

We decided that I should keep score of the runs and extras and that he should keep the bowling analysis, and at the fall of every wicket we should copy from each other. This made story-telling possible.

Richard awoke one morning saying to Rachel: 'But what an unusual dream.'

'Tell me, my dear,' she said, 'and hurry, because I want to tell you mine.'

'I was having a conversation,' he said, 'with a person (or persons, because he changed his appearance so often) of great intelligence, and I can clearly remember the argument. Yet this is the first time I have ever been able to remember any argument that came to me in sleep. Usually my dreams are so different from waking that I can only describe them if I say: "It is as though I were living and thinking as a tree, or a bell, or middle C, or a five-pound note; as though I had never been human." Life there is sometimes rich for me and sometimes poor, but I repeat, in every case so different, that if I were to say: "I had a conversation," or "I was in love," or "I heard music," or "I was angry," it would be as far from the fact as if I tried to explain a problem of philosophy, as Rabelais's Panurge did to Thaumast, merely by grimacing with my eyes and lips.'

'It is much the same with me,' she said. 'I think that when I am asleep I become, perhaps, a stone with all the natural appetites and convictions of a stone. "Senseless as a stone" is a proverb, but there may be more sense in a stone, more sensibility, more sensitivity, more sentiment, more sensibleness, than in many men and women. And no less sensuality,' she added thoughtfully.

It was Sunday morning, so that they could lie in bed, their arms about each other, without troubling about the time; and they were childless, so breakfast could wait. He told her that in his dream he was walking in the sand hills with this person or persons, who said to him: 'These sand hills are a part neither of the sea before us nor of the grass links behind us, and are not related to the mountains beyond the links. They are of themselves. A man walking on the sand hills soon knows this by the tang in the air, and if he were to refrain from eating and drinking, from sleeping and speaking, from thinking and desiring, he could continue among them for ever without change. There is no life and no death in the sand hills. Anything might happen in the sand hills.'

Rachel said that this was nonsense, and asked: 'But what was the argument? Hurry up!'

He said it was about the whereabouts of the soul, but that now she had put it out of his head by hurrying him. All that he remembered was that the man was first a Japanese, then an Italian, and finally a kangaroo.

In return she eagerly told her dream, gabbling over the words. 'I was walking in the sand hills; there were rabbits there, too; how does that tally with what he said of life and death? I saw the man and you walking arm in arm towards me, and I ran from you both and I noticed that he had a black silk handkerchief; he ran after me and my shoe buckle came off and I could not wait to pick it up. I left it lying, and he stooped and put it into his pocket.'

'How do you know that it was the same man?' he asked.

'Because,' she said, laughing, 'he had a black face and wore a blue coat like that picture of Captain Cook. And because it was in the sand hills.'

He said, kissing her neck: 'We not only live together and talk together and sleep together, but it seems we now even dream together.'

So they laughed.

Then he got up and brought her breakfast.

At about half past eleven, she said: 'Go out now for a walk, my dear, and bring home something for me to think about: and be back in time for dinner at one o'clock.'

It was a hot morning in the middle of May, and he went out through the wood and struck the coast road, which after half a mile led into Lampton.

('Do you know Lampton well?' asked Crossley. 'No,' I said, 'I am only here for the holidays, staying with friends.')

He went a hundred yards along the coast road, but then turned off and went across the links: thinking of Rachel and watching the blue butterflies and looking at the heath roses and thyme, and thinking of her again, and how strange it was that they could be so near to each other; and then taking a pinch of gorse flower and smelling it, and considering the smell and thinking, 'If she should die, what would become of me?' and taking a slate from the low wall and skimming it across the pond and thinking, 'I am a clumsy fellow to be her husband'; and walking towards the sand hills, and then edging away again, perhaps half in fear of meeting the person of their dream, and at last making a half circle towards the old church beyond Lampton, at the foot of the mountain.

The morning service was over and the people were out by the cromlechs behind the church, walking in twos and threes, as the custom was, on the smooth turf. The squire was talking in a loud voice about King Charles, the Martyr: 'A great man, a very great man, but betrayed by those he loved best,' and the doctor was arguing about organ music with the rector. There was a group of children playing ball. 'Throw it here, Elsie! No, to me, Elsie, Elsie, Elsie!' Then the rector appeared and pocketed the ball and said that it was Sunday; they should have remembered. When he was gone they made faces after him.

Presently a stranger came up and asked permission to sit down beside Richard; they began to talk. The stranger had been to the church service and wished to discuss the sermon. The text had been the immortality of the soul: the last of a series of sermons that had begun at Easter. He said that he could not grant the preacher's premiss that *the soul is continually resident in the body*. Why should this be so? What duty did the soul perform in the daily routine task of the body? The soul was neither the brain, nor the lungs, nor the stomach, nor the heart, nor the mind, nor the imagination. Surely it was a thing apart? Was it not indeed less likely to be resident in the body than outside the body? He had no proof one way or the other, but he would say: Birth and death are so odd a mystery that the principle of life may well lie outside the body which is the visible evidence of living. 'We cannot,' he said, 'even tell to a nicety what are the moments of birth and death. Why, in Japan, where I have travelled, they reckon a man to be already one year old when he is born; and lately in Italy a dead man – but come and walk on the sand hills and let me tell you my conclusions. I find it easier to talk when I am walking.'

Richard was frightened to hear this, and to see the man wipe his forehead with a black silk handkerchief. He stuttered out something. At this moment the children, who had crept up behind the cromlech, suddenly, at an agreed signal, shouted loud in the ears of the two men; and stood laughing. The stranger was startled into anger; he opened his mouth as if he were about to curse them, and bared his teeth to the gums. Three of the children screamed and ran off. But the one whom they called Elsie fell down in her fright and lay sobbing. The doctor, who was near, tried to comfort her. 'He has a face like a devil,' they heard the child say.

The stranger smiled good-naturedly: 'And a devil I was not so very long ago. That was in Northern Australia, where I lived with the black fellows for twenty years. "Devil" is the nearest English word for the position that they gave me in their tribe; and they also gave me an eighteenth-century British naval uniform to wear as my ceremonial dress. Come and walk with me in the sand hills and let me tell you the whole story. I have a passion for walking in the sand hills: that is why I came to this town... My name is Charles.'

Richard said: 'Thank you, but I must hurry home to my dinner.'

'Nonsense,' said Charles, 'dinner can wait. Or, if you wish, I can come to dinner with you. By the way, I have had nothing to eat since Friday. I am without money.'

Richard felt uneasy. He was afraid of Charles, and did not wish to bring him home to dinner because of the dream and the sand hills and the hand-kerchief: yet on the other hand the man was intelligent and quiet and decently dressed and had eaten nothing since Friday; if Rachel knew that he had refused him a meal, she would renew her taunts. When Rachel was out of sorts, her favourite complaint was that he was overcareful about money; though when she was at peace with him, she owned that he was the most generous man she knew, and that she did not mean what she said; when she was angry with him again, out came the taunt of stinginess: 'Tenpence-halfpenny,' she would say, 'tenpence-halfpenny and three-pence of that in stamps'; his ears would burn and he would want to hit her. So he said now: 'By all means come along to dinner, but that little girl is still sobbing for fear of you. You ought to do something about it.'

Charles beckoned her to him and said a single soft word; it was an Australian magic word, he afterwards told Richard, meaning *Milk:* immediately Elsie was comforted and came to sit on Charles' knee and played with the buttons of his waistcoat for awhile until Charles sent her away.

'You have strange powers, Mr Charles,' Richard said.

Charles answered: 'I am fond of children, but the shout startled me; I am pleased that I did not do what, for a moment, I was tempted to do.'

'What was that?' asked Richard.

'I might have shouted myself,' said Charles.

'Why,' said Richard, 'They would have liked that better. It would have been a great game for them. They probably expected it of you.'

'If I had shouted,' said Charles, 'my shout would have either killed them outright or sent them mad. Probably it would have killed them, for they were standing close.'

Richard smiled a little foolishly. He did not know whether or not he was expected to laugh, for Charles spoke so gravely and carefully. So he said: 'Indeed, what sort of shout would that be? Let me hear you shout.'

'It is not only children who would be hurt by my shout,' Charles said. 'Men can be sent raving mad by it; the strongest, even, would be flung to the ground. It is a magic shout that I learned from the chief devil of the Northern Territory. I took eighteen years to perfect it, and yet I have used it, in all, no more than five times.'

Richard was so confused in his mind with the dream and the handkerchief and the word spoken to Elsie that he did not know what to say, so he muttered: 'I'll give you fifty pounds now to clear the cromlechs with a shout.'

'I see that you do not believe me,' Charles said. 'Perhaps you have never before heard of the terror shout?'

Richard considered and said: 'Well, I have read of the hero shout which the ancient Irish warriors used, that would drive armies backwards; and did not Hector, the Trojan, have a terrible shout? And there were sudden shouts in the woods of Greece. They were ascribed to the god Pan and would infect men with a madness of fear; from this legend indeed the word "panic" has come into the English language. And I remember another shout in the *Mabinogion,* in the story of Lludd and Llevelys. It was a shriek that was heard on every May Eve and went through all hearts and so scared them that the men lost their hue and their strength and the women their children, and the youths and maidens their senses, and the animals and trees, the earth and the waters were left barren. But it was caused by a dragon.'

'It must have been a British magician of the dragon clan,' said Charles. 'I belonged to the Kangaroos. Yes, that tallies. The effect is not exactly given, but near enough.'

They reached the house at one o'clock, and Rachel was at the door, the dinner ready. 'Rachel,' said Richard, 'here is Mr Charles to dinner; Mr Charles is a great traveller.'

Rachel passed her hand over her eyes as if to dispel a cloud, but it may have been the sudden sunlight. Charles took her hand and kissed it, which surprised her. Rachel was graceful, small, with eyes unusually blue for the blackness of her hair, delicate in her movements, and with a voice rather low-pitched; she had a freakish sense of humour.

('You would like Rachel,' said Crossley, 'she visits me here some-times.')

Of Charles it would be difficult to say one thing or another: he was of middle age, and tall; his hair grey; his face never still for a moment; his eyes large and bright, sometimes yellow; sometimes brown, sometimes grey; his voice changed its tone and accent with the subject; his hands were brown and hairy at the back, his nails well cared for. Of Richard it is enough to say that he was a musician, not a strong man but a lucky one. Luck was his strength.

After dinner Charles and Richard washed the dishes together, and Richard suddenly asked Charles if he would let him hear the shout: for he thought that he could not have peace of mind until he had heard it. So horrible a thing was, surely, worse to think about than to hear: for now he believed in the shout.

Charles stopped washing up; mop in hand. 'As you wish,' said he, 'but I have warned you what a shout it is. And if I shout it must be in a lonely place where nobody else can hear; and I shall not shout in the second degree, the degree which kills certainly, but in the first, which terrifies only, and when you want me to stop put your hands to your ears.'

'Agreed,' said Richard.

'I have never yet shouted to satisfy an idle curiosity,' said Charles, 'but only when in danger of my life from enemies, black or white, and once when I was alone in the desert without food or drink. Then I was forced to shout, for food.'

Richard thought: 'Well, at least I am a lucky man, and my luck will be good enough even for this.'

'I am not afraid,' he told Charles.

'We will walk out on the sand hills tomorrow early,' Charles said, 'when nobody is stirring; and I will shout. You say you are not afraid.'

But Richard was very much afraid, and what made his fear worse was that somehow he could not talk to Rachel and tell her of it: he knew that if he told her she would either forbid him to go or she would come with him. If she forbade him to go, the fear of the shout and the sense of cowardice would hang over him ever afterwards; but if she came with him, either the shout would be nothing and she would have a new taunt for his credulity and Charles would laugh with her, or if it were something, she might well be driven mad. So he said nothing.

Charles was invited to sleep at the cottage for the night, and they stayed up late talking.

Rachel told Richard when they were in bed that she liked Charles and that he certainly was a man who had seen many things, though a fool and a big baby. Then Rachel talked a great deal of nonsense, for she had had two glasses of wine, which she seldom drank, and she said: 'Oh, my dearest, I forgot to tell you. When I put on my buckled shoes this morning while you were away I found a buckle missing. I must have noticed that it was lost before I went to sleep last night and yet not fixed the loss firmly in my mind, so that it came out as a discovery in my dream; but I have a feeling, in fact I am certain, that Mr Charles has that buckle in his pocket; and I am sure that he is the man whom we met in our dream. But I don't care, not I.'

Richard grew more and more afraid, and he dared not tell of the black silk handkerchief, or of Charles' invitations to him to walk in the sand hills. And what was worse, Charles had used only a white handkerchief while he was in the house, so that he could not be sure whether he had seen it after all. Turning his head away, he said lamely: 'Well, Charles knows a lot of things. I am going for a walk with him early tomorrow if you don't mind; an early walk is what I need.'

'Oh, I'll come too,' she said.

Richard could not think how to refuse her; he knew that he had made a mistake in telling her of the walk. But he said: 'Charles will be very glad.

At six o'clock then.'

At six o'clock he got up, but Rachel after the wine was too sleepy to come with them. She kissed him goodbye and off he went with Charles.

Richard had had a bad night. In his dreams nothing was in human terms, but confused and fearful, and he had felt himself more distant from Rachel than he had ever felt since their marriage, and the fear of the shout was gnawing at him. He was also hungry and cold. There was a stiff wind blowing towards the sea from the mountains and a few splashes of rain. Charles spoke hardly a word, but chewed a stalk of grass and walked fast.

Richard felt giddy, and said to Charles: 'Wait a moment, I have a stitch in my side.' So they stopped, and Richard asked, gasping: 'What sort of shout is it? Is it loud, or shrill? How is it produced? How can it madden a man?'

Charles was silent, so Richard went on with a foolish smile: 'Sound, though, is a curious thing. I remember once, when I was at Cambridge, that a King's College man had his turn of reading the evening lesson. He had not spoken ten words before there was a groaning and ringing and creaking, and pieces of wood and dust fell from the roof; for his voice was exactly attuned to that of the building, so that he had to stop, else the roof might have fallen; as you can break a wine glass by playing its note on a violin.'

Charles consented to answer: 'My shout is not a matter of tone or vibration but something not to be explained. It is a shout of pure evil, and there is no fixed place for it on the scale. It may take any note. It is pure terror, and if it were not for a certain intention of mine, which I need not tell you, I would refuse to shout for you.'

Richard had a great gift of fear, and this new account of the shout disturbed him more and more; he wished himself at home in bed, and Charles two continents away. But he was fascinated. They were crossing the links now and going through the bent grass that pricked through his stockings and soaked them.

Now they were on the bare sand hills. From the highest of them Charles looked about him; he could see the beach stretched out for two miles and more. There was no one in sight. Then Richard saw Charles take something out of his pocket and begin carelessly to juggle with it as he stood, tossing it from finger tip to finger tip and spinning it up with finger and thumb to catch it on the back of his hand. It was Rachel's buckle.

Richard's breath came in gasps, his heart beat violently and he nearly vomited. He was shivering with cold, and yet sweating. Soon they came to an open place among the sand hills near the sea. There was a raised bank with sea holly growing on it and a little sickly grass; stones were strewn all around, brought there, it seemed, by the sea years before. Though the place lay behind the first rampart of sand hills, there was a gap in the line through which a high tide might have broken, and the winds that continually swept through the gap kept them uncovered of sand. Richard had his hands in his trouser pockets for warmth and was nervously twisting a soft piece of wax around his right forefinger – a candle end that was in his pocket from the night before when he had gone downstairs to lock the door.

'Are you ready?' asked Charles.

Richard nodded.

A gull dipped over the crest of the sand hills and rose again screaming when it saw them. 'Stand by the sea holly,' said Richard, with a dry mouth, 'and I'll be here among the stones, not too near. When I raise my hand, shout! When I put my fingers to my ears, stop at once.'

So Charles walked twenty steps towards the holly. Richard saw his broad back and black silk handkerchief sticking from his pocket. He remembered the dream, and the shoe buckle and Elsie's fear. His resolution broke: he hurriedly pulled the piece of wax in two, and sealed his ears. Charles did not see him.

He turned, and Richard gave the signal with his hand.

Charles leaned forward oddly, his chin thrust out, his teeth bared, and never before had Richard seen such a look of fear on a man's face. He had not been prepared for that. Charles' face, that was usually soft and changing, uncertain as a cloud, now hardened to a rough stone mask, dead white at first, and then flushing outwards from the cheek bones red and redder, and at last as black as if he were about to choke. His mouth then slowly opened to the full, and Richard fell on his face, his hands to his ears, in a faint.

When he came to himself he was lying alone among the stones. He sat up, wondering numbly whether he had been there long. He felt very weak and sick, with a chill on his heart that was worse than the chill of his body. He could not think. He put his hand down to lift himself up and it rested on a stone, a larger one than most of the others. He picked it up and felt its surface, absently. His mind wandered. He began to think about shoemaking, a trade of which he had known nothing, but now every trick was familiar to him. 'I must be a shoemaker,' he said aloud.

Then he corrected himself: 'No, I am a musician. Am I going mad?' He threw the stone from him; it struck against another and bounced off.

He asked himself: 'Now why did I say that I was a shoemaker? It seemed a moment ago that I knew all there was to be known about shoemaking and now I know nothing at all about it. I must get home to Rachel. Why did I ever come out?'

Then he saw Charles on a sand hill a hundred yards away, gazing out to sea. He remembered his fear and made sure that the wax was in his ears: he stumbled to his feet. He saw a flurry on the sand and there was a rabbit lying on its side, twitching in a convulsion. As Richard moved towards it, the flurry ended: the rabbit was dead. Richard crept behind a sand hill out of Charles' sight and then struck homeward, running awkwardly in the soft sand. He had not gone twenty paces before he came upon the gull. It was standing stupidly on the sand and did not rise at his approach, but fell over dead.

How Richard reached home he did not know, but there he was opening the back door and crawling upstairs on his hands and knees. He unsealed his ears.

Rachel was sitting up in bed, pale and trembling. 'Thank God you're back,' she said; 'I have had a nightmare, the worst of all my life. It was frightful. I was in my dream, in the deepest dream of all, like the one of which I told you. I was like a stone, and I was aware of you near me; you were you, quite plain, though I was a stone, and you were in great fear and I could do nothing to help you, and you were waiting for something and the terrible thing did not happen to you, but it happened to me. I can't tell you what it was, but it was as though all my nerves cried out in pain at once, and I was pierced through and through with a beam of some intense evil light and twisted inside out. I woke up and my heart was beating so fast that I had to gasp for breath. Do you think I had a heart attack and my heart missed a beat? They say it feels like that. Where have you been, dearest? Where is Mr Charles?'

Richard sat on the bed and held her hand. 'I have had a bad experience too,' he said. 'I was out with Charles by the sea and as he went ahead to climb on the highest sand hill I felt very faint and fell down among a patch of stones, and when I came to myself I was in a desperate sweat of fear and had to hurry home. So I came back running alone. It happened perhaps half an hour ago,' he said.

He did not tell her more. He asked, could he come back to bed and would she get breakfast? That was a thing she had not done all the years they were married.

'I am as ill as you,' said she. It was understood between them always that when Rachel was ill, Richard must be well.

'You are not,' said he, and fainted again.

She helped him to bed ungraciously and dressed herself and went slowly downstairs. A smell of coffee and bacon rose to meet her and there was Charles, who had lit the fire, putting two breakfasts on a tray. She was so relieved at not having to get breakfast and so confused by her experience that she thanked him and called him a darling, and he kissed her hand gravely and pressed it. He had made the breakfast exactly to her liking: the coffee was strong and the eggs fried on both sides.

Rachel fell in love with Charles. She had often fallen in love with men before and since her marriage, but it was her habit to tell Richard when this happened, as he agreed to tell her when it happened to him: so that the suffocation of passion was given a vent and there was no jealousy, for she used to say (and he had the liberty of saying): 'Yes, I am *in love* with so-and-so, but I only *love* you.'

That was as far as it had ever gone. But this was different. Somehow, she did not know why, she could not own to being in love with Charles: for she no longer loved Richard. She hated him for being ill, and said that he was lazy, and a sham. So about noon he got up, but went groaning around the bedroom until she sent him back to bed to groan.

Charles helped her with the housework, doing all the cooking, but he did not go up to see Richard, since he had not been asked to do so. Rachel was ashamed, and apologized to Charles for Richard's rudeness in running away from him. But Charles said mildly that he took it as no insult; he had felt queer himself that morning; it was as though something evil was astir in the air as they reached the sand hills. She told him that she too had had the same queer feeling.

Later she found all Lampton talking of it. The doctor maintained that it was an earth tremor, but the country people said that it had been the Devil passing by. He had come to fetch the black soul of Solomon Jones, the gamekeeper, found dead that morning in his cottage by the sand hills.

When Richard could go downstairs and walk about a little without groaning, Rachel sent him to the cobbler's to get a new buckle for her shoe. She came with him to the bottom of the garden. The path ran beside a steep bank. Richard looked ill and groaned slightly as he walked, so Rachel, half in anger, half in fun, pushed him down the bank, where he fell sprawling among the nettles and old iron. Then she ran back into the house laughing loudly.

Richard sighed, tried to share the joke against himself with Rachel – but she had gone – heaved himself up, picked the shoes from among the nettles, and after awhile walked slowly up the bank, out of the gate, and down the lane in the unaccustomed glare of the sun.

When he reached the cobbler's he sat down heavily. The cobbler was glad to talk to him. 'You are looking bad,' said the cobbler.

Richard said: 'Yes, on Monday morning I had a bit of a turn; I am only now recovering from it.'

'Good God,' burst out the cobbler, 'if you had a bit of a turn, what did I not have? It was as if someone handled me raw, without my skin. It was as if someone seized my very soul and juggled with it, as you might juggle with a stone, and hurled me away. I shall never forget last Monday morning.'

A strange notion came to Richard that it was the cobbler's soul which he had handled in the form of a stone. 'It may be,' he thought, 'that the souls of every man and woman and child in Lampton are lying there.' But he said nothing about this, asked for a buckle, and went home.

Rachel was ready with a kiss and a joke; he might have kept silent, for his silence always made Rachel ashamed. 'But,' he thought, 'why make her ashamed? From shame she goes to self-justification and picks a quarrel over something else and it's ten times worse. I'll be cheerful and accept the joke.'

He was unhappy. And Charles was established in the house: gentle-voiced, hard-working, and continually taking Richard's part against Rachel's scoffing. This was galling, because Rachel did not resent it.

('The next part of the story,' said Crossley, 'is the comic relief, an account of how Richard went again to the sand hills, to the heap of stones, and identified the souls of the doctor and rector – the doctor's because it was shaped like a whiskey bottle and the rector's because it was as black as original sin – and how he proved to himself that the notion was not fanciful. But I will skip that and come to the point where Rachel two days later suddenly became affectionate and loved Richard she said, more than ever before.')

The reason was that Charles had gone away, nobody knows where, and had relaxed the buckle magic for the time, because he was confident that he could renew it on his return. So in a day or two Richard was well again and everything was as it had been, until one afternoon the door opened, and there stood Charles.

He entered without a word of greeting and hung his hat upon a peg. He sat down by the fire and asked: 'When is supper ready?'

Richard looked at Rachel, his eyebrows raised, but Rachel seemed fascinated by the man.

She answered: 'Eight o'clock,' in her low voice, and stooping down, drew off Charles' muddy boots and found him a pair of Richard's slippers.

Charles said: 'Good. It is now seven o'clock. In another hour, supper. At nine o'clock the boy will bring the evening paper. At ten o'clock, Rachel, you and I sleep together.'

Richard thought that Charles must have gone suddenly mad. But Rachel answered quietly: 'Why, of course, my dear.' Then she turned viciously to Richard: 'And you run away, little man!' she said, and slapped his cheek with all her strength.

Richard stood puzzled, nursing his cheek. Since he could not believe that Rachel and Charles had both gone mad together, he must be mad himself. At all events, Rachel knew her mind, and they had a secret compact that if either of them ever wished to break the marriage promise, the other should not stand in the way. They had made this compact because they wished to feel themselves bound by love rather than by cere-mony. So he said as calmly as he could: 'Very well, Rachel. I shall leave you two together.'

Charles flung a boot at him, saying: 'If you put your nose inside the door between now and breakfast time, I'll shout the ears off your head.'

Richard went out this time not afraid, but cold inside and quite clear-headed. He went through the gate, down the lane, and across the links. It wanted three hours yet until sunset. He joked with the boys playing stump cricket on the school field. He skimmed stones. He thought of Rachel and tears started to his eyes. Then he sang to comfort himself. 'Oh, I'm certainly mad,' he said, 'and what in the world has happened to my luck?'

At last he came to the stones. 'Now,' he said, 'I shall find my soul in this heap and I shall crack it into a hundred pieces with this hammer' – he had picked up the hammer in the coal shed as he came out.

Then he began looking for his soul. Now, one may recognize the soul of another man or woman, but one can never recognize one's own. Richard could not find his. But by chance he came upon Rachel's soul and recognized it (a slim green stone with glints of quartz in it) because she was estranged from him at the time. Against it lay another stone, an ugly misshapen flint of a mottled brown. He swore: 'I'll destroy this. It must be the soul of Charles.'

He kissed the soul of Rachel; it was like kissing her lips. Then he took the soul of Charles and poised his hammer. 'I'll knock you into fifty fragments!'

He paused. Richard had scruples. He knew that Rachel loved Charles better than himself, and he was bound to respect the compact. A third stone (his own, it must be) was lying the other side of Charles' stone; it was of smooth grey granite, about the size of a cricket ball. He said to himself: 'I will break my own soul in pieces and that will be the end of me.' The world grew black, his eyes ceased to focus, and he all but fainted. But he recovered himself, and with a great cry brought down the coal hammer crack, and crack again, on the grey stone.

It split in four pieces, exuding a smell like gunpowder: and when Richard found that he was still alive and whole, he began to laugh and laugh. Oh, he was mad, quite mad! He flung the hammer away, lay down exhausted, and fell asleep.

He awoke as the sun was just setting. He went home in confusion, thinking: 'This is a very bad dream and Rachel will help me out of it.'

When he came to the edge of the town he found a group of men talking excitedly under a lamppost. One said: 'About eight o'clock it happened, didn't it?' The other said: 'Yes.' A third said: 'Ay, mad as a hatter. "Touch me," he says, "and I'll shout. I'll shout you into a fit, the whole blasted police force of you. I'll shout you mad." And the inspector says: "Now, Crossley, put your hands up, we've got you cornered at last." "One last chance," says he. "Go and leave me or I'll shout you stiff and dead."'

Richard had stopped to listen. 'And what happened to Crossley then?' he said. 'And what did the woman say?'

'"For Christ's sake," she said to the inspector, "go away or he'll kill you."'

'And did he shout?'

'He didn't shout. He screwed up his face for a moment and drew in his breath. A'mighty, I've never seen such a ghastly looking face in my life. I had to take three or four brandies afterwards. And the inspector he drops the revolver and it goes off; but nobody hit. Then suddenly a change comes over this man Crossley. He claps his hands to his side and again to his heart, and his face goes smooth and dead again. Then he begins to laugh and dance and cut capers. And the woman stares and can't believe her eyes and the police lead him off. If he was mad before, he was just harmless dotty now; and they had no trouble with him. He's been taken off in the ambulance to the Royal West County Asylum.'

So Richard went home to Rachel and told her everything and she told him everything, though there was not much to tell. She had not fallen in love with Charles, she said; she was only teasing Richard and she had never said anything or heard Charles say anything in the least like what he told her; it was part of his dream. She loved him always and only him, for all his faults; which she went through – his stinginess, his talkativeness, his untidiness. Charles and she had eaten a quiet supper, and she did think it had been bad of Richard to rush off without a word of explanation and stay away for three hours like that. Charles might have murdered her. He did start pulling her about a bit, in fun, wanting her to dance with him, and then the knock came on the door, and the inspector shouted: 'Walter Charles Crossley, in the name of the King, I arrest you for the murder of George Grant, Harry Grant, and Ada Coleman at Sydney, Australia.' Then Charles had gone absolutely mad. He had pulled out a shoe buckle and said to it: 'Hold her for me.' And then he had told the police to go away or he'd shout them dead. After that he made a dreadful face at them and went to pieces altogether. 'He was rather a nice man; I liked his face so much and feel so sorry for him.'

'Did you like that story?' asked Crossley.

'Yes,' said I, busy scoring, 'a Milesian tale of the best. Lucius Apuleius, I congratulate you.'

Crossley turned to me with a troubled face and hands clenched trembling. 'Every word of it is true,' he said. 'Crossley's soul was cracked in four pieces and I'm a madman. Oh, I don't blame Richard and Rachel. They are a pleasant, loving pair of fools and I've never wished them harm; they often visit me here. In any case, now that my soul lies broken in pieces, my powers are gone. Only one thing remains to me,' he said, 'and that is the shout.'

I had been so busy scoring and listening to the story at the same time that I had not noticed the immense bank of black cloud that swam up until it spread across the sun and darkened the whole sky. Warm drops of rain fell: a flash of lightning dazzled us and with it came a smashing clap of thunder.

In a moment all was confusion. Down came a drenching rain, the cricketers dashed for cover, the lunatics began to scream, bellow, and fight. One tall young man, the same B.C. Brown who had once played for Hants, pulled all his clothes off and ran about stark naked. Outside the scoring box an old man with a beard began to pray to the thunder: 'Bah! Bah! Bah!'

Crossley's eyes twitched proudly. 'Yes,' said he, pointing to the sky, 'that's the sort of shout it is; that's the effect it has; but I can do better than that.' Then his face fell suddenly and became childishly unhappy and anxious. 'Oh dear God,' he said, 'he'll shout at me again, Crossley will. He'll freeze my marrow.'

The rain was rattling on the tin roof so that I could hardly hear him. Another flash, another clap of thunder even louder than the first. 'But that's only the second degree,' he shouted in my ear; 'it's the first that kills.'

'Oh,' he said. 'Don't you understand?' He smiled foolishly. 'I'm Richard now, and Crossley will kill me.'

The naked man was running about brandishing a cricket stump in either hand and screaming: an ugly sight. 'Bah! Bah! Bah!' prayed the old man, the rain spouting down his back from his uptilted hat.

'Nonsense,' said I, 'be a man, remember you're Crossley. You're a match for a dozen Richards. You played a game and lost, because Richard had the luck; but you still have the shout.'

I was feeling rather mad myself. Then the Asylum doctor rushed into the scoring box, his flannels streaming wet, still wearing pads and batting gloves, his glasses gone; he had heard our voices raised, and tore Crossley's hands from mine. 'To your dormitory at once, Crossley!' he ordered.

'I'll not go,' said Crossley, proud again, 'you miserable Snake and Apple Pie Man!'

The doctor seized him by his coat and tried to hustle him out.

Crossley flung him off, his eyes blazing with madness. 'Get out,' he said, 'and leave me alone here or I'll shout. Do you hear? I'll shout. I'll kill the whole damn lot of you. I'll shout the Asylum down. I'll wither the grass. I'll shout.' His face was distorted in terror. A red spot appeared on either cheek bone and spread over his face.

I put my fingers to my ears and ran out of the scoring box. I had run perhaps twenty yards, when an indescribable pang of fire spun me about and left me dazed and numbed. I escaped death somehow; I suppose that I am lucky, like the Richard of the story. But the lightning struck Crossley and the doctor dead.

Crossley's body was found rigid, the doctor's was crouched in a corner, his hands to his ears. Nobody could understand this because death had been instantaneous, and the doctor was not a man to stop his ears against thunder.

It makes a rather unsatisfactory end to the story to say that Rachel and Richard were the friends with whom I was staying – Crossley had described them most accurately – but that when I told them that a man called Charles Crossley had been struck at the same time as their friend the doctor, they seemed to take Crossley's death casually by comparison with his. Richard looked blank; Rachel said: 'Crossley? I think that was the man who called himself the Australian Illusionist and gave that wonderful conjuring show the other day. He had practically no apparatus but a black silk handkerchief. I liked his face so much. Oh, and Richard didn't like it at all.' ·

'No, I couldn't stand the way he looked at you all the time,' Richard said.

Avocado Pears

TOM'S FATHER WAS a respectable chemist in Birmingham, an old-style Christian Socialist, and Tom, who went as day-boy to a local grammar-school and did brilliantly and came up to Oxford with a scholarship and had no friends there except among the serious Labour crowd at Ruskin College, was surprisingly ignorant of certain perverse but familiar facts of life. One day he came to borrow my French dictionary. I asked him what he wanted to look up. 'Just the name of a fruit,' he said carelessly. But someone else had borrowed the dictionary. 'It doesn't matter,' he said. Then he told me the story.

'A month ago I was in Paris for a week-end, and I was wandering about vaguely looking at things the evening I arrived – I had never been in Paris before. I walked steadily in one direction until I came to a very poor quarter – I don't know where, but it was somewhere in the northern part. The streets were narrow and full of garbage. After a time I came on two policemen: they were busy kicking a man who was lying in the gutter. He had a pretty long wound in his scalp and looked bad; certainly he hadn't any fight left in him. I ran up and took a flying kick at the bigger of the policemen, from behind, and sent him sprawling, and then I took a standing kick at the other and sent him sprawling, too. They were lovely kicks; modelled on those long shots at goal by Dorrell of "The Villa". The policemen saw I was angry so they ran away.

'I wasn't wearing a hat – I never do – and wore a muffler round my neck so the man's friends came up from where they had been hiding in a doorway – they were Communists – and began embracing me and slapping me on the back. When I answered in English they were surprised at first, but said: "*Vous êtes bon camarade, tout de même.*" They explained that they hadn't attacked the policemen, because they carried revolvers and generally weren't afraid to use them. This was all right for me. So we went to a pub and they gave me coffee I don't drink, as you know. The brother of the man whom I had rescued came up later. He was a printer's foreman, he told me, and could talk a little English. He said how grateful he was and offered to show me the sights of Paris. First he took me round the slum parts – my God ! it *was* a filthy place. It even beat what I saw while I was helping with that survey of housing conditions in Glasgow for the Labour Research Bureau. "Well, now let's look at the prettier part," I said. "I'll find the money." The printer laughed and said that we must disguise ourselves first as good bourgeois. So I went back to my hotel and changed and met him later over at Montmartre. He was a big hefty fellow and looked magnificent; he had borrowed a dinner jacket from another brother who was a waiter; and for a joke he had put a ribbon of the Legion of Honour in his button-hole to make it look more realistic.

'We went to a show called *La Revue Ultra-Nue*, and it was; I don't care for that sort of thing so we didn't stay there long. Then he took me to see a fashionable brothel. His sister was the concierge there, so there was no gate-money to pay and we had some champagne with the women who happened to be disengaged; the printer explained that I was not a customer but a serious young man studying social conditions. The women were all Communists, so we got on well together; they were quite simple about their profession: *"Il faut vivre,"* they said, shrugging, and one of them who was an Italian – I talk a little Italian, you know – told me what their ambitions were. They would save up for five or six years until they had put by quite a decent sum and could retire. It was a house frequented by Americans, and *Madame la Propriétaire*, though a Royalist, was a decent sort, and didn't take too high a percentage of their earnings. So when they had put by so-and-so many francs – It came to about £500 I reckoned – they would advertise for a husband in the matrimonial papers: *"Jeune Fille Avec Tâche Désire Mari Affectueux,"* and be sure to find a good one. *"Avec Tâche"* means "slightly soiled". "And after all," said the Italian girl, "this is the best possible school to learn *'comment plaire à son mari.'* Men are all the same."

'Then we went to a wrestling match, and there were two enormously fat practically naked men rolling about on the floor. They were carefully greased, so that they couldn't get a decent hold on each other, but at last one did and began slowly breaking the other fellow's arm. I couldn't bear to wait for the crack! so we went out. The filthy look on the faces of the young bloods who were watching !

'After that we watched the crowd coming out of the *Opéra*, and the printer spat and muttered *Assassins!* There was one absolute caricature-group of four men with opera-hats, monocles and canes and I said: "Let's follow them." So we followed them to a swell restaurant; it was a dreadful place, all plush and mirrors and salon pictures of nymphs and satyrs. We sat in a corner and the printer ordered oysters and said something to the waiter: it was a Communist password or something because when I paid for the oysters with a twenty-franc note, I got twenty francs change.

'Well, we sat there and I watched the four comics out of the corner of my eye while the printer told me all the ins and outs of Communism. Apparently he was an important official of the Party; I had noticed that his friends, though they called him Comrade, made it a sort of title. I wish I could have understood it all. He got excited and talked too fast. He told me he had been foreman of a munitions works during the war and sabotaged output for two or three years until he had been caught; then he had to disappear quickly into one of the Apache quarters of Paris where army-deserters lived in a sort of fortress, and the police didn't dare round them up because they knew that they had bombs and rifles and even machine-guns. At least, that's what I made out of the story.

'While we were talking I saw a chap about my own age – no, he was a bit younger, say about nineteen – looking in at the food in the window. He was a good-looking kid, but he seemed hungry. I was listening to the printer who had his back to the window, and waiting for him to finish the story: then I thought I'd invite the kid in to give him a meal. Well, I was surprised. The oldest-looking of the four comics, a fattish fellow with a falsetto voice, saw the kid, dashed out of the door and came back, pulling him in. He made him sit down at their table and called to the waiter to lay a place for him. The waiter laid a place, trying not to look furious, but I could see that he was: he was digging the fingers of his disengaged hand into the palm. The kid looked embarrassed but happy at the idea of something to eat. So this fattish fellow put him at his ease by introducing him. It was about an hour after the opera and these comics were half-tight. As he called their names in turn they pulled themselves up unsteadily, and said in a nasty sneering sort of voice: "*À votre service, monsieur.*" One was the Count of something and another the Marquis of something else, and the third was the nephew of the Minister of War. The fat fellow was the editor of one of the chief Royalist papers.

'He ordered oysters for the kid, and the kid obviously didn't want oysters: he wanted a big lump of meat and potatoes and cabbage and things. He ate the oysters in an awkward sort of way, trying not to look hungry: but first he ate the little bits of brown bread and butter that they serve with them. Then he wiped his mouth and thanked them. The fat fellow and the nephew of the War Minister were talking in Italian about the kid; I couldn't make it out at all. It seemed quite mad to me. They got all soppy and talked about his beautiful eyes, and how strong his body was; they might have been a couple of grandmothers discussing their soldier grandson just going off with the draft for his military service. The Marquis and the Count were not interested in the kid. They were talking about women's breasts, very seriously and intensely, as though they were in the corset business. They were making drawings on the table-cloth with the Count's gold pencil; they had tried the Marquis's fountain-pen first, but the ink ran too much.

'The waiter passed and slipped a piece of paper into the printer's hand. He read it, crumpled it up and stuffed it into his shoe. Then he stopped his story about that morning's fight – I didn't tell you that this was the first of May – in which he had half-killed one Royalist by hitting him on the head with another Royalist, because the Royalists had tried to spoil their parade, and began to pay attention to the other table.

'The kid, having had his oysters, wanted to excuse himself, say good-night and go off – probably to sleep in the Bois. He looked as though he needed sleep. But the fat fellow whom they called *"Mon cher Grégoire"* wouldn't let him. He said that the little angel, meaning the kid, must have some dessert. I ought to have mentioned that they had already given him two or three glasses of old brandy and the kid was feeling a bit dizzy, by the look of him. The way he had eaten the brown bread and butter, he can't have had much in his stomach to begin with. *Mon cher Grégoire* and the nephew of the War Minister had now changed places with the other two and were sitting next to the kid and gently detaining him, holding his arms in a sickly affectionate sort of way.

'Grégoire called the waiter; the waiter looked angrier than ever, but obviously didn't want to lose his job by refusing to do what he was told. Grégoire asked him what fruit he had, and he said: "Every sort, sir." "Good," said Grégoire, "and now what angel's food would my little Cupid like to eat?" (The printer translated this for me; I didn't recognize the word *cupidon*.) Would he have Guava or Persimmon or Pampelmousse? The kid shook his head.

'*"Alors une pêche?"*

'*"Merci, monsieur!"*

'*"Alors, ananas?"*

'*"Merci, merci, monsieur!"*

'*"Alors, une poire d'Avocado?"*

'*"Merci, merci, monsieur."*

'The kid was almost in tears with embarrassment, gratitude mixed with a rising shame, even fear. The nephew of the War Minister had laid his sleek yellow head on the kid's shoulder, and was quoting a bit of Racine or something. Grégoire filled the kid's glass again, and said with some impatience that Monsieur Pierre – Pierre was the kid's name – was remarkably fastidious about his dessert. He went on with the list of fruits – mandarins and medlars and mangoes and God knows what. Then the nephew got hold of Pierre's hand and began admiring it, what strong, firm fingers, what a slender wrist and actually picked it up and began kissing it. It was the funniest thing you ever saw. He was probably the drunkest of the four. The Count and the Marquis were still discussing breasts, but in a very inconsequential way. Grégoire wasn't so drunk, though.

'Well, at last the kid shouted out in a hysterical but somehow proud way: "JE SUIS OUVRIER! AU DIABLE AVEC VOS POIRES D'AVOCADO!" He tried to get up, but couldn't, because the nephew was clawing on to him and kissing his neck. But Grégoire did not seem in the least put out; he turned to the waiter and said: *"Alors, garçon. De la merde pour ce monsieur.*" Well, at that the printer picked up a carafe of water, and, walking over to Grégoire, broke it over his head. Then he detached the nephew, and jerked him backward on the floor, and grabbing the kid, pulled him out. He got him into a taxi that happened to pass, and off they went at full speed. The waiter had pretended to stop us, but had allowed me to push him over with a bang against a door. As soon as he saw the kid and the printer safe in the taxi he began to blow a police whistle. But, of course, the taxi got away. I had thrown a loaf of bread at the Marquis, which hit him on the cheek, and that made me feel good. As it happened, I had only a few hundred yards to walk to my hotel, so I escaped all right.

'I never saw the printer again, or the kid. I was thinking of them just now and wondering what sort of a fruit *merde* was.'

Old Papa Johnson

IN JULY 1916 I was in hospital with one Captain H.H. Johnson of the Army Service Corps, who had a habit of referring to himself in the third person as 'Old Papa Johnson'. I was in with a lung wound, and he with a badly fractured pelvis. 'Of all the inappropriate happenings!' he said. 'Imagine, Old Papa Johnson, of all people, being laid out by the kick of an Army mule in the middle of a European war!' He added, to remove any misunderstanding: 'No, the A.S.C. isn't my corps, except just now for convenience. I'm cavalry, really – did fifteen years off and on in the Lancers. I was with them at Le Cateau and got wounded. And then rejoined them at Ypres and got it again. This time it was shell, not bullet, and the medical board gave me "Permanently unfit for Combatant Service". So I transferred to the A.S.C. – yes, I know you fire eating young infantry officers look down on that worthy corps – and I hadn't any great passion for acting as baker's boy and butcher's delivery man myself. Still, it was better than being in England. But now that ridiculous mule...'

Papa Johnson was about forty-five years old; very broad shoulders, medium height, I judged (but it is difficult to judge the vertical height of a man whom one sees only in a horizontal position), and a comedian's face. I only once saw it as anything but a comedian's face, and that was when a hospital orderly was impertinent. Then it set hard as stone, and his voice, which was ordinarily a comedian's voice, too, rasped like a drill instructor's; the orderly was terrified. Papa Johnson talked the most idiotic patter half the time and kept the nurses in hysterics. I had to ask him once to stop it, because it was bad for my wound to laugh like that; it might start a haemorrhage again. He had a small make-up box with a mirror and grease paints, and an assortment of beards and moustaches. While Sister Morgan was taking his temperature he would get under the blankets with a pocket torch – the thermometer in his mouth – and when the two minutes were up he would emerge in some new, startling character. A handkerchief and a towel were his only other stage properties. Sister Morgan would take the thermometer from him gravely, and he would say: 'Hello, boys and girls, I'm Queen Victoria as a young wife and mother!' or 'Beware, you wicked old men, I'm the Widow Twankey,' or

'Give ear, O Benjamin, I am Saul the son of Kish in search of his father's asses,' and she couldn't help laughing. And he would insist on talking in character until breakfast came up. Biblical parts were his speciality.

One day I was watching him at work on a complicated paper-cutting trick. He folded a sheet of newspaper this way and that, snipping it carefully here and there with a pair of nail scissors; he had told me that when it opened out it was going to be what He called 'Bogey-Bogey Ceremony in Sumatra'. He was full of tricks of this sort. I quoted a verse of the Psalms at him about it – I forget which it was – and he said, shaking his head at me sorrowfully: 'No, no, little Gravey-spoons, you've got that all awry. Never misquote the Psalms of David to Old Papa Johnson, because he knows them all off by heart.' And so he did, as I found when I challenged him, and Proverbs, too, and St Mark's Gospel ('It's the one that reads truest to me,' he said, 'the others seem to me to have been played about with by someone who wanted to prove something'), and most of Isaiah and the whole of Job. Also Shakespeare's *Sonnets*. I was astonished. 'Where on earth did you come to learn all that?' I asked. 'At a Jesuit College as a punishment for independence of character?'

'No, no, no; bethink yourself, child! Do Jesuits use the *Sonnets* as a textbook? I learned most of my stuff in the Antarctic – I was on two expeditions there – while we were snowed up. Some of it in the Arctic. But I learned most when I was Crown Agent on Desolation Island.'

'Where's that? Is that one of the Fiji group?'

'No, no, no, child. That's in the Antarctic, too. It's the most southerly land under the British flag. The appointment is made yearly – it's well paid, you would say – but others wouldn't agree – £1,000 a year and everything found. Usually a Scot takes it on. The Scots don't mind living entirely alone in a howling wilderness as much as we English do; they are a very, very sane people. But my Scottish predecessor stuck it only for nine months, and I stuck it for two years: you see Old Papa Johnson is just a little bit insane. Always was so from a child. So he didn't come to any harm there. Besides, he had company for the last ten months.'

'If the island's a wilderness, what's the sense of keeping an agent there and wasting all that money on him? Is it just to keep the British claim from lapsing? Mineral deposits waiting for development?'

Johnson carefully laid down his 'Bogey-Bogey' business before answering. It was, by the way, a birthday present for Sister Morgan. Johnson went out of his way to be friendly with Sister Morgan, though I couldn't understand why. She was a V.A.D. nurse, middle-aged, incompetent, and always trying to play the great lady among the other nurses; they detested her. But with Johnson she behaved very well after a time and I came to like her, though when I was in another ward I had thought her impossible.

'As Crown Agent, I would have you understand, Captain Graves, I had to supervise His Majesty's customs, and keep a record of imports and exports, and act as Postmaster-General and Clerk of Works, and be solely responsible for maintaining the Pax Britannica in Antarctic regions – if necessary with a rope or a revolver.'

I never knew when Papa Johnson was joking, so I said: 'Yes, your Excellency, and I suppose the penguins and reindeer needed a lot of looking after; and what with their sending each other so many picture postcards and all, you must have had your hands full at the office.'

'Hignorance!' snapped Papa Johnson, in the idiotic tones that he used for the Widow Twankey, 'Reindeers hindeed! Hain't no sich hanimals hin hall Hant-harctica. Them dratted reindeers honly hinhabitates *Harctic* hareas. Which there wasn't no penguins neither, not a penguin hon hall that hisland. There was prions, and seahawks, and sea helephants come a-visiting; but they wasn't no trouble, not they.' Then he continued in his usual voice: 'The gross value of imports and exports in the two years I was there amounted to... guess, child!' I refused to guess, so he told me that the correct answer was something over one million seven hundred thousand pounds sterling.

'For I should have told you, little Gravey-spoons, that Desolation island has a harbour which is more or less ice-free for a month or two round Christmas every year. The whalers put in there then. It isn't every ship that can deal, like the *Larssen* can, with an unlimited quantity of whale; so when the smaller ships have more oil than they can manage comfortably and don't want to go back to Norway yet – half the world away – they dump it in barrels on Desolation Island, in care of the Crown Agent, and get a chit from him for it. There are big store caves blasted out of the rock. The oil tankers come to collect the stuff. Also, a Norwegian company had put a blubber-boiling plant on the island for the convenience of its smaller boats – three great metal cauldrons, each about twice the size of this room, and weighing I don't know how many hundred tons. They must have been landed in sections and welded together on the spot; but that was before my time.

'When those fellows came ashore to boil down their blubber, I always had a busy time. I had to watch that they didn't pinch Government property or the oil belonging to other ships that I had in bond, or raid my house when my back was turned. I carried my revolver loose and loaded and hardly had time to sleep. But I was the sole representative of His Majesty, and he had given me unlimited power to make laws for the entire period of my stay, and to see that they were kept. After my first experience with a blubber party, which ended in a death and a fire, I issued an edict that henceforth Desolation Island was to be the driest as well as the coldest of His Majesty's possessions. I couldn't stop the brutes from boozing themselves silly aboard their own vessels in the harbour, but I saw to it that not a drop was landed on British soil. (Tough! you wouldn't believe how tough these Norwegian whalingmen were. But their ships' officers were tougher still and kept them under.)

'One day a tanker put in and two unexpected visitors came off her. One of them, a tall fellow with a Guards' Brigade moustache (here Papa Johnson made one up to show me, from his make-up box) and a quarrelsome sort of face (here Papa Johnson made the sort of face he meant) came up to me and said in superior tones (here Papa Johnson imitated them): "Mr Henry Johnson, the British Crown Agent, I believe? My name's Morgan, Major Anthony Morgan of the Indian Army. I have come to live here with you. This is Professor Durnsford, who is on the staff of the New York Museum of Natural History," and he pulled forward a harmless-looking little fellow with a snubnose and the expression of a Pekinese. "We intend to do research work here." He handed me an introductory letter from the Government of New Zealand. I was too busy with customs business to read it, so I put it into my pocket – you see I disliked the man at first sight and didn't like having his company forced on me without a please or thank you – and I said: "Well, I can't refuse you, I suppose, if you have decided to dwell among me. There's my house; it's the only one on the island. Make yourselves at home while I attend to these papers. I'll send your stuff ashore when I've examined it."

'Morgan flared up. "You will certainly do no such thing as to tamper with my personal luggage."

'I shrugged my shoulders and said: "It's my job; I'm Customs here. Give me your keys."

'He saw that I was serious, and realized that the tanker was still in the harbour and able to take him off; I could refuse to put him up at my house and so he would have to go back in her. He threw me the keys with very bad grace, and Durnsford politely handed me his. They were numbered keys, so I had no trouble finding the right boxes for them.

'That evening I cooked the supper and Morgan got a mess kit out of his tin trunk to eat it in. The man Morgan actually tried to old-soldier Papa Johnson with his row of ribbons. And do you know what they were? Child, one was the Coronation ribbon and one was the Durbar ribbon and one was the Osmanieh, which one gets almost as a matter of routine if one is seconded to the Egyptian Army, and the fourth and last was the M.V.O. of the Third Class. So, pretending to be dazzled, I went off with the frying pan in my hand and changed into my old campaigning tunic, which sported Ashanti, Egypt, China, King's and Queen's medals South Africa, and North-West Frontier. Not a routine ribbon among them; they made his display look pretty sick. But I had only two stars up, so he tried to high-hat me with his crown.

'Believe me, child, there was the devil to pay about my embargo on wines and spirits; he had brought out twenty cases of Scotch. At first he didn't realize that Scotch was not drunk on Desolation Island. He said that in his opinion it would have been courteous of me, perhaps, to have put a bottle of my own stuff on the table, since I had not taken off any of his with the first boatload. But when I explained how it was, he went up in the air and bellowed at me as though he was in his Orderly Room and I was a poor devil of a Sudanese recruit. I won't repeat what he said, child, because a nurse might come in and catch a word or two and misunderstand. I was pleasant but firm; reminding him that I was Lord Chief Justice and Lord High Executioner and everything else on the island and that what I said went. Professor Durnsford had been a witness to his threats, I said, and I would subpoena him, if necessary, for the trial. And I quoted *Alice in Wonderland:* "I'll be judge, I'll be jury," said cunning old Fury, "I'll try the whole cause and condemn you to death."

"'You can't prevent me bringing it ashore," he said at last.

"'Can't I?" I said, in nasty tones, showing my Colt.

'He broke into worse language than ever and the only true things he said about me were that I must be a little insane and that I had a face like Dan Leno on one of his off-nights. He ended: "Remember these words, for they are the last I shall address to you while I remain on this island." I answered, improving on poor Dan Leno: "Ha, Comma, Ha, among the trumpets. I'm Job's war horse, and I scent the battle from afar."

'Morgan kept it up throughout the meal. If he wanted the salt or beans or mustard when they happened to be right close to my plate, he would ask Durnsford, who sat between us, to pass them to him. I had decided to ship Morgan back home with his whiskey the very next day, but when he started this baby game of sending me to Coventry, I was so pleased that I decided to keep him with me. As you know, child, I love baby games. It was a nice game, because Morgan and I held the cards and Durnsford was pool for the winner to take. Not that I cared much about Durnsford then, but he seemed a decent little Pekinese of a man, too good to go coupled with an ill-tempered great mastiff like Morgan. They had arranged to come on this expedition together, by letter, before actually meeting. Morgan had written that he could get permission from the New Zealand Government for them both to put up at my house; and Pekey Durnsford was glad of a companion. Neither of them had been in the Antarctic before.

'Durnsford was the best possible "kitty" for our game of nap; he tried to be so neutral. Of course, I didn't go out of my way to make myself pleasant to him; that would have been no sort of game – an auction with the bidding in sugar plums and the prize to go to the men who bid highest. No, no, no! I answered his questions civilly, though not always pertinently, I supplied him with necessaries, and saw that he didn't run into danger: but I allowed him no loose conversation. Little Pekey Durnsford felt ever so uncomfortable (and even, I believe, went so far as to ask Morgan to apologize to me), but I felt perfectly happy. You see, child, having got accustomed to the deathly silence of Desolation Island when I was by myself for months at a time, I thoroughly enjoyed the very lively silence of the man Morgan. Often he was on the point of asking me something important about the island which only I could tell him, but then his haughty pride choked back the question. And so next day the question would come innocently enough through Durnsford. I would put on my "Schoolgirls we" voice and say: "Darling, that's a *great* secret. But if you promise *on your honour* never to tell anyone else in the world about it, I'll whisper it to you." Durnsford would smile unhappily, and Morgan would scowl.

'There were several rooms in my shack, but mostly storerooms, and only one big stove. Morgan made a show of moving his belongings into another room; but he got too cold and had to sneak back. It was a log-built shack, by the way, with steel doors and steel window shutters. It had an airtight lining and it was anchored to the rock with four great steel cables that went right across the roof. Understand, child, that in the Antarctic we keep a special and unique sort of blizzard, so these were necessary precautions.

'Well! The oil tanker had steamed off and the whalers had come and dumped their barrels and had their blubber parties and said goodbye; so unless there came a chance call from a vessel that was built pretty sturdy against the ice, like the one my predecessor went away in – he'd been killing himself with Scotch and couldn't lay off it because nobody was at hand to tell him not to make a beast of himself – unless a chance vessel called, you see, there we were together for another nine or ten solid months. I had a wireless apparatus, but it hadn't much of a range, and it was rarely I picked up a passing ship except in the season.

'For five solid months the man Morgan kept it up' (here Papa Johnson resumed the moustache, which had fallen off). '"Durnsford, old fellow, do you think that you could prevail on that comedian friend of yours to disencumber the case he's sitting on? It happens to contain the photographic plates. He has apparently taken a three-year lease on it, with the option of renewal. Haw! Haw! Haw!" Durnsford looked at me apologetically. I didn't get off the packing case, of course... I never asked Durnsford to relay a message to Morgan. I pretended he didn't exist, and if he had been sitting on the packing case and I had wanted anything inside it, I should simply have opened it with him on it. He was afraid of me and careful not to start a roughhouse.

'They didn't get on too well with their natural-history studies, because they didn't know where to look. I knew my island well and there's a surprising amount of life on it, if you look in the right places, besides the prions and the other creatures I mentioned before, which don't take much finding, and a few ratlike animals that spend most of their life hibernating, and even a few honest-to-God birds. In the interior are fresh-water pools with all sorts of little bugs living in the ice. Heaven knows how they keep alive, but when you thaw them out they wriggle nicely. Durnsford didn't know that I knew and I didn't let on; his big friend took him round to see the sights, but he wasn't by any means so good a guide as Old Papa Johnson would have been.

'One day, it was twelve noon on Midsummer Eve with the thermometer forty-five below and the stars shining very prettily – you have heard of our beautiful long Polar night, I expect, that goes on month after month without a spot of daylight to help it out? Well, one day – or one night, if you prefer – after breakfast – or after supper if you like – the man Morgan puts on his snowshoes and says to Durnsford: "Coming out for a shuffle, professor?" "All right, major," Durnsford answers, putting down his book and reaching for his snowshoes.

'"Durnsford," I said, "don't go out!" He asked: "Why?" in a surprised voice, so I said: "Look at the barometer!" Morgan interrupted, saying to Durnsford: "Your imbecile acquaintance has no understanding of barometers. This one has been rock-steady for the last twenty-four hours."

'"Durnsford," I said again, "don't go out!"

'Morgan haw-hawed: "Oh, don't listen to it; come along for a bit of exercise. Leave old Red Nose with his string of sausages and his red-hot poker; he's not in his best vein these days."

'Durnsford hesitated, with one snowshoe already on. He hesitated quite a long time. Finally he took it off again. "Thank you, Mr Johnson," he said. "I'll take your advice. I don't know what you mean about the barometer, but you must certainly understand conditions here better than Major Morgan."

'That was good to hear; I had won my game of nap with the man Morgan at last and scooped the kitty. And it wasn't bluff: the unnatural steadiness of the barometer meant trouble. I had made sure that the shutters were fast some hours before.

'So Morgan went alone, whistling "Oh, it's my delight on a starry night in the season of the year," and two minutes later a creaking and groaning and humming began. Durnsford looked puzzled and thought I was playing a trick. "No," I said, "it's only the house moving about a little and the cables taking the strain. A capful of wind. But have a look at that rock-steady barometer."

'He went over to it, and behold! the creature had gone quite off its chump and was hopping about like a pea in a saucepan. Durnsford was silent for a minute or two and then he said: "Johnson, I know that the major has behaved abominably to you. But don't you think – ?"

'"No, dearie," I said, "your poor old granny is very, very sleepy at the moment, and simply hasn't got it in her to think thoughts about troublesome majors and the likes of them."

'"Oh, stop your jokes, for once!" he shouted, "I'm going out to look for him."

'He grabbed his shoes again. So I spoke to him severely and showed him my gun. I said that I didn't mind his slaying himself if he felt so inclined, but that I drew the line at his killing Old Papa Johnson too. They were double doors; the outer one was steel and the inner one solid two-inch oak planking, with an airlock between them. The moment he unbolted the outer door the wind would get into the air-lock and blow the inner one in and then tear the shack to pieces in three seconds.

'"But the major?" he gasped. "Won't he get frozen to death?"

'"Your intelligent friend was killed by the first gust of wind a few seconds after leaving the shack," I said.

'That blizzard blew without stopping for seventy-two hours; any moment I expected the cables to go. I set myself to learn the Book of Ruth to keep my mind from dwelling on our imminent fate. Then it stopped as suddenly as it began. We found the body only fifty yards from the shack, wedged between two rocks. And you wouldn't believe it, but that blizzard had got inside one of those big metal cauldrons – twice the size of this room, I'm telling you – and blown it clean into the harbour! As local registrar of births, deaths, and marriages I reported all these occurrences to a distant whaler, a month or two later, and when the tanker eventually turned up, it came with a letter from the man Morgan's sister, asking me to put her brother's remains in the lead coffin which she enclosed. So I had to dig them up again, though I had said the burial service over them and left nothing out.

'As for Pekey Durnsford, he was so full of gratitude to me for saving his life that he slobbered all over me. And soon I found that he liked silly games, just like I did. It was he who first taught Old Papa Johnson how to do this paper-folding business, though Papa's improved on Pekey's methods a lot since. And in return Papa showed him where to scare up all the living creatures in our kingdom. Pekey found one quite new species of fresh-water cheese mite which he called Something-or-other Papa-john-sonensis. And you should have seen the letter of thanks that I got from the New York Museum of Natural History!

'Morgan's sister – now child, for goodness' sake don't remind her who H.H. Johnson is – I recognized her handwriting when she put my name on the fever chart – is not a bad woman in spite of her airs, though it's taken me three weeks and a lot of patience to coax her to be my playmate. And do you know, little Gravey-spoons? if it hadn't been for that whiskey business I verily believe that Old Papa Johnson could even in time have made a playmate of her ill-tempered brother.'

Interview with a Dead Man

AFTER A WHILE the dead man, recognizing my voice, began to whistle and imitate the masters of his old school, many of whom, bicentenarians, survived him. 'Though perhaps no longer, ahem, in the active pursuit of pedagogy,' he intoned in a mock-clerical voice.

'What's the news?' I asked.

'News?' he said. 'Well, for a start here's a letter that came last night from my executors informing me that I am expected to write a posthumous Anthem for the League of Nations suitable for translation into at least twenty-seven languages.'

He went on to say that he had indeed already executed the commission: early that morning he had written a marching song of hope, to rhythms heavily stressed for percussion purposes, and poked it up through the letter slit of the stout Welsh-quarried slabs of slate, inscribed 'HE BEING DEAD YET LIVETH', which formed the roof of his quasi-eternal resting place. He had, however, recollected the nearness of the church, where the song would undoubtedly be sung at Christmas and Easter, on Empire Day, the King's Birthday, and all similar semireligious, semipolitical feasts; and had slowly pulled the composition back and torn it up before the sexton had caught a glint of it.

'It was an ironic production,' he said, 'but the living can never believe that the dead have a sense of humour, so whenever any reference had been made to the song in my hearing or whenever it was sung or whistled, I should have been forced to chuckle audibly to disprove this popular fallacy.'

'I am beautifully embalmed,' he continued. 'They were obliged, of course, to remove my digestive and sexual organs, which are corruptible, but I still have my fingers free to pick my nose in the old absent fashion, to scratch my head when it itches and to use a pencil thoughtfully when the itch is eased. This is a lidless coffin allowing me plenty of elbowroom. My eyes are shut with coins, but that is no handicap in the decent darkness of the vault; even when alive, I always had the knack of writing with my eyes shut. I lay the left hand flat as a margin to the paper and, pricking the skin with my pencil each time, know by sensory indication just where to begin the new line.'

Thus he rattled on, remarking among other things that at least he had no more financial worries. He had benefited handsomely under his own will and paid the lease of the vault and of a small plot of land around it for ninety-nine years in advance. Unfortunately the freehold, the property of the Ecclesiastical Commissioners, was not for sale; he had, however, secured the option for renewal at the same terms when the ninety-nine years should have expired. He asked for news of his wife and children and of their stepfather.

In short, he was perfectly dead, and his daily postbag, because of the recency of his death, was enormous; he used the blank pages of letters and the back of envelopes for his replies. He was in no position to buy stationery, even if his signature to cheques or letters had been valid, which it was not. However, he calculated that the serviceability of his large gold propelling pencil (which held, screwed in its base, a copious supply of refills) could even at the present extravagant rate of daily use be prolonged for fully another three hundred years.

'With care, for as long as three thousand years,' he cried, 'and by that time who will care for my work except antiquarians?'

His mood was now so hilarious that I had no compunction in leaving him without another word of commiseration or encouragement. His parting joke was one about the legal impossibility of the dead libelling the living.

'But,' he said, 'I am careful not to trade on my immunity. I flatter myself that I died a sportsman and lie buried as such.'

Está en su Casa

'HOLA – SEÑOR!'

The sudden summons came from a thin hook-nosed man in a baggy white shirt, blue striped cotton trousers, and a black felt hat, who rose suddenly from behind a mastic bush a few yards off. I had been sitting for ten minutes or more on the stone bench of the *mirador*, a look-out platform built on the cliff edge, idly watching a tall-funnelled Spanish destroyer disengage itself from the horizon and disappear behind the distant headland to the north-east. Below me was a drop of nearly a thousand feet to a glaring white stony beach. I sprang up, startled, and may have answered in English; but I do not remember. He forced a reassuring smile, spread out both hands to show that he was unarmed and said in Spanish: 'Please forgive my disturbance of your tranquillity. You are an American?'

I answered: 'No, *señor*, you must not judge me by my elegant straw hat, a gift from a friend in the United States. Judge me rather by my old shirt and patched trousers. I am one of the victorious but bankrupt English. What a stifling day, is it not?'

This put him at his ease. 'Yes, it is very hot,' he said. But he stayed where he was, so I strolled over to him.

' Your first visit to Majorca?' he asked.

'The first time since the troubles started in 1936, when I had to leave my house and lands. And I remember you well, even if you do not remember me. Surely you are Don Pedro Samper, the proprietor of Ca'n Samper on the other side of the mountain spur?'

We shook hands heartily as I went on: 'I visited you once in the company of your neighbour Don Pablo Pons, back in 1935. I needed some really good cuttings to graft on two young apricot trees that had proved to be of poor quality, and Don Pablo informed me that you had the best tree on the island. I had the pleasure of meeting your charming and sympathetic wife. I hope she is in good health?'

'Thanks be to God, we are well, and so are the children.' He apologized several times for not having recognized me, explaining that my sunglasses, the greying of my hair and the thinness of my face had deceived him. In return he enquired after my health, that of my family, and the condition of my property after ten years' absence. And of course he wanted to hear about the flying bombs in London. The Spanish Press had played up the havoc of the flying bomb until it was difficult for anyone to believe that there could be a single survivor. 'And is it true that in England now potatoes sell at a hundred pesetas a kilo?'

'No, at about one peseta. The farmers are subsidized by the Government.'

'Well, well!' he said. 'Our journalists seem to have been misinformed about many things... But, tell me, did those apricot cuttings take?'

'Divinely well. I found a barbaric crop of apricots waiting for me – the branches had to be tied up to prevent them from breaking off – and wonderfully tasting apricots they are. Like orange-blossom honey. I sold a great quantity and bottled the remainder.'

'I am delighted... Have you perhaps visited Don Pablo since your return? You must know that he no longer lives in these parts but has taken a house in Palma?'

'Between ourselves, I have no intention of calling upon him. When I quitted the island at an hour's notice with only a suitcase and a wallet, I left a certain small affair for him to settle on my behalf. He neglected it, and his neglect has cost me a thousand pesetas or more. But I do not intend to recall the matter to his memory; it is already ancient history. And, finding my house in perfect condition, with everything in its place, I have reason to be grateful that his conduct is not characteristic of Majorcans in general.'

'No, indeed! His is a very special case. You know perhaps of my former disagreements with him?'

'You disputed about some irrigation rights.'

'We did indeed.'

'May I ask whether you are still on bad terms with him? In our village I find that the effect of the Troubles has been to end all personal and family feuds and unite the people as never before.'

'*Está en su casa!*, as we say here. He is in his own house; I am in mine.' ·

'I am sorry. I should be interested to hear the story if it doesn't inconvenience you to tell it.'

'It is a long one. But, Don Roberto – may I first ask a favour of you?'

'Anything that lies in my power.'

'I wish to seat myself on the bench of the *mirador* where you have been. I have been trying to reach it all morning since ten o'clock. Will you help me?'

'But, man, are you lame?'

'Not in my legs. In my belly.'

'You mean that you are scared? Then why go? The view is as good from that rock over there as from the *mirador* itself.'

'My doctor orders it – Doctor Guasp of Sóller, a specialist. He knows a great deal about psychology, having studied in Vienna as well as in Madrid. Once I have gone there, he says, and remained calmly for a while on the bench, making my peace with a certain important Saint, my nerves will recover and I shall once more sleep all night. He even offered to come with me, but I was ashamed to put him to the trouble. I said: "No, I will go alone. I am no coward." But now I find that I cannot walk the last few steps.'

He began to stutter and a light sweat broke from his forehead. 'Excuse me,' he said, 'the heat is excessive. You will perhaps take me there in a little while when we have smoked a cigarette or two in the shade of this rock? Meanwhile I will tell you about the irrigation dispute. Have you tobacco?'

'I stupidly left my pouch at home.'

'No matter. Here is good tobacco, and cigarette paper.'

'Contraband?'

'Did I not say it was good tobacco? You cannot buy this sort at any *estanco*. Allow me, you seem to have lost the habit of rolling cigarettes. In England you smoke only Luckies and Camels?'

He began his story between puffs. 'Well, if you know anything of the matter, you will know that I had been for fifteen years the tenant farmer of the estate called Ca'n Sampol, which Don Pablo Pons acquired by his marriage with Doña Binilde.'

I nodded.

'He dispossessed me, though I had an agreement with Doña Binilde's late husband that I was secure in my life-tenancy. Don Cristóbal Fuster y Fernández was a *caballero*, a man of the strictest honour. When he inherited the estate from his brother who was killed in the Rif War, he told me in the presence of his wife: "There will be no changes here. You may cultivate Ca'n Sampol for the rest of your life, friend Pedro. You have transformed the place since you took it over, and I am happy to leave it in your hands." In the island, as you know, a verbal agreement is sufficient between neighbours, and if there is a witness present it becomes binding in law. To ask to have it put in writing is bad manners. We pride ourselves on being men of our word. Well, a catastrophe! In 1934, Don Cristóbal died in a road accident, and Doña Binilde fell in love, at the funeral itself, with a profligate adventurer – this same Don Pablo – and married him on the very first day that the law permitted.'

'I did not know that there are restrictions in Spain on immediate marriage in such cases.'

'There is a law that safeguards the rights of posthumous children. Well, as you can imagine, the marriage caused a scandal, and I, for one, did not attend the wedding – out of respect for the memory of Don Cristóbal. Not a week later Don Pablo served me notice to quit the farm, which he proposed to cultivate himself.'

'And Doña Binilde?'

'She was infatuated with the man. He could do nothing wrong. And she was angry with me for my coolness towards her. When I appealed to her about the agreement made in her presence between Don Cristóbal and me, she answered: " Upon my word, peasant, I can remember nothing. I have a bad head for business matters."'

'But the Law protected you?'

'Certainly it did. In those days six years' notice was necessary. But I chose not to take the case to court. It is an uncomfortable position for a man to be tenant to a landlord who has a grudge against him, especially if the wife has instigated it. So I said to him, mildly enough: "Since Doña Binilde has lost her memory for the sayings of the best husband in Majorca, how can I press the matter? My word is not good enough for you, I see. Well, then, pay me ten thousand pesetas and I will leave on St Anthony's Day, when I have passed the olives safely through the mill." For it was not a bad olive year.

'"Ka, man! Why should I pay you ten thousand pesetas?" asked Don Pablo.

'"It is customary to compensate a tenant in lieu of notice. I am asking two years' rent."

'"Two years' rent! How two years' rent? You have ruined the estate by your mismanagement!" he yelled.

'I insisted: "The respected Don Cristóbal – may his soul rest in peace – thought otherwise. He knew that I found Ca'n Sampol in a derelict condition and added many thousands to its value. He told me so in the presence of Doña Binilde."

'"I remember nothing of that. I have a bad head for business matters," the lady said very stubbornly. "And, in the Virgin's Name, who are you to decide who is the best husband in Majorca and who the worst?"

'I should not have believed it possible that a decent woman could change so, even with the help of peroxide and red nail-varnish; but some women are as accommodating as chameleons.'

'But you got some compensation, surely?'

'Not two *reales*. I will explain. Don Cristóbal, like so many gentlemen of a generous nature, had been slack about keeping accounts. He had a good memory for sums due, and sums owing, but disliked committing his memory to paper, and either demanding, or making out, receipts. Don Pablo was aware of this peculiarity and therefore asked me to show the rent receipts for the last few years of my Ca'n Sampol tenancy. Four half-yearly receipts were missing. So he set those against the two years' compensation that I asked, and I had no redress, having always paid in cash, not by cheque, and having no witness to the payments.'

'What a nasty insect! And then you went to live at Ca'n Samper?'

'Yes. It had been bequeathed me by my old uncle some three years before: family property descended from my great-grandparents. They had once owned Ca'n Sampol too, though that was before the big house had been built there in Carlist times. You have seen Ca'n Samper. It is a small place but the soil is good, there is plenty of water and the orchard is valuable.'

'Someone told me a local proverb about its position... something about twitching hairs from a beard – I forget.'

He laughed nervously: 'Yes, that is right. St Peter, we say in our village, sits on St Paul's neck and twitches the hairs from his beard. The proverb refers to the two saints' sharing the same feast day. St Peter takes precedence and robs St Paul of the glory. And in the geographical sense Samper – the name is a contraction of the Majorcan words *San Per*, or St Peter – sits on the neck of Sampol, or *San Pol*, namely St Paul, because of my farm's situation just above the small western bulge of the Ca'n Sampol terraces. Yes, *señor*, though not showing any animosity, I decided to put a tight collar round Don Pablo's neck, a regular martingale, and pluck out a few bristles from his chin. Meanwhile, my wife and I could live comfortably enough at Ca'n Samper and enjoy the respect and affection of the village, who soon knew all about the negro's trick that Don Pablo had played us. Now we come to the story of the irrigation rights.'

He paused for a minute while he rolled and lighted another cigarette.

'"Water is gold,"' I quoted in the sententious local style which keeps conversation on the move.

'"And land without water is stones and dust,"' he agreed. 'Well, while I had been farming Ca'n Sampol, secure in my life-tenancy, I had not made much distinction in my mind between it and my own farm; in fact, I had rather robbed Peter to keep Paul fat. At Ca'n Sampol I had planted a very fine grove of orange trees – Florida seedless navels, brought from Valencia, the first seen in the island. They need a lot of water about midsummer, but if well tended they yield fruit the size of canteloupes and of a marvellous juiciness. Well, St John's Day came around and Don Pablo's bailiff greeted me in the Church porch after mass, and asked me to let down the water from Ca'n Samper every Monday and Friday, if that suited me. And I said, playing the innocent: "Ka, man, why do you want water? You have plenty in Ca'n Sampol. Enough for goldfish ponds and fountains and a turbine for the electric light."

'"Yes," said he, "God be thanked that the greater part of the farm is well watered. But the part separated by the Rock of the Ass from the rest of the terraces, lying directly below Ca'n Samper, does not enjoy the benefit of the spring which rises on the other side of the rock. And that is precisely where you sited the new orange plantation."

'"Of course," I said. "I had almost forgotten that I planted about a hundred Florida navel oranges while I was the tenant of Ca'n Sampol.

They no longer interest me." Many people were present and smiled at my words.

"'But those terraces have a right to the water from Ca'n Samper."

"'Certainly, they have. But only to the residue. Naturally in the winter and spring, when there is plenty of rain, you can have as much as you please because I cannot possibly use it all, not being a great water-drinker. But in June, July, August and September I intend to use it all. There will be no residue."

"'Master Pedro, that is a bad thing to say. You should never have planted those orange trees if you intended to starve them."

"'Be reasonable, man! Who is to starve first, myself or the orange trees? Now that I have to make a living for my children from a small place like Ca'n Samper, I must intensively cultivate every square metre of it. I can no longer afford to rob Peter to make Paul fat. If Don Pablo had considered things well he would have built a small reservoir to catch the winter residue."

"'It is a hold-up. This is midsummer, and unless you let down the water the trees will die. There is no great depth of soil in the plantation. The roots are touching rock already."

"'No, they will not die, but they will lose their leaves and shed their fruit, and be greatly discouraged until that reservoir is built. A pity, because they are beautiful trees."

"'What are you going to cultivate so intensively this midsummer? This is not the season for planting vegetables or trees, and your terraces are not by any means fully sown."

"'What is it to you whether I grow twitch-grass or coconuts?" That raised a loud laugh.

"'You are ill-advised to quarrel with Don Pablo."

"'I am not quarrelling with him. He is in his own house; I am in mine. If he wishes to buy water let him come and talk to me, and we will call up a squadron of lawyers from Palma to write the affair down in a manner so clear that neither he nor I can escape our commitments." The occasion, Don Roberto, when you came with him to my house a fortnight later for the apricot cuttings – that was when he finally prevailed on himself to talk to me. As you yourself have recalled, it was St Peter's Day and my fiesta; but it was also St Paul's Day and his fiesta. He brought you with him as a protection, trusting that my courtesy to foreigners would restrain me from making a scandal or slamming the door in his face. You may remember that, while you were chatting with my wife, and showing my little boy your watch that opened with a secret spring and also chimed the hour, I went out with Don Pablo to fetch you the cuttings. He did his utmost to soothe and caress me, pleading that I should let bygones by bygones, and give him at any rate a loan of the water until it was time to build a reservoir. "Have you no shame, man?" he asked. "Do you wish to lose the esteem of your neighbours? What will the village say if you let my trees die out of spite." I laughed loudly.

"'I laugh in your face," I said, " your neighbours are laughing behind your back."

"'It is not Christian behaviour," he said. " One would take you for a *chueta*."[1]

"'Distinguished Don Pablo, even Christians disagree at times, and your Saint with my Saint. For the Hermit of the Moorish Tower, who knows the Scriptures like any priest – he was once on the point of being ordained when he boxed the Superior's ears and was thrown out of the Seminary – the Hermit, I tell you Don Pablo, was explaining something of importance to me last Sunday. He said that according to the Epistle to the Galatians, St Paul entered upon a public argument at Antioch with St Peter, declaring that he was much to be blamed and a regular *chueta*, trying to make everyone else into a *chueta*. But what did St Peter answer? He refused to be drawn into a scandalous scene (says the Hermit), and instead, like St Michael when insulted by the Devil, left the matter to be decided by God. And what was the result? He was preferred to St Paul in all things, and entrusted with the gold and silver keys of Paradise which St Paul was not allowed to touch, not even with one finger. I am Peter, you are Paul, and the silver key at my belt is water. Call me *chueta*, by all means, but if you want water, pay for it you must."

'So he asked me to name a price. And I said: "It is not much that I ask. Merely a written statement from your wife that I was never behind-hand with my rent. That will be worth ten thousand pesetas to me. In return, I will cease to water my young coconut palms and you can have what water you require, summer and winter, and be saved the expense of building a reservoir." But he refused to do anything of the kind and called me a bad name. It was at this point that I made a great mistake, as Doctor Guasp has since pointed out to me. If I had been content to refer historically to the quarrel between the two Saints, long ago patched up in Heaven, no great harm would have been done. But before I parted with Don Pablo on this occasion I forgot the Hermit's moral about not answering in kind when insulted. I championed my own Saint, as was right, but in expressing my disgust of Don Pablo I foolishly sneered at the "Great Apostle to the Gentiles," as Doctor Guasp calls St Paul, in provocative words that I now deeply regret. Well, as I expected, Don Pablo was thoroughly incensed and fetched me before the tribunal.'

'And you won your case?'

'That was easy. Not only did I have justice and documents and important witnesses on my side, but I happened to be a friend of the prosecuting attorney's secretary, so that I knew in advance exactly what questions

---

[1] A Jew in Christian disguise.

would be asked and had all my witnesses well primed, and a series of very cutting replies ready for my own use. Moreover, I had subpoenaed Doña Binilde and she had to take the oath. Despite her love for Don Pablo she was not going to risk her salvation by committing perjury; I knew that well. So my counsel forced her to admit that, so far as she knew, I had never been in arrears and that her husband had expressed great satisfaction with my labour. The prosecuting attorney protested that these questions were irrelevant, but the Judge, who knew of the case beforehand from Doña Binilde's brother, who was very much ashamed of his sister, overruled him. Then my counsel asked me in cross-examination, whether I intended to bring a counter-charge for non-payment of my compensation.

'I replied: "No. Since there has clearly been a misunderstanding between Don Pablo and his distinguished wife, it will not be necessary. He will obviously pay me, as a matter of personal honour, and shake hands with me in Court." Don Pablo grew very red, seeing that the dog was dead, as they say, and came out with the money. We shook hands, and I said in front of everybody: "Many thanks. Now I will see whether I can spare a few bucketsful of water for your orange plantation. My coconut palms are doing nicely now, and I can perhaps water them a little less intensively." Everyone laughed, including the Judge, because the coconuts of Ca'n Samper were already a byword. But Don Pablo had to pay costs... Well, then came the matter of his Large Black pigs, you may have heard of that?'

'They trespassed, did they not?'

'They trespassed gravely, stealing the mast from under my oak-trees. I went to the Mayor, and served Don Pablo a formal injunction to keep his pigs under restraint, but he told the Mayor that he had a legal right to the mast. It was lying on the New Road, which was built to connect the Upper and Lower roads while the two farms were still under the same ownership, and the proprietor of Ca'n Sampol had, he said, a right of free passage through it and could graze his animals on their way through Ca'n Samper. So the Mayor brought this message back to me and I said: "If the answer is 'no,' then he must come to the Tribunal! And I lay you a hundred pesetas to one that I will win my case." And I won it.'

'Did he not have any grazing rights?'

'Certainly he had. One cannot stop a mule or an ass snatching a mouthful of grass as he goes along a road to which he has a right. And, to forestall all possible arguments on this head, the deed referring to the New Road – a deed drawn at the time that my grandparents sold Ca'n Sampol – contained a clause making the grazing rights reciprocal: my beasts equally had a right to graze in their passage along the New Road through Ca'n Sampol. But the Ca'n Samper oaks, planted since the deed was drawn, bore acorns of the sweet variety that are sold roasted on tile barrows in the market. The ordinary bitter acorns rank legally as "pasture"; these ranked as fruit. So, having disregarded my injunction, he was ordered to pay damages and costs, and undertake that his pigs kept to their sty in future... That was another hair twitched from St Paul's beard. What date was it that you left the island?'

'It was August 2, 1936.'

'A few days only before the catastrophe of the Invasion of Majorca. I daresay you read all about it in the newspapers. One Captain Bayo had advertised in Barcelona for volunteers to reconquer Majorca for the Republican Government, and he arrived, with a few ships and a few thousand Catalans and Valencians and Frenchmen, one Sunday morning at Puerto Cristo on the other side of the island from here. He met with little opposition, and had he chosen to march directly on Palma, the city would have been his. But he did not, or he could not, for his scallywags – and upon my word, though there may have been high-minded and idealistic revolutionaries among them, these were certainly a small minority – his scallywags preferred to loot the shops and cafés and villas of that little seaside place and outraged the feelings of all those who might otherwise have welcomed them and marched in their ranks. Soon they were all drunk, and the acting Captain-General of the islands collected the coast-guards and civil guards in lorries, and sent them to block the roads. By the time that Bayo had reorganized a part of his force and got them on the move, it was too late. The Italian war-planes had flown to the Palma airport, refuelled and came humming into action. The battle was lost, and much blood was shed, some of it by the peasant women who came out with butchers' knives to defend their property against Bayo's deserters, scattering them in twos and threes across the Plain.'

'A great disappointment to the Liberals and Socialists of the island! Before I left they were saying: "Now that General Goded has failed to secure Barcelona, the rebellion will be over in three weeks."'

'They were disappointed to tears. The precipitate and disorderly Bayo invasion was the worst possible advertisement for their cause, and they had no resistance left when it came to the Terror. The hotheads of the Falange soon got busy on the Reds and hunted them like thrushes. Not merely· the few Communists and militant Socialists, not merely the Socialist mayors and councillors and their supporters, but all sympathizers with what was, after all, the legal government. Of this I do not wish to say much except that the military commanders, who were in control, behaved correctly for the most part and discouraged lynch law. But for many months terrible things happened, in revenge for the terrible things said to have been done to the Anti-Republicans in Minorca, Catalonia and elsewhere; and as propaganda became fiercer on both sides, so the acts of revenge became more horrible. In all, about four thousand men died in Majorca, for the Nationalists were numerically weak and could take no risks of a counter-revolt. Majorca with its natural riches, its air-fields and sea-plane base must be held at all costs. "To be relentless now," they said, "is to be merciful in the long run." Trials became tragically brief. A civil war is like the shaking of a bottle of clear wine. It froths and grows dark with unsuspected dregs. I tell you, there are men who die here every month in remorse for their deeds of that day, though the doctors diagnose tuberculosis or heart trouble.'

'Private feuds become complicated with public causes,' I suggested.

'That is well said. In peace time, jealousy and rancour pass unnoticed or find vent in petty ways, but in a civil war it is different. If a bad man – and every village has one or two bad men, and many sour old women of the devout sort we call " Saints" – had been worsted in a bargain by his neighbour, or been passed over in a legacy in favour of a cousin, that was enough. The unfortunate rival would be denounced as a Red who had expressed sorrow at the news of Bayo's defeat, and off he would have to go to the overcrowded and insanitary Castle prison until his case came up months later. Sometimes he never even reached prison. He would "resist arrest" or "attempt to escape" and be found dead by the roadside with a bullet in him, or with a broken neck at the foot of a cliff.'

'Where were your own political sympathies?'

'I have no politics. I voted for the Socialists at the election which was the cause of the war, because the candidates for our Council had undertaken to build a new school for the girls and to bring the telephone to the village. My politics are the same, I suppose, as any peace-loving man's: I hate disorder, graft and inefficiency in government, and I dislike change. But when a thing stinks it must be thrown away.'

'And Don Pablo?'

'He came out as an ultra-patriotic Right-winger, talking as valiantly and immoderately as the famous "General Manzanilla," the self-appointed Nationalist spokesman, himself. He was so far to the Right that he nearly dipped over the horizon and came to China. Our village is isolated, as you know. No telephone, no telegraph, and at that time we did not even have a Civil Guard stationed there. And nobody had heard of the Falange except from the newspapers. But the priest preached the necessity of rallying to the Church against the miscreants who had murdered children and violated nuns and crucified priests in their own churches and wished to destroy every vestige of decent civilization. So Don Pablo stepped into the breach, as the largest landowner, and formed a League for Defence against the Reds. He said that since we had no armed forces in the village, we must get help from the Falange Headquarters at Palma. The next thing that we knew, he had two gunmen installed in the barn next to the Church, and was soliciting subscriptions to maintain them there at ten pesetas apiece a day until the danger had passed. He collected a large sum with the priest's help, so now we were thoroughly secure. The men were not of the island; the younger was an Aragonese, the elder a Valencian. Well, of course, in times like those, it was not enough for them to sit still and draw their pay. Defence was understood as offence, and since it happened that the Socialist candidates for the local council were all men of property and well-connected – the one who had hoped to be mayor was married to the priest's sister and had freely given a plot of his ground to make an extension of the crowded churchyard – well then, less prominent victims had to be found. There was a harmless one-eyed ancient, a bit silly, but the village bee-expert; he boasted that he had been a Socialist since the year of the Second International – whatever that may have been – and that all his bees were Socialists too. He was hauled off to prison with the face of a martyr and died there a few weeks later of peaceful senility. It's now ten years since there has been honey in the village. And the schoolmaster, who was not from these mountains, but a nobody from the Plain, he too suffered. He was altogether too independent and progressive in his views for Don Pablo's taste. He even favoured careers for women and, instead of attending mass in the parish church, used to go for confession to a friend of his, a retired priest with an interest in antiques and literature, who lived five kilometres away. Don Pablo had him lodged in the "Grand Hotel", as we called the prison, for six months before his trial came off. He was acquitted, but asked the Ministry of Education for an exchange of posts, and is now teaching in Palma, where he has a school of some importance.'

Don Pedro was now coming to the part of the story that made painful telling. Tears started to his eyes and he had difficulty in controlling his voice. But he continued: 'After these routine arrests, others followed of a different sort altogether. Bernat Martí, a schoolfellow of mine, who kept a café and butcher's shop near the Church and was a great wag, was arrested late one night by the two gunmen, despite the frantic cries of his daughter, a deaf-mute, and carried off in Don Pablo's car. He was shot in the back while trying to escape. "A dangerous Red," Don Pablo subsequently reported to the military officer at the Port. But if Bernat was a Red, then I am a negro. The truth was that on St Anthony's Day, when we have a bonfire and the beasts and cars are blessed by the priest, it is the custom in our village to make *copeos* – that is to say scurrilous rhymes to the accompaniment of an ancient jig. And on St Anthony's Day, two years before this, Bernat had rhymed about the indecent haste with which Doña Binilde had rushed to the Church with Don Pablo. When I heard the news of his death, I went at once to my cousin Amador, a good fellow but impulsive. I said to him: "The shameless wretches have murdered Bernat. Take my advice, go off at once to stay with your brother-in-law, the coastguard Lieutenant, at the other end of the island."

'"Why should I go? I am no Red."

'"Because you went to the trouble of indirectly warning Doña Binilde, before she married, of the profligate record of Don Pablo which you had discovered during your recent visit to the Continent."

"'Ka! I am not afraid of the man. If you suspect him of framing Bernat, why do you not clear out yourself?" But I could not convince Amador, and two nights later the gunmen took him off in Don Pablo's car as he was returning from a game of cards at the café. He tried to escape, they reported afterwards, and fell into the ravine, breaking his neck.'

I asked: 'Well, Don Pedro, and why did you not clear out?'

'For the same reason that my cousin Amador did not: for pride. My reason told me "go"; my pride said "stay". I stayed. So they picked me up the very next night, just before dawn, while I was coming home from Amador's father's house, where I had sat with the family to condole with them, as the custom is. They slowed down the car and shouted: "Jump in, we are going your way." But while the younger drove, the elder kept me covered with his pistol from the back seat. "I have a warrant for your arrest," he remarked casually.

"'It would interest me much to see that," said I. "Before you take me to prison, please have the goodness to conduct me to my house. There I can read the document by a better light than the moon, and also collect bedding, clothing and food. You understand that I must let my wife know what has become of me and give her instructions about managing my affairs if I should happen to be away for a long time."

"'No, no, we are in a hurry and the New Road would cut our tyres to pieces. You can read the warrant at the prison guard-house. You are a dangerous Red and supported Socialists in their candidature..."

"'And twice defeated Don Pablo at the tribunal," I interrupted.

"'Not another word," said the elder gunman, "or I shall use the butt first, and then the barrel."

'So I kept quiet and thought only of escape. As we passed the Mayor's house, where the car had to slow down to turn an awkward corner, I took a chance. I knew that they would not dare to shoot me in the middle of the village. I slipped off my heavy signet ring and flung it at his bedroom window; by luck my action was not noticed, because the elder gunman at that moment was leaning forward and muttering instructions into his companion's ear. And my aim was good; as usually happens when one is in danger, with no time to reason or calculate. The shutters were open, and the windows too, because it was a very hot night, and my ring flew straight in and rang on the wash basin. The Mayor leaped up with a start, lighted a candle and rushed to the other window. He recognized Don Pablo's car by its make and the beat of its engine as it disappeared down the road to the port; it was a German Opel, nearly worn out. Then he searched the floor and found my ring.

"'Bless my soul!" he cried. "A P. and an S. This is Pedro of Ca'n Samper's signet ring. The assassins have taken him for a ride."

'His wife, now wide awake, though at first she had grumbled at his making such a disturbance when she wanted to sleep, sat up in bed and said: "Man, there is no time to lose. Don't stand there gaping and saying: 'He is taken for a ride.' Hurry into your trousers, never mind your shoes; and unlock the garage, take the car and go after them."

"'I am unarmed,'" the poor man bleated.

"'You are a great coward. If I could drive I should go myself. Pedro is a good man, besides being your maternal cousin and the godfather of your eldest son. Have you no shame? You have nothing to fear. Drive fast, until you catch them up – yours is the better vehicle – and keep close behind them to make sure that Pedro reaches the prison safely. They will not dare to do anything with witnesses about and will hold their fire until they reach the desolate stretch of road between the *mirador* and the Moorish Tower. For the Virgin's sake, get busy!'"

"'Alas, woman,'" he said, getting into his trousers, "there is not a drop of gasolene in the tank, and it would take me more than five minutes to rouse a neighbour and fill up."

"'In the name of God, have you no sense? Take Tomeu's motorcycle – it is in our garage. You can ride a motor-cycle. And if I hear tomorrow that Pedro is dead, I swear to you by all the Saints and Blessed Ones that I will be your woman no longer. You can sleep in the kitchen with the cats." In Majorca, it is the women who command in the home, just as Solomon prophesied.

'Meanwhile, Don Roberto, you can imagine that I was far from comfortable with the pistol barrel between my shoulders and the car bumping and rattling along the road. We continued to the Port and then turned around the mountain-spur by the coast road past your house, and reached Ca'n Bi; then there were no more houses for some kilometres. But I could not see what I hoped to see across the valley as we turned the corner, namely the headlights of the Mayor's car coming in pursuit. So I addressed the elder gunman: " Friend, here we are in a conveniently desolate place. Before you kill me, will you allow me to address a few words to an old acquaintance of mine?"

"'Where is he?'"

"'Far enough from here.'"

"'What do you mean? Do you want to telephone?'"

"'I only want a word or two with my patron saint, St Peter.'"

"'He is dead,'" sneered the younger man. " You will not get through."

"'Shot while resisting arrest?'" I asked, mimicking his Aragonese accent.

'The elder gunman laughed. "This is a courageous peasant. I am sorry that we have to cancel his account. Very well, Master, we will stop here and you can kneel in peace on the *mirador* yonder and put your call through while I smoke a cigarette. Though, upon my word, I cannot make out why you should take the trouble to telephone one whom you will be confronting in person the moment I throw away my cigarette butt." They stopped the car and we got out, and walked to where we are now sitting.

'This is country that I know very well, by day and by night. When I was young I bought myself out of military service with the money I made by smuggling here. I used to hump forty kilos' weight of tobacco up from the beach below us, by way of the cliff track, and take it across the road past the Moorish Tower and away over the mountains. My hope was that perhaps I could break away from my captors and escape down the cliff where, being ignorant of the footholds and handholds they would be unable to follow me. But they knew their trade and kept me covered with both pistols; unfortunately, too, the moon was very bright and the first signs of dawn were already showing beyond the headland. I tried bribery, but could not interest them. The younger gunman said: "If we took you back alive you would certainly inform the Mayor, or the priest, and claim his protection and we should lose not only the money but also the confidence of Don Pablo."

'At this I suddenly solved a problem that had been troubling me for a long time. I cried out: "Chests full of gold ! Why did I not think of it earlier? You are a pair of Bayo's deserters, and you have hoodwinked the District Party-leader and Don Pablo and everyone else into accepting you as Falangist incorruptibles. Well now, that is very funny and I must laugh, even if it is the last joke that I am ever confronted with."

'"It is very funny, very funny indeed," agreed the elder. "My companion and I took the Falangist badges off a couple of young gentlemen whom we sandbagged in Barcelona during General Goded's visit, and kept them in our pockets in case of need. But get on with your prayer, without unseemly laughter, because the dawn, of which you will not see the corresponding sunrise, is nearly here."

'I was trembling like a valley poplar in the sea-breeze, yet would not admit to myself that my last five minutes had come. There was still hope of rescue; for, as I say, I know this region well, and all that normally happens here, day and night. So I advanced alone to the *mirador* and made my genuflexion to the East, as if in Church, and then settled down to pray with my head on the bench where you were seated just now. I prayed in a low, clear voice so that the gunmen should hear every word. My brain was working with great clarity, though my body was shaken with spasms.

'"Most blessed and illustrious Saint Peter," I prayed, "you who jangle at your belt the great keys of Heaven, the silver and the gold! Most merciful and humane Saint, once the chief of sinners – your colleague Paul alone excepted – insomuch as you cursed and swore from first cock-crow to second cockcrow, denying our Saviour Jesus Christ. Deign to listen to one who is neither a great saint nor a great sinner, but a villager of villagers who calls upon you in his extreme hour of necessity. Permit me respectfully to remind your Holiness that your servant has a peculiar lien upon your care. He is called by your name; he was born upon the very day which you share with your colleague St Paul; he was baptized in the Parish Church of which you are patron; and for the last ten years, as the senior Pedro in the village has been your *Obrero* – he has been charged with the organization of your annual fiesta, when we glorify your name with a religious service, a candled procession, and with dances, fireworks, a football match and agreeable diversions for the children in the Plaza."

"'Eloquent, is he not?" interrupted the younger gunman, tossing a pebble at me. "He prays like a bishop's bastard."

"'Leave him alone," said the elder. "This is as good as the graveyard scene in *Don Juan Tenorio*."

"'Peter, Peter!" I continued. "Magnanimous Apostle, who alone of the Twelve had the guts of a man and dared draw a sword in defence of your innocent Master, when the gangsters came to arrest him a little before dawn on Holy Friday. Glorious Saint, whose name signified 'The Rock,' upon you I build my hopes, and call upon you with all my heart and soul. It is for no favour at the Celestial Gates that I am pleading: I ask for immediate help. I conjure you, beloved Patron, by the blue waters of the Galilean Lake, and the blue waters that surround our island, until the other day called 'The Island of Calm'; I conjure you, Saint, by the nets that you spread from the boat of Zebedee, your father, and by the nets that we spread from our boats at the Port for *salmonete* and the tunny; I conjure you by the silver coin which you found in the fish's mouth, and by the silver coins which I yearly pay towards the upkeep of your Church and the glory of your name – Peter, my Peter, come, be present, appear ! Help, Peter, help!" These last words I shouted with such passion that they could be heard a kilometre away.

"'Silence, man!" exclaimed the elder gunman, flinging away his cigarette butt. "Come, Miguel, over the cliff with him."

'But I pointed with my finger: "Lo! Behold!" I cried.

'They looked, and gaped with astonishment, and the younger gunman whimpered like a dog: "Alas! See who comes! You should never have allowed him to pray with such force." Both stood irresolute, and in the silence that ensued I heard the distant crowing of a cock from Ca'n Bi, and the distant *pam-pam-pam* of a fishing boat as it chugged towards the Port with the night's catch. I closed my eyes again, and waited.

"'Hand over those pistols," cried St Peter, waving his bundle of fishing-rods menacingly. He stood nearly two metres high and the keys clanked loudly at his belt as he sprang towards us through the rosemary and mastic, his beard blowing wildly in the dawn breeze. They gave up their pistols like little boys caught in an act of naughtiness. He tossed one over the cliff in a high arc and handed the other to me. "Accompany me back to your car, rogues," he said, "lest I cast the pair of you where I cast that pistol!"

'They stumbled back, the Saint not saying a word but flogging them at intervals with his rods while I kept them covered with the pistol. He was red with wrath. When we reached the road there was the Mayor, barefooted but with the motor-cycle, waiting by Don Pablo's car, and we were three to one. So the Mayor left the motorcycle on this side of the wall, and climbed into the car, and drove us straight to the District Barracks, where he demanded to see the Commanding Officer at once. From that moment everything went very well indeed. The Commandant knew the Saint well, and knew the Mayor by name and reputation, and had once bought a cob from me which fortunately had proved as sound and sweet-tempered as I had guaranteed it to be. When the gunmen had made a full confession and had been put into the guardroom, the Saint said to the Commandant: "Don Pablo of Ca'n Sampol, when he hears of this, will laugh with one side of his face only."

'Believe it or not, that was precisely what happened. When the Civil Guards came later in the day to arrest him, he suffered a sort of paralytic stroke, which screwed up the left half of his face in a grin which has not since left him. After he had spent some months in the Grand Hotel, waiting his turn, he was sentenced to death for conspiracy against the life of an innocent man, but by the influence of Doña Binilde's relations, one of whom was the Vicar-general of Palma, the sentence was commuted to life-imprisonment, and they let him out after three years. *Está en su casa.* And I am in mine. But ever since then I have had recurrent nightmares of the *mirador*, and have felt myself tossed in a high arc over the cliff by a furious Saint whom I suppose, by the portfolio of documents at his side, to be St Paul. It comes upon me just before dawn and afterwards I cannot sleep a wink.'

It is one of the beauties of Majorcan story-telling that the point is never laboured. Don Pedro counted on my knowledge of local affairs to supply the details which he omitted. The gunmen, being newcomers to the district, were unaware that in the ruined Moorish Tower on the rock pinnacle high above the coast road, lives a Hermit, who just before dawn every morning – Sundays and important feasts excepted – locks his great nail-studded Hermitage door, scrambles through the evergreen oak glades and olive groves, crosses the road close to the *mirador* and climbs down by the smugglers' track to his boat-house at the bottom. There he says his matins, attends to his lobster pots in season, collects driftwood and sometimes gathers samphire from the cliff face, or caper buds for pickling, and goes fishing with rod and line. He is a very tall, strong, quick-tempered man, formerly a sailor, and disdains to wear shoes or sandals. Pilgrims visit his Hermitage often, to leave little gifts when they know he will be at home. They kiss the rope that girds his rough brown habit and sometimes consult him about difficult matters with which they do not wish to trouble the parish priest who, they say, is a good man but inexperienced in the ways of the world.

'Come, friend Pedro,' I said. 'You have recovered from your lameness. Up with you to the *mirador*! Lean right over and you will be able to tell Doctor Guasp from what a fall you were saved. Here is my arm.'

'A thousand thanks, friend. If you will pardon me, I can dispense with help.'

He went leisurely up the steps to the *mirador* and leaned over the parapet with bowed head, humbly making his peace with the energetic Saint whom he had insulted.

Bins K to T

I WAS MORE amused than shocked when I first realized that I was a matchbox and pencil pocketer: it seemed a harmless enough form of absent-mindedness. Why matchbox and pencil pocketers – the aberrancy is quite a common one – should not also take cigarette lighters and fountain pens, no psychologist has been able to explain; but in practice they never do. Another odd thing about them is that, however slow and stupid on other occasions, they are quick as lightning and as cunning as weasels when they go into action.

'Sign, please!' the errand boy would call at the door of my flat in Hammersmith Mall, and when I came out, fumbling half-heartedly in my pockets for a pencil, he would offer me his. Then, after scribbling my name on the chit, I would perform some ingenious sleight-of-hand – but exactly how and what must remain unknown, because I never caught myself at it. All I can say is that he went off whistling, convinced that the pencil was back behind his ear, while I retired indoors with a clear conscience; and that, when I emptied my pockets before going to bed, the nasty chewed stub of indelible was there, large as life, along with other more handsome trophies. As for matches: I would stop a stranger in the street, politely ask for a light, strike a match on the box he offered and, after hypnotizing him (and myself) into the belief that I had returned it, thank him and stroll slowly off. I often wonder what a film-take of the incident would have shown.

Pencils are cheap, matches are cheaper still. My friends remained seemingly unaware of my depredations, or at any rate never accused me of them, until one Easter I went to stay at Kirtlington near Oxford with one F.C.C. Borley, a Wadham don who lectured on moral philosophy and was an expert on French literature and wine.

Borley was youngish, with an unwholesome complexion, lank hair, and so disagreeable a voice and manner that he literally had not a friend in the world – unless one counted me, and neither of us really liked the other. His fellow-dons couldn't stand him, though he had a well-stored and accurate mind, praiseworthy loyalty to the College, and no obvious vices – except to dress like a stage-Frenchman and always to be in the right. He gave them the creeps, they said, and agreed that his election had been a major disaster. I had met him by chance on a walking tour in Andalusia, where I nursed him through an illness because nobody else was about; and now I was helping him with the typescript of a book he had written on drinking-clubs at the English Universities. I never pretended to compete with him in vintage scholarship or to share his rhetorical raptures over such and such a glorious port-wine year – Borley always chose to call it 'port wine' – or the peculiar and Elysian bouquet of this or that little known *Château*. And never let on that, in fact, I considered port primarily an invalid's drink and preferred an honest Spanish red wine or brandy to the most cultivated French. The only subject on which I claimed to be knowledgeable was sherry, a wine singled out for praise in the Fellows' grace at Wadham, and therefore not to be lightly disregarded by Borley, even though it meant nothing to his palate.

He had a Savoyard chef called Plessis whose remarkable ragouts and crêmes and soufflés these elegant wines served well enough to wash down. Out of respect for Plessis I never contradicted Borley or listened with anything but close attention to his endless dissertations on food, wine, the French classics and eighteenth-century drinking habits. In exchange, he accepted my suggested amendments to his book readily enough wherever style, not fact, was in question; but that was because I had left him his affectations and perverse punctuation and everything else that gave the book its unpleasant, personal flavour, and concentrated merely on cutting out irrelevancies and repetitions and taking him up on the finer points of grammar.

Over coffee and brandy one evening, when our work on the book was all but finished, he suddenly unmasked his batteries. 'Fellow-drinker,' he said – he had a nauseating habit of calling people 'fellow-drinker' at table and 'fellow-gamester' at cards – 'I have a crow to pluck with you, and what could be a more suitable time than this?'

'Produce your bird,' I answered, and then in a pretty good imitation of Borley himself: 'When we've plucked, singed and gutted it like good scullions, and set aside the tail-feathers for pipe-cleaners, we'll summon Plessis from his cabinet and leave him to the fulfilment of his genius. I have no doubt but he'll stuff the carrion with prunes soaked in rose-water, chopped artichoke hearts, paprika, and grated celeriac – then stew gently in a swaddling of cabbage-leaves and serve with hot *mousseron* sauce... What wine shall we say, fellow-drinker? *Maître Corbeau*, 1921? Or something with even more body?'

But Borley was not to be side-tracked. 'Frankly,' he continued, jutting out his pointed chin with its silly black imperial, 'it goes against my conscience as a host to make the disclosure, but in *vino veritas*, you know: you're a damned thief!'

I flushed. 'Go and count your German-silver teaspoons, check your forged fore-edge paintings, send Mme Plessis upstairs to go through my linen in search of your absurd Sulka neck-ties. There's not an object in this house that I'd accept as a gift, except some of your sherry – though not all of that. Your taste in furnishings and *objets d'art is* almost as bad as your manners, or your English grammar.'

He was prepared for some such come-back and met it calmly. 'Yesterday, friend Reginald Massie,' he said pompously, 'you stole every match I possessed. To-day I sent to the grocer for another packet of a dozen boxes. Tonight there's only a single box left, that one on the mantelpiece... Just Heavens, and now that too has disappeared! It was there two minutes ago, I'd stake my reputation – and I never saw you leave your chair! However, nobody's come in, so pray hand it over!'

He was trembling with passion. Caught on the wrong foot, I began emptying my trouser-pockets, and out came the matchboxes; but, I was glad to see, no more than seven of them.

'There,' I said, 'count! You lie; I did not take the whole dozen. Where are the other five? I believe you're a match-pocketer yourself.'

'You were courteous enough to change for dinner,' he reminded me. 'The rest of the loot will be found in your tennis trousers. And now for the pencils!'

I felt in my breast-pocket and pulled out eight or nine. 'The perquisite of my profession,' I explained lightly. 'Think of the trouble I've taken in correcting your illiterate English, not to mention your more than sketchy Spanish. I needed a whole fistful of pencils. You'd probably have had them all back before I left.'

'Tell me, how often in your life have you either returned a borrowed pencil or bought a new one?'

'I can't say off-hand. But once, at a Paddington book-stall, I remember...'

'Yes, felonious Massie, I can well picture the scene. Just before the train started you asked the attendant to show you an assortment of propelling-pencils, drew your purse, made a couple of passes and, hey presto, levanted with the whole tray.'

'I have never in my life pocketed a propelling-pencil. That would be theft. You insult me.'

'It's about time someone did, fellow-drinker! What a pettifogging rogue you are, to be sure. Convinced that nobody's going to haul you into Court for the sake of a penny pencil or a ha'penny matchbox, you lose all sense of decency and filch wholesale. Now, if you were to set your covetous eyes on something only a little larger and more valuable, such as, as – let us say this corkscrew –'

'I wouldn't be found dead with that late-Victorian monstrosity!'

'– I repeat, with this corkscrew, I'd have a trifle more respect for you. But you stick to your own mean lay. In the criminal world, *on dit*, William

Sikes, the master-burglar, looks down his nose at the ignoble sneak-thief and tuppeny tapper. William's scorn for you, O lower than Autolycus, would be an easterly blast to wither every flower in the summer's garden of your self-esteem.' He leaned back in his ornate chair, placed the tips of his fingers together and eyed me malevolently.

It is a fallacy that good wine makes one less drunk than bad. Borley would never have dared to talk to me like that, if he hadn't had a skinful of his special Pommard; and if I hadn't been matching him glass for glass I should probably have kept my temper. I'd once heard him remark after a post-mortem at a North Oxford bridge-table: '... *And if* the King of Hearts had worn a brassière and pink bloomers, he'd have been a Queen! So what, fellow-gamesters?' But there was no *And if* on this occasion.

Frowning, I poured myself another brandy, tossed it over his shirt front, and then tweaked his greasy nose until it bled. I ought to have remembered that he had a weak heart; but then, of course, so ought he.

Borley died, ten days later, after a series of heart-attacks. Nobody knew about the tweaked nose – it isn't the sort of thing the victim boasts about – and though I think Plessis and his wife guessed from the brandy on their master's clothes that there had been a brawl, they did not bring the matter up. They benefited unexpectedly from the will: a legacy of a thousand pounds, free of death duties. To me, in spite of my disparagement of his wine, Borley left 'the Worser Part' of his Cellar – it was another of his affectations to capitalize almost every other word – while 'the Better' was to go to Wadham Senior Common Room. I had also been appointed his sole executor, which entailed a great deal of tiresome work: it fell to me to organize his funeral and act as chief mourner. The bulk of his estate went to a second cousin, a simple-minded Air Force officer at Banbury, who took one look at the Kirtlington house, pulled a comic face and took the next train back. The will, I should mention, had been a last-minute scrawl, on the fly-leaf of a cookery book, which was grudgingly accepted for probate because the nurse and doctor had witnessed it and the intentions were clear enough.

I felt a bit guilty about Borley. Once or twice in the course of the next few weeks I had a novel twinge of conscience when I stowed away my day's catch of pencils and matches in the bottom drawer of my desk. Then one day a letter came from Dick and Alice Semphill reminding me that I was to spend a yachting holiday with them in August, and that *Psyche* would be found moored in Oulton Broad on the fifteenth, if that suited me. I wrote back that I'd be there without fail, accompanied by a dozen of Borley's burgundies and clarets which, though the Worser Part of his Cellar, were well worth drinking; and a bottle or two of my own Domecq *Fundador* brandy.

Psyche is a comfortable craft, though rather slow, and the Semphills were glad to see me again. Both of them are mad on sailing. Dick's an architect and Alice and I once nearly got married when we were both under age; we're still a little more than friends. I think that's all I need to say about them here.

The first night in the saloon, just before supper, eight-year-old Bunny Semphill watched me produce a bottle of Beaujolais and offered to uncork it. But he found the job too stiff for him, so I had to finish it.

As I was twisting the cork from the corkscrew, I started as though I had been stung. 'Bunny,' I asked, 'where the deuce did this come from?'

He stared at me. 'I don't know, Mr Massie. I took it from the rack behind you.'

'Dick,' I called, trying not to sound scared, 'where did you get this ivory-handled corkscrew?'

Dick, busy mixing the salad in the galley, called back: 'I didn't know we possessed such a thing. I always use the one on my pocket knife.'

'Well, what's this?' And I showed it to him.

'Never set eyes on it until now.'

Neither, it proved, had Alice Semphill or Captain Murdoch, an Irish Guardsman who was the fifth member of the party.

'You look as though you'd seen a ghost,' said Alice. 'What's so extraordinary about the corkscrew, Reggie? Have you come across it before?'

'Yes: it belonged to the chap who bequeathed me the wine. But the trouble is that it wasn't part of the bequest. I can't make out how it got here.'

'You must have brought it along by mistake. Perhaps it got stuck into one of the bottle-covers.'

'I'd have seen it when I packed them.'

'Not necessarily.'

'Besides, who put it on the rack?'

'Probably yourself. You know, Reggie, you do a lot of pretty absent-minded things. For instance, you pinched all our matches almost as soon as you came aboard. Not that I grudge you them in the least; but I mean...'

'How do you know? Did you see me pick up so much as a single box?'

'No, I can't honestly say I did. But I was wildly looking for a light and saw your raincoat hanging up and tapped the pockets, and they positively rattled...'

'I brought a lot of matches with me. Useful contribution, I thought.'

She let that go with a warning grimace. But the corkscrew mystery remained unsolved. I sincerely hoped that I hadn't suddenly become a major thief, as Borley had wished I would. It might land me in a police-court – and eventually in a home for kleptomaniacs. I picked up the corkscrew, which I'd have recognized in a million. It was a stout eighteeneightyish affair, with an ivory handle and a brush at one end, I suppose for whisking away the cobwebs from the necks of 1847 port bottles.

'Who were the people who chartered *Psyche* last week?' I asked.

'The Greenyer-Thoms; friends of Dick's brother-in-law George. He's an estate-agent; she paints. They live near Banbury.'

'Aha!' I said, 'that explains it. They must have been at the sale of Borley's effects. The principal legatee is his Air Force cousin, who lives there.'

'Violent T.T. types, the Greenyer-Thoms, both of them,' Alice objected.

'Secret drinkers,' I countered, replacing the corkscrew on the rack. 'That's why they wanted the yacht. It's easy to dispose of the empties; just drop them into the water under cover of night.'

After supper Murdoch asked me jocosely whether he might be allowed to smell the cork of one of my famous brandies. I roused myself from a dark-brown study, fetched a bottle and reached for the corkscrew. It was not on the rack. I glanced sharply from face to face and asked: 'Who's hidden it?'

They all looked up in surprise, but nobody spoke.

'I put it back on the rack and now it's gone. Hand it over, Bunny! You're playing a dangerous game. I'm foolishly sensitive about that corkscrew.'

'I haven't touched it, Mr Massie – drop dead, I haven't – I swear!'

'Tap Massie's pockets, Mrs Semphill,' Murdoch invited. 'They're positively wriggling with corkscrews.'

Dick caught a nose-tweaking glint in my eye. 'Gentlemen, gentlemen!' he cried warningly. Then he pulled out his pocket knife.'–This will do, Reggie,' he said.

Dick's a decent fellow.

As I silently uncorked the brandy, Bunny went down on his hands and knees and searched among our feet. Then he rummaged among the cushions behind us.

'*Couldn't* it be in one of your pockets, Mr Massie?' he asked at last.

'Certainly not!' I snapped. 'And for God's sake don't fidget so, child! Go on deck if you're bored with adult conversation.'

'I was only trying to help.'

'Well, don't try so hard.'

Alice didn't like the way I pitched into the boy and came to his rescue. 'I really think he had a right to ask you that,' she said. 'Especially as I can see the end of my best drawing-pencil peeping out of your breast-pocket.'

'It's not yours, woman; it's mine!'

'Let me umpire this tug-of-war,' said Murdoch. 'I'm the fairest-minded man in all East Anglia.'

'Keep out of this, Murdoch!' I warned him.

'Oh, forget it, chaps, for Christ's sake!' said Dick. 'If we're going to squabble about matches and pencils on the very first night of our sail...'

Under the influence of the Domecq, which everyone praised, we soon recovered our self-possession – but half an hour later, when we had finished washing-up and were going on deck, Bunny looked at me curiously.

'Who hung the corkscrew on that hook?' he asked. 'Did you?'

'Captain Murdoch has a devious sense of humour,' I told him, 'and if you find yourself catching it, lay off!' But a cold shiver went through me and I stayed below for a supplementary drink. The blasted thing was dangling from a hook above the galley-door. If I had been sure who the practical joker was, I'd have heaved him overboard.

For the sake of peace Dick must have asked the others not to comment on the corkscrew's reappearance, because the next day there was an eloquent silence, unbroken by myself, when I borrowed Dick's knife to uncork another bottle of claret. But for the rest of the holiday I was careful to go through my pockets, morning, afternoon and night, to make sure that I had left enough matches and pencils lying about for general use. I had a superstitious feeling that, if I did, the corkscrew would stay on its hook. And I was right.

I am a little vague about where we went, or what weather we had; but I know that when the time came to say goodbye, Alice couldn't resist asking: 'Haven't you forgotten your trick corkscrew? It's still hanging up in the saloon.'

'No,' I said. 'It isn't mine and never was. The Greenyer-Thoms left it here. Anyhow, *Psyche* can do with an ivory-handled corkscrew.'

'Thank you,' said Alice quizzically. 'But I don't think Borley intended it for us.'

That evening, back in my flat, I found that in the hurry of my departure I had forgotten to frisk myself for matches and pencils. Among the day's collection I found an outsize box of Swan Vestas boldly marked in ink *John Murdoch, his property; please return to the Guards Club*, and Alice's double-B Koh-i-Noor pencil with her initials burned on it – with a red-hot knitting needle? – at both ends and in the middle. This made me cross. 'Bunny must have planted them on me,' I reassured myself. 'It couldn't have been Murdoch – he went off yesterday morning – and Alice wouldn't have been so unkind.'

'Nice gentlemanly corkscrew you've brought back, Sir,' my Mrs Fiddle remarked as she bustled in with the soup.

'Oh, I have, have I?' I almost yelled. 'Then throw it out of the window!'

She looked at me with round, reproachful eyes. 'Oh, Sir, I could never do such a thing, Mr Massie, Sir. You can't buy a corkscrew like that nowadays.'

I jumped up. 'Then I'll have to throw it away myself. Where is it?'

'On the pantry-shelf, next to the egg-cups,' she answered resignedly, picking up my fallen napkin. 'But it seems such wicked waste.'

'*Where* did you say it was?' I called from the pantry. 'I don't see it.'

'Come back, Mr Massie, and eat your soup while it's hot,' she pleaded. 'The corkscrew can wait its turn, surely?'

Not wanting to look ridiculous, I came back and restrained myself until dessert, when I asked her curtly to fetch the thing.

She was away some little time and showed annoyance when she returned.

'You're making game of me, Sir. You've hid that corkscrew; you know you have.'

'I have done nothing of the sort, Mrs Fiddle.'

'There's only the two of us in the flat, Sir,' she said, pursing her lips.

'Correct, Mrs Fiddle. And if you want the corkscrew yourself, you're welcome to it, so long as you don't bring it back here. I should, of course, have offered it to Mr Fiddle before I talked of throwing it out of the window.'

'Are you accusing me of hiding it with intent to deceive you, Mr Massie?'

'Didn't you accuse *me* of that, just now?'

The thrust went home. 'I didn't mean anything rude, Sir, I'm sure,' she said, weakening.

'I should hope not. But, tell me, Mrs Fiddle, are you certain you saw a corkscrew? What was it like?'

'Ivory-handled, Sir, with a sort of shaving brush at one end, and a little round silver plate set in the other with some initials and a date.'

This was too much. 'That's the one,' I muttered, 'but, upon my word, I never noticed the initials.'

'Well, look again, Mr Massie, and see if I'm not right,' she said. And then, plaintively, as she retired into the kitchen with her apron to her eyes: 'But you oughtn't to pull my leg, Sir! I take things so seriously, ever since my little Shirley died.'

I poured her a drink, and we made peace.

Next day the corkscrew turned up in the pantry at the back of the napkin-drawer. Mrs Fiddle produced it in triumph. 'Here it is, Sir. Now see if I wasn't right about the initials.'

I took it gingerly from her, and there was the silver plate all right. I couldn't understand how I had missed it. *F.C.C.B. 1928*, the silver slightly tarnished.

'Yes, Sir, it could do with a nice rub-up.'

I saw no way out of this awkward situation but to earn credit as a practical joker. 'The fact is,' I blustered, 'I bought it at Lowestoft as a present for Mr Fiddle. I didn't intend you to see it, and that's why I made a bit of a mystery of the whole affair. I meant to keep it for his birthday. First of next month, isn't it?'

'No, Sir. Fiddle's birthday was the first of last month. Very kind of you, Sir, all the same, I'm sure.'

But she still seemed dissatisfied. 'Fiddle isn't a wine or spirit drinker, Sir,' she explained after a pause, 'and bottled beer comes with screw-tops these days.'

'How very stupid of me! All right, let's chuck it out of the window, after all.'

'Oh, no, Sir! You might hurt someone passing in the street. Besides, it's a nice article. Keep it for yourself, and give Fiddle a couple of bottles of stout, instead. He'd take that very kindly, though belated. And so would I, if it comes to that, Mr Massie, Sir.'

Late that evening I walked along the Mall with a neat package in my hand until I came to Hammersmith Bridge. When no one was about, I hurled it into mid-stream. What a load off my mind! But that night I dreamed that a nasty-looking corpse floating in the water had grabbed the parcel just as it sank and shouted to me to come back and collect my property. He rose dripping from the Thames; it was F.C.C. Borley himself. I turned and fled screaming towards the Broadway, but he came after me. 'It's yours, you damned thief!' he bawled. 'Wait! I've brought it!' And then, as a parting shot, heard indistinctly through the rumble of traffic: 'And the Worser Part (Bins K to T) for Mr Reginald Massie.' That was the operative phrase in his will.

I awoke with chattering teeth, jumped out of bed, switched on all the lights in the flat, poured myself a stiff drink, and went along to see whether the corkscrew were back again on the pantry hook. Thank God, it wasn't!

I re-packed my suitcase and read myself to sleep again.

In the morning when Mrs Fiddle brought my tea I told her that I had been rung up by another set of yachting friends in South Devon, and was catching the morning train there. I'd send her a wire to let her know when I was returning, and what to do with my letters. This was nothing unusual; I frequently leave home on a sudden impulse.

I booked for Brixham, where I knew that a regatta was in progress. Also, a bachelor-uncle of mine lived on the hill overlooking the harbour: an ex-Marine Colonel whom I had not seen for years and whose chief interest was British freshwater molluscs. We exchanged cards at Christmas and his were always superscribed: 'Come and visit a lonely old man.' I thought: 'Here's my chance to show a little family feeling; besides, all the pubs are sure to be full because of the regatta.'

Uncle Tim was delighted to see me and discuss his molluscs and his rheumatism. That evening he took me in a taxi to the Yacht Club for an early supper. 'You look depressed, my boy,' he said, 'and not too well in spite of your holiday. You ought to get married. Man isn't meant to live by himself. Marriage would tone you up and give you a motive in life.' He added sadly: 'I put it off too long. Molluscs and marriage don't go together. Children would have played the deuce with my aquarium and cabinets.'

'Oh, they grow up,' I said airily. 'Seven years' patience, and your collection would have been safe enough.'

'You may be right; but the poor little blighters couldn't wait.'

'Who? The children?'

'No, no, stupid! The molluscs!'

'I beg your pardon. But why ever not?'

'River pollution: those confounded chemical manures washed off the soil, you know. A regular massacre of the innocents: whole species destroyed every year.'

I shook my head in sympathy.

'But there's nothing to prevent *you* from marrying, is there?' he persisted.

'I collect matchboxes,' I answered, rattling my pockets gloomily. 'Mine is one of the finest collections in Europe. It would hardly be fair to bring up children among so much incendiary material, would it?'

Presently Uncle Tim, reaching for the menu, said that his rheumatism be damned: with our Dover sole and roast chicken we'd have a bottle of the Club's famous hock, tacitly reserved for resident members. 'I know that you appreciate a sound wine, Reginald,' he said. 'Not many young men do, with all these confounded mixed drinks about. Gin and vermouth – gin and tonic – gin and bitters: that's what it's come to. Even in the Navy. Pollution, I call it!' He finished enigmatically: 'Whole species destroyed every year.'

'Did you ever come across a youngster called Borley?' he went on. 'Chap I met once, here at the Club. He wore a floppy hat and an absurd tie like a Frenchman; said he was writing a book. A mind like a corkscrew – went round and round, and in and in, and then pop! out would come something wet. But, for all that, he had a remarkable knowledge of wine; and consented to approve of our hock.'

A waiter tip-toed in, cradling the bottle, and ceremoniously dusted its neck with the brush at the end of an ivory-handled corkscrew. 'I've brought it, fellow-drinker,' he whispered with a confidential leer.

'Good Heavens, boy!' cried Uncle Tim. 'What's amiss? Are you taken ill?'

I had dashed out of the Club, and was half-running, half-flying, down the slope to the Fish Market. The evening crowds in Fore Street blocked my way but I swerved and zigzagged through them like an international wing-threequarter.

'Hey, Reggie, stop!' a woman shouted almost in my ear.

I handed her off and darted across the narrow street, where I found myself firmly tackled around the waist.

'For God's sake, Reggie, what's the hurry? Have you murdered someone?'

It was Dick Semphill! I stopped struggling and gaped at him. 'Come into this café and tell Alice and me what's happened.'

I followed him in, still gaping, and sat down. 'What on earth are you doing in Brixham?' I asked, when I found my voice.

'The regatta, of course,' Alice answered.

'But why aren't you up in Lowestoft?'

'That's not till next month. We've been here since Friday. *Psyche's* not distinguished herself yet, but there's still hope.'

'*Psyche*? But she can't possibly have sailed from Suffolk in the time!'

'I don't know what you're driving at. She's not been in the Broads since last year. You're coming up there next month – at least we hope you are – and we're going to have a wonderful time. By the way, you haven't yet told us whether Oulton Broad on the fifteenth suits you.'

'Where's Bunny?'

'At school in Somerset. Murdoch will collect him when he breaks up.'

'Dick – Alice, I believe I'm going off my head.' I told them the whole story from the beginning, even making a clean breast of the matchbox business. They both looked thoroughly uncomfortable when I had finished.

Alice said: 'Obviously, it was a dream, but I can't make out exactly at what point it began and ended. Listen: I'll ring up the Yacht Club and find out if your Uncle Tim's there.'

The 'phone was close to our table. Presently I heard her say: 'You're sure? Not since last Tuesday? Laid up with rheumatism? Oh, I'm so sorry. No, no message. Thanks very much.'

She put back the receiver. 'It's not so bad, Reggie,' she said. 'You haven't let your uncle down. As a matter of fact, they don't serve meals at the Yacht Club; and the only cellar there is the Commodore's personal bottle they keep under the counter. So your dream didn't end until Dick·woke you up a moment ago. It was a bit more than a dream, of course; a sort of sleep-walk, probably due to worrying about that chap Borley. Lucky we met you. Do you mind turning out your pockets, Reggie, dear? That may give us a clue to how long you've been away from your flat.'

I obeyed dazedly. Out came eight matchboxes of different sorts, seven pencils and, among other odds and ends, the return half of a railway ticket from Paddington, and an unposted letter to Alice herself, written from my flat and confirming the Oulton Broad rendezvous.

'You came down here only this afternoon,' she said, showing me the date on the ticket.

There was also a bulky envelope containing all the documents concerned with my winding-up of Borley's affairs. Alice ran through them. 'I see you duly delivered the wine to the Warden and Fellows of Wadham College,' she said. 'And here's the itemized bill for the funeral at Kirtlington Parish Church. Oh, and a note from Squadron-leader Borley of Banbury, saying that if you'd like any souvenir from his cousin's effects before the auctioneer disposes of them, you're very welcome, but will you please let him know as soon as possible. He wrote on Thursday; I don't suppose you've answered him yet. Hullo, here's a photostat of the will itself! What beastly wriggly writing! Yes, it's witnessed by –'

Dick had kept quiet all this time. Now he grabbed the will and read it. 'It's all right, Reggie,' he said. 'You've not gone nuts, and we won't even have to get you psycho-analysed. You've merely been haunted – by a ghost which it ought to be easy enough to lay.' Then he burst out: 'You dolt, why didn't you take the trouble to find out whether your friend Borley was a Protestant or a Catholic?'

'I did take a great deal of trouble, but nobody knew. Even the College couldn't tell me, so I followed the line of least resistance and had him buried C. of E.'

' Exactly. That's what all the trouble's been about ! You see now why in your dream he called you a damned thief?'

'I don't understand.'

'Read the will again. Read it aloud!'

I read:

'I appoint Reginald Massie to be my executor... the Better Part of my Cellar (Bins A to J) are for the Warden and Fellows of Wadham College, Oxford. The Worser Part (Bins K to T) are for Mr Reginald Massie...'

'Not "*for Mr Reginald Massie,*" idiot; if he'd meant you he'd have written "the said Reginald Massie." It's "*for the Requisite Masses*"! Masses for his soul's repose, don't you see?'

The exhumation was not easy to wangle, hut I got it fixed up in the end. Then I handed over the wine to the St Aloysius people at Oxford and they agreed to do the rest. And on Alice's insistence, I wrote to Squadron-leader Borley, asking for the corkscrew as a keepsake. Since he sent it I haven't pocketed a single matchbox or pencil – so far as I know, that is...

School Life in Majorca 1955

DEAR Mrs HAMPSTEAD-HENDON:

Mother asks me to answer about schools for your children when you come to see us in Majorca, because they are the same age as Richard and me. First we lived in a village called Binijiny where they do nothing but grow tomatoes. I and Richard were sent to the Franciscan nuns, and I looked after him until he was old enough to do up his own buttons. Then he went to the State school because the Bishop won't let girls and bigger boys learn together, although at Binijiny there were only ten boys in the boys' school and only four girls in the girls' school. The Franciscans had the other eight girls, mostly with baby brothers. Richard's headmaster got 800 pesetas a month, not quite £2 a week, which he couldn't live on. So he spent his school hours at home translating William Shakespeare into Spanish; but as he knew no English, he translated a French translation. He had learned French when he was a waiter-boy in a Marseilles Economical Restaurant which his uncle had; he didn't like the life because his uncle used to buy the left-overs in the market, stinky fish and rotten vegetables, and say: 'We must show our clients an example by eating no better than they do.' That's how he came to be a schoolmaster.

You can see the Inspector's car coming up to the Binijiny mountain from two kilometres away, and it always stops halfway to cool down the radiator; so Jaime Frau, the boy who knew the lessons best, used to teach the little boys, and Juan Grau, the boy who knew least, kept watch from the Calvary outside. The Master said: 'This is good training for your careers, if you don't like growing tomatoes. Jaime can be a schoolmaster like me and Juan can be a *guardia* like his father.' Juan never missed the car and when it arrived the Master had rushed from his house to the school and was busy giving a lecture on the glorious days of Philip II - which is where history really stops in the school books until it starts again with Franco and the glorious liberation of the *Patria*. So the Inspector who was a *Madrileño* had a lovely *arroz paella* at the *Fonda,* and lots of wine, and then lots of *licores,* and a cigar, and said that Binijiny had the best school in his district. Once he sent for ten *ensaimadas,* which are a sort of very light sugar bun in the shape of a whirligig, and said: 'Now, my little friends, see which of you can eat the quickest. This will be a useful lesson to you in this island of bandits.' When Juan Grau won easily, the Inspector shouted '*Olé!*' and then grabbed Richard's *ensaimada* and asked: 'What is wrong with you, little English boy, are you ill? You have taken only one bite.' Richard said: 'No, sir! But we English can't eat so fast as you Spaniards.' Then the Inspector laughed and swallowed the *ensaimada* himself at one gulp. Then he made Richard kneel down with his arms stretched out like the penitents on Holy Thursday and said: 'Stay like that until you have given me back Gibraltar.'

Mother kept me with the Franciscans, because at the Girls' State School there was too much religion and also politics. One day the Señorita of the Girls' School saw me sitting on the convent steps eating my lunch, and said in a loud voice that all Protestants will go to Hell and burn for ever. But Sor Juana came out and told the Señorita that I was top of the class in Sacred History. At the back of our arithmetic book which we had to use was the Spanish eagle holding the Falangist arrows in its claws, and that day Sor Juana told the little ones: 'That's the *Demonio* who comes for naughty children.' In Spanish schools one learns everything off by heart and chants it, and nobody explains what anything means, and nobody cares. Mother paid the nuns fifty pesetas a term for Richard and me, and they were very contented. We talked Majorcan in the playground. It is an easy language, a sort of Italianish French, but one has to shout it or they think you are ill and want to give you a purge.

Two years ago we moved to Palma, which is a large city, and were sent to State schools near our flat. They never opened our windows and I had sixty in my class, mostly poor girls. There was no fireplace but the room soon warmed up even when there was snow on the mountains, and we sat three girls to every desk made for two. My Señorita was very sweet, but I got fleas and sore throats. One day, when a steamroller passed, a window pane fell out and broke; and it never got mended, which was a good thing, of course. Richard's boys in the school next door were lucky to have a playground where they played bullfights and 'hit me harder'; we girls had to stay at our desks (taking turns to go to the *retrete*) and embroider. He got into trouble because his friends caught the steamroller in a booby-trap and burst the water-main, so that the whole suburb was without water for a month. And he learned to throw stones at cars and insult policemen.

Mother took us both away and now we go to the two best schools in the Island. Mine is a convent, and we wear sailor suits and learn French and I am actually allowed out early to learn ballet - because my ballet teacher is a Catholic *refugiada* from the Russians - but I have to be very industrious to make up. One gets ribbons and coloured scarves to wear for being that, and now I am so dressed up that the girls nickname me 'The Capitán General of the Baleares'. Richard's new headmaster is a priest who knows Piccadilly in London and says: 'To everyone his own religion!' and asked

Mother about Richard's psychology before he went. He built the school on an English plan with windows that go up and down, and lavatories with water; and he gives gymnastics and basket-ball. There's an old grey cockatoo who knows the whole *Grado Elemental* book off by heart, and a huge black dog who wanders in and out of the classrooms. Mother pays a lot for us - more than £3 a month each, including school dinners and school books; but we are supposed to make valuable friendships with the daughters and sons of rich businessmen. The playground language is Spanish, because the rich businessmen don't like to have their children mistaken for ordinary Majorcans, even though they are. I think your children would be happy in our schools and soon learn Spanish, but they might not like having to eat bread and oil rubbed with garlic at dinner. We are accustomed to it; but not to the *garbanzo* soup, which is filthy. When it comes round I ask the girls at my table: 'Does anyone know the third person plural past definite tense of the verb *avoir?*' And they shout it out, and it sounds like everyone being sick, and the nun gets cross.

Love from Margaret

P.S. I enclose the *Bulletin* of St Modesto of Bobbio's College in case you are interested.

Bulletin of the College of St Modesto of Bobbio
No. 119 Autumn 1955

THE COLLEGE, IN its stony immobility, gives signs of awakening life. Somnolent, it casts off the lethargy of a long summer siesta, and makes ready to receive you, dearest young collegians, to its throbbing bosom... At last it is the first week of October, and the end of our annual course in June becomes a retrospect of centuries. The piles of exuberant text-books impatiently await the caress of your industrious hands, while over the now no longer silent cloisters and the already noisy classroom broods the benign and gentle spirit of our illustrious Patron, the incomparable Saint Modesto of Bobbio.

So to work, my friends !

If you are a student and are made to study, this is no sort of injury. Far contrariwise. Learning and the results of learning are absolutely necessary for a man of superior station. If you study with all your forces you will amass a vast capital, on the interest of which you will one day be able to live in voluptuous ease. A student who abandons himself to beachcombing and the gipsy life, prejudices not only himself but his future sons and grandsons, and educated society in general.

With this little prologue I shall present you to the students who have crowned themselves with glory by passing with distinction their Baccalaureat. Let the presentation take the form of a few distinct interviews:

Alonzo García

I found Alonzo rolling dice, left hand against the right, in the Hall of Seraphic Youth. He is a serious adolescent in white trousers and khaki shirt, as absorbed in his game as when he played goal last spring in our football team that knocked such lumps of flesh out of our rivals of St Dominic's.

'Tell me, Alonzo - to what career will you dedicate yourself ?'

'Well, at the moment, I shall respect my good Uncle's desire that I should join him as a humble assistant in the business which has given him so portly a belly.'

'Of course: he is a director of the Madrid Bull Ring management, is he not?'

'Exactly: he contemplates to present to the public more valiant and dependable cornupeds than ever were seen before in the history of Spain, and more valiant and brilliant artists of killing. If, in some modest way, I can contribute to the glories of the National Fiesta...'

'You have chosen well, Alonzo. Moreover, I greatly applauded your organization of the end-of-term bullfight, which was full of colour and passion. Everything for the Fatherland... Perhaps there will be reduced fees for your old teachers.'

We parted smiling.

Diego Vásquez
Diego was discovered in a romantic corner of the cloisters. He explained to us that he had his eye on a career which would be not only momentarily profitable, but would lead to a splendid future: that of interpreter-guide to tourists visiting the public buildings of our city.

'I think you have chosen well, Diego. Although one cannot occasionally repress a feeling of disgust at a sight of these ill-mannered sightseers, especially young women who often do not hesitate to enter sacred edifices without decently shrouding their heads, or their upper arms, or their semi-bare bosoms, and who even wear tight shorts like footballers, it is necessary to forgive them. They are doubtless Protestants or Jews and therefore totally without culture. It will be your duty and privilege to instruct them, with true Spanish courtesy, in decent comportment. After all, the tourist trade is most necessary to the national economy, as the Ministers of State never fail to remind us.'

'I will try to feel no resentment towards these savages.'

'Noble boy!'

Jaime and Cayetano Bobadilla, also Antonio Alemán
The three new bachelors who are about to enter the Royal Military Academy were found in the Health and Faith Gymnasium, tossing the medicine-bag one to the other.

As I entered unexpectedly, the said bag happened to strike me on the side of the head and I fell prostrate. The three comrades made the most chivalrous excuses and explanations...

It appears that the Bobadilla brothers intend to follow in the footsteps of their illustrious ancestors and carve a way to Fortune with the shining sword. Both are super-aces in the Gymnasium referred to; but Antonio Alemán, though the son of an historical professor, almost excels them in the flame-like loyalty which he consecrates to the military life.

'I dedicate myself to repairing a historical injustice nearly three centuries old.'

'You refer to Gibraltar?'

[An audible gnashing of resentful teeth.]

'If I have to tear down the alien flag with fingers ensanguined from scaling that truly Spanish crag, I will do so.'

'May God go with you, Antonio!'

The Bobadilla brothers echo this correct sentiment fervently.

Francisco Maura

As I entered the Library, where Francisco, a dwarfish but brilliant student, was consulting a new work of algebra recently set upon the shelves, I uncovered myself; for I knew that I stood in the presence of a future Atomic Physicist!

'And the cobalt bomb ?' I asked.

'It will not be long before we Castilians are able to construct bombs of transcendental power from even the cheapest materials, which Spain and her colonies can supply in prodigal quantities. Nothing can then hold back our glorious march of scientific progress...'

'Among these materials... ?'

'I will begin with tin-plate, of which this country has an excess, owing to the growing and natural preference of the public for aluminium coffee-pots and galvanized iron watering-cans.'

'May the noise of your explosions reach this Library only as a distant reverberation from the evil cities of Moscow and Leningrad - the Sodom and Gomorrah of today!'

Francisco's good-natured grin nearly halved his cherub's face.

Mauricio Venturoso

I had envisaged Mauricio, our exalted young philosopher, as a future occupant of the Chair of Logic at the Central University, not to mention making complimentary visits to Oxford, where he would expound Hegel and Kant or refute the theories of the late Ortega y Gasset. But this is not to be, he tells me, philosophically enough.

'What alternative profession, Mauricio?'

'The simple one of entering my father's business: the fabrication of innumerable plastic novelties.'

'Demark a few, if you please.'

'What shall I say...? Plastic flower-pots, plastic infantile night-vases, plastic back-scratchers for export to the Moroccans, plastic cock-spurs.'

'Did you say "cock-spurs"?'

'Yes, indeed, they are very necessary in the cock-fighting industry, since the humanity of the present regime forbids the use of metal ones; but they serve very well, being not only sharp but resistant.'

'Perhaps, after all, it is better that you should consider the nation's material interests, Mauricio, than waste your inherited talents on such difficult problems in philosophy as often entice to views incompatible with true belief.'

'Ah, flaming youth! Each to the conquest of his own ideal!'

Curiosities

An Appetite

The American soldier Chester Salvatori costs the Army authorities large sums on account of the quantity of alimentation which is a daily necessity to him. Although the aforesaid soldier weighs no more than 158 lb (or say 70 kilos), he is accustomed to breakfast off 40 eggs, eight rashers of bacon, a ration of oatmeal, with three litres of milk and one of coffee. On a certain occasion he devoured a 16-1b (or say $7^1/_2$ kilos) turkey at a sitting. On another he disposed of 38 pork chops. What about posting him to the Commissariat ?

A unique training programme

A prisoner in the *Santé* at Paris has evolved a very original training programme. His mattress was infested with bed-bugs, and he decided to train a large-sized spider to hunt them. He succeeded remarkably well, and the spider devoured the bed-bugs with such expedition that he soon was able to pass a few excessively tranquil nights.

Cure for seasickness

A Portuguese diplomat was so subject to seasickness that he feared that he would never reach the country to which he was destined. In the midst of his anxieties he threw himself from his bunk, whereupon it occurred to him to look at himself in a mirror - which cured him instantly. He made diverse proofs with sundry other seasick passengers, all with the same success.

The remedy is both cheap and easy.

Congratulations! His Excellency the Civil Governor and Provincial Chief of the Falange, Comrade Lorenzo Jurado Hurtado, has personally presented the First Prize of the Juvenile Pigeon-Shooting Championship to Felipe González, alumnus of this College. He felled not less than ten of the enemy in twelve discharges.

Notice: It is with sorrowful anger that the Reverend Father charged with the Direction of this Sacred College spews out the scandalous and painful charge that the Mercedes-Benz automobile, in which he takes his needful journeys, was purchased with College Funds. It is sufficiently well known that this splendid vehicle - impudently and blasphemously nicknamed 'The Sandals of St Modesto' - was won, equally with the Vespa motor-scooter possessed by the College Librarian, in a bona fide public lottery organized for Charity under ecclesiastical auspices.

To conclude this little bulletin, collegians! You must apply yourselves seriously to your studies in the present autumn. If you do the contrary, you will be a hazard and disturbance to your companions; a despair to your professors; a disgrace to your family and country. And how to explain your miserable frowardness to our Patron, who watches over us all and whose hot tears fall reproachfully on all unworthy heads?

Treacle Tart

THE NEWS TRAVELLED from group to group along the platform of Victoria Station, impressing our parents and kid-sisters almost as much as ourselves. A lord was coming to our prep-school. A real lord. A new boy, only eight years old. Youngest son of the Duke of Downshire. A new boy, yet a lord. Lord Julius Bloodstock. Some name! Crikey!

Excitement strong enough to check the rebellious tears of home-lovers, and make our last good-byes all but casual. None of us having had any contact with the peerage, it was argued by some, as we settled in our reserved Pullman carriage, that on the analogy of policemen there couldn't be boy-lords. However, Mr Lees, the Latin Master (declined: *Lees, Lees, Lem, Lei, Lei, Lee*) confirmed the report. The lord was being driven to school that morning in the ducal Rolls-Royce. Crikey, again! *Cricko, Crickere, Crikey, Crictum!*

Should we be expected to call him 'your Grace', or 'Sire', or something? Would he keep a coronet in his tuck-box? Would the masters dare cane him if he broke school rules or didn't know his prep?

Billington Secundus told us that his father (the famous Q.C.) had called Thos a 'tuft-hunting toad-eater', as meaning that he was awfully proud of knowing important people, such as bishops and Q.C.'s and lords. To this Mr Lees turned a deaf ear, though making ready to crack down on any further disrespectful remarks about the Rev. Thomas Pearce, our Headmaster. None came. Most of us were scared stiff of Thos; besides, everyone but Billington Secundus considered pride in knowing important people an innocent enough emotion.

Presently Mr Lees folded his newspaper and said: 'Bloodstock, as you will learn to call him, is a perfectly normal little chap, though he happens to have been born into the purple – if anyone present catches the allusion. Accord him neither kisses nor cuffs (*nec oscula, nec verbera*, both neuter) and all will be well. By the way, this is to be his first experience of school life. The Duke has hitherto kept him at the Castle under private tutors.'

At the Castle, under private tutors! Crikey! *Crikey, Crikius, Crikissime!*

We arrived at the Cedars just in time for school dinner. Thos, rather self-consciously, led a small, pale, fair-haired boy into the dining-hall, and showed him his seat at the end of the table among the other nine new-comers. 'This is Lord Julius Bloodstock, boys,' he boomed. 'You will just call him Bloodstock. No titles or other honorifics here.'

'Then I prefer to be called Julius.' His first memorable words.

'We happen to use only surnames at Brown Friars,' chuckled Thos; then he said Grace.

None of Julius's table-mates called him anything at all, to begin with, being either too miserable or too shy even to say 'Pass the salt, please.' But after the soup, and half-way through the shepherd's pie (for once not made of left-overs) Billington Tertius, to win a bet, leant boldly across the table and asked: 'Lord, why didn't you come by train, same as the rest of us?'

Julius did not answer at first, but when his neighbours nudged him, he said: 'The name is Julius, and my father was afraid of finding newspaper photographers on the platform. They can be such a nuisance. Two of them were waiting for us at the school gates, and my father sent the chauffeur to smash both their cameras.'

This information had hardly sunk in before the third course appeared: treacle tart. Today was Monday: onion soup, shepherd's pie and carrots, treacle tart. Always had been. Even when Mr Lees-Lees-Lem had been a boy here and won top scholarship to Winchester. 'Treacle. From the Greek *theriace*, though the Greeks did not, of course...' With this, Mr Lees, who sat at the very end of the table, religiously eating treacle tart, looked up to see whether anyone were listening; and noticed that Julius had pushed away his plate, leaving the oblong of tough burned pastry untouched.

'Eat it, boy!' said Mr Lees. 'Not allowed to leave anything here for Mr Good Manners. School rule.'

'I never eat treacle tart,' explained Julius with a little sigh.

'You are expected to address me as "sir",' said Mr Lees.

Julius seemed surprised. 'I thought we didn't use titles here, or other honorifics,' he said, 'but only surnames?'

'Call me "sir",' insisted Mr Lees, not quite certain whether this were innocence or impertinence.

'Sir,' said Julius, shrugging faintly.

'Eat your tart,' snapped Mr Lees.

'But I never eat treacle tart – sir!'

'It's my duty to see that you do so, every Monday.'

Julius smiled. 'What a queer duty!' he said incredulously.

Titters, cranings of necks. Then Thos called jovially down the table: 'Well, Lees, what's the news from your end? Are the summer holidays reported to have been wearisomely long?'

'No, Headmaster. But I cannot persuade an impertinent boy to sample our traditional treacle tart.'

'Send him up here,' said Thos in his most portentous voice. 'Send him up here, plate and all! Oliver Twist asking for less, eh?'

When Thos recognized Julius, his face changed and he swallowed a couple of times, but having apparently lectured the staff on making not the least difference between duke's son and shopkeeper's son, he had to put his foot down. 'My dear boy,' he said, 'let me see you eat that excellent piece of food without further demur; and no nonsense.'

'I never eat treacle tart, Headmaster.'

Thos started as though he had been struck in the face. He said slowly: 'You mean perhaps: "I have lost my appetite, sir." Very well, but your appetite will return at supper time, you mark my words – and so will the treacle tart.'

The sycophantic laughter which greeted this prime Thossism surprised Julius but did not shake his poise. Walking to the buttery-table, he laid down the plate, turned on his heel, and walked calmly back to his seat.

Thos at once rose and said Grace in a challenging voice.

'Cocky ass, I'd like to punch his lordly head for him,' growled Billington Secundus later that afternoon.

'You'd have to punch mine first,' I said. 'He's a... the thing we did in Gray's *Elegy* – a village Hampden. Standing up to Lees and Thos in mute inglorious protest against that foul treacle tart.'

'You're a tuft-hunting toad-eater.'

'I may be. But I'd rather eat toads than Thos's treacle tart.'

A bell rang for supper, or high tea. The rule was that tuck-box cakes were put under Matron's charge and distributed among all fifty of us while they lasted. 'Democracy', Thos called it (I can't think why); and the Matron, to cheer up the always dismal first evening, had set the largest cake she could find on the table: Julius's. Straight from the ducal kitchens, plastered with crystallized fruit, sugar icing and marzipan, stuffed with raisins, cherries and nuts.

'You will get your slice, my dear, when you have eaten your treacle tart,' Matron gently reminded Julius. *'Noblesse oblige.'*

'I never eat treacle tart, Matron.'

It must have been hard for him to see his cake devoured by strangers before his eyes, but he made no protest; just sipped a little tea and went supperless to bed. In the dormitory he told a ghost story, which is still, I hear, current in the school after all these years: about a Mr Gracie (why 'Gracie'?) who heard hollow groans in the night, rose to investigate and was grasped from behind by an invisible hand. He found that his braces had caught on the door knob; and, after other harrowing adventures, traced the groans to the bathroom, where Mrs Gracie...

Lights out! Sleep. Bells for getting up; for prayers; for breakfast.

'I never eat treacle tart.' So Julius had no breakfast, but we pocketed slices of bread and potted meat (Tuesday) to slip him in the playground afterwards. The school porter intervened. His orders were to see that the young gentleman had no food given him.

Bell: Latin. Bell: Maths. Bell: long break. Bell: Scripture. Bell: wash hands for dinner.

'I never eat treacle tart,' said Julius, as a sort of response to Thos's Grace; and this time fainted.

Thos sent a long urgent telegram to the Duke, explaining his predicament: school rule, discipline, couldn't make exceptions, and so forth.

The Duke wired back non-committally: 'Quite so. Stop. The lad never eats treacle tart. Stop. Regards. Downshire.'

Matron took Julius to the sickroom, where he was allowed milk and soup, but no solid food unless he chose to call for treacle tart. He remained firm and polite until the end, which came two days later, after a further exchange of telegrams.

We were playing kick-about near the Master's Wing, when the Rolls-Royce pulled up. Presently Julius, in overcoat and bowler hat, descended the front steps, followed by the school porter carrying his tuck-box, football boots and hand-bag. Billington Secundus, now converted to the popular view, led our three cheers, which Julius acknowledged with a gracious tilt of his bowler. The car purred off; and thereupon, in token of our admiration for Julius, we all swore to strike against treacle tart the very next Monday, and none of us eat a single morsel, even if we liked it, which some of us did!

When it came to the point, of course, the boys sitting close to Thos took fright and ratted, one after the other. Even Billington Secundus and I, not being peers' sons or even village Hampdens, regretfully conformed.

Weekend at Cwm Tatws

I SHOULDN'T BRING the story up – there's nothing in it really, except the sequel – if it wasn't already current in a garbled form. What happens to me I prefer told my own way, or not at all. Point is: I fell for that girl at first sight. So much more than sympathetic, as well as being in the beauty queen class, that...

In spite of my looking such a fool, too.

And probably if she'd had a wooden leg, a boss eye and only one tooth... Not that I was particularly interested in teeth at the moment, or in any position to utter more than a faint ugh, or even to smile a welcome. But how considerate of her to attend to me before taking any steps to deal with the heavy object on my lap! Most girls would have gone off into hysteria. But *she* happened to be practical; didn't even pause to dial 999. Saw with half an eye that... Put first things first. Besides looking such a fool, I was a fool: to get toothache on a Saturday afternoon, in a place like Cwm Tatws. As I told myself continuously throughout that lost week-end.

The trouble was my being all alone: nobody to be anxious, nobody to send out a search party, nobody in the township who knew me from Adam. I had come to Cwm Tatws to fish, which is about the only reason why anyone ever comes there, unless he happens to be called Harry Parry or Owen Owens or Evan Evans or Reece Reece or... Which I'm not. Tooth had already stirred faintly on the Friday just after I registered at the Dolwreiddiog Arms; but I decided to diagnose neuralgia and kill it with aspirin. Saturday, I got up early to flog the lake, where two- and three-pounders had allegedly been rising in fair numbers, and brought along my bottle of aspirins and a villainous cold lunch.

No, to fish doesn't necessarily mean being a Hemingway fan; after all, there was Izaak Walton, whom I haven't read either.

By mid-afternoon Tooth woke up suddenly and began to jump about like... I hooked a couple of sizeables, though nothing as big as advertised; both broke away. My error was waiting for the lucky third. That, and forgetting that it was Saturday afternoon. It was only when I got back to Cwm Tatws, which has five pubs (some bad, some worse), a police station, a post office, a branch bank and so forth – largish place for that district –

that I decided to seek out the town tooth-drawer, Mr Griffith Griffiths, whose brass plate I had noticed next to 'Capel Beulah 1861'.

Not what you thought. Mr Griffith Griffiths was at home all right, most cordial, and worked Saturday afternoons and evenings because that was the day when everyone... But he had recently slipped on a wet rock in his haste to gaff a big one and chipped a corner off his left elbow. Gross bad luck: he was left-handed.

'Let's look at it,' he said. And he did. 'No hope in the world of saving that poor fellow. I must yank him out at once. Pity on him, now, that he's a hind molar, indeed!'

What should X do next? Mr Griffith-heard-you-the-first-time will be out of action for the next month. X could of course hire a motor-car and drive thirty miles over the hills to Denbigh, where maybe tomorrow...

I pressed and pleaded. 'Is there nobody in this five-pub town capable of... A blacksmith, for instance? Or a barber? Why not the vet? Under your direction?'

'Well now, indeed, considering the emergency, perhaps, as you say, Mr Rowland Rowlands the veterinarian might consent to practise on you that which he practises on the ewes.'

Unfortunately Mr Rowland-say-it-twice had driven off to Denbigh himself in the last 'bus-motorr' (as they call it in Cwm Tatws), to visit his whatever she was.

Mr Griffith Griffiths right-handedly stroked his stubby chin. He couldn't shave now and thought the barber saloon vulgar and low. Said: 'Well, well, now, I shouldn't wonder if dear old Mr Van der Pant might peradventure play the good Samaritan. He is English too, and was qualified dental surgeon in Cwm Tatws, not altogether fifteen years ago; for it was from Mr Van der Pant that I bought this practice. A nice old gentleman, though a confirmed recluse and cannot speak a single word of Welsh.'

Welshlessness being no particular disadvantage in the circumstances, I hurried off to Rhododendron Cottage, down a wet lane, and up an avenue of wetter rhododendrons. By this time my tooth was...

You are wrong again. I found Mr Van der Pant also at home, and he had not even broken an arm. But took ten minutes to answer the bell, and then came out only by accident, having been too deaf to hear it.

Let us cut short the dumb-show farce: eventually I made him understand and consent to...

The room was... Macabre, isn't it? 'Only Adults Admitted.' Had been locked up since whenever, by the look of it. Cobwebs like tropical creepers. Dental chair deep in dust. Shutters askew. No heating. Smell of mice. Presence of mice. Rusty expectoration bowl and instrument rack. Plaster fallen in heaps from the ceiling. Wallpaper peeled off. Fascinating, in a way.

I helped him screw in an electric light bulb, and said: 'No, please don't bother to light a fire!'

'Yes, it must come out,' he wheezed. 'Pity that it's a posterior molar. Even more of a pity that I am out of anaesthetics.'

Fortunately he discovered that the forceps had been put away with a thin coating of oil, easily wiped off with... He eyed it lovingly. Might still be used.

Was used.

By this time the posterior molar... Or do I repeat myself? It could hardly have been more unfortunate, he complained. That forceps was not at all the instrument he should have chosen. Mr Griffith Griffiths had bought his better pair along with the practice. Still, he'd do his best. Would I mind if he introduced a little appliance to fix my jaws apart, so that he could work more cosily? He was getting on in years, he said, and a little rusty.

And please would I keep still? Yes, yes, most unfortunate. He had cut the corner of my mouth, he was well aware, but that was because I had jerked.

Three minutes best unrecorded. Not even adults admitted.

Mr Van der Pant then feared that we were getting nowhere. That forceps!

Tooth was rotten and he had nipped off the crown. Now we must go deeper, into the gum. It might hurt a little. And, please, would I keep still this time? I should experience only a momentary pain, and then... Perhaps if I permitted him to lash me to the chair? His heart was none too good, and my struggles...

Poor blighter! 'You can truss me up like an Aylesbury duckling, if you care, so long as you dig this... tooth out,' I said. He couldn't hear, of course, but guessed, and went out to fetch yards and yards of electric light flex.

Trussed me up good and proper: sailor fashion. 'Had he ever been dentist in a man-of-war?' I asked. But he smiled deafly. It was now about six-thirty on Saturday evening, and curiously enough he had begun telling me of the famous murderer – one Crippen, before my time – who had been his fellow dental-student when... His last words were: 'And I also had the privilege once of attending his wife and victim, Miss Belle Ellmore, an actress, you will remember. She had split an incisor while biting on an...'

I wish people would finish their sentences.

So, as I say, *she* turned up, providentially, at about eleven-fifteen, Monday, Mr Van der Pant's grand-niece, on a surprise visit. Lovely girl, straight out of Bond Street, or a band-box.

And there I sat in that dank room, on that dusty dental chair, with a dead dentist across my knees; my jaws held apart by a little appliance, a chill, a ripening abscess, my arms and legs and trunk bound tightly with yards of flex; not to mention, of course...

Yes, I like to tell it my own way, though there's not much in it. Might have happened to any other damned fool.

But the sequel! Now that really was...

The Full Length

WILLIAM ('THE KID') Nicholson, my father-in-law, could never rid himself of the Victorian superstition that a thousand guineas were a thousand guineas; income tax seemed to him a barbarous joke which did not, and should not, apply to people like myself. He had a large family to support, and as a fashionable portrait painter was bound to keep up appearances which would justify his asking the same prices for a full length as his friends William Orpen and Philip de Laszlo. He excelled in still-lifes and, though complaining that flowers were restless sitters, would have liked to paint nothing else all day except an occasional landscape. But full-length commissions were what he needed. 'Portraits seldom bounce,' he told me.

When I asked him to explain, he said: 'I have been painting and selling, and painting and selling for so many years now that my early buyers are beginning to die off or go bankrupt. Forgotten W.N. masterpieces keep coming up for auction, and have to be bought in at an unfair price, five times as much as they originally earned, just to keep the W.N. market steady. Some of them are charming and make me wonder how I ever painted so well; but others plead to have their faces turned to the wall quick. Such as those!'

It had come to a crisis in Appletree Yard. The Inland Revenue people, he told me, had sent him a three-line whip to attend a financial debate; also, an inexpert collector of his early work had died suddenly and left no heirs, so that his agent had to buy in three or four paintings which should never have been sold. 'Be sure your sin will find you out,' the Kid muttered despondently. 'What I need now is no less than two thousand guineas in ready cash. Pray for a miracle, my boy!'

I prayed, and hardly two hours had elapsed, before a ring came at the studio door and in walked Mrs Mucklehose-Kerr escorted by one Fulton, a butler, both wearing deep mourning. The Kid had not even known of her existence hitherto, but she seemed solid enough and the name Mucklehose-Kerr was synonymous with Glenlivet Whisky; so he was by no means discourteous.

The introductions over, Mrs Mucklehose-Kerr pressed the Kid's hand fervently, and said: 'Mr Nicholson, I know you will not fail me: you and you alone are destined to paint my daughter Alison.'

'Well,' said the Kid, blinking cautiously, 'I am pretty busy at this season, you know, Mrs Mucklehose-Kerr. And I've promised to take my family to Cannes in about three weeks' time. Still, if you make a point of it, perhaps the sittings can be fitted in before I leave Town.'

'There will be no sittings, Mr Nicholson. There *can* be no sittings.' She dabbed her eyes with a black-lace handkerchief. 'My daughter passed over last week.'

It took the Kid a little while to digest this, but he mumbled condolences, and said gently: 'Then I fear that I shall have to work from photographs.'

Mrs Mucklehose-Kerr answered in broken tones: 'Alas, there *are* no photographs. Alison was so camera-shy. She used to say: "Mother, why do you want photographs? You will always have me to look at – me myself, not silly old photographs!" And now she has passed over, and not left me so much as a snapshot. On my brother's advice I went to Mr Orpen first and asked him what I am now asking you; but he answered that the task was beyond him. He said that you were the only painter in London who could help me, because you have a sixth sense.'

Orpen was right in a way. The Kid had one queer parlour trick. He would suddenly ask a casual acquaintance: 'How do you sign your name?' and when he answered: 'Herbert B. Banbury' (or whatever it was), would startle him by writing it down in his own unmistakable handwriting.

'Look, here is her signature; this is the cover of her history exercise book.'

As he hesitated, his eye caught sight of the bounced canvases, leaning against the table on which lay the Income Tax demand. 'It is a difficult commission, Mrs Mucklehose-Kerr,' he said.

'I am willing to pay two thousand guineas,' she answered, 'for a full length.'

'It is not the money...' he protested.

'But Fulton will tell you all about dear Alison,' pleaded Mrs Mucklehose-Kerr, weeping unrestrainedly. 'Miss Alison was a beautiful girl, Fulton, was she not?'

'Sweetly pretty,' Fulton agreed with fervour. 'Pretty as a picture, madam.'

'I *know* you will consent, Mr Nicholson, and of course I will choose one of her own dresses for her to wear. The one I liked best.'

There was nothing for it but to consent.

The Kid took Fulton to the Café Royal that evening and plied him with whisky and questions.

'Blue eyes?' – 'Bluish, sir, and a bit watery. But sweetly pretty.'

'Hair?' – 'Mousy, sir, like her nature, and worn in a bun.'

'Figure?' – 'So, so, Mr Nicholson, so, so! But she was a very sweet young lady, was Miss Alison.'

'Any physical peculiarities?' – 'None, sir, that leaped to the eye. But I fear I am not a good hand at descriptions.'

'Had she no friends who could sketch her from memory?' – 'None, Mr Nicholson. She lived a most retired life.'

So the Kid drew a blank with Fulton, and his parlour trick did not help at all because he lacked the complementary faculty (with which Mrs Mucklehose-Kerr credited him, but which, in his own phrase, was a different pair of socks altogether) of conjuring up a person from a signature. The next day, in despair, he consulted his brother-in-law, the painter James Pryde. 'Jimmy, what on earth am I to do now?'

Jimmy thought awhile and then, being a practical Scot, answered: 'Why not find out from Fulton whether the girl ever went to a dentist?'

Sir Rockaway Timms happened to be a fellow-member of the Savile, and the Kid hurried to Wimpole Street to consult him.

'Rocks, old boy, I'm in a fearful hole.'

'Not for the first time, Kid.'

'It's about a girl of eighteen called Alison Mucklehose-Kerr, one of your patients.'

'You should leave 'em alone until they reach the age of discretion. Oh, you artists!'

'I never set eyes on her. And now, it seems, she's dead.'

'Bad, bad! By her own hand?'

'I want to know what you know about her.'

'I can only show you the map of her mouth, if that's any morbid satisfaction to you. I have it in this cabinet. Wait a moment. M... Mu... Muck... Here you are! Crowded incisors; one heavily and clumsily stopped rear molar; one ditto lightly and neatly stopped by me; malformed canines; wisdom teeth not yet through.'

'For Heaven's sake, Rocks, what did she *look* like? It's life or death to me.'

Sir Rockaway glanced at the Kid quizzically. 'What do I get out of this?' he asked.

'An enormous box of liqueur chocolates swathed in pink ribbon.'

'Accepted, on behalf of Edith. Well, this Alison whom you betrayed in the dark forest was a sallow, lumpish, frightened Scots lassie with a slight cast in the off eye – but, for all that, the spitting image of Lillian Gish!'

The Kid wrung Sir Rockaway's hand as violently as Mrs Mucklehose-Kerr had wrung his own at parting. Then he rushed out to his waiting taxi.

'Driver,' he shouted. '*The Birth of a Nation*, wherever it's showing, as fast as your wheels will carry us!'

Mrs Mucklehose-Kerr, summoned to Appletree Yard a week later, uttered a moan of delight the moment she entered the studio. 'It is Alison, it is my Alison to the life, Mr Nicholson!' she babbled. 'I knew your genius would not fail me. But oh! how well and happy she is looking since she passed over!... Fulton, Fulton, tell Mr Nicholson how wonderful he is!'

'You have caught Miss Alison's expression, sir, to the dot!' pronounced Fulton, visibly impressed.

Mrs Mucklehose-Kerr insisted on buying two of the bounced and unworthy early Nicholsons which happened to be lying face-up on the floor. The Kid had been on the point of painting them over; and his obvious reluctance to sell made her offer twelve hundred guineas for the pair.

He weakly accepted; forgetting what a terrible retribution the Inland Revenue people would visit on him next year.

God Grant Your Honour Many Years

I SLIT OPEN the flimsy blue envelope and, pulling out an even flimsier typewritten slip, began to read without the least interest; but recoiled like the man in *Amos* who carelessly leans his hand on a wall and gets bitten by a serpent. The Spanish ran:

> With regard to a matter that should prove of interest to your Honour: please be good enough to appear in person at this Police Headquarters on any working day of the present month between the hours of 10 and 12. Business: to withdraw your Residence Permit.
> God grant your Honour many years!
>> *Signed:* Emilio Something-or-other.
>> *Stamped in purple:* The Police
>> Headquarters, Palma de Mallorca.

For two or three minutes I sat grinning cynically at the nasty thing. *'Para retirar la Autorización de Residencia!'* Well, that was that!

Though often warned that in a totalitarian state anything might happen, without warning, without mercy, without sense, I had imagined it could never happen to me. I first came to Majorca, twenty-five years ago, during Primo de Rivera's dictatorship; and stayed on throughout the subsequent Republic. Then one fine summer's day in 1936 small bombs, and leaflets threatening larger bombs, began to fall on Palma; soldiers hauled down the Republican flag; unknown young men with rifles invaded our village of Binijiny and tried to shoot the Doctor by mistake for a Socialist politician; the boat service to Barcelona was suspended; coffee and sugar disappeared from the shops; all mail ceased; and one day the British Consul scrawled me a note:

Dear Robert,

This afternoon H.M.S. *Grenville* will evacuate British nationals: probably your last chance of leaving Spain in safety. Luggage limited to one handbag. Strongly advise your coming.

I.L.

I hastily packed my handbag with manuscripts, underclothes and a Londonish suit.

An hour later Kenneth, two other friends and I were heading for the port in the taxi which the Consul had considerately sent out to us. Thus we became wretched refugees, and wretched refugees we continued to be for ten years more until the Civil War had been fought to a bloody close, until the World War had broken out and run its long miserable course, and finally until the Franco Government, disencumbered of its obligations to the Axis, had found it possible to sanction our return. Reader, never become a refugee, if you can possibly avoid it, even for the sake of that eventual happy homecoming in an air-taxi, with a whole line of bristly village chins awaiting your fraternal salute. Stay where you are, kiss the rod and, if very hungry, eat grass or the bark off the trees. To live in furnished rooms and travel about from country to country – England, Switzerland, England, France, the States, England again – homesick and disorientated, seeking rest but finding none, is the Devil's own fate.

This brings the story up to 1946. I came back to Binijiny, and thanks to the loyalty of the natives found my house very much as I had left it. Certain ten-year-old Kilner jars of homemade green tomato pickle had matured wonderfully, and so had a pile of *Economists* and *Times Literary Supplements*. 'Happily ever after,' I promised myself. Then in 1947 Kenneth joined me again, and we resumed work together.

And now this! '*Para retirar la...*'

But why? I belong to no political organization, am not a *frémasón*, have always refused to write either against, or for, any particular form of Spanish Government, and if ever people ask me: 'What is it like on your island?' am careful to reply: 'It is not mine; it is theirs.' As a foreigner who must apply every two years for a renewal of his residence permit, I try to be the perfect guest: quiet, sober, neutral, appreciative and punctilious in money matters. Then of what crime could I be accused? Had someone perhaps taken exception to a historical novel of mine about Spanish colonization under Philip II? Or to the rockets I release every July 24th, which happens to be my birthday as well as the anniversary of the capture of Gibraltar? Had some cathedral canon denounced me for having acted as Spanish-English interpreter at a serio-comic meeting of solidarity between the corn-fed Protestant choir of the U.S. aircraft-carrier *Midway* and the bleak encatacombed Evangelical Church of Majorca? Where could I find out? The police would doubtless refuse an explanation. What means had I of forcing them to say more than 'Security Reasons', which is about all that our own democratic Home Office ever concedes?

Nobody had invited me to settle in Majorca; almost anyone had a right to object to my continued presence there.

... So this was why they had brooded so long over my application for renewing the damned permit!

My wife probably wouldn't much mind a change of house and food and climate. But how could I break the news to Kenneth? Although I should be sunk without him, he could scarcely be expected to share my exile again; the poor fellow had hardly enjoyed a day's happiness, I knew, during those ten long years. And what if our long association put him on the black list too? And just as he was buying that motor-cycle!

Yet why the hell should I take this lying down? After twenty-five years – after all the sterling and dollars I had imported – and my four children almost more Majorcan than the Majorcans! I'd hire a car, drive to Palma at once, visit the Chief of Police and ask, very haughtily, who was responsible for what was either a tactless practical joke or a cruel *atropellada*. (*Atropellada*, in this sense, has no simple familiar English equivalent, because it means deliberately running over someone in the street.) Afterwards I'd ring up the British Embassy at Madrid. And the Irish Embassy. And the American Embassy. And...

Here came the car. Poor Kenneth! Poor myself! Poor children! It would have to be England, I supposed. And London, I supposed, though in my previous refugee days I had always been plagued by abscesses and ulcers when I tried to live there. My wife loves London, of course. But how could we find a house large enough and cheap enough for us all? And what about schools for the children? And a nurse for the baby? And who would care for our cats in Binijiny?

I had forgotten that, this being a total fiesta in honour of San Sebastián, the Patron Saint of Palma, all offices would be closed. Nothing doing until the next day; meanwhile church bells rang, boot-blacks pestered me, Civil Guards sported their full-dress poached-egg head-dresses and stark white gloves, and the population drifted aimlessly about the streets in their Sunday best.

As I stood check-mated outside the Bar Fígaro, a dapper Spaniard greeted me and asked politely after my health, my family and my busy pen, remarking what a pity it was that so few of my books were available in Spanish and French translation. I couldn't place him. He was probably a shirtmaker, or a hotel receptionist, or a Tennis Club Committeeman, or a senior Post Office clerk, whom I would recognize at once in his proper setting. Awkward!

'Come, Don Roberto, let us take a coffee together!' I agreed miserably, suspecting that, like everyone else, he wanted to cross-examine me on contemporary English literature. But, after all, why shouldn't I continue to humour these gentle, simple, hospitable people? It was their island, not mine. And the Bar Fígaro has sentimental memories for me.

We sat down. I offered him my pouch of black tobacco and a packet of *Marfil* papers. He rolled cigarettes for us both, handed me mine to lick and stick, snapped his lighter for me, and said: 'Well, distinguished friend, may we expect your visit soon? I ventured to send you an official reminder only yesterday. When will you find time to withdraw your Residence Permit – *"para retirar la Autorización de Residencia"* – from our files? It has been waiting there, duly signed, since late October.'

In my gratitude I gave Don Emilio an hour's expert literary criticism of the works of such English *gran-novelistas* as Mohgum, Ootschley, Estrong and Oowohg, promising not only to visit him at the earliest opportunity with the necessary 1 peseta 55 céntimos stampage but to lend him a contraband Argentine edition of Lorca's *Poems*.

God grant him many years! What a sleepless night he saved me!

6 Valiant Bulls 6

DEAREST AUNT MAY,

You will never guess what happened to me yesterday, which was Ascension Day, besides being my birthday! I met our new postman at the front door and collected your 'Now you are 11' birthday card – thanks awfully! He was a young man with very long hair, and wanted to know what the card meant. So I told him. Then he asked if I was acquainted with the foreign family Esk. I said 'No, but show me the letters, please!' and they were all for Father, ten of them – 'William Smith, Esq' – the postman had had them for a week! So we were both very pleased. Then I mentioned that Señor Colom was taking me to the bullfight for a birthday treat, and his face lighted up like a Chinese lantern. I asked: 'Are they brave bulls?' and he said: 'Daughter, they are an escandal!' and I asked: 'How an escandal?' And he explained that Poblet, the senior matador, had written to his friend Don Ramón, who had a bull farm near Jerez and was supplying the six bulls for the fight, to send him under-weight ones, because he wasn't feeling very well after grippe and neither were the two other matadors, Calvo and Broncito; and he'd pay Don Ramón well and arrange things quietly with the Bull Ring Management. So everything was fixed; until the new Captain-General of Majorca, who's President of the Ring and very correct, went to see the bulls as they came ashore. He took one look and said: 'Weigh them!' So they put them on the scales and they weighed about half a ton less than the proper weight. So he said: 'Send them back at once and telephone for more.' The second lot had just arrived by steamer. The new postman told me that they were a disaster, and looked like very especial dangerous insects.

My friend Señor Colom is really a music critic, but that position is worth nothing, only a few pesetas a week; he gets his living from being a bull critic. A regular matador earns about two or three thousand pounds a fight, so his agent can afford to pay the critics well to say how much genius and valour he has, even if he hasn't. Señor Colom writes exactly what he really thinks about concerts, but bullfights are different; he makes the agent himself write the review, then reads it over for grammar-faults and puts in a few extra bits, and signs it. That is the custom.

Anyhow, Señor and Señora Colom and I went, and the U.S.A. fleet was in port and two American sailors sat next to us. It seems that the Captain-General had measured the bulls' horns himself and told the herdsman: 'When these beasts are dead I will measure their horns again. If they have been shortened and re-pointed, someone will go to prison.' Then he had checked the pics to see that they didn't have longer points than is allowed, and also sent a vet to see that nobody gave the bulls a laxative to make them weak. So it was going to be fun to watch.

The Captain-General was in the President's box and after the march-past he waved his handkerchief and the trumpets blew and the first bull was let loose. He was a great cathedral of a bull, and rushed out like the Angel of Death. But when the cape-men came out and began to cape him, there was a sudden growl and loud protests and everyone shouted 'Bizgo! Bizgo!' which meant that the bull was squint-eyed and wouldn't answer to the cape. So the Captain-General sent the bull away, and Poblet, who should have fought it, gave a nasty grin, because there were no substitute bulls. One had got drowned when he slipped off the gangplank of the steamer, and another had got horned by a friend. The Captain-General looked furious.

The next bull was very fierce, and the cape-men ran for their lives behind the shelters. One of them couldn't quite get there, so he dashed for the wooden wall and shinned up and escaped into the passage behind. The bull jumped right over the wall after him and broke a news-photographer's camera and spectacles, and gave him an awful fright. The crowd laughed like anything. Then the trumpets blew again and 'in came the cavalry' as Señor Colom always calls the picadors. The bull went smack at the first horse, before the peon who led it had got it into position, and knocked all the wind out of its body. The picador was underneath kicking with his free boot at the bull's nose. One of the two American sailors fainted, and his friend had to carry him out. Four more American sailors fainted in different parts of the ring; they are a very sensitive class of people.

This bull was Broncito's.

Broncito is a gipsy and engaged to Calvo's sister. He is very supersti-tious, and that morning had met three nuns walking in a row, and told Calvo he wouldn't fight. Calvo said: 'Then you will never be my brother-in-law. Would you disgrace me before the public? Would you have me kill your bulls for you as well as my own? I don't like them any more than you do.' So Broncito promised to fight. Well, the picador wasn't hurt, they never are. The cape-men drew the bull away and the peons got the horse up again, and it seemed none the worse. And the picadors did their work well and so did the banderilleros. But Broncito was trembling. He made a few poor passes, standing as far away as he could, and then offered up a prayer to the Virgin of Safety, the one who saves matadors from death by drawing the bull away with a twitch of her blue cape. The bull happened to be in the right position, standing with his legs apart, so Broncito lunged and actually killed it in one. The public was furious because he hadn't played the bull at all, hardly, and the play is what they pay to see.

The third bull was Calvo's, and Calvo was terribly valiant because he was so ashamed of Broncito. He made dozens of beautiful passes, high and low, also veronicas and some butterfly passes which everyone but Señor Colom thought wonderful. He had known the great Marcial Lalanda who first perfected them and said that Calvo's were both jerky and ungenial; though, of course, he couldn't *write* that for his paper. Calvo killed after two tries and was rewarded with both ears. His chief peon cut off the tail too, and gave it to him, but the Captain-General had signalled only for the ears, so the peon got fined 500 pesetas for presumption.

After the interval, with monkey-nuts and mineral water, it was Poblet's turn again. His bull came wandering in very tranquilly, had a good look round and then lay down in the middle of the ring. After a lot of prodding and taunting of which he took no notice, they had to send for a team of white and black oxen, with bells, who came gambolling into the ring and coaxed him out again. Do you know the story of Ferdinand the Bull? It ends all wrong. Bulls like Ferdinand don't go back to the farm to eat daisies. I'm afraid they get shot outside the ring by the Civil Guard, like deserters in battles.

The public was getting impatient. It booed and cat-called like anything, but the fifth bull (Broncito's again) was a supercathedral; soap-coloured and with horns like an elephant's tusks. Broncito was sick with horror, and when both the horses had been knocked down before the picadors could use their pics, and only one banderillero had been tall enough to plant his pair of darts well, he went white as a sheet. He pretended to play the bull but it chased him all over the place and the crowd roared with laughter and made rude jokes. So he shook his fist at them and called for the red *muleta* and sword and then, guess what! He *murdered* the bull, with a side-pass into his lungs instead of properly between the shoulder-blades. There was an awful hush from the Spaniards, who couldn't believe their eyes – it was like shooting a fox; but tremendous cheers came from the American sailors who thought Broncito had been very clever. Then of course the cheers were drowned by a most frantic booing, and the Captain-General sprang to his feet and cursed terribly. The next thing was that two *guardias* arrested Broncito and marched him off to prison.

The last bull was easily the best of the six and Calvo was more anxious than ever to show off. He wanted both ears *and* the tail *and* the foot (which is almost never given) and when he came to play the bull he dedicated it to the public and did wonderful, wonderful, fantastic things. There's a sort of ledge running round the wooden wall which helps cape-men when they scramble to safety. He sat down on it, to allow himself no room to escape from a charge, and did his passes there. Afterwards he knelt and let the bull's horns graze the gold braid on his chest. And did several *estupendous* veronicas and then suddenly walked away, turning his back to the bull, which was left looking silly. Calvo had waved all his cape-men far away and the crowd went wild with joy. But some idiot threw his hat into the ring, which took the bull's attention from the *muleta*, and Calvo got horned in the upper leg and tossed up and thrown down. Then the bull tried to kill him. I don't know how many more sailors fainted; I was too busy to count.

Suddenly an *espontáneo* in grey uniform with long hair simply hurled himself into the ring and grabbed Calvo's sword and red *muleta* and drew the bull off. It was our sloppy new postman! And while the peons carried Calvo to the surgery, he played the bull very valiantly and got apotheosistical cheers, louder even than Calvo's, and the Captain-General himself applauded although the postman was committing a crime. Everyone expected Poblet to enter and finish off the bull, but Poblet had now also been arrested for insulting the Lieutenant of the Civil Guard for insulting Broncito; so there was no other proper matador left. But Calvo petitioned that the postman should be allowed to finish off the bull, for having saved his life. The Captain-General consented and, when I waved madly, the postman recognized my yellow frock and rededicated the bull to me – me, Aunt May! Because it was my birthday and because of the Esq. And though the poor boy was rustic and quite without art, as Señor Colom said (and wrote), he managed to kill his enemy at the second try.

Then, of course, he was arrested too. All *espontáneos* are.

But the Captain-General let him off with a caution and a big box of real Havana cigars.

Ever your loving niece,
Margaret

Flesh-coloured Net Tights

DEAREST AUNT MAY,

I must at last explain that long telegram I sent you from Olga, who's my ballet teacher, asking for all those pairs of flesh-coloured net tights to be put on the B.E.A. plane. I hope you didn't think that they were for the Dolorous Nuns to wear themselves. It is a story rather like the 'Belle of the Ballet' serial in *Girl*, though nobody gets kidnapped or locked into a spidery cellar. Olga's a Polish *refugiada*, who escaped from the Russians to Sadler's Wells in England and said: 'I'm a prima ballerina from Warsaw. Please, can I have a job?' So they gave her a scrubbing-brush and a pail. Olga scrubbed floors for ages, but three years ago she escaped from the English to Majorca. The Governor allowed her to start a school for Classical Ballet here, because his wife had seen Moira Shearer's *Red Shoes* and thought that it was very artistic and in good taste; but Brunhilda Schwarzfuss, the German lady who has a *Tanzgruppe* here, wasn't at all pleased by the news.

Brunhilda is square and bouncy and wears a sort of deerstalker hat. She waves her drumstick and shouts: 'Now, *niñas*, I'll put on the gramophone today and you'll all be little horses galloping along the sands and suddenly putting your heads down and kicking up your heels. Bang, bang, bang! Off you run! *Muy bien! Muy bien!*' After two goes of that, she changes the record and they play at being soldiers, or else rabbits. Then the bigger girls express their emotions in dances they invent themselves, which means waggling their arms and tossing their heads back and giving a few backward kicks, or pretending to be terribly afraid of something and push it off without looking at it. Or they play at shepherdesses and fawns. The shepherdesses are the neat girls; the fauns are the clumsy ones, whose mothers have asked Brunhilda to run some of the fat off them and make them easier to marry. The shepherdesses waltz around and the fauns jump after them and pretend to blow pipes. It is all rather awful, because they don't learn a single *one* of the 120 basic positions of ballet, and the windows are tight shut to prevent draughts and most of the girls are afraid of the cold showers afterwards and rub themselves with Majorcan eau de Cologne instead.

Last year Olga married an American called Bill, the nice poor sort of American. He is a composer and was a trumpeter. But he sold his trumpet to marry Olga and had to teach English for a living instead. Bill said to Olga: 'We must advertise if we want this school to pay. The best way is to put on a good show at the Plaza.' Olga said: 'Oh, no, Bill, my girls aren't ready. After only three years I should be ashamed.' Bill said: 'Nonsense, nobody here will know the difference, and the girls will get experience. Let's do Glasnov's *Four Seasons* and aim for early April.'

How Olga worked us! We almost hated her sometimes, though she's so sweet really, because we had to go straight from our various convents to ballet class and never had time for a sit-down supper and came home nearly dead at about ten o'clock. But the Nuns thought that dancing was idleness, and made us work dreadfully hard at Visigothic Kings and Principal Exports of Spain and The Properties of Solid Bodies, to show we were industrious. We had to get 'Outstanding' on our weekly reports instead of just 'Approved'. And Sor Juana one day reprobated me for practising ballet steps in the playground and called me presumptuous; but I said I was just cold. And she said: 'Don't answer back, my daughter. You ought to bear the cold bravely!' Well, that afternoon we found a hot-water bottle lying about in a corner of the playground. It must have fallen from under Sor Juana's skirts; so my companions chose me to give it back to her, which I did very politely without a word.

I'm at the Sacred Tunics, but the Little Flowers who have a big new convent down the road pay Brunhilda to give their girls dancing lessons. Of course, I don't really *know* who had said what; only it's certain that the Mother Superior of the Little Flowers took aside all the girls who go to Olga's and warned them that she was of doubtful antecedents and that, if they took part in the public performance of the *Four Seasons,* they'd all get zero on their term's report. Luckily one of the girls was the daughter of the man who fabricated the convent beds and tables and chairs and things. They are six months behindhand with paying. So she went crying to her father and said: 'Father, will you let them insult Olga? After you and Mother, she's the best person in Majorca.' And he answered: 'Enough, child, I'll tell them things.' So he did, and after that the Little Flowers even let the girls go off early to rehearsals.

Bill hired the Plaza Theatre for April 1st and taught the orchestra the *Four Seasons* music. It had taken him weeks to prepare it for the right number of instruments and copy out the parts. Then about New Year we read an 'interviu' in the *Prensa Palmesana* in which Brunhilda said that Classical Ballet was very bad for the legs and very monotonous and already going out of fashion, and that she would put on a performance in the Plaza early in March with all her *Tanzgruppe* pupils. When the man from the *Prensa* asked what would she show, she answered: 'The *Four Seasons,* danced with all naturalness and liberty of expression.'

One of Olga's girls is the niece of the man who has a mortgage on the Plaza Theatre, and she went crying to her father and said: 'Father, will you let them insult Olga? After you and Mother she's the best person in Majorca.' And he answered: 'Enough, child, we'll tell them things, the insects.' So next day his brother made the theatre owner warn Brunhilda that the Plaza would probably be out of action all March because it was to be altered for 3-D. So that was all right. Then suddenly the convent of Dolorous Nuns started giving Olga's pupils zero even if they were top of the class. I found out from the bus-man who collects the Dolorous day-girls from the other side of Palma that someone had told terrible lies about Olga's being a Protestant and in love with the theatre-owner. But Olga's confessor happened to be the Dolorous Nuns' confessor too, so *he* told them things. Don't think that our Majorcan nuns aren't good people. They are terribly good; but the trouble is they just don't like Classical Ballet.

Meanwhile Brunhilda and Carmen Carabel the *flamenco* teacher had made a sort of alliance against the Ballet School. Carmen teaches American lady tourists to manage castanets and stamp their heels and chew roses and make proud gipsy faces full of hate, so as to win fancy-dress prizes when they get home. And her father, who owns a night club, is a great friend of the Millionairess, whose husband owns the *Prensa*. That was why the *Prensa* had printed Brunhilda's 'interviu'. The Millionaire allows the Millionairess to censor the art and music and liter-ature pages, to keep her out of mischief. He censors the news and the sports, to keep himself out of mischief.

Anyhow, two days before the show the Dolorous Nuns and the Little Flowers and my own Sacred Tunics said that all the girls over twelve years old would be expelled if they danced bare-legged on the stage. That was when we telegraphed you for the tights, which can't be bought here. You were splendid, Aunt May! They arrived five hours before the perfor-mance, but it was a public holiday with the customs office shut. The chief customs man happened to be the father of one of our Rain Fairies and a very kind man. He opened the office and wrote something in the book. Then he handed Olga the tights and said: 'This is now tomorrow; the duty is fifty-four pesetas sixty céntimos. Pay me when you like.'

It was simply a marvellous show. Olga danced herself, and Bill borrowed a dress suit and conducted wildly and we all got encores and flowers and everyone said nobody would have believed Palma could produce anything so memorable and artistic. But of course there wasn't a single word about it in the *Prensa Palmesana* next day, although their photographer had been photographing like mad and Señor Colom the music critic congratulated Olga afterwards on our great and genial display. Luckily the Admiral's niece, who is also the Governor's god-daughter, was one of our Dead-Leaf fairies. She went crying to the

Governor – you can guess the rest – and next day we found a whole page of photographs in the *Prensa*.

That's all, really, except for Brunhilda's show ten days later. It wasn't Glasnov's *Four Seasons* at all, but a lot of potty little dances, done to German music, with Snowflakes and Bunnies jumping about to a gramophone which had a loudspeaker in front of it. And then these *Bailes Creativos* by the bigger girls! And the shepherdesses and fauns! And the joke was, their legs were as bare as on the beach!

Olga took us all to watch and we clapped until our hands were sore, it was so terrible. And now a cathedral canon has written a long article in the *Semana Católica*, about the proclivious immorality of dancing; which means Brunhilda too. I don't know how this serial will continue.

Much love and thanks,
Margaret.

Thy Servant and God's

DEAR UNCLE GEORGE,

Don't ask me whether Spanish is easy to learn; because Spain is where I live and I can't remember when I couldn't talk it. And I don't know if it's as like Latin as you think, because I haven't done much Latin yet. But Father says that when the Roman soldiers came here to fight Aníbal and taught Latin to their allies the Ibéricos, they used an awful dog-Latin like the dog-English our sailors talk to Chinese men and undiscovered tribes who sell them coconuts. So I don't suppose the Latin you learned at Winchester will get you very far. But as you say you don't know a word of Spanish, except *fiesta* and *siesta* and *Tío Pepe* and *mañana*, I thought I'd give you an idea of what it's like, by using a letter from my friend Anita Fons y Pons. I've made two translations with Father's help: first what you'd think it means, and then what it does mean.

Most desired little friend Margarita:

I write this little card with the motive of rendering thee graces in respect of thy most attentive target which fills me with gaiety, since the same informs me that thou rejoicest in perfect health. Thus the same I lament that thou canst not make us grateful by visiting our house the other week for a pair of days at least, as I was hoping, for the fifteen days beginning after the Easters of the Nativity.

[Dearest Margaret,

This is to thank you for your kind card. I am so pleased to hear you're well, though disappointed that you can't stay with us for a bit. I'd been hoping that you'd come next week, as soon as Christmas is over, for at least a fortnight.]

But look, man, I am estranged by this that in it thou so unconsciously depreciatest the mothers, above all our own little sisters. I consider it almost as grave as to mock your fathers. I encounter them goodest (bonísimas) *persons, and my mamma opinionates that it is convenient always to treat them as intimate parents, even if one or other of them has a genius.*

[But, darling, I'm surprised that you say such impolite and wild things about the nuns, especially our own Sisters. In my opinion that's almost as bad as being rude to your father and mother. I find them awfully kind people and mother says we should always treat them like our own relations even if one or two of them do have bad tempers.]

Actually I suffer from a grain on my little beard, which holds pus, owed to a disgrace which I suffered while Ricardito, who is a veritable uncle, was pulling my dietary at me; which, when the people's medical, who is only a practitioner and very donkey, examined, he declared that it wasn't nothing of importance, but that at the best a little pomade of penicillin might not go badly.

[At present, I have a rather nasty spot on my chin, due to an accident: Dickie, who's a very nasty boy, threw my diary at me. The village doctor, who isn't really qualified and very stupid, looked at it and said it was nothing really, though perhaps it might be a good idea to use a little penicillin ointment.]

Precisely at the hour of his arrival, it passed that thy servant had commenced practising the paces in her dietary class of ballet, utilizing the tablet of the ancient hennery to stamp upon with more commodity than the little responsive portland of the cave; and he gave me a good hour, affirming that much dance had rendered my legs curious, and counselled me not to inflame my little bottom with the small candles. He always goes with seeming groceries to give fear.

[When he came along I was just beginning to practise my daily ballet steps. I had borrowed some boards from the old chicken house to make a better dancing floor than the terribly hard cement in the cellar. He congratulated me on the improvement which all this dancing has made in the shape of my legs and warned me not to let my ballet skirt catch fire from the footlights. He always teases me in this frightfully rude way.]

In exchange, the Chief of the Library who, since then, is a very formal cavalier, said when I entered his tent to buy a head-breaker of those that join themselves and form infantile caprices, that in the theatrical function to which he had given his presence, I had merited in an imposing manner the homage which the respectable obsequiated me, and for this he most charmingly regaled me with an imposing coloured gum.

[On the other hand, when I went to the bookshop to buy one of those 'Children's Fun' jigsaw puzzles, the manager, who's a very polite man of course, said that I had thoroughly earned my applause at the last show he watched; so he very nicely gave me a wonderful red india-rubber.]

In these moments I come from touching my instrumental duty and from concluding the Apology which touched me to write of the much-spoken-of Don Quijote. In brief, I go to play with my little companions of the vicinity, passing the corner, the 'wheel of the potatoes', which is very diverted and holds much grace.

[I have just been doing a piano exercise, and finishing the Eulogy which I had to write about that dreary Don Quixote. I'm off soon to play 'Potato Ring' with the girls round the corner; it's great fun and pretty to watch.]

I was very content to assure myself of the reality of the leaping out of thy ingress. To me also they accorded a diploma for the holy writings, and with that a bend azure, and a precious rosary of variously formed accounts. But I lament to inform thee that from my cosmological sciences I sacked no more than a regular.

[I was so pleased to see that you really did get 'outstanding' in your entrance exam. I was given a diploma too, in Scripture, also a blue sash and a lovely rosary of different shaped beads. But I'm sorry to say that I got only a 'fair' in general science.]

Good, I haven't nothing more to communicate to thee. Salute thy papas affectionately, give a little kiss to Hieronimito, and do thou accept, my most desired Margarita, a most strong embrace from the best of all thy little friends, desiring for thee that thou wilt learn much Latin in these vacations and utilize the good time to take many baths. Good-bye until another.

Anita, Thy servant and God's.

[Well, that's all. My love to your father and mother, a kiss for little Jeremy, and a big hug for yourself from your best friend. I hope you'll learn plenty of Latin these holidays and swim a good deal while the weather holds. Good-bye till next time.

Ever your Anita.]

I expect you think that Anita is silly and affected and old-fashioned. She isn't, Uncle George, I promise. She's my best friend, and very modern and rather naughty, and I write to her in just the same correct style as this. You have to, in Spanish; otherwise it doesn't make sense.

Lots of love to you and Aunt May, from

Margaret.

P.S. 'Lots of love' *would* sound silly in Spanish!

A Man May Not Marry His...

YOUR CORRESPONDENT, TELEPHONING from 'The Twelve Commandments', a charming little public house not a hundred yards from the gates of Lambeth Palace, reports that deep concern has been caused in that edifice by an examination of the quarterly report of the Archbishops' Standing Committee on Matrimony. This highly technical and still secret report, signed by Prebendary Palk, D.D., the biggest troublemaker in the whole Anglican Confession, emphasizes certain deficiencies in the *Table of Kindred and Affinity*: a legal document which your correspondent in his childhood used to study attentively during sermon time as a relaxation from the ardours of the Litany, and on which he is still something of an expert.

Half an hour ago, the bald and booming Prebendary unbosomed himself to your correspondent, who had invited him to a double gin-and-lime in the discreet bar-parlour. 'The Church,' he said, 'has hitherto been content to accept Genesis i, 27: "male and female created he them" as definitive; to believe that every human being is predestined before birth to one sex or the other. Insufficient credit has been given, however, to the mystery and evolutionary wonder of the Divine Scheme, and the remarkable skill with which, ahem, Providence has been pleased to endow certain outstanding surgeons and physicians. It has now been proved that a man or woman, even after consummating his or her marriage by an act of procreation, may experience a partial change of sex which these physicians and surgeons are empowered to make total.'

Pressed tactfully by your correspondent, the Prebendary enlarged on this theme: 'The Standing Committee,' he allowed himself to be quoted as saying, 'are by no means satisfied that the prohibited degrees listed in the *Table of Kindred and Affinity* have been defined with sufficient exactitude to prevent what may seem – I must emphasize, *seem* – scandalous marriages from taking place: unions which are, *prima facie*, incestuous in spirit, if not in letter. It is, for instance, a law of almost platitudinous force that a man may not marry his deceased wife's grandmother, nor (as he may more readily be tempted to do, if his grandfather has married a young girl and left her all the family cash) his deceased grandfather's wife. Yet since a certificate, signed by two or three qualified doctors and approved by a magistrate, now enables a man legally to register himself at Somerset House as a woman, what – pray, tell me that? – prevents him, as the Law stands, from marrying his deceased wife's grandfather, or his own grandmother's husband who may well be in his vigorous sixties?'

'Provided always that there is no consanguinity, and the spouses evince a genuine desire for the procreation of children,' your correspondent put in, sympathetically but doubtfully, from behind a pink gin.

'Quite, quite,' agreed the Prebendary, who is, by the way, a confirmed bachelor. 'Though in a civil marriage, you know, the registrar does not insist on the moral safeguard you very properly mention. But the question arises: should such a marriage, even between Christians of the highest principles and the deepest devotion for each other, be solemnized in a church? What troubles us committee-men is that, if such a man, now legally a woman, has been christened as a man, and if, worse – or I should say "better", I suppose – he has solemnized a Church marriage and begotten children on his wife now deceased, he must necessarily remain a male in the Church's sight, since these sacraments cannot be annulled or disregarded, even if the subject becomes a declared renegade to the faith. This consideration implies that in accordance with I Corinthians xi, 4, he would be obliged to appear in church with his head uncovered, not covered as in verse 5.'

'Don't let a little thing like that trouble you, Prebendary. In these days of empty pews, parsons admit women bareheaded, barefooted, and even in two-piece bathing suits. Besides, ritualistic changes of sex among physically normal women are already legalized in this country.'

'Ha! How's that?' he asked sharply.

'Well,' explained your ingenious correspondent. 'One Sunday, Jane Doe, a Bishop's daughter, greets the Queen with a low curtsy when, as Head of the Church, she lays the foundation stone of a new cathedral. On the following Sunday, the same Jane Doe, a sergeant-major in the W.R.A.C., assists at a Church Parade and salutes the Queen, as her Colonel-in-Chief. The salute is, in theory, a removal of the hat, which Jane Doe performs as an honorary man, but which would have been forbidden her, as a Bishop's daughter, on the previous Sunday.'

Here the Prebendary tried to argue the toss, but your correspondent reminded him that the symbolic removal of the hat is emphasized by Queen's Regulations, which make it a punishable offence to salute bareheaded.

Prebendary Palk then grunted with less than conviction, and returned to his marriage hypothesis: 'Granted that the Divine Law, as starkly laid down in Leviticus xx, 13, prevents the Church from recognizing a physical union between man and man; yet if one partner in this union be physically a female, is not the spirit of the Law observed? And would this spirit not be flouted were the union one between a woman who was legally and physically a man, and a man who had retained his physical male nature?'

Your blushing correspondent was obliged to agree that, in his opinion, flouting would have occurred.

'And, to take an extreme instance: what of a marriage solemnized in church between a man who has been physically and legally, but not spiritually, changed to a woman, and a woman who has been physically and legally, but not spiritually, changed to a man? I can see no possible moral objection to a match of this sort, because the spouses belong to opposite sexes whichever way you look at it. But, if the ex-woman prove her intrinsic masculinity by begetting children on the ex-man, and if the ex-man proves his intrinsic femininity by bearing and suckling these, to which of the two are the offspring to yield obedience as the spiritual male authority (Genesis iii, 16) in the household? And which of the two should be churched after the birth of each legitimate offspring?'

'Search me,' replied your correspondent gravely, signing to the tapster, who at once refilled the Prebendary's glass. 'Perhaps the decision would be better left to the individual conscience?'

'These are indeed thorny problems,' declared Prebendary Palk, 'but they must be resolutely faced, and not only by the Protestant Churches. Heaven knows what the Vatican reaction will be, but only yesterday I was talking to a Greek Orthodox dignitary – the Lesbian Patriarch in point of fact...'

'Off record,' interrupted your correspondent boldly, 'what counsel would you give to a legalized ex-man if he were to fall honourably in love with his deceased grandmother's husband and find his feelings tenderly reciprocated?'

'Strictly off record,' the Prebendary answered, venting a non-ecclesiastical chuckle, 'I should advise him to get on with it while the going is good, publish the banns in a remote parish, and not disclose the relationship to the officiating priest. It is, after all, as the Chief of Sinners pointed out, better to marry than to burn; and whatever legislation may be called for will not retrospectively illegitimize the offspring of such a union – we can promise your friend that.'

'I assure you, the case is quite hypothetical,' your correspondent stammered, meeting the Prebendary's shrewdly curious gaze with some embarrassment.

An Appointment for Candlemas

HAVE I THE honour of addressing Mrs Hipkinson?

That's me! And what can I do for you, young man?

I have a verbal introduction from – from an officer of your organization. Robin of Barking Creek was the name he gave.

If that isn't just like Robin's cheek! The old buck hasn't even dropped me a Christmas card since the year sweets came off the ration, and now he sends me trouble.

Trouble, Mrs Hipkinson?

Trouble, I said. You're not one of us. Don't need to do no crystal gazing to see that. What's the game?

Robin of Barking Creek has been kind enough to suggest that you would be kind enough to...

Cut it out. Got my shopping to finish.

If I might perhaps be allowed to carry your basket? It looks as if it were rather heavy.

O.K., you win. Take the damn thing. My corns are giving me gyp. Well, now, out with it!

The fact is, madam, I'm engaged in writing a D. Phil. thesis on Contemporary Magology...

Eh? What's that? Talk straight, *if* you please!

Excuse me. I mean I'm a University graduate studying present-day witchcraft; as a means of taking my degree in Philosophy.

Now, that makes a bit more sense. If Robin answers for you, I don't see why we couldn't help – same as I got our Deanna up into O level with a bit of a spell I cast on the Modern School examiners. But don't trouble to speak in whispers. Them eighteenth-century Witchcraft Acts is obsolescent now, except as regards fortune-tellers; and we don't touch that lay, not professionally we don't. Course, I admit, we keep ourselves to ourselves, but so do the Masons and the Foresters and the Buffs, not to mention the Commies. And all are welcome to our little do's, what consent to be duly pricked in their finger-tips and take the oath and give that there comical kiss. The police don't interfere. Got their work cut out to keep up with motoring offences and juvenile crime, and cetera. Nor they don't believe in witches, they say; only in fairies. They're real down on the poor fairies, these days.

Do you mean to say the police wouldn't break up one of your Grand Sabbaths, if...

Half a mo'! Got to pop into the Home and Commercial for a dozen rashers and a couple of hen-fruit. Bring the basket along, ducks, if you please...

As you were saying, Mrs Hipkinson?

Ah yes, about them Sabbaths... Well, see, so's to keep on the right side of the Law, on account we all have to appear starko, naturally we hire the Nudists' Hall. Main festivals are quarter-days and cross quarter-days; them's the obligatory ones, same as in Lancashire and the Highlands and everywhere else. Can't often spare the time in between. We run two covens here, used to be three – mixed sexes, but us girls are in the big majority. I'm Pucelle of Coven No. 1, and my boy-friend Arthur o'Bower (radio-mechanic in private life), he's Chief Devil of both. My husband plays the tabor and jew's-trump in Coven No. 2. Not very well up in the book of words, but a willing performer, that's Mr H.

I hope I'm not being indiscreet, but how do you name your God of the Witches?

Well, we used different names in the old days, before this village became what's called a dormitory suburb. He was Mahew, or Lug, or Herne, I seem to remember, according to the time of year. But the Rev. Jones, our last Chief Devil but two, he was a bit of a scholar: always called the god 'Faunus', which is Greek or Hebrew, I understand.

But Faunus was a patron of flocks and forests. There aren't many flocks or forests in North-Eastern London, surely?

Too true, there aren't; but we perform our fertility rites in aid of the allotments. We all feel that the allotments is a good cause to be encouraged, remembering how short of food we went in the War. Reminds me, got to stop at that fruit stall: horse-radish and a cabbage lettuce and a few nice carrots. The horse-radish is for my little old familiar; too strong for my own taste... Shopping's a lot easier since Arthur and me got rid of that there Hitler...

Please continue, Mrs Hipkinson.

Well, as I was saying, that Hitler caused us a lot of trouble. We don't hold with politics as a rule, but them Natsies was just too bad with their incendiaries and buzz-bombs. So Arthur and I worked on him at a distance, using all the strongest enchantments in the *Book of Moons* and out of it, not to mention a couple of new ones I got out of them Free French Breton sailors. But Mr Hitler was a difficult nut to crack. He was *protected*, see? But Mr Hitler had given us fire, and fire we would give Mr Hitler. First time, unfortunately, we got a couple o' words wrong in the formula, and only blew his pants off him. Next time, we didn't slip up; and we burned the little basket to a cinder... Reminds me of my great-grandmother, old Mrs Lou Simmons of Wanstead. She got mad with the Emperor Napoleon Bonapart, and caused 'im a horrid belly-ache on the Field of Waterloo. Done, at a distance again, with toad's venom – you got to get a toad scared sick before he'll secrete the right stuff. But old Lou, she scared her toad good and proper: showed him a distorting looking-glass – clever act, eh? So Boney couldn't keep his mind on the battle; it was those awful gripings in his stomjack what gave the Duke of Wellington his opportunity. Must cross over to the chemist, if you don't mind...

For flying ointment, by any chance?

Don't be potty! Think I'd ask that Mr Cadman for soot and baby's fat and bat's blood and aconite and water-parsnip? The old carcase would think I was pulling his leg. No, Long Jack of Coven No. 2 makes up our flying ointment – Jack's assistant-dispenser at the Children's Hospital down New Cut. Oh, but look at that queue! I don't think I'll trouble this morning. An aspirin will do me just as well as the panel medicine.

Do you still use the old-style besom at your merrymakings, Mrs Hipkinson?

There's another difficulty you laid your finger on. Can't get a decent besom hereabouts, not for love nor money. Painted white wood and artificial bristles, that's what they offer you. We got to send all the way to a bloke at Taunton for the real thing – ash and birch with osier for the binding – and last time, believe it or don't, the damned fool sent me a consignment bound in nylon tape! Nylon tape, I ask you!

Yes, I fear that modern technological conditions are not favourable to a spread of the Old Religion.

Can't grumble. We're up to strength at present, until one or two of the older boys and girls drop off the hook. But TV isn't doing us no good. Sometimes I got to do a bit of magic-making before I can drag my coven away from that Children's Hour.

Could you tell me what sort of magic?

Oh, nothing much; just done with tallow dolls and a bit of itching powder. I raise shingles on their sit-upons, that's the principle. Main trouble is, there's not been a girl of school-age joined us since my Deanna, which is quite a time. It's hell beating up recruits. Why, I know families where there's three generations of witches behind the kids, and can you guess what they all say?

I should not like to venture a guess, Mrs Hipkinson.

They say it's *rude*. *Rude!* That's a good one, eh? Well now, what about Candlemas? Falls on a Saturday this year. Come along at dusk. Nudists' Hall, remember – first big building to the left past the traffic lights. Just knock. And don't you worry about the finger-pricking. I'll bring iodine and lint.

*This is very kind of you indeed, Mrs Hipkinson. I'll phone Barking Creek
tonight and tell Robin how helpful you have been.*

Don't mention it, young man. Well, here's my dump. Can't ask you in,
I'm afraid, on account of my little old familiar wouldn't probably take to
you. But it's been a nice chat. O.K., then. On Candlemas Eve, look out for
three green frogs in your shaving mug; I'll send them as a reminder...
And mind, no funny business, Mister Clever! We welcome good sports,
specially the College type like yourself; but nosy-parkers has got to watch
their step, see? Last Lammas, Arthur and me caught a reporter from the
North-Eastern Examiner concealed about the premises. *Hey presto!* and we
transformed him into one of them Australian yellow dog dingoes. Took
him down to Regent's Park in Arthur's van, we did, and let him loose on
the grass. Made out he'd escaped from the Zoological Gardens; the
keepers soon copped him. He's the only dingo in the pen with a kink in his
tail; but you'd pick him out even without that, I dare say, by his hang-dog
look. Yes, you can watch the dingoes free from the 'Scotsman's Zoo',
meaning that nice walk along the Park railings. Well, cheerio for the
present!

Good-bye, Mrs Hipkinson.

The Five Godfathers

DEAR AUNTIE MAY,

About that christening. The baby's father, Don Onofre Tur y Tur, was a lawyer; but that doesn't mean much here in Majorca. Only a few lawyers have offices and clerks and things. The rest take law degrees because their fathers want to make gentlemen of them that way; though there isn't enough law work to go around among them all. And once they become gentlemen they are ashamed to sell melons in the market, or plough olive terraces with a mule-plough; so most of them waste their time in cafés, or make love to foreign lady-tourists who look lonely.

Onofre's father, Don Isidoro, had earned lots and lots by selling ice-cream outside the boys' colleges in the summer and doughnuts in the winter. Afterwards he bought a dance-house called 'The Blue Parrot' and a souvenir shop called 'Pensées de Majorque', and thus became immensely rich, like Charles Augustus Fortescue in the *Cautionary Tales*. But Onofre fell in love with Marujita, one of the taxi-girls at 'The Blue Parrot' and secretly married her. (The taxi-girls' job is to dance with the customers and make them buy gallons of expensive drink, and then sit in corners and cuddle them all night.) Don Isidoro was furious when he found out; he banished Onofre to Binijiny with an allowance of a hundred pesetas a day, telling him never to show his face in Palma again.

Of course, everyone at Binijiny knew the story; and the mayor's wife and the secretary's wife were awfully catty to Marujita. But Onofre said she mustn't pay any attention to these low people. He managed to be quite happy himself: he had a motor-bicycle, and an apparatus for spearing fish under water, and a gun for shooting rabbits, and a quail for decoying quail, and a net for netting thrushes. He also used to play poker every day with two American abstract painters and one New Zealand real painter. Marujita may have been a bit lonely, but she loved having a home of her own, after being a taxi-girl, and a hundred pesetas a day seemed like riches.

One day the rumour went round that Marujita was 'embarrassed and soon going to give light', meaning she expected a baby, and presently Onofre asked mother to arrange things with the midwife, a kind woman from Madrid who thinks Binijiny very rustic. So mother did. Marujita couldn't manage the housework towards the end, but the neighbours pretended to be too terribly busy to look in, and we live on the other side of the valley. So, because a Spanish man doesn't help in the house, especially if he's a gentleman like Onofre, Marujita cabled for her younger sister Sita. Don Isidoro had dismissed Sita from 'The Blue Parrot', where she was dancing too, for fear the men customers found out that she was his relative; he gave her a day's notice and her boat fare, third-class, to Valencia. Wasn't that mean? Well, Sita turned up in Binijiny a month before the baby was expected, and though she seemed scared of mother and us at first, as though we'd certainly be unkind to her, we liked her awfully. The two sisters were always crying over each other and kissing, and saying rosaries; and Sita knitted vests and socks all day.

Anyhow, the baby got safely born, and because it was a boy Onofre simply had to call it after the grandfather; that's a rule here, just as the second son has to be called after the other grandfather. Sita was splendid. She helped the midwife with Marujita, and didn't scream or run in circles like the Binijiny women do; but she made the baby feel at home, and washed it and changed it and sang it lovely Flamenco songs. She also cooked the meals and did all the other housework. Onofre had told her on the first day: 'Sister-in-law, you're a very good girl; you shall be godmother.' When the New Zealand painter was asked to be godfather he answered, 'Look here, I'm a Protestant.' But Onofre said, 'No matter, it's all the same. Priests are priests everywhere.'

Of course, Onofre had announced the birth to the grandparents, first with a respectful telegram, and then with a flowery letter, enclosing an invitation card to the christening. He never expected to get any answer; it was just to keep his allowance safe.

Well, on the day of the christening, Sita put on her Sunday dress and wiped off her make-up and arranged the drinks and cakes and biscuits and *tapas* for the baptismal party in the sitting-room. Then she wrapped the baby like a mummy in four or five thick shawls and Doña Isabel the midwife accompanied her because she had never been a godmother before. Marujita wasn't well enough to go, so she stayed in bed. Onofre had sent out a whole packet of invitations to the christening, but nobody else came at all except mother and father and me and Richard, and the two American abstract painters and the New Zealand real painter.

The priest was waiting at the church door but the acolytes hadn't arrived. We waited about for nearly an hour talking and joking, while the baby slept. At last the priest said he had other business to do and he must start without the acolytes, and perhaps Onofre would condescend to assist? So he did, to save time. Sita already had the lighted candle in her hand, which every godmother carries, when a large, splendid car drew up in the Plaza, and Don Isidoro and Doña Tecla entered. Onofre turned pale, and the beastly old man said at once: '*I* am godfather here and no one else, understand, Onofre? What's more, this immodest woman is not going to be godmother by my side. Unless she goes away I'll cut off your allowance and the child will starve.' Onofre turned paler still, but Sita kept calm. She said to the priest: 'Father, I renounce my rights. Nobody will ever say that I prejudiced the good fortune of this precious infant.' Then she handed the candle to Doña Isabel and went home to tell Marujita. The New Zealand painter also gave up, of course, so the priest started; but as soon as he turned his back and bowed to the altar Doña Tecla seized the baby from Doña Isabel, and said '*I* am godmother here, woman, and no one else, understand?'

But Doña Isabel hung on to the candle, and told the grandparents in a loud whisper that Sita was worth forty basketfuls of *canaille* like them. Doña Tecla screeched back at her, cackling like an old hen, which made the priest lose his place in the book and start reading prayers for missionaries in foreign parts. He had just found out his mistake and said 'Caramba, what a folly!' when in ran the acolytes without their surplices and laughing fit to burst. The manager of the hotel had sent them to fetch Doña Isabel at once, because two Belgian ladies insisted on sunbathing naked by the fishermen's huts, and if the Guardias caught them *he'd* be fined two hundred and fifty pesetas for each woman, because they were guests in his hotel, and that is the law. Doña Isabel asked 'Why me?' And they answered 'Because you are accustomed to deal with undressed women.' So Doña Isabel said 'Patience, in a moment!'

The priest took the baby and put the usual salt in its mouth to drive out the Devil, but for some reason or other it didn't cry. Perhaps it liked the taste. So Don Isidoro said 'Put in more, man; the Devil's still inside!' and Doña Tecla reached forward under the shawls and pinched the poor little baby on purpose to make it yell. Onofre noticed that and said in a loud voice 'Mother, you may insult my sister-in-law, and the certificated midwife of this village; these are women's affairs in which I don't meddle. But you will *not* pinch my son's bottom.'

The priest hurriedly made the sign of the cross on the baby's forehead, and called it Onofre, by mistake for Isidoro. Then Onofre took it from him and gave it to mother, who hurried it out of church before worse could happen. Doña Isabel went with her, still holding the candle.

Naturally Don Isidoro disowned Onofre, and Doña Tecla slapped his face before they stamped out of the church and drove off in their large splendid car. The rest of us trailed along to the baptismal party. Onofre did his best to be cheerful, and said 'Come along, friends, and help me drink up the brandy, because tomorrow we're all beggars.'

Sita was there when we arrived, rocking the baby and looking very pretty and pale without her make-up. Everyone began at once to drink and dance. Our family went away early because Richard had eaten too much cake and drunk half a glass of *anis*; but presently another guest invited himself in, an officer of the Spanish Blue Division whom the Russians had just let out of prison after fourteen years. He had no friends left and wanted to celebrate his return. Doña Isabel also came. She had frightened the Belgian women into putting on their clothes and then gone back to the church, where she found that Doña Tecla hadn't signed the register as the baby's godmother. So she signed it herself; because, after all, she'd held the candle. And the name would be Onofre, she said, not Isidoro, and that was God's will.

Just before midnight Onofre beat his head with his fist and shouted 'I had almost forgotten; my beast of a father did not sign the book either. Quick, gentlemen, to the Rectory, before the clock strikes twelve and the day becomes extinct!' So the Blue Division prisoner and the two abstract painters, and the real one, all trooped up to the Rectory, very intoxicatedly, and insisted on signing the register as little Onofre's joint godfathers. The priest had to let them, to avoid a scandal.

And guess what? In April they're all going to the Seville Fair at the invitation of Sita's new *novio*, who's a Chilean millionaire called Don Jacinto; I have met him. Don Jacinto is also lending Onofre and Marujita five million pesetas to start a much more luxurious Palma dance-house than 'The Blue Parrot'. He says 'That will teach Don Isidoro not to insult poor beautiful dancing-girls who are positively saints!' It's going to be called 'Los Cinco Padrinos', which means 'The Five Godfathers', because Don Jacinto has added his name to the list too, for solidarity.

All the same, I can't say I trust him, somehow, and Marujita doesn't either; but we hope for the best.

Lots of love,
Margaret

The White Horse or
'The Great Southern Ghost Story'

THERE HAD ALWAYS been a Colonel Flack at Sophie, Georgia, even while it was still called Sophiaville, and a Doc Halloran, too; not to mention a Lawyer Pritchard. For generations it was a vexed question 'who got there the fustest', the Flacks or the Hallorans, and many a hasty word was spoken on account of it, until at last the Lawyer Pritchard who flourished under President Polk summoned his Colonel Flack and his Doc Halloran to the County Court House. 'Gentlemen,' he said, 'all the relevant documents are right here in that safe; and if this tomfool argument crops up again, I'll publish a certificated extract of them in every paper south of the Line, which won't do neither of you-all a heap of good.'

The Flacks came from the county of Somerset in England, and owned a regular coat of arms, with the motto *Nec Flacci Mortem*, meaning: 'I don't care a straw for death.' And they certainly did not.

We Doc Hallorans – for I'm the present holder of the title – originate in Co. Meath, Ireland. We're charged with the protection of the said Flacks in the matter of setting their broken bones, plugging their bullet holes with medicated cotton, scaring away their green rats and pink elephants (especially after Thanksgiving), and also seeing that they get born in good shape. We take the task pretty seriously, because the Flacks, when they're not in liquor, are the best folks for a hundred miles around; and our debt to them, to quote Lawyer Pritchard, is inassessable and unrepudiatable.

The Flacks suffered as heavily as any Georgian family in the Civil War; lost nearly every male of the younger generation in this battle or that, and Colonel Randolph Flack was fuming and pining because he had to stay home and mind the plantation, instead of riding out with General Lee. The principal tie was his lady: she'd been widowed in the first skirmish of the war, he'd married her a year later, and now she was expectant. The Colonel couldn't very well leave his lady in the big mansion, all alone except for the slaves; there were plenty of deserters and bad men around at the time. So he continued to pine and fume, and my great-grandfather had to bear the brunt of his tantrums.

General Sherman took Atlanta early in September, and began moving across Georgia on his notorious march to the sea; destroying, as he went, everything that could be destroyed. The Colonel took it into his head that Sherman was the Beast of Revelations, and that the South's only hope lay in putting that Beast out of the way. Moreover, he was going to do it himself, in gentlemanly fashion. He would ride up to the General, salute him with a sweep of his beaver hat, and ask point blank: 'Sir, are you man enough to shoot it out?'

My great-grandfather did his best to dissuade him from his project. 'May I venture to doubt, Colonel Flack,' he said, 'whether you'd be permitted to approach within parleying distance of General Sherman? He's reckoned to have a bodyguard of Maine hunters about him who'll drill you clean at a thousand paces.'

'Those goddam Yankees can't shoot!' shouted the Colonel, who was certainly in liquor at the time.

'They can't miss!' answered my great-grandfather.

'We'll see about that,' said the Colonel. *'Nec Flacci Mortem!'*

'And what of your lady?' asked my great-grandfather.

'Why, she's a Southerner, Doc; she'll understand.'

'And what of your child?'

'That's your business, Doc,' says the Colonel. 'But I'll be along at the birth, never you fear, to see fair play.'

Nothing could stop the obstinate fellow. He sent for his case of duelling pistols; he sent for his white horse; he made his coloured valet stuff the saddlebags with bourbon, corn bread, bacon and a couple of clean shirts. Then off he trotted, clippety-clop, up the dirt-road, over the brow of the hill, then down through the sweet-potato patch, splash across the creek and away into the pine wood...

What took place at the encounter, nobody ever learned: whether the Maine hunters drilled him clean, or whether General Sherman was even quicker on the draw than he... But Colonel Flack didn't come riding home that week, nor that month neither, though Sherman's sixty thousand were now well on their way to Savannah. Sophie, I am glad to report, lay a good twenty miles off the track of destruction and escaped without losing so much as a hog.

The day before Twelfth Night, the Colonel's lady was brought to bed, and this being her first child, my great-grandfather felt a certain anxiety; he arrived early with his black bag, and had twenty-four hours to wait – from midnight to midnight. But as the clock struck at last, a noise of hooves was heard approaching at a gallop from the pine woods and then splashing across the ford through the creek, which was mighty deep at that season, and up through the sweet-potato patch, and down over the brow of the hill to the mansion. My great-grandfather was working like a demon now to save the child, and the sweat streaked his face. However, he stole a glance out of the window and recognized both horse and rider; so

he cried to the lady: 'Courage, ma'am, all's well! Your husband's home!'
And with that they made a concerted effort and another male Flack was
brought into the world; which saved the family name from extinction, for
all the rest had been killed. But he didn't dare tell her until many months
later that the breast of the Colonel's shirt was stained with red, and that
his face shone white as clay in the moonlight.

Now, this posthumous child happened to be the Colonel's seventh; and
a tradition arose at Sophie that whenever a seventh Flack came to be born
(it could be counted on to be a boy) the Colonel's ghost would attend the
accouchement. If it hadn't appeared on such occasions, or if no Doc
Halloran had been in attendance on the lady, Sophie would have reckoned
it mighty queer.

Well, this is where I enter the story. The Flacks, as usual, had been
breeding fast, but the current expenditure of life was well above the
average; three boys gone in the First World War, and two in the Second;
and several other deaths from miscellaneous causes had reduced the line
to the widow and two daughters of the late Colonel Randolph Flack, killed
with the Marines on Iwo Jima. But a posthumous child was expected
around Twelfth Night, to make the seventh.

Lawyer Pritchard waited below, trampling up and down the parlour,
like a bear in a cage, muttering to himself and anticipating the worst. I had
been upstairs for twenty-four hours, but with plenty to occupy my hands
and mind; though it looked to be a losing battle.

Finally the clock struck midnight, and the moment of crisis came. I
heard the sound of hooves galloping out from the wood, plunging down
into the creek, then through, and up, and over, and along the dirt-road.
'Fine,' I thought, as they clattered to a stop. But then came sounds of a
scuffle, and when I dared steal a glance through the window, I saw my
own black gelding in the driveway, and on that black gelding sat Colonel
Flack, dressed exactly as my father had described him to me – beaver hat,
pistol case, bloodstain and all – but I have never in my life seen a more
dejected face! What is more, it was the face of the Colonel Flack whom I
knew, Randolph Flack, of the Marines!

It all seemed so wrong and so out of key with tradition that I heard
myself hollering madly at him: 'Hi there, Colonel, you turned hoss-thief?
That's my beast! Where's your own?' And as true as I'm standing here, he
hollers back: 'It's the Commander-in-Chief, Doc! He's grabbed mine and
told me to shift for myself.'

Another mounted figure moved into the light of the french window,
and you will excuse me for not describing him, for though I have seen
Death often in the course of my professional activities, and wearing many
disguises, that is not a subject on which I care to dwell in company. I'll say
no more than this: he was riding the Colonel's white horse.

'Call yourself a Flack?' I hollered again. 'So you're a coward after all, is that it? Forgotten the family motto, eh? You, who never before let your-self be pushed around by the Top Brass? *Nec Flacci Mortem* indeed! My word, I'm downright ashamed of you, Randy Flack! And no Doc Halloran ever said that before to a man of your name.'

It worked. I saved the mother and I saved the boy. Then, when I could look up again, I watched the Colonel trotting away out of sight, mounted on his own horse; and the duelling pistol smoked in his hand.

Epics Are Out of Fashion

PETRONIUS DID HIS best. He wasn't a bad fellow at heart, though he had the foulest mind in Rome and drank like a camel. And he was such an expert in the art of modern living that the Emperor never dared buy a vase or a statue, or even sample an unfamiliar vintage, without his advice.

One evening Petronius dropped in to dinner at the Palace and was handed a really repulsive-looking sauce, of which herb-benjamin and garlic seemed to be the chief ingredients. Since the waiter actually expected him to pour it over a beautifully grilled sole, Petronius made Nero blush to the roots of his hair by asking in his silkiest tones: 'My dear Caesar, can this be *exactly* what you meant?' Nero's eager, anxious glances, you see, made it quite obvious that he had invented the sauce himself; and if Petronius had been weak enough to approve, every noble table in Rome would soon have stunk with the stuff. Our hearts went out to him in gratitude.

My brother-in-law Lucan notoriously lacked Petronius's poise, and yet was far too pleased with himself. I had always regretted my sister's marriage: Lucan, the son of rich Spanish provincials, never ceased to be an outsider, although his uncle Seneca, Nero's tutor, had now risen to the rank of Consul and become the leading writer and dramatist of his day. Seneca doted on young Lucan, an infant prodigy who could talk Greek fluently at the age of four, knew the *Iliad* by heart at eight; and before he turned eleven had written an historical commentary on Xenophon's *Anabasis* and translated Ibycus into Ovidian elegiacs.

He was now twenty-five, two years older than Nero, who had taken him as his literary model. Lucan repaid this kindness with a wonderful speech of flattery at the *Neronia* festival. But when that same night Petronius visited our house – Lucan was staying with us at the time – on the pretext of congratulating him, I guessed that there was something else in the wind. So I dismissed the slaves, and out it came.

'Yes, Lucan, a most polished speech; and I am too discreet to inquire how sincerely you meant it. But... well... a rumour is about that you're working on an important historical poem.'

'Correct, friend Petronius,' Lucan answered complacently.

'For the love of Bacchus, you aren't after all writing your *Conquests of Alexander*, are you?'

'No, I scrapped that, except for a few fine passages.'

'Wise man. You might have inspired our Imperial patron to emulate the Macedonian by marching into Parthia. Despite his innate military genius, and so on, and so forth, I cannot be sure that the army would have proved quite equal to the task. Those Parthian archers, you know...' He let his voice trail off.

'No, since you ask, the subject is the Civil Wars.'

Petronius threw up his hands. 'That's what I heard, and it alarmed me more than I can say, my dear boy! It's a desperately tricky subject, even after a hundred years. At least two-thirds of the surviving aristocratic families fought on the losing side. You may please the Emperor – I repeat *may* and underline it – but you'll be sure to tread on a multitude of corns. How long is the poem?'

'An epic in twelve books. Nine are already written...'

'An *epic*, my very good sir?'

'An epic.'

'But epics are ridiculously out of fashion!'

'Mine won't be. I make my warriors use modem weapons; I rule out any absurd personal intervention of the gods; and I enliven the narrative with gruesome anecdotes, breath-taking metaphors, and every rhetorical trope in the bag. Like me to read a few lines?'

'If you insist.'

While Lucan is away fetching the scroll, Petronius plucks me by the sleeve. 'Argentarius, you must stop this nonsense somehow – anyhow! The Emperor has just coyly asked me: "What about those *Battle of Actium* verses I showed you the other night? Were you too drunk to take them in?" "No, Caesar," I assured him, "your remarkable hexameters sobered me up in a flash." "So you agree that I'm a better poet than Lucan?" To which I replied: "Heavens above, there's no comparison!" He must have taken this all right, because his next remark was: "Good, because those lines form part of my great modern epic."'

Re-enter Lucan. Petronius breaks off the sentence dramatically and reaches for the scroll. Lucan watches him read. After an uncomfortable quarter of an hour Petronius lays the scroll down and pronounces: 'This will take a lot of polishing, Lucan. I don't say it's not good, but it must be far, far better before it can go to the copyists. Put it away in a drawer for another few years. In my opinion (which you cannot afford to despise) the modern epic is a form that only retired statesmen or young Emperors should attempt.'

Lucan turns white. 'What do you mean?' he asks.

'I have nothing to add to my statement,' replies Petronius, and waves his hand in farewell. Petronius was so drunk, by the way, that he almost seemed sober.

Lucan tried to cut Petronius in the Sacred Way early next morning; but found himself forcibly steered into the back-room of a wine shop. 'Listen, imbecile,' Petronius said, 'nobody denies that you're the greatest poet in the world, *with one exception;* but that exception has got wind of your project, and he'll be very cross indeed if you presume to compete with him. For the love of Vulcan, light the furnace with that damned papyrus! Write a rhymed cookery-book instead – I'll be delighted to help you – or some more of your amatory epigrams about negresses with lascivious limbs and hair like the fleece of Zeus's black Laphystian ram; or what about a Pindaresque eulogy of the Emperor's skill as a charioteer? Anything in the world – but *not* an epic about the Civil Wars!'

'Nobody has a right to curb my Pegasus.'

'Those were Bellerophon's famous last words,' Petronius reminded him. 'The Thunderer then sent a gadfly which stung Pegasus under the tail, and Bellerophon fell a long way, and very hard.'

Lucan flared up. 'Who are you to talk about caution? You satirize Nero as Trimalchio in your satiric novel, don't you? Nobody could mistake the portrait: his flat jokes, his rambling nonsensical talk, his grossly vulgar taste, his heart-breaking self-pity. Oh, that squint-eyed, lecherous, illiterate, muddle-pated, megalomaniac, morbid, top-heavy mountain of flesh!'

Petronius rose. 'Really, Spaniard, I think this must be good-bye! There are certain things that cannot be decently said in *any* company.'

'But which I have nevertheless said, and will say again!'

It proved to be their last meeting. A month later Lucan invited a few friends to a private banquet where, after dessert, he declaimed the first two or three hundred lines of his epic. It started by describing the Civil Wars as the greatest disgrace Rome ever suffered, but none the less amply worth while, since they guaranteed Nero's eventual succession. Then it promised Nero that on his demise he'd go straight up to the stars, like the divine Augustus, and become even more of a god than he already was – with the choice, though, of deciding whether to become Jove and wield the Olympian sceptre, or Apollo and try out the celestial Sun-chariot.

This was all very well so far; but then came the pay-off. You must understand that Petronius had got away with the Trimalchio satire because he was an artist: careful not to pick on any actual blunder or vulgarity of Nero's that had gone the rounds, but burlesquing the sort of behaviour which (under our breaths of course) we called a Neronianism. Nero would never have recognized the *nouveau-riche* Trimalchio as himself; and, obviously, nobody would have dared enlighten him. But Lucan wasn't an artist. He soon let his mock-heroic eulogy degenerate into ham-handed caricature: he begged Nero when deified not to deprive Rome of his full radiance by planting himself in the Arctic regions of

Heaven or in the tropical South, whence his fortunate beams would reach us only *squintingly*; and he was, please, not to lean too *heavily* on any particular part of the aether for fear his *divine weight* would tilt the heavenly axis off centre and throw the whole universe out of gear. And the idiot emphasized each point with a ghastly grimace – which caused such general embarrassment that the banquet broke up in confusion.

Nero, as it happened, heard only a vague rumour about the affair, but enough to make him ask Petronius whether Lucan had been warned not to trespass on the Imperial preserve. Petronius answered without hesitation: 'Yes, Caesar. I explained that it would be ridiculous for him to compete with his master in literature.' So Nero sent a couple of Guards officers to Lucan's house with the curt message: 'You will write no more poetry until further notice!'

The sequel is well known. Lucan persuaded a few other hot-heads to join his plot for assassinating the Emperor in the name of artistic freedom. It miscarried. His friends were arrested; and Lucan had his veins opened by a surgeon in the usual warm bath, where he declaimed a tragic fragment from his *Conquests of Alexander*: about a Macedonian soldier dying for loss of blood.

Lucan's father naturally had to follow his dreary example, and so did old Seneca. (Rather hard on my poor sister, that!) Moreover Lucan had left a rude letter behind for the Emperor, if rude be a strong enough word, incidentally calling Petronius a coward for pulling his punches in the Trimalchio portrait. So Petronius was in for it too!

But I had run straight from the banquet down to Ostia – a good twelve miles – with all the gold I could cram into a satchel, and taken ship to Ephesus; where I dyed my hair, changed my name, and lay low for three or four years until Vespasian had been securely invested with the purple. Thank goodness I was stupid at school, and never felt any literary ambitions whatsoever! But nobody in Rome could touch me as a long-distance man...

Earth to Earth

YES, YES AND yes! Don't get me wrong, for goodness' sake. I am heart and soul with you. I agree that Man is wickedly defrauding the Earth-Mother of her ancient dues by not putting back into the soil as much nourishment as he takes out. And that modern plumbing is, if you like, a running sore in the body politic. And that municipal incinerators are genocidal rather than germicidal... And that cremation should be made a capital crime. And that dust bowls created by the greedy plough...

... Yes, yes and yes again. *But!*

Elsie and Roland Hedge – she a book-illustrator, he an architect with suspect lungs – had been warned against Dr Eugen Steinpilz. 'He'll bring you no luck,' I told them. 'My little finger says so decisively.'

'You too?' asked Elsie indignantly. (This was at Brixham, South Devon, in March 1940.) 'I suppose you think that because of his foreign accent and his beard he must be a spy?'

'No,' I said coldly, 'that point hadn't occurred to me. But I won't contradict you.'

The very next day Elsie deliberately picked a friendship – I don't like the phrase, but that's what she did – with the Doctor, an Alsatian with an American passport, who described himself as a *Naturphilosoph;* and both she and Roland were soon immersed in Steinpilzerei up to the nostrils. It began when he invited them to lunch and gave them cold meat and two rival sets of vegetable dishes – potatoes (baked), carrots (creamed), bought from the local fruiterer; and potatoes (baked) and carrots (creamed), grown on compost in his own garden.

The superiority of the latter over the former in appearance, size and especially flavour came as an eye-opener to Elsie and Roland. Yes, and yes, I know just how they felt. Why shouldn't I? When I visit the market here in Palma, I always refuse La Torre potatoes, because they are raised for the early English market and therefore reek of imported chemical fertilizer. Instead I buy Son Sardina potatoes, which taste as good as the ones we used to get in England fifty years ago. The reason is that the Son Sardina farmers manure their fields with Palma kitchen-refuse, still available by the cartload – this being too backward a city to afford effective modern methods of destroying it.

Thus Dr Steinpilz converted the childless and devoted couple to the Steinpilz method of composting. It did not, as a matter of fact, vary greatly from the methods you read about in the *Gardening Notes* of your favourite national newspaper, except that it was far more violent. Dr Steinpilz had invented a formula for producing extremely fierce bacteria, capable (Roland claimed) of breaking down an old boot or the family Bible or a torn woollen vest into beautiful black humus almost as you watched. The formula could not be bought, however, and might be communicated under oath of secrecy only to members of the Eugen Steinpilz Fellowship – which I refused to join. I won't pretend therefore to know the formula myself, but one night I overheard Elsie and Roland arguing in their garden as to whether the planetary influences were favourable; and they also mentioned a ram's horn in which, it seems, a complicated mixture of triturated animal and vegetable products – technically called 'the Mother' – was to be cooked up. I gather also that a bull's foot and a goat's pancreas were part of the works, because Mr Pook the butcher afterwards told me that he had been puzzled by Roland's request for these unusual cuts. Milkwort and pennyroyal and bee-orchid and vetch certainly figured among the Mother's herbal ingredients; I recognized these one day in a gardening basket Elsie had left at the post office.

The Hedges soon had their first compost heap cooking away in the garden, which was about the size of a tennis court and consisted mostly of well-kept lawn. Dr Steinpilz, who supervised, now began to haunt the cottage like the smell of drains; I had to give up calling on them. Then, after the Fall of France, Brixham became a war-zone whence everyone but we British and our Free French or Free Belgians allies were extruded. Consequently Dr Steinpilz had to leave; which he did with very bad grace, and was killed in a Liverpool air-raid the day before he should have sailed back to New York. But that was far from closing the ledger. I think Elsie must have been in love with the Doctor, and certainly Roland had a hero-worship for him. They treasured a signed collection of all his esoteric books, each called after a different semi-precious stone, and used to read them out aloud to each other at meals, in turns. Then to show that this was a practical philosophy, not just a random assemblage of beautiful thoughts about Nature, they began composting in a deeper and even more religious way than before. The lawn had come up, of course; but they used the sods to sandwich layers of kitchen waste, which they mixed with the scrapings from an abandoned pigsty, two barrowfuls of sodden poplar leaves from the recreation ground, and a sack of rotten turnips. Looking over the hedge, I caught the fanatic gleam in Elsie's eye as she turned the hungry bacteria loose on the heap, and could not repress a premonitory shudder.

So far, not too bad, perhaps. But when serious bombing started and food became so scarce that housewives were fined for not making over their swill to the national pigs, Elsie and Roland grew worried. Having already abandoned their ordinary sanitary system and built an earth-closet in the garden, they now tried to convince neighbours of their duty to do the same, even at the risk of catching cold and getting spiders down the neck. Elsie also sent Roland after the slow-moving Red Devon cows as they lurched home along the lane at dusk, to rescue the precious drop-pings with a kitchen shovel; while she visited the local ash-dump with a packing case mounted on wheels, and collected whatever she found there of an organic nature – dead cats, old rags, withered flowers, cabbage stalks and such household waste as even a national wartime pig would have coughed at. She also saved every drop of their bath-water for sprinkling the heaps; because it contained, she said, valuable animal salts.

The test of a good compost heap, as every illuminate knows, is whether a certain revolting-looking, if beneficial, fungus sprouts from it. Elsie's heaps were grey with this crop, and so hot inside that they could be used for haybox cookery; which must have saved her a deal of fuel. I call them 'Elsie's heaps', because she now considered herself Dr Steinpilz's earthly delegate; and loyal Roland did not dispute this claim.

A critical stage in the story came during the Blitz. It will be remem-bered that trainloads of Londoners, who had been evacuated to South Devon when war broke out, thereafter de-evacuated and re-evacuated and re-de-evacuated themselves, from time to time, in a most disorganized fashion. Elsie and Roland, as it happened, escaped having evacuees billeted on them, because they had no spare bedroom; but one night an old naval pensioner came knocking at their door and demanded lodging for the night. Having been burned out of Plymouth, where everything was chaos, he had found himself walking away and blundering along in a daze until he fetched up here, hungry and dead-beat. They gave him a meal and bedded him on the sofa; but when Elsie came down in the morning to fork over the heaps, she found him dead of heart-failure.

Roland broke a long silence by coming, in some embarrassment, to ask my advice. Elsie, he said, had decided that it would be wrong to trouble the police about the case; because the police were so busy these days, and the poor old fellow had claimed to possess neither kith nor kin. So they'd read the burial service over him and, after removing his belt-buckle, trouser buttons, metal spectacle-case and a bunch of keys, which were irreducible, had laid him reverently in the new compost heap. Its other contents, he added, were a cartload of waste from the cider-factory, salvaged cow-dung, and several basketfuls of hedge clippings. Had they done wrong?

'If you mean "will I report you to the Civil Authorities?" the answer is no,' I assured him. 'I wasn't looking over the hedge at the relevant hour, and what you tell me is only hearsay.' Roland shambled off satisfied.

The War went on. Not only did the Hedges convert the whole garden into serried rows of Eugen Steinpilz memorial heaps, leaving no room for planting the potatoes or carrots to which the compost had been prospectively devoted, but they scavenged the offal from the Brixham fish-market and salvaged the contents of the bin outside the surgical ward at the Cottage Hospital. Every spring, I remember, Elsie used to pick big bunches of primroses and put them straight on the compost, without even a last wistful sniff; virgin primroses were supposed to be particularly relished by the fierce bacteria.

Here the story becomes a little painful for members, say, of a family reading circle; I will soften it as much as possible. One morning a policeman called on the Hedges with a summons, and I happened to see Roland peep anxiously out of the bedroom window, but quickly pull his head in again. The policeman rang and knocked and waited, then tried the back door; and presently went away. The summons was for a blackout offence, but apparently the Hedges did not know this. Next morning he called again, and when nobody answered, forced the lock of the back door. They were found dead in bed together, having taken an overdose of sleeping tablets. A note on the coverlet ran simply:

> Please lay our bodies on the heap nearest the pigsty. Flowers by request. Strew some on the bodies, mixed with a little kitchen waste, and then fork the earth lightly over.
>
> E.H.; R.H.

George Irks, the new tenant, proposed to grow potatoes and dig for victory. He hired a cart and began throwing the compost into the River Dart, 'not liking the look of them toadstools', as he subsequently explained. The five beautifully clean human skeletons which George unearthed in the process were still awaiting identification when the War ended.

They Say... They Say

THIS IS SATURDAY, listeners, and here I am standing beside the old recording van in a Spanish seaport town on the Costa Brava. The sun is pretty hot, even for this time of year: several scores of farmers and dealers, mainly from outlying districts, have taken possession of the Market Square cafés. Nice fellows, too. Not a knife, pistol or unkind thought in the whole crowd. That hoarse buzz you hear is their usual exchange of views on the price of tomatoes, olive futures, the effects of drought on the regional economy, and so on. The overtones are excited argument about the Grand Tour of Catalonia – on push-bike – and the fearful struggle of the local *fútbol* team to avoid relegation to the Third Division of the League.

Now, suppose we bring the microphone over to a corner table and listen to what those two very relaxed-looking types are saying to each other over their coffee and *anís*. The melancholy-looking fellow in black corduroys, sporting a massive silver watch-chain, is Pep Prat. Pep breeds mules; and his rubicund *vis-à-vis* with the blue sash, by name Pancho Pons, grows carnations for the Barcelona market.

PANCHO: Well, Master Pep! Been along Conception Street lately?

PEP: And if not, have I missed much, Master Pancho?

PANCHO: Nothing, nothing. I was only making conversation.

PEP: Make some more by all means.

PANCHO: I went this morning to change a one-hundred-*duro* note at the Banco Futurístico.

PEP: Did they short-change you? Mistakes often happen on a Saturday.

PANCHO: No, indeed. Don Bernardo Bosch was in a very good humour. He now has an enchanting little office with three easy chairs, a mahogany desk and a window overlooking the street.

PEP: Of course... Of course... Ah, Master Pancho! That poor woman's face comes back to me so clearly!

PANCHO: What courage, eh? I should never have dared address him as she did.

PEP: It is now more than a year ago.

PANCHO: Yet the words still ring in my ears. I happened to be doing some business with the cheesemonger next door, and poor saintly Margalida never spoke in a low voice, even at the worst of times. On that occasion she might have been missionizing the heathen. She said: 'Don Bernardo, not another word! I have this shop on a hundred years lease, with eighty-six more to run and since (thanks be to God!) I am now only thirty years old and enjoy good health, it should last out my life. I am not selling, I do not need to sell, and though the shop may measure only twenty-five and a half square metres it suffices for my modest business.'

PEP: She had spirit.

PANCHO: And Don Bernardo answered: 'You are a bloodsucker, you are a negress, Margalida Mut, you are Jael and Sapphira rolled into one. I offer you fifteen hundred *duros* a square metre to surrender your lease and you dare refuse it!' And the poor creature answered: 'I am not selling, you gipsy! But if you and your colleagues think of selling the Banco Futurístico equally cheap, let me know – I may need it as a lumber room. *Adiós!*" That ended the comedy.

PEP: But tell me: exactly why would she not sell?

PANCHO: Ask me, rather, why she should sell. Should she sell just because the Banco Futurístico had bought up the rest of the site, and did not wish her rusty shutters and peeling sign to interrupt their beautiful marble façade in Conception Street? Margalida was a martyr to principle.

PEP: Nevertheless, principle puts no bacon in the stew. Her trade was beggarly. She called herself an antique-dealer but I have seen better stuff spread out on a sack in the Flea Market: nails, horseshoes, a broken sewing machine, three cracked dishes, books without covers, half a Salamonic bedrail.

PANCHO: Mind, I know nothing, but they say... very unjustly no doubt... that the excellent woman was a receiver of stolen goods, a usuress at compound interest, a blackmailer, a Protestant!

PEP: They say! Ah, the hypocrites! They said nothing like that at her funeral. What a display! A thousand people at least walked in it, besides priests and acolytes. And an epidemic of tall wax candles. Also columns in the *Heraldo* about her good works and devotion and saintliness. I recall how shocked Don Bernardo was when he heard the news. He hurried at once in his very pyjamas to condole with the deceased's afflicted sister Joana Mut.

PANCHO: It was well done, although Margalida had not been on speaking terms with either of the two sisters since their parents' death – some dispute about the inheritance, they say.

PEP: Yes, they say. And they say... But never mind.

PANCHO: An extraordinary end, eh? Altogether baffling. It happened, you will remember, at precisely seven o'clock, when all the shutters in the street were clanging down; and her protests, if any, must have been drowned in the noise. Nobody was aware that anything unusual had occurred until nine o'clock next morning when someone noticed the gap at the bottom of the shutter – which showed that she had not locked it as was her custom when she went home to her solitary flat. A pity, because it was then too late to telephone the station-police at Port Bou and have the passengers searched as they crossed the frontier. You may be sure that the assassin was French.

PEP: My brother-in-law at Police Headquarters disagrees.

PANCHO: No Catalan of the Costa Brava would murder even a supposed usuress for her money!

PEP: Certainly not! But no money was taken. A two-hundred-*duro* note was left untouched in the open cash-box. They say that the assassin was a married lady who wished to retrieve some compromising document from it. They say that a long strand of hair was found in poor Margalida's fingers...

PANCHO: Yes, they say! But they also say it was Margalida's own hair, torn out in the struggle.

PEP: Of the same colour and thickness, I admit. It certainly seemed to be Mut hair... What I cannot understand is why my brother-in-law had orders from high up to post an armed guard at either end of the street for a whole month; as if to prevent a disturbance.

PANCHO: It is, of course, a theory that murderers revisit the scene of their crimes. But what I should have liked to ask your brother-in-law was, why he allowed that picture of poor Isidoro Núñez to appear in the *Heraldo* entitled: 'Wanted, dead or alive, for the Conception crime!' Isidoro is not a bad fellow. Once he got drunk and borrowed the mayor's bicycle and ran it into a tree, so they jailed him for a couple of months; but that was his one crime. Actually, it was well known that he had gone off, two days before, to visit his father in Galicia; and when he returned the police did not even interrogate him. They say...

PEP: Oh yes, they say! They also say that it was a love tragedy, that the poor woman was killed by an amorous and impulsive youngster whom she had rejected.

PANCHO: Ka! Margalida was as ugly as a fisherman's boot.

PEP: Pancho, you must not speak disrespectfully of the dead. Very well, let us suppose that the amorous youngster was really after her money...

PANCHO: Good! And that he believed her to have already closed the bargain with Don Bernardo. Tell me, by the way, did her heirs sell the lease for those fifteen hundred *duros* the square metre?

PEP: No. You see, Margalida had not been quite accurate: she had the shop on a life tenure only. When she died it reverted to the landlord. A pity, because under the Rent Restriction Law the landlord could never have made the lessee pay more than the price originally agreed on – a mere ten *duros* a month. That law is a great protection to poor people.

PANCHO: Who was the landlord, by the way?

PEP: By a remarkable coincidence it was Joana Mut herself. And since she had no aptitude for the family antique business, she regretfully parted with the freehold. The Bank paid a thousand *duros* a square metre, they say, but that may be an exaggeration. The other sister got nothing except Margalida's stock and personal effects, poor child!

PANCHO: Garlic and onions, Pep! Do you know what I think?

PEP: Tell me.

PANCHO: I think that the unfortunate angel pulled down the shutters and choked herself with her own hands in mortification for having turned down Don Bernardo's offer!

PEP: It is very possible. Indeed, they say...

Well, listeners, I expect you have heard enough. But before I return you to the Studio let us cross the street and hear what that vigorous but charming-looking fishwife has to say for herself. The one with the spotted handkerchief round her hair. Well, well, what a coincidence! If she isn't Aina, the youngest of the three Mut sisters! I wish you could watch her now, knife in hand, ripping the tough brown skin off an ugly-looking sting-ray! My word, personally I shouldn't like... And, look, if that isn't Don Bernardo himself buying prawns at the next stall! Good Heavens! Aina has recognized him! She has laid down the sting-ray...

Oh! Oh! I'm glad you missed that, listeners! Garlic and onions!

The Abominable Mr Gunn

ONE MONDAY MORNING in September 1910, the abominable Mr J.O.G. Gunn, master of the Third Form at Brown Friars, trod liverishly down the aisle between two rows of pitch-pine desks and grasped the short hairs just above my right ear. Mr Gunn, pale, muscular and broad-faced, kept his black hair plastered close to the scalp with a honey-scented oil. He announced to the form, as he lifted me up a few inches: 'And now Professor Graves will display his wondrous erudition by discoursing on the first Missionary Journey of St Paul.' (Laughter.)

I discoursed haltingly, my mind being as usual a couple of stages ahead of my tongue, so that my tongue said 'Peter' when I meant 'Paul', and 'B.C.' when I meant 'A.D.', and 'Crete' when I meant 'Cyprus'. It still plays this sort of trick, which often makes my conversation difficult to follow and is now read as a sign of incipient senility. In those days it did not endear me to Mr Gunn...

After the disaster at Syracuse, one Athenian would often ask another: 'Tell me, friend, what has become of old So-and-so?' and the invariable answer came: 'If he is not dead, he is school-mastering.' I can wish no worse fate to Mr J.O.G. Gunn – father of all the numerous sons-of-guns who have since sneered at my 'erudition' and cruelly caught at my short hairs – than that he is still exercising his profession at the age of eighty-plus; and that each new Monday morning has found him a little uglier and a little more liverish than before.

Me erudite? I am not even decently well read. What reading I have done from time to time was never a passive and promiscuous self-exposure to the stream of literature, but always a search for particular facts to nourish, or to scotch, some obsessive maggot that had gained a lodgement in my skull. And now I shall reveal an embarrassing secret which I have kept from the world since those nightmare days.

One fine summer evening as I sat alone on the roller behind the cricket pavilion, with nothing much in my head, I received a sudden celestial illumination: it occurred to me that I knew everything. I remember letting my mind range rapidly over all its familiar subjects of knowledge; only to find that this was no foolish fancy. I did know everything. To be plain: though conscious of having come less than a third of the way along the path of formal education, and being weak in mathematics, shaky in Greek grammar, and hazy about English history, I nevertheless held the key of truth in my hand, and could use it to open any lock of any door. Mine was no religious or philosophical theory, but a simple method of looking sideways at disorderly facts so as to make perfect sense of them.

I slid down from the roller, wondering what to do with my embarrassing gift. Whom could I take into my confidence? Nobody. Even my best friends would say 'You're mad!' and either send me to Coventry or organize my general scragging, or both; and soon some favour-currier would sneak to Mr Gunn, which would be the end of everything. It occurred to me that perhaps I had better embody the formula in a brief world-message, circulated anonymously to the leading newspapers. In that case I should have to work under the bedclothes after dark, by the light of a flash-lamp, and use the cypher I had recently perfected. But I remembered my broken torch-light bulb, and the difficulty of replacing it until the next day. No: there was no immediate hurry. I had everything securely in my head. Again I experimented, trying the key on various obstinate locks; they all clicked and the doors opened smoothly. Then the school-bell rang from a distance, calling me to preparation and prayers.

Early the next day I awoke to find that I still had a fairly tight grasp of my secret; but a morning's lessons intervened, and when I then locked myself into the privy, and tried to record it on the back of an old exercise-book, my mind went too fast for my pen, and I began to cross out – a fatal mistake – and presently crumpled up the page and pulled the chain on it. That night I tried again under the bedclothes, but the magic had evaporated and I could get no further than the introductory sentence.

My vision of truth did not recur, though I went back a couple of times to sit hopefully on the roller; and before long, doubts tormented me, gloomy doubts about a great many hitherto stable concepts: such as the authenticity of the Gospels, the perfectibility of man and the absoluteness of the Protestant moral code. All that survived was an after-glow of the bright light in my head, and the certainty that it had been no delusion. This is still with me, for I now realize that what overcame me that evening was a sudden infantile awareness of the power of intuition, the supralogic that cuts out all routine processes of thought and leaps straight from problem to answer.

How easily this power is blunted by hostile circumstances Mr Gunn demonstrated by his treatment of one F.F. Smilley, a new boy, who seems, coincidentally, to have had a vision analogous to mine, though of a more specialized sort. Smilley came late to Brown Friars; he had been educated at home until the age of eleven because of some illness or other. It happened on his first entry into the Third Form that Mr Gunn set us a problem from Hilderbrand's *Arithmetic for Preparatory Schools*, which was to find the square root of the sum of two long decimals, divided (just for cussedness) by the sum of two complicated vulgar fractions. Soon everyone was scribbling away except F.F. Smilley, who sat there abstractedly polishing his glasses and gazing out of the window.

Mr Gunn looked up for a moment from a letter he was writing, and asked nastily: 'Seeking inspiration from the distant church spire, Smilley?'

'No, sir. Polishing my glasses.'

'And why, pray?'

'They had marmalade on them, sir.'

'Don't answer me back, boy! Why aren't you working out that sum?'

'I have already written down the answer, sir.'

'Bring your exercise-book here!... Ah, yes, here is the answer, my very learned and ingenious friend Sir Isaac Newton' – tweaking the short hairs – 'but where is it worked out?'

'Nowhere, sir; it just came to me.'

'Came to you, F.F. Smilley, my boy? You mean you hazarded a wild guess?'

'No, sir, I just looked at the problem and saw what the answer must be.'

'Ha! A strange psychical phenomenon! But I must demand proof that you did not simply turn to the answer at the end of the book.'

'Well, I did do that afterwards, sir.'

'The truth now slowly leaks out.'

'But it was wrong, sir. The last two figures should be 35, not 53.'

'Curiouser and curiouser! Here's a Brown Friars' boy in the Third Form who knows better than Professor Hilderbrand, Cambridge's leading mathematician.'

'No, sir, I think it must be a misprint.'

'So you and Professor Hilderbrand are old friends? You seem very active in his defence.'

'No, sir, I have met him, but I didn't like him very much.'

F.F. Smilley was sent at once to the Headmaster with a note: 'Please cane bearer for idleness, lying, cheating and gross impertinence' – which the Headmaster, who had certain flaws in his character, was delighted to do. I cannot tell the rest of the story with much confidence, but my impression is that Mr Gunn won, as he had already won in his battle against J.X. Bestard-Montéry, whose Parisian accent when he was called upon to read 'Maître Corbeau, sur un arbre perché' earned him the name of 'frog-eating mountebank', and a severe knuckling on the side of the head. Bestard was forced to put a hard Midland polish on his French.

Mr Gunn, in fact, gradually beat down F.F. Smilley's resistance by assiduous hair-tweakings, knucklings and impositions; and compelled him to record all mathematic argument in the laborious way laid down by Professor Hilderbrand. No more looking out of the window, no more guessing at the answer.

Whether the cure was permanent I cannot say, because shortly before the end of that school-year the Chief of County Police gave the Headmaster twenty-four hours to leave the country (the police were more gentlemanly in those Edwardian days), and Brown Friars broke up in confusion. I have never since heard of F.F. Smilley. Either he was killed in World War I, or else he is schoolmastering somewhere. Had he made his mark in higher mathematics, we should surely have heard of it. Unless, perhaps, he is so much of a back-room boy, so much the arch-wizard of the mathematical-formula department on which Her Majesty's nuclear physicists depend for their bombs and piles, that the Security men have changed his name, disguised his features by plastic surgery, speech-trained him into alien immigrance, and suppressed his civic identity. I would not put it past them. But the mathematical probability is, as I say, that Gunn won.

The Whitaker Negroes

HAUNTINGS, WHETHER IN waking life or dream, are emotionally so powerful, yet can be so rarely ascribed to any exterior agency, that they are now by common consent allotted to the morbid pathologist for investigation – not, as once, to the priest or augur. A number of hauntings 'yield to treatment', as the saying is. The great Dr Henry Head told me once about a patient of his who was haunted by a tall dark man, always standing on the bedside mat. Head diagnosed a trauma in the patient's brain, of which the tall dark man was a projection, and proved his case by moving the bed slowly around; the tall dark man swung with it in a semicircle until he ended on a veranda just outside the french-window. An operation removed him altogether. And I read in an American medical paper the other day of a man who, as a result of advanced syphilis, was haunted by thousands of women every night; after he had been given extract of snake-root they were reduced to the manageable number of one.

There are also occasional hauntings which most psychologists would tend to dismiss as fantasies or, however grotesque, as symbols of some inner conflict; but which deserve to be accepted at their face value and placed in the correct historical context. Let me describe a persistent haunting from my own case-history. I am glad to say that it did not originate in my ghost-ridden childhood and is therefore easier to assess, though I cannot claim to have been in good mental and physical health at the time; on the contrary, I was suffering from vivid nightmares and hallucinations of the First World War, in which I had fought. Shells used to burst on my bed at night, by day I would throw myself flat on my face if a car backfired, and every rose garden smelt terrifyingly of phosgene gas. However, I felt a good deal better now that the War seemed to be over: an armistice had been signed, and the Germans were not expected to renew the struggle.

January 1919, found me back again with the Royal Welch Fusilier reserve battalion, at Limerick; where twenty years before my grandfather had been the last Bishop of the Established Protestant Church of Ireland. Limerick was now a stronghold of Sinn Fein, King George Street had become O'Connell Street, and when our soldiers took a stroll out of

barracks they never went singly and were recommended to carry
entrenching-tool handles in answer to the local shillelaghs. This return as
a foreign enemy to the city with which my family had been connected for
over two hundred years would have been far more painful but for old
Reilly, an antique dealer, who lived near the newly-renamed Sarsfield
Bridge. Reilly remembered my father and three of my uncles, and gave me
fine oratorical accounts of my Aunt Augusta Caroline's prowess in the
hunting field, and of the tremendous scenes at my grandfather's wake – at
which his colleague, the Catholic Bishop, had made attendance compul-
sory in tribute to his eminence as a Gaelic scholar and archaeologist. I
bought several things from Reilly: Irish silver, prints, and a century-old
pair of white, elbow-length Limerick gloves, left by the last of the Misses
Rafferty and so finely made (from chicken-skin, he told me) that they
folded into a brass-hinged walnut shell.

The shop smelt of dry rot and mice, but I would have gone there to chat
more often, had it not been for a nightmarish picture hanging in the shop
entrance: a male portrait brightly painted on glass. The sitter's age was
indeterminate, his skin glossy-white, his eyes Mongolian, their look imbecile; he had two crooked dog-teeth, a narrow chin, and a billy-cock hat
squashed low over his forehead. To add to the horror, some humorist had
provided the creature with a dudeen pipe, painted on the front of the
glass, from which a wisp of smoke was curling. Reilly said that the picture
had come from the heirs of a potato-famine emigrant who had returned
with a bag of dollars to die comfortably of drink in his native city. Why
this face haunted and frightened me so much I could not explain; but it
used to recur in my imagination for years, especially when I had fever. I
told myself that if I ever saw a midnight ghost – as opposed to midday
ghosts, which had been common enough phenomena during the later,
neurasthenic stages of the War, and less frightening than pathetic – it
would look exactly like that.

In the spring of 1951, when Reilly had been thirty years in his grave,
Julia Fiennes visited me in Majorca. She was an American: Irish-Italian
on her father's side, New Orleans-French on her mother's; a textile
designer by profession; young, tall, good-looking, reckless and romantic.
She had come 'to take a look at Europe before it blows up'. When we first
met, a shock passed between her and me of the sort usually explained in
pseudo-philosophic terms as 'We must have met in a previous incarna-
tion.' Psychologists postulate 'compatible emotion-groups'. I am content
to call it 'Snap!' Indeed, as it proved, Julia and I could converse in a joking
verbal shorthand, which meant little to anyone else, but for us expressed a
range of experience so complex that we could never have translated it into
everyday language. An embarrassing, if exhilarating discovery, because
this rapport between us, strong as it was, proved inappropriate both to her
course of life and mine. We wanted nothing from each other except a

humorously affectionate acknowledgement of the strength of the link; thirty-three years separated us; we belonged to different civilizations; I was perfectly happy in my own life, and she was set on going on and on until she came to a comfortable stop in either contentment or exhaustion; which she has since done.

With Beryl, to whom I am married, I enjoy the less spectacular but more relevant rapport that comes of having all friends in common, four children, and no secrets from each other. The only eccentric form which our rapport takes is that sometimes, if I am working on some teasing historical problem and go to bed before I reach a solution, its elements may intrude not into my dream but into hers. The classic instance was when she woke up one morning, thoroughly annoyed by the absurdity of her nightmare: 'A crowd of hags were swinging from the branches of a large tree in our olive grove and chopping off the ends with kitchen knives. And a horde of filthy gipsy children were waiting below to catch them...' I apologized to Beryl. I had been working on textual problems in the New Testament, and established the relation between Matthew xviii, 20 and Isaiah xvii, 6 which ran: 'As the gleaning of an olive-tree: two or three berries at the top of the topmost branch'; and of this with Deuteronomy xxiv; 20: 'When thou beatest thine olive-trees thou shalt not go over the boughs again: the gleanings shall be for the stranger, the fatherless and the widow.' I went to bed wondering idly how the fatherless and the widow managed to glean those inaccessible olives, if no able-bodied stranger happened to be about.

'Well, now you know!' Beryl answered crossly.

Once when Julia and I were taking a walk down a dark road not far from the sea, and exchanging our usual nonsense, I suddenly asked her to tell me something really frightening. She checked her pace, clutched my arm and said: 'I ought to have told you, Robert, days ago. It happened when I was staying with my grandmother in New Orleans, the one who had the topaz locket and eyes like yours. I guess I must have been twelve years old, and used to ride off to school on my bicycle about half a mile away. One summer evening I thought I'd come home by a different route, through a complicated criss of cross-streets. I'd never tried it before. Soon I lost my way and found myself in a dead-end, with a square patio behind a rusty iron gate, belonging to an old French mansion overgrown with creepers. The shutters were green too. It was a beautifully cool, damp place in that heat. And as I stood with my hand on the latch, I looked up, and there at an attic window I saw a face... It grinned and rapped on the glass with its leprous-white fingers and beckoned to me...'

By Julia's description it was the identical face that had been painted on glass in Mr Reilly's shop. When I told her about it, we broke into a run of perfect terror, hurrying towards the nearest bright light.

I thought it over afterwards. Perhaps Julia had become aware of my long-buried fear, which then became confused in her imagination with childhood memories of New Orleans; and it stood out so vividly that she really believed that she had seen the face grinning at her. She mentioned no pipe; but then the pipe could be discounted as extraneous.

After supper, an American called Hank, a New York banker's son, burst into the house, in a state of semi-collapse. Since he came of age Hank had fallen down on every job found for him by his father, and now drifted about Europe as a remittance-man. He wanted to write, though without an inkling of how to begin, and was more than a bore about his problems. Hank told me once: 'The night before I sailed my father said a very cruel thing to me. He said: "Hank, you're a good watch, but there's a part missing somewhere."' As a regular time-piece Hank was certainly a dead loss; and the place of the missing part had been filled by an erratic ancillary movement which by-passed time altogether. For instance, a few days before this, Hank had begun to jabber hysterically about a terrifying earthquake, and wondered whether the world were coming to an end. Next morning the papers mentioned a very limited earthquake in Southern Spain, which had swung pictures on walls, dislodged cornices from half a dozen buildings in a small town, and made several girls in the telephone exchange faint for terror. Now, Hank could hardly have felt the distant shock, although Majorca is said to form part of a range, mostly submerged, which continues south-westward to the mainland; but he had certainly caught the emotion of the frightened telephone girls.

'What's new, Hank?' I asked coldly.

'I've had a most horrible experience,' he gasped. 'Give me a drink, will you? I took a car to Sóller this afternoon. The heel had come off my walking shoe and I wanted to get it fixed. You know Bennasar the shoe-maker, off the market square? I was just about to go in when I happened to look through the window...'

Julia and I glanced at each other. We both knew what Hank was going to say. And he said it: 'I saw a frightful face...'

That made us feel more scared than ever.

Soon afterwards Julia went off on a rambling tour through France, Austria and Italy, and next year revisited Majorca with her mother. That was September 1952. She found me collaborating in a film-script with Will Price. Will comes from Mississippi; but New Orleans is one of his family's stamping grounds, so he and Mrs Fiennes were soon discussing third and fourth cousins. One day as we all sat outside a café, Julia happened to mention Hank. 'Who's Hank?' the others wanted to know. We explained, and Julia repeated the story of the New Orleans face. Her mother gasped and shook her roughly: 'Darling, why in Heaven's name didn't you tell me about it at the time?'

'I was terrified.'

'I believe you're making it up from something I told you, sweetie. I saw the same face myself before you were born – *and* the rusty iron gate – *and* the creepers and the shutters.'

'You never told me anything of the sort. Besides, I saw it myself. I don't have other people's visions. You mustn't confuse me with Hank.'

It occurred to me: 'Probably her mother had the vision, or whatever it was, first. And then Julia as a child must have heard her telling the story to somebody, and incorporated it in her own private nightmare world.'

But Will eased back in his chair and, turning to Mrs Fiennes, asked in the playful Southern accent that they were using: 'Honey, did you ever hear them up there in the old attic, sloshing water all over the place?'

None of us understood what he meant.

That night, when we were sitting about, drinking *coñac*, Will raised his voice: 'Ladies and gentlemen, may I have your permission to spin a yarn?'

'Why, of course.'

Will started: 'A good many years ago my father's law firm, Price & Price, acted for the mortgagees of a bankrupt property in Mississippi. Money was not forthcoming, so my father consented to take his fees in real estate – about eighty acres of almost worthless land at Pond near Fort Adams. Fort Adams was once a prosperous river port for the cotton country east of the River; the town itself was perched on the high bluffs which overhang the water hereabouts. But the River suddenly chose to change course five miles to the west and left Fort Adams with a wide frontage of swamp, so that all trade moved along to Natchez and Baton Rouge, which were still ports. These bluffs form the edge of a three-hundred-mile line of hills raised, they say, by prehistoric dust storms blowing in from the Great Plains, and cut up by streams and swamps. There used to be dozens of rich plantations in the hills, but when the River deserted Fort Adams they were abandoned and allowed to revert to jungle.

'A victim of this catastrophe was Pond, a village that had got its name from the cattle-pond which its leading citizen, old man Lemnowitz, dug and surrounded with two-storey frame stores and warehouses. It used to be a tough job to fetch cotton over the hills from the plantations in the interior. The bales were loaded on enormous, sixteen-wheeled wagons drawn by from six to ten yoke oxen. Teamsters and planters would camp at Pond before making the final drive up-hill to Fort Adams. Old man Lemnowitz hired them extra oxen for the effort, and carried on a thriving trade in supplies of all sorts which he had hauled up from the River in the off-season.

'There were still traces of ancient wealth near Pond when I visited it – ruins of the ante-bellum mansions and slave-quarters, with huge, twisted vines writhing up through the floors – and at Pond itself Lemnowitz's warehouse, formerly a sort of Macy's, was still in business under the same name. But only one corner was now occupied: by a small, not very elegant, store that sold tobacco, notions, staples and calico. It also called itself the Pond Post Office.

'The rest of Pond was jungle. My mother had come down there to see whether Price & Price owned any camellias; because sometimes these old planters collected rare flowers, and camellias could still be found growing wild in their deserted gardens. No! No orchids in that area, but camellias had been imported from all over the world, including even the Chinese mountains where they originally belonged. I was there to keep my mother company and check the land lines. Well, I went to buy a pack of cigarettes in the Lemnowitz store, and before I could get my change, a Thing walked in.

'It was undoubtedly human, in a weird way – walked upright and had the correct number of limbs. It even strode up to the counter and held out a dime for a can of snuff. But for the rest... The face was a glazed greenish white, with four fangs that crossed over the lips, and a protruding underlip. It had dark-brown hair, dripping with wet, under a black felt hat – the sort that gave the po' white trash from Georgia their nick-name of "wool-hats". Long arms ending in gauntlets – the local work-gloves of canvas and leather with stiff cuffs – which hung below its knees as it walked. Muddy "overhawls", leather brogans called "clod-hoppers", and a stink as if fifty cess-pools had been opened simultaneously. I said nothing, except perhaps "Oh!" What would any of you have said in the circumstances? Imagine the dark cavern of a mouldering warehouse behind you, with acres of empty shelves lost in the gloom, and then in It comes through the door with the blazing sun behind it. When It vanished again, I ran to the window to make sure that my mother had not fainted, and then tip-toed back to the counter. *"What was that?"* "Why, that was only a Whitaker Negro," Mr Lemnowitz said casually. "Never seen one before?" He seemed to be enjoying the situation.'

As Will told the story my old terrors came alive again. 'Well, what was it really?' I croaked.

'I guess it was just a Whitaker Negro,' said Will. 'Later, I decided to check up on my sanity. Mr Lemnowitz told me that for a couple of nickels Boy Whitaker, who was only a half-Whitaker, would guide me to where his folk lived. And he did. There are, or were, several families of Whitaker Negroes near Pond, tucked away in the jungle swamps where nobody ever ventures, not even the Sanitary Inspector. You have to understand the geography of these hills and reckon with their amazing verdancy and complete lack of vistas. One can march in a straight line up and down hills and over swamps for scores of miles without seeing a self-respecting horizon. The jungle is so thick in places that whole families have grown up and died within a mile of neighbours whose existence they didn't even suspect; and we Mississippians are noted for our gregariousness. I don't

know how I ever reached the place myself, because I was working to wind-
ward and the stench spread for half a mile around the place. I nearly threw
up even before I arrived. They live tax-free and aren't mentioned in the
census, and don't of course have to send their kids to school, still less get
drafted for military service. The kids live in wallows under their huts,
which are built on piles: apparently they don't come out much until
they're fourteen years old or so – can't stand the sun. A good documentary
sequence could be taken of a sow and her litter wallowing in the slime with
a bunch of young Whitaker monsters: you could title it *Symbiosis* – which
is what we call a "fo'bit" word.

'The adults make a sort of living by raising hogs and chickens: enough
to keep them in snuff and brogans and gauntlets and other necessities.
The hair proved to be mostly spanish-moss clapped wet on the head to
keep it cool – it comes grey-green and goes dark when you soak it; but
their real hair is also long, brown and wavy, not kinky in the usual negroid
style. The brogans and gauntlets were filled with water. You see, they
have no sweat-glands – that's their trouble. It's a hereditary condition and
their skin needs to be kept wet all the while, or they die. They're Negroes;
but said to be mixed with Choctaw Indian, also perhaps a strain of
Chickasaw and Natchez.'

Someone asked: 'Didn't the snuff get a bit *damp*, Will?'

Will answered blandly: 'No, sir, it did not! Snuff is "dipped" not
snuffed, in those parts. It's sold in cans about an inch and a half high. The
lid of the can is used to dip a little snuff into the buccal pouch – which is
another "fo'bit word" meaning the hollow under your nether lip, excuse
me for showing off.'

Most of the *coñac*-drinkers grinned incredulously, but Will turned to
me: 'Did you ever hear of Turtle Folk? That's what they call whites
afflicted by the same disease. There are quite a few cases up and down the
Mississippi – Natchez, Vicksburg, Yazoo City, Baton Rouge – kept a close
secret, though. Once I was in a house at Natchez where they kept a turtle-
man in the attic, and I heard him sloshing water about overhead. That was
what Julia must have seen in New Orleans, and Mrs Fiennes before her.
And I guess what you saw in Limerick was a portrait of a turtle-man
brought back from the South as a curiosity.'

We asked Will: 'How did they get there? And why are they called
"Whitaker Negroes"?'

He answered: 'I was coming to that. Around 1810, or so the story goes,
a big planter named George Whitaker grew disgusted with his labour
problems. He was an intelligent, wide-eyed, gullible New Englander, with
Christian leanings, who wanted to reform the South and incidentally get
even richer than he already was. He disliked the business of buying slaves
and breeding them like cattle – with the result, he said, that they had no
traditions, no morals, and no discipline but what could be instilled into

them by fear. Ideally, he thought, a planter should be able to take a long vacation, like a European landlord, and come back to find work proceeding smoothly under coloured overseers – only petty crimes to punish, and the crops properly harvested. He argued that if the early slave-traders had kept families and clans together under their African chiefs, the labour problem would not have existed. Then it occurred to him: "Why not experiment?" And he went down to New Orleans, where he interviewed the famous pirate Jean Lafitte. "Sir," he said, "I wish you to visit Africa on my behalf and bring me back a whole tribe of Negroes. Two hundred is the figure I aim at, but a hundred would do. I'll pay you two hundred dollars a head: men, women and children. But mind, it must be a whole tribe, not samples from a score of them, or I don't buy."

'George was a serious man, and Jean Lafitte decided to take his offer. He sailed to the Gold Coast with his brother Pierre on the next tide and there, almost at once, as luck would have it, surprised a whole tribe on the march. The Negroes had been expelled from somewhere in the interior, and being in a pretty poor way, offered no resistance. The Lafittes got two hundred of them aboard, made ingenious arrangements for their welfare on the voyage, and brought across alive one hundred and fifty – smuggled them through Fort Adams and the Bayou St John until Pond came in sight. This constituted, you see, fraudulent evasion of the 1808 Federal embargo on the importation of slaves; so two hundred dollars a head was not an unreasonable price, considering the risk. But think of it in terms of modern money! Well, Mr Lemnowitz told me, at Pond, that when George Whitaker saw the livestock that the Lafittes had brought back from Africa, and realized they were now his responsibility – though because of their constitution, of no more use as field workers than the bayou alligators – he turned deathly white. He paid Jean Lafitte without a word; then he went home, made out his will, bequeathing the bulk of his land to the then "Territory of Mississippi" – after which he and his young wife jumped into the River, hand in hand, and were not seen again.

'Someone took over the plantation, but allowed the Whitakers to remain in a swamp and make out as best as they could. And they hung on there long after the Whitaker mansion was swallowed up by the jungle. Their "forty" is tax-free and inviolable because the original deed of gift represented taxes paid in perpetuity. About fifteen years ago a Whitaker went crazy – they are none of them very bright – and hit the trail for he didn't know where. He travelled from swamp to swamp, living off the land, and eventually reached the town of Woodville which is not very far away as the crow flies, but a thousand miles as the jungle grows. The good people of Woodville, who normally publish an extra of their local paper only when a war is declared or a President assassinated, hurried one through the press with the banner headline: "MAN FROM MARS!" because the poor wretch was half-dead and couldn't explain himself, and all the horses in the town were bolting, and the women screaming their heads off.'

'And the Choctaw blood?'

'The Choctaws and Chickasaws were the local Indians, who obligingly moved away from the neighbourhood to make room for cotton. I was told that a few rogue males stayed behind in the swamps, mostly pox-cases, and intermarried with the Whitaker Negroes for want of other women.'

'Did your mother find any camellias?'

Will, detecting a hint of irony in the innocent question, answered: 'Thank you, ma'am. She got a lapful.'

Then he turned to me again. 'Do you know anyone on *Time* magazine?'

'Only the editor,' I said. 'I happened to rent Tom Matthews a house here in 1931, while he was still a book reviewer.'

'Then ask him to send you a copy of a piece about Turtle Folk published that year'

'I certainly will.'

And in due course of time Tom sent me the medical column of *Time*, December 14th, 1931, and this is what I read:

TURTLE FOLK

At Houston, Miss., A Mrs C. keeps a tub of water in her back yard for an extraordinary purpose. It is a ducking tub for her five-year-old son. Every time he feels uncomfortable he jumps in, clothes and all. Mrs C. does not scold. For that is the only way the boy can keep comfortable. He lacks sweat glands, which in normal people dissipate two to three quarts of cooling perspiration every day.

Mrs C. has another son, an infant, who likewise lacks sweat glands. He is too young to go ducking himself. So she dowses him from time to time with scuppers of water. Neither child can sleep unless his night clothes and mattress are wet. They take daytime naps in their damp cellar, with moist sacks for pillows.

Nearby at Vardaman, Miss., are two farmer brothers similarly afflicted. Each works alternate half days. While one plows the other soaks himself in a creek. Every once in a while the worker saunters to the creek for a cool dowsing. The brothers have a sister who dunks herself in the cistern back of their house.

They have a sweatless neighbour woman who must also wet herself for comfort.

At Vicksburg, Miss., there is a seventh of these folk who, like turtles, must periodically submerge themselves. The Vicksburg case is a 12-year-old boy, handled by Dr Guy Jarrett. The others are cases of Dr Ralph Bowen of Memphis.

Dr Bowen last week had on hand a medical report concerning the phenomenon. The seven suffer from 'hereditary ectodermal dysplasia of the anhydrotic type'. That is, they lack sweat glands, and the lack is hereditary. However, the seven Mississippi cases are related only as indicated above. This suggests that the failing is not so uncommon as heretofore believed (only 23 cases have been reported in medical literature). The ailment must often escape medical attention. Along with the lack of sweat glands goes a lack of teeth. None of the seven Mississippi cases has more than two teeth.

Tom also sent me a typescript from *Time's* research files:

FROM ANDREWS' DISEASES OF THE SKIN
Hereditary ectodermal dysplasia
There are numerous anomalies of the epidermis and appendages due to faulty evolution of the epiblastic layer of the blastoderm. The term 'ectodermal defect' has been limited to those conditions arising from incomplete development of the epidermis or its appendages, or its absence in circumscribed areas, thus excluding the keratodermias and the nevi. Atrichosis congenitalis with or without deformities of the nails and teeth is common, and is accompanied at times by nevi and other congenital anomalies. Congenital absence or malformation of the nails and teeth is also of frequent occurrence, and in circumscribed areas it is not out of the ordinary to find that the sebaceous and sweat glands are absent or impaired. In restricted areas there may be a complete absence of the epidermis and appendages at birth. It is more rare to encounter cases of extensive deformation or complete absence of all, or nearly all, of the cutaneous structures originating from the epiderm, to which group the term 'congenital ectodermal defect' is given. Guilford, an American dentist, was the first to report a case of this kind. The appearance of these patients is typical and conspicuous, as they have a facies that is suggestive of congenital syphilis. The skin is hairless, dry, white, smooth, and glossy. The teeth are entirely absent or there may be a few present, but the development is always defective.

There are dystrophic disturbances in the nails. The scalp hair is sparse and of a fine soft texture. The cheek bones are high and wide, whereas the lower half of the face is narrow. The supraorbital ridges are prominent; the nasal bridge is depressed, forming a 'saddle-back nose'. The tip of the nose is small and upturned, while the nostrils are large and conspicuous. The eyebrows are scanty, none being present on the outer two thirds. The eyes slant upwards, producing a Mongolian facies. At the buccal commissures radiating furrows, 'pseudorhagades', are present, and on the cheeks there are telangiectases and small papules simulating milium and adenoma sebaceum. The lips are thickened, the upper one being particularly protrusive.

The patient studied by Dr MacKee and myself never sweated. He was uncomfortable during hot weather due to elevation of body temperature and was unable to play baseball and running games with other boys of his age, because of great fatigue induced by such exertions. These symptoms resemble those in other cases reported in the literature, and not uncommonly the subjects find it necessary during the summer to have pails of water thrown over them if they are to keep comfortable.

The affection is familial, generally affecting males, and seems to be due to an injury during the third month of uterine life. Some of these patients are mentally deficient, but the majority of them have normal mentality because the anlage of the nervous system is distinct from the cutaneous ectoderm long before the injury occurs. MacKay and Davidson report 4 cases occurring respectively in a woman, aged thirty-four years, and her two sons and one daughter, aged six, eleven, and thirteen years. A comprehensive article with good references on this subject has been written by Gordon and Jamieson.

I was now in a position to review the story from the beginning. In 1919, I had been neurotic, as a result of having spent thirteen months in the trenches under continuous bombardment, and had begun to 'see things' in France even before a fragment of eight-inch shell went clean through my right lung and knocked me out. Limerick was a dead-alive city haunted by family ghosts, and the glass picture focused my morbid fears of the past and future – yes, it must have been the portrait of a turtle-man brought back to Ireland from the Southern States.

Julia and I: because of the unusually close rapport between us, partly explained by her Irish blood, it was not surprising that we should be scared by the same sort of face. Will had testified that the original was highly terrifying to any but a physician who could look coldly at it and characterize it as a *facies*. ('When am a face not a face, Massa Bones?' 'When it's a *facies*.') And why should Julia's mother not have stumbled across the same old house in New Orleans, and seen the same turtle-man peering through the attic window twelve years previously?

Hank: no natural sympathy existed between him and me, or between him and Julia. But he did have a remarkable receptivity for the emotions of people at a distance, and the trick of converting them into waking visions of his own. Clearly, he had subjectivized the fright which Julia and I conveyed to each other into something horrible that he had himself seen at Soller. I need hardly add that Señor Bennasar keeps no tank in his patio for dunking turtle-folk in.

Will Price: he had a keen dramatic sense, but I found him far more accurate than most of my friends about names, dates and facts, and could not disbelieve his story. That is to say, I could accept what he saw with his own eyes. And what Mr Lemnowitz told him about George Whitaker and the Lafitte brothers was, Will himself confessed, 'shrouded in local myth'. On principle I suspect any legend about the Lafittes, as I do any legend about Paul Revere, Paul Jones, or Paul Bunyan. Besides, what connection could there be between the Whitaker Negroes and the white Turtle Folk who occur spasmodically on the Lower Mississippi? Nobody had suggested that sophisticated white women of Natche, Vicksburg, Vardaman, Baton Rouge, Yazoo City and New Orleans ever paid clandestine visits to Pond in search of a new sexual *frisson*. It therefore seems probable that if the Lafittes did indeed smuggle a shipload of Negroes to Pond, these were healthy enough when they arrived, but proved susceptible to the turtle-disease, which is endemic to the Mississippi; and because of inbreeding it became hereditary among them. The families affected were disowned by their masters but permitted to camp on the swampy fringes of the Whitaker estate, after George dragged his wife with him into the River – which he probably did, if at all, for some simple, domestic reason. And because high cheek-bones and a weak growth of hair are characteristic of the turtle-folk *facies* – which resembles that of the congenital syphilitic – there seems to be no reason for bringing the pox-stricken Choctaws and Chickasaws into the story either.

But what about the numerous coincidences which hold the story together? Julia, her mother, Will, Hank, and myself had all been frightened, directly or indirectly, by the same rare phenomenon; and we met accidentally in Deyá, a village of four hundred inhabitants commendably unknown to history, which lies three or four thousand miles away from Pond, an even smaller place, to the geographical existence of which only Will among us could testify. Moreover, Tom Matthews who clarified the phenomenon (scientifically at least) for all of us – both Julia and her mother were immensely relieved to know that it was a real face after all – had also been living at Deyá when the *Time* article appeared. But these coincidences do not amount to much, perhaps, and would never have come to light had not the Whitaker *facies* been so unforgettably frightening. (It occurs to me as I write that the real explanation of the Glamis Monster – the reputedly 'Undying Thing' which used to peer out from one of the attic windows at Glamis Castle – may have been hereditary ectodermal dysplasia in the Bowes-Lyon family, hushed up because one of its victims was heir to the earldom.) Finally, I suspect myself of having exaggerated the telepathic sympathy between Julia and myself. Did the face she described so vividly superimpose itself, perhaps, on the fading memory of the one I had seen in Mr Reilly's antique shop? My imagination is not that of a natural liar, because my Protestant conscience restrains me from inventing complete fictions; but I am Irishman enough to coax stories into a better shape than I found them.

This is not yet all. In 1954, I broadcast a short summary of the foregoing story for the B.B.C. As a result, a doctor wrote to tell me that he once had under observation, in a Liverpool hospital, a white child suffering from this rare disease; but that occasional sponging was sufficient relief for its discomfort, except in unusually hot weather. Another letter came from Mrs Otto Lobstein, an Englishwoman who was going off some months later with her husband for a tour of the Southern States, and proposed to check up on the Whitaker Negroes. 'Where did you say that they lived?' she wrote.

I provided the necessary map-references, not really expecting to hear from Mrs Lobstein again; but in due process of time she sent me a letter and a photograph. The photograph showed a Mississippi finger-post pointing south to Woodville, north to Pinckneyville, east to Pond and Fort Adams; and the fine condition of the three roads suggested that prosperity had returned to the neighbourhood since Will Price's visit there more than twenty years previously. This was the letter, which I have been kindly allowed to print here.

New Orleans,
February 1st, 1955.

DEAR ROBERT GRAVES,

We spent an interesting day tracking down the Whitaker-negroes, after camping for a night in the Mississippi woods – a wretched night because this was the hardest frost of the winter. But the early morning sun was startlingly warm and the fields beautiful; no wind blew and thin, erect strings of smoke came from the small shacks along the road.

Pond is not on the map, so we took the road to Fort Adams until we came to a very lovely old plantation home, where one Rip White directed us to the Whitaker plantation. But he was far more anxious to tell us about his own house, which 'had been granted to Henry Stewart, son of Mary Queen of Scots about 180 years ago'. Henry was 'a contender to the Throne', so they shipped him off to America, where he was given this plantation of 2,200 acres to keep him quiet and occupied. The house did have a royal air, but I was a little troubled by the discrepancy in date between Mary Queen of Scots and King George III, and between the names Stewart and Stuart!

When we reached the plantation, we met Mr Whitaker, the owner, who was going somewhere in a hurry, but told us that the old mansion some way back in the fields had been demolished a few years before. (Its place was now taken by a large, hard-looking, unromantic modern bungalow.) He also told us that the land had been split up at the same time between the various Whitaker sons – which didn't seem to coincide with Will Price's story that the land had been deeded to the State, unless perhaps a brother of the man who committed suicide had contested the deed of gift and won it back. Anyhow, Mr Whitaker advised us to ask Mrs Ray about the story; she had raised all the Whitaker whites for two or three generations.

Dear old Mrs Ray gave us interesting recollections of what her mother and father had told her as a child: how, when the overseer had whipped a slave over a log for not picking enough cotton, the rest would creep out of the plantation after dark and go into a 'holler' – bending their heads low down so as not to be heard, they would sing and pray for freedom. But she had no stories about Whitaker-negroes.

At Woodville, a small town on the way to Pond, we visited the Court House to look for records of the original George Whitaker. There we found an intelligent official, Mr Leek, who had actually met some of the Whitaker-negroes, when he helped them to fill up questionnaires during the Second World War. He told us that they were dying out fast. In winter, he said, they wore ordinary clothes; in summer, heavy underclothes soaked in water. The Court House records, however, did not show that any Whitaker land had been deeded to the State since 1804, when they began. Mr Leek's explanation of why the Whitaker-negroes were so called was that the first sufferer had 'Whitaker' as his Christian name.

At last we reached Pond. Pond Post Office is a big, barn-like structure which, as in the days of trading-posts, carries everything and deals in sacks of flour and rolls of cotton; the large, serene pond mentioned by Will Price lay at the foot of the hill. Mr Carroll Smith, the postmaster in succession to Mr Lemnowitz, sold us some safety-pins. He was small and silver-haired, with sensitive brown eyes. At first he showed a certain reticence when we questioned him, but gradually shed it. He confirmed that very few Whitaker-negroes are left, and said that they lived on the plantations, not in the swamps. Nowadays, only one member of a family of five or six children would inherit the disease. Occasionally a Whitaker-negro visited the Post Office, which was always an unpleasant experience, because the glandular excretions emitted through his mouth conveyed an appalling odour of decay. Mr Smith had never heard the story of George Whitaker's suicide and believed, with Mr Leek, that the original sufferer was an immigrant negro from Virginia. He suggested that we should visit a Mr McGeehee in Pinckneyville, the nearest village, who had a couple of Whitaker-negroes working for him. He would say no more on the subject, after that, though we talked for some time about share-cropping. So we drove on.

Mr McGeehee's plantation was very English, with a tree-lined driveway running through park-like meadows (where Herefords and Red Devons grazed) to a big, unpretentious house. Mr McGeehee himself was most hospitable; so was his mother, a gentle old lady, looking like a pressed flower. We chatted politely in the spacious drawing-room about farming and children and plantation houses; but both the McGeehees remained emphatic that we must not meet the two Whitaker-negroes working for them. Mr McGeehee, very rightly, felt responsible for his employees and said that too many sightseers had come to stare at the pair recently, which made them sensitive. So my husband and I did not press the point; and, in any case, we felt the point slipping away from us. A group of people with a strange history, living in odd conditions and with a bizarre inheritance, are one thing; and a few sufferers from skin disease, who happen to have been born into normal families, are quite another.

In the 1930s, apparently, Will Price found them living in a group, and this was natural because they are not popular with the other negroes, for obvious reasons; and he must have gone there in the summer, when their distinctive habits were more conspicuous. As for the story of their origin, it seems probable that Mr Lemnowitz heard it from some source, now lost, which was as untrustworthy as that of Rip White's legend about 'Henry Stewart, the Contender to the Throne'.

A novel feature of the countryside which may interest you is that plantation owners have begun to import Brahmini cattle – instead of orchids – from the Far East. These withstand heat and drought better than other breeds, and make good store cattle; I saw many of them grazing in the fields – silky-grey in colour, with huge horned heads. The bulls were humped like camels, and added a richness to the Pond landscape.

Yours sincerely,
Anna Lobstein.

This calm and practical travelogue has dispelled my haunting nightmare for ever. Terror gives way to pity; the pirates Jean and Pierre Lafitte, together with the rogue Choctaws and Chickasaws, are banished to the realms of macabre legend. Only the hospitable Mr McGeehee and his gentle old mother, who resembles a pressed flower, are left on the stage; in charge of two sensitive sufferers from hereditary ectodermal dysplasia of the anhydrotic type, whose principal purpose in life is to herd silky-grey Brahmini cattle in lush parkland – a far more agreeable example of *symbiosis* than the one reported by Will Price.

Trín-Trín-Trín

– TRIN-TRIN-TRIN!
– *Speak to me!*
– Is that the house of Gravés? Can one talk with Don Roberto?
– *At the apparatus! On behalf of whom?*
– I am Don Blas Mas y Mas. –
– *A thousand pardons, Don Blas. In consequence of the bad telephone connection I did not fix in my mind that it was you.*
– How do you find yourself, Don Roberto?
– *Very rickety well, thanks be to God!*
– I celebrate it. And your graceful spouse?
– *Regrettably she is a trifle catarrhed.*
– I much lament it. And the four beautiful children?
– *For the present, thanks be to the saints, well enough. I feel overwhelmed by your amicable inquiries. But you, Don Blas? How goes it with you?*
– A stupidity has occurred to me. I am speaking from my uncle's private clinic, having broken my arm in various places.
– *Ai, Ai, Ai! I feel it painfully... What a most disgraceful event! I wager that it somehow had relations with motor-bicycles.*
– Mathematically correct, Don Roberto!
– *Does the arm molest you so much as to prevent you from recounting me the accident?*
– Confiding it to so formal and sympathetic a friend as Don Roberto would be an alleviation, although truly the wound is painful enough. Well, it began on San Antonio's festival when I was strolling along the Borne with that shameless robber Francisco Ferragut.
– *The celebrated racing cyclist who finished first of his class during the Tour of Majorca?*
– The identical one. As you know, Francisco is a formidable jokester and said to me there on the Borne: 'Come to watch me eat pastries!' I answered: 'Is that such a rare thing?' He explained that it was not the technique of eating that would be of interest, so much as the technique of eating without payment. Nothing! We went across the street and there he gazed into the display window of a travel agency. I asked: 'Are we obliged

to fly to Sweden for your pastries?' 'Patience!' he answered. 'All fishermen have first to wait for a bite.' Presently a servant girl passed with a tray and entered the Widow Dot's pastry shop. Francisco said: 'There's a fish under that rock !'

PAUSE

– Are you listening, Don Roberto?

– *Attentively. Continue, please!*

– And you remember what day that was?

– *You mentioned San Antonio, if I do not deceive myself.*

– Exact! Well, when the girl comes out, carrying her tray heaped with exquisite pastries, he stops her and says: 'Pretty girl, I recognize you, surely? You work in the house of Don Antonio... ? Don Antonio...? *Caramba!* What has happened to my memory today?' The girl murmurs helpfully: 'He calls himself Don Antonio Amaro,' and Francisco exclaims: 'What a fool I am! Of course: Don Antonio Amaro! Now, child, I have a most important message for Don Antonio - please pay attention! Say that Doctor Eusebio Busquets after all regrets with much pain his inability to obsequiate Don Antonio on his name day according to the kind invitation handed him yesterday – Doctor Eusebio Busquets, understand? – but he is obliged to perform a critical throat operation at the precise hour named for the feast. Nevertheless, assure him that I have now taken the liberty of eating his health with one of these delicious pastries.' Then he seizes the largest and creamiest of the confections on the tray, crams it into his mouth, and says thickly: 'Now, don't forget the name, please – Doctor Eusebio Busquets!'

– *I am a stupid Englishman, I do not see how your accident is related...*

– We are coming to that. Being ashamed to stand and watch Francisco play the same trick on two dozen or so innocent servant girls, who would be coming with trays from all the big houses of the vicinity to collect pastries each for her own Don Antonio, I called a taxi and went after the girl...

– *Who was very pretty, a real salad? They always are in your histories.*

– She was no exception. And on overtaking her, I handed her a pastry which I had bought, of the identical class stolen, and explained that Don Francisco was a robber and a charlatan, etcetera, etcetera, and that I had chivalrously come to save her from playing a ridiculous part before her employers, and having three pesetas docked from her wages...

– *In short, you asked her what afternoon she would be free to come for a spin to Cas Catalá on the back of your new motor-bike?*

– You are not by any means so stupid as you pretend, Don Roberto.

– *And eventually you crashed with her on the pillion?*

– Little by little, please! No, no, that would have been a very vulgar and quotidian history.

– *Pardon me, dear Blas! Of course nothing quotidian or vulgar could ever happen to* you *in these amorous hazards.*

– Do not laugh at me, I am in great pain. But listen, it was a comedy! Three days later I met the girl by the Cavalry Barracks at about two o'clock; she climbed up behind and I set off. Well, we precipitated ourselves with a noise like a dawn bombardment down the Marine Drive, but as we reached the Hotel Mediterráneo, she said: 'Friend, excuse me, I must dismount for a moment!' I did not ask why, because that question might perhaps embarrass a simple girl; I merely stopped and let her get down. She crossed the street and, while pausing to light a cigarette, I suddenly heard the noise of a motor-bike starting up. I looked around casually to see what make it might be, and there was Francisco Ferragut with my sweetheart on the pillion of his racer roaring back to Palma, and she was waving good-bye at me.

– *O la, la, la! A trifle violent, such behaviour in simple girls, eh?*

– I grew cross, I confess it to you, and went in pursuit. Francisco had 100 metres start, but he's a smart boy and trusted in his bike to escape; it was more powerful than mine – yet, on the other hand, he carried twice the weight. Then followed a transcendental chase through the streets of Palma, where there is a pretended speed limit of twenty kilometres an hour. We both drove forward magisterially, registering at least 140 and causing much emotion on both sides of the Avenue until we reached the Barón de Pinopar turning, where a khaki-coloured military auto cut in, caught my rear lamp and sent me into an irrecoverable roll. These soldiers, they think the world is theirs! They always behave as if manoeuvring on the battlefield where civilians have no right to exist. In effect, the bicycle was shattered. I was thrown against a plane-tree, they continued their journey without a backward glance!

– *How infamous! Some people should be refused permission to hold a driving licence. And the girl? What?*

– Nothing... Nothing at all... I met her again five minutes later in the *Mare Nostrum* emergency ward. Francisco had shocked with an air force lorry half a minute later; he was rendered unconscious; she fractured only a rib or two. So, before he recovered his senses, I magnanimously arranged for her to be translated here with me to my uncle's clinic, and after a week of interesting convalescence we now understand each other divinely well. She loves me with madness and repudiates that it would ever have been possible for her to abandon me; she was merely about to lure Francisco far out into the country, and there be revenged on him for his love of sweet things by dropping a spoonful of sugar into his petrol tank. She and I are now securely affianced.

– *In a fortunate hour! I celebrate it...!*

– Now if you have a moment, my sweetheart insists on giving you a much fuller and incomparably more graphic version of these events. Hold on, I beg of you, dear friend...

Cambridge Upstairs

As a child, psychopath R.G. was conditioned to despise the Light Blues. First became aware of the concept 'Cambridge' at the commencement of a long series of Oxford victories on the river. Reveals that no boy either at his dame-school or preparatory school (unless two-fisted and two-booted and having some elder relative closely connected with Cambridge) dared oppose local opinion, which was devoutly Oxonian. Recalls snatches of playground song:

> *Oxford upstairs, eating cherry pie –*
> *Cambridge downstairs, beginning to cry.*

> *Oxford upstairs, drinking pints of beer –*
> *Cambridge downstairs, feeling very queer.*

> *Oxford upstairs, having lots of fun –*
> *Cambridge downstairs, how their noses run!*

Psychopath R.G., reclining on couch, exclaims to his *alter e*go, Herr Professor Doctor R.G.: 'I tell you, Herr Professor Doctor, that in those days God loved Oxford. And I loved Oxford; moreover, my brother Philip, the left-handed demon bowler, and my brother Dick, the brilliant batsman with his terrible drives to long on, not only loved Oxford, but were actually up there. God loved Oxford, as He once loved and favoured Israel, and the boat race was an annual rite confirming this fact. I even thought it odd that Cambridge still had the nerve to compete in that fatedly unequal struggle.'

Q. 'How long did this delusion persist?'

A. 'My first set-back came when once Downing, C., a new boy at Brown Friars, appeared in the playground wearing a Cambridge favour. This, of course, we at once snatched from his lapel and hurried into the blue-black inkwell to turn it Oxford. Tears burst from his eyes, and gazing wildly about him, he shouted in impassioned tones: "Anyhow, I don't care what you stinkers say. The *Sky*'s Cambridge!" I was busily thinking up a crushing come-back to this blasphemy, when the rest of Oxford University set on Downing, C. and man-handled him; but Mr Orrery, the new maths master, rushed up like a thunderstorm, and rescued Downing, C., throwing my companions around like sacks.' Here psychopath R.G. began to perspire and evince great agitation. Coaxed by Herr Professor Doctor he continued: 'Mr Orrery, who was seen to be wearing a light blue tie, took Downing, C.'s evidence, and awarded us one hundred lines each, to be shown up by teatime: "I must not bully defenceless new boys." Mr Orrery then escorted Downing, C. to the shop at the corner with sixpence to purchase a new Cambridge favour, which he wore undisturbed for the rest of the day. Naturally, we sent Downing, C. to Coventry for sneaking to Mr Orrery.'

Q. 'What effect did the subsequent series of Oxford defeats have on your adolescence?'

A. 'A most disheartening effect. The world was no longer the same. The sun had, as it were, set for ever. By the waters of Babylon we sat down and wept, while the hosts of Midian prowled and prowled around. Everyone I met seemed to be Cambridge-minded and Cambridge-hearted.'

Q. 'Did you doubt that God still loved Oxford?'

A. 'I knew that "whom He loveth, He chasteneth", Herr Professor Doctor. But Oxford was no longer upstairs, Cambridge was upstairs.'

Q. 'Hold that! Hold it! Your hand is trembling with redoubled violence! We'll unearth that phobia in a jiffy. What do *stairs* mean to you?'

Herr Professor Doctor Robert Graves, though only a quack psychiatrist, did not need to look up the word *Stairs* in *The Grosser Lexicon of Gross Symbolology*. He simply handed psychopath R.G. a nip of centenarian Spanish brandy and out came the whole story.

A. 'I recall reading a novel called *Darkness of the Soul* at the age of eight or nine, which made a deep impression on me. It told of a country vicar's son who had lost money on horses, taken to drinking in taverns, and forged a cheque for no less than £100. While awaiting arrest, the young rake had a painful interview with the vicar, in the course of which he cried out bitterly: "O Father, if only you had put me into trade, instead of sending me to Cambridge, this shame would never have fallen on our house!" He continued: "There was a little man on my staircase who offered me books to read, wicked books, materialistic books, books that poured scorn on Holy Writ, books that should never have been allowed to exist. And I fell, Father, miserable sinner that I am! I took them, I read them, I absorbed the poison, I lost my faith." Even as he spoke there came a loud rap at the front door... Thereafter, every night when I climbed the stairs to bed, a shadowy figure lurked on the upstairs landing. He had a pedlar's tray full of wicked, wicked books, books that should never have been allowed to exist, books bound in light blue, and he wore Mr Orrery's gown and mortar-board and pepper-and-salt suit and light blue tie – oh, it was *frightful*...'

Questioned further, sobbing psychopath R.G. recalled how, while up at Oxford in 1923, he had been persuaded to visit Cambridge (which he then knew jocularly as 'Tabland') for a few hours; and had been scared by all he saw.

Q. 'In what way scared?'

A. 'Everything was so much the same and yet so disturbingly different, Herr Professor. As when I first went to the U.S.A. and visited rural Pennsylvania. The perils of that countryside! I remember sitting down in the corner of a meadow and getting poison ivy on my wrists and jiggers in my toes; and a series of the most extraordinary animals appeared – a skunk, two snapping turtles, three robins the size of thrushes, and a small, ill-favoured pig which I afterwards identified as a ground-hog and hadn't known existed.'

Q. 'Never mind about North American zoology. What about Cambridge?'

A. 'The College porters all wore top-hats! Imagine! And it seemed that all the oldest colleges were built of brick, instead of the newest ones, as at Oxford; and the pleasure punts were propelled backwards, not forwards – that is, they were pointed the wrong way round. It was all so Looking-Glassy. The undergraduates treated me well enough, I grant; but each in turn said with a certain icy reserve: "We hear you are from the other place." Since I had hitherto heard the phrase applied only to Hell and the House of Lords, I felt acutely embarrassed.'

Herr Professor Doctor cut short the inquiry at this point and advised the patient, on behalf of them both, to accept the unexpected and generous invitation from the Master and Fellows of Trinity College, Cambridge, which had prompted this successful analysis. Furthermore, to take with him his children, Lucia (aged 11) and Juanito (aged 9) as a prophylaxis against any similar phobia that they might have inherited, their mother too being devotedly Oxonian. This advice he took.

Yes. I had a wonderful time, and came away cured. They had dined and wined me, and listened patiently to my lectures on English Literature which were, I admit, far from urbane. I became a convert to top-hats as the only decent wear for college porters, and to brick as a highly suitable material for ancient colleges. And though, after dinner, at Trinity, the great silver laver was borne in empty, as a mere signal for grace after meat – its counterpart at Pembroke still brimmed with fair water – I was invited to dip a fine linen napkin in it and dab myself behind the ear for coolness. And how charming that on a Friday at Trinity, no flesh nor fowl might be served in Hall, but only fish, fish, beautiful fish, even to Protestants! And that a long Latin grace was still declaimed antiphonically in the old pronunciation, with no *weeny, weedy, weaky* nonsense. I even heard gallant talk, at a high Level, of putting the College brew-house, now a lumber-room, back into commission.

Lucia and Juanito had a wonderful time too – in the Egyptian Room at the Fitzwilliam, and on the swings in the municipal playground – and admitted that they had never in their lives been in a grander house than the Master's Lodge at Trinity... Yet, as I leaned over the bridge at Clare College, gazing at the pellucid waters of the Backs, and the glowing autumnal flower beds, and the green lawns, and the dignified college architecture, I heard a pleasure punt approaching. The children, in dark-blue jerseys, were punting it right end foremost (or wrong end foremost) and I heard Juanito's embarrassingly loud question: 'When are we going to get somewhere *really* pretty?' The good people of Clare were not to know that Juanito is accustomed, when he goes boating at home, to cliffs five hundred feet high, rich in sea-eagles' nests, and to rocks green with samphire and wild caper, and violet-tinted backwaters full of striped fish, and pinewood headlands crowned by mediaeval watch-towers of golden limestone.

'Ha, Ha!' Chort-led Nig-ger

'I'VE GIVEN UP the old rag in utter disgust,' growled Haymon Fugg, Q.C. 'And you, Admiral?'

Admiral of the Fleet Sir St Clair Fopp-Jalopy sighed uncomfortably. 'It's a little difficult for an old salt like myself to break the habit of a lifetime, my dear fellow, and I still hope it may not come to that. After all, they've not gone Walt Disney yet; show no signs of it either, praise be! However, as I was telling you, I did write Fleetway House a couple of stingers, on Club notepaper too, and got two quite civil, though not altogether satisfactory replies. The editor at least did me the courtesy to answer in his own fist – not one of those jelligraphed form-letters – to the effect that analysis of the correspondence received (mainly, he admitted, from the Sex) showed 83 per cent in favour of permanent substitution. Last night I wrote to Rupert direct, hadn't done such a thing since the second year of the Peacemaker's reign! Maybe *he*'ll be able to arrange matters for us.'

' Not a hope, I'm afraid, Admiral. In my opinion, Rupert's been quietly dethroned by a palace revolution. Because he made the journal what it is, and named it too, they couldn't decently rob him of that column; but anything he and his friends do is only back-page stuff now.'

'Still in full colour, you must admit.'

'Oh, yes, still in full colour... Clearly, there was no immediate course between that and liquidation. It would have been going a bit too far to print him in red on the middle page, along with Fay and Eddie and similar riff-raff.'

'Fay and Eddie, riff-raff? Choose your words, please, Fugg! I couldn't disagree with you more strongly.'

'Very well, "riff-raff" is unreservedly withdrawn. But I shall, with the very greatest respect, characterize Fay and Eddie as caviare for the Admiral.'

'I gladly accept your rectification. Well, let us agree that Rupert may be slipping, like "Nyet" Molotoff; but surely he still has a deal of pull in the Fleetway House Politburo? Probably owns quite a block of shares, don't you think?'

'I wonder... And I also wonder (forgive me) whether a commendable loyalty to the Senior Service has not perhaps coloured your judgement on the whole shocking affair... ?'

'A little hard on me, aren't you, Fugg? I confess that it could have been worse if our old Ethiopian friend had elected to become a damned pongo or an Air Force erk, instead of a red-haired matelot; but I am hardly the man to be swayed by sentiment in a case where tradition has been so wilfully flouted.'

'To revert for a moment. You must surely have noticed that pressure has recently been exerted on Rupert to make him omit the hyphens in his two- and three-syllabled words, and change his familiar form of address. "Hullo, boys and girls!" indeed! A disgusting neologism! They'll be changing the name of the paper next.'

'Wouldn't dare. Remember that sensational drop in circulation when the old *Nineteenth Century* tried to give itself a new look? No, you're a little too young perhaps... But I can still hear the angry sputter of my father's quill pen when he resigned his subscription.'

'Quill pen in 1900?'

'Yes, indeed. My father was one of Her Majesty's Inspectors of Schools under the Board of Education, and every year around April 1st they dealt him out not only sealing wax and red tape but packets of goose-feather quills; and a little black pen-knife, every five years, to trim them with. However, what do you think is at the back of this... this... transmogrification? Colour prejudice?'

'That, I fear, may be the correct diagnosis, Admiral. First, we had the Mau-Mau trouble, then this friction in our ports and industrial centres due to the influx of cheap and unrestricted West Indian labour. And it cannot have escaped your attention that our poor saucer-eyed blackamoor hero is said to have undergone his denigration – no, that's the wrong word; should I say *catamelanesis?* – because of a confessed inferiority complex about his complexion. Yet I cannot quite take that statement *au pied de la lettre*. He had all our hearts, and knew it.'

'Indeed he had. Personally, I never thought of him as one of what Kipling used undemocratically to call "the lesser breeds within the Law". Golly was Nature's own gentleman, and if he had an ugly mug, why, I'm no beauty myself; and if you'll forgive me...'

'Certainly, Admiral, I too have a face like a clumbungus...'

'Thank you kindly! My point is that Rupert cannot have been consulted in the matter. He would never have let down the journal with such a bump. And the girl's unhappy too – you can read it in her face... Look here, I believe with the help of fellow-chicks in the Savage and White's and perhaps the Athenaeum, and the Rag of course, we could put pressure on the top brass at Fleetway House to set that damned spell in reverse, and get the poor fellow back again as he used to be? We might also have a smack at restoring the hyphenization, while we're about it.'

Major Spinks, a garrison gunner, who was acting Club Secretary coughed apologetically from a near-by armchair. 'Don't want to butt in on a private discussion, gentlemen, but the fact is, I felt equally bad about this how-d'ye-do – at first. Then I had a word with Doubleday Durkins, who keeps his private line to the Street. Apparently, the case is even worse than you suppose. What happened seems to have been that Rupert Chick took Betty out to a night-club, with Nigger, Stripey and the rest of the Soho gang. There she danced with a very personable young member of the Lower Deck and fell for him like a ton of chocolates. Our Golly, of course, felt more than a trifle peeved and, being already a bit high, threw a gin-and-tonic in her face. The sailor then landed him one on the mark. Betty giggled and asked: "What price the Black Hope?" The next thing, the rivals began breaking chairs on each other; but Golly is as tough as they come and the sailor got hospitalized. Betty, just like a woman, announced that she was through with Golly for ever and would rather die than go through the farce of pretending that she wasn't, just to soothe the pie-faced public. Doubleday reports harrowing days at Fleetway House, with even talk about the paper folding up. Betty had meanwhile issued a statement; said she loved the sailor boy heart and soul and would cancel her contract unless their friendship were officially recognized. She also accused Golly of submitting her to forty years of mental cruelty. Rupert Chick got into fearful hot water for first introducing Betty to the other fellow and then not intervening in the rough house. He pleaded bumble-foot, but they nearly threw him out on his ear, all the same. At last, late on Monday evening, only a few hours before *Chicks' Own* hit the newsstalls, some clever type – I believe it was Eddie of "Fay and Eddie" – thought up this ingenious story of a kind fairy waving a wand and changing Golly into Sailor Boy. Fooled me, fooled you, fooled all of us! Meanwhile Golly has turned Trappist monk and can't be reached by phone or letter; he's just trying to forget, Doubleday says. So now we see Betty and the Sailor Boy at their carefree domestic antics, in full colour on the front page. Seems to me the acme of bad taste. Apparently she's bought him out of the Navy.'

No comment came from the Q.C., none from the Admiral. They waited stony-eyed until the Major had cleared his throat three or four times and finally shuffled off with some excuse about seeing a librarian about a book.

The Admiral broke the silence at last. 'I don't know whether an action lies, my learned friend – that's for you to say. My guess would be a clear case of slander: hatred, ridicule, contempt, and all the trimmings. Moreover, what this insufferable pop-gun-wallah – calls himself an acting-Secretary – relays from that thundering ass Fiddlehead Durkin isn't worth a moment's thought; between you and me, both of them are secret *Tiger Tim* fans!'

Ditching in a Fishless Sea

– PABLO, THE DIRECTORS desire this office to supply a little folder of simple recommendations for English-speaking passengers in the Espanish Air Service, that they may not drown. You have studied English with a professor for two years; I for one only. It is your duty to compose the text, no?

– Well, it is certain that I am better qualified than you; but why should English-speaking passengers fear to drown?

– In case that an Espanish plane should accidentally land in the sea.

– It is illogical that such a plane should thus land (as you call it) in the sea, our Service having a 100 per cent record of absolute safety.

– No one can deny it, Pablo; yet the Directors point out that planes of other lines often fall into the sea, so that, for solidarity, they say, we must pretend that extraordinary precautions are needful also for us. The foolish passengers expect it.

– I cannot see why they should expect that our safety is less absolute than 100 per cent, just because we feel chivalrously inclined to our foreign competitors.

– Enough, this comes as an order from the Directors. We must accept it. Come, scribble out those simple recommendations. Start perhaps with a little philosophy. Improvise, man! Your imagination was never unfertile.

– If it is an order, I obey. Here we go now!

Provision and an elementary knowledge of the ambient protect the man in his activities; ignorance on the contrary, attracts, makes or increases danger inherent to all existing. In communities and regarding transportation, shows, sports, etc., rules leading to a better result are published by their representative organizations, always that these rules are kept wholly. Today this is a must in the air services. In the most improbable case of ditching, passenger's life depends upon his conduct as the crew know quite well what they have to do in such cases not only for their own reputation but for the Company's and in first place for the life of the passenger.

How is that for philosophy?.

– Not so bad. As for the practical side, let us presuppose some sort of life-saving waistcoat and one or two boats of the sort one blows up. We shall need to provide them, I suppose (what a nuisance), in case the passengers demand tactile confirmation of this fantasy.

– Remember that with a few exceptions, there is time enough to get ready in case of ditching and that the life waistcoats may keep afloat any person without danger even in the state of unconsciousness and dinghies are fit to hold overweight as well; they are inflated with great rapidity and revised carefully periodically.

How is that?

– Not so bad. Now for the reassurance that there is no danger.

– Oh, this accursed solidarity that breeds fears on the pretext of smothering them! *In case of sinking passengers should know that the radio listening station on duty does not even miss the lack of reports and therefore the aid is immediate taking only a short time to come to the spot; furthermore the water the plane is flying over is not dangerous either by large fish or by extreme temperatures. Therefore the passenger, if following the instructions below and those supplementary given him from the cockpit with order and confidence, he will succeed in his own safety.*

How is that?

– Not so bad. Now for the detailed recommendations. Improvise boldly, man!

– Should a ditching have to be faced the following instructions will be given to passengers. Take off your spectacles. Loose your tie and collar as well as belts, braces, etc. Empty your pockets of all pointed articles as pens, pencils, etc. Wear light clothes.

– But, Pablo, if they are already wearing heavy clothes and their light ones are packed in the hold ?

– So much the worse for them. Are you criticizing me, Pepe? Do you perhaps wish to write the rest yourself?

– No, no, I have no literary talent. How could I criticize you? Please continue.

– Very well, do not interrupt me further:

Put on the life waistcoat. Place the bulks under the legs and adopt the position according to the number of seat. Fix up your belt. Passengers before an imminent ditching should have to do the following. To contract hardly their muscles. To breathe deeply. To keep motionless and quiet until the plane is absolutely stop still. Soon after this, they will loose the belts and shoes to leave the plane by the nearest exit. When head and body have gone complete through the door or the window, passengers will pull from the inflation string of the waistcoat throwing themselves into the water without fear being sure they are safe.

Passengers should not worry if the transfer is difficult directly into the dinghy because the string with reel will be thrown to take them on board bearing in mind that this is an easy operation.

Do not disinflate your waistcoat until you are on the boat that will take you to the harbour; passengers must avoid slippering on the stairs rubber or wet wood to prevent falling again into the water.

– That is a very thoughtful warning, Pablo. Recommend them also to procure sandwiches in water-proof boxes, also cough pastilles and hot-water bottles, from the air-hostess, lest rescue be unaccountably delayed.

– No, no, Pepe. That would be less than reassuring. In theory rescue will come in two or three minutes, since in practice no accident can occur.

– Very well. Now only the question of priority troubles me. It is clear that all passengers have equal priority since the fares are paid equal. But do the men go out first, or do the women go first? If we recommend the men, it will seem unchivalrous; if the women, it will seem as though they were sacrificed as test-victims. Better then say nothing, perhaps, and let chance, quickness and mobility of spirit decide the precedence!

– Naturally, the pilot and crew go out first, to blow up the boats and fish the passengers into them. But better not mention even this, lest our Espanish employees be accused of putting their own lives before those of the beloved passengers.

– You will leave that question also open, then ? Now what of children travelling separately?

– *Children in their life waistcoat (not the breast-fed ones) should be left to persons keeping a better spirit and nearest the exit.*

Is that well put?

– Magisterially. And a word perhaps about invalids and the fat.

– *Fat persons as well as invalids should leave the plane by the main exit but always letting the others to come out first.*

How's that?

– I am doubtful, Pablo. Both illness and fatness are relative conditions. Fat people love life as much as the thin and think themselves robust while calling the thin 'emaciated'. Can you imagine an ugly great cathedral of a capitalist's wife telling a slender gipsy dancer: 'You go first, you will not block the door so much as I'? And the invalids - who will admit that he is such if the admission gives him less chance of life?

– Very well, there will be no invalids. But fat people must have a low priority, I insist. If the sea were rough, they might overturn the boat while trying to struggle aboard.

– But the sea is, in theory, not rough nor cold nor full of large fish. Nevertheless, have it your way! Imagine having to give precedence to my Aunt Curra, that calamity of fatness! Not only would a waistcoat of enormous girth be needed for her, but she would be sure to put it on upside down and back to front.

– Your Aunt Curra, Pepe, would float like a buoy even without a waistcoat, and we could anchor the boats to her to keep them from drifting. What more shall I write?

– Let each passenger sing his individual national anthem to encourage himself and show defiance of danger.

– Might that not rather encourage international hatreds and cause confusion?

– It is possible. Let us rather, then, recommend strict silence.

– Very well. And for a finish, a little propaganda, eh?

Passengers should also know that Espanish Air Service whose results without accidents is so wonderful and yet so natural is trying to better everything regarding transportation and specially in connection with safety.

– Very lucent and cogent, Pablo! The Directors should promote you for this. But oh, that the fantastic and impossible might come to pass! That an Espanish plane might accidentally land on the sea and that I might watch you, with your braces undone and your spectacles gone, holding one non-breast-fed baby on either arm, keeping a better spirit in your heart and breathing deeply as you throw a string with a reel to my Aunt Curra where she floats in strict silence, perhaps upside down, in the warm, fishless Mediterranean Sea!

Period Piece

IT WAS ONE July in the reign of Edward the Good, *alias* Edward the Peacemaker, and I went for the long week-end to Castle Balch – fine place in Oxfordshire – my cousin Tom's roost. Tom was a bit of a collector, not that I ever held that against Tom, and Eva must take the principal blame, if any: meaning that the people she invited for house-parties were excessively what the Yankees call (or called) 'high-toned' – artist-fellows, M.P.s, celebrities of all sorts, not easy to compete against. On this particular occasion, Eva had flung her net wide and made a stupendous haul. To wit: Nixon-Blake, R.A., who had painted the picture of the year – do they have pictures of the year nowadays? It's years since I visited Burlington House – and Ratface Dingleby, who had taken his twenty-foot *Ruby* round the Horn that same February. Saw his obituary in *The Times* a couple of years ago: lived to ninety, not born to be drowned. And, what the devil was his name? the elephant-hunter who won the V.C. in the Transvaal? – Captain Scrymgeour, of course! He got killed under Younghusband in Tibet a year or two later. And Charlie Batta, the actor-manager. None of whom I could count as cronies. *Homines novi*, in point of fact. Fortunately, Mungo Montserrat was there; my year at Eton. And Doris, his spouse, a bit stuffy, but a good sort: another cousin of mine. I teem with cousins.

This being described as a tennis week-end, we had all brought our flannels and rackets, prepared to emulate the Doherty brothers, then all the go. Both Castle Balch courts played admirably – gardener a magician with turf – but being July, of course it rained and rained ceaselessly from Friday afternoon to Monday afternoon and the tournament was literally washed out. We enjoyed pretty good sport none the less – Tom had a squash court for fellows like Mungo and me who were too energetic to content themselves with baccarat and billiards. And Charlie Batta sent to Town for some pretty actresses who happened to be seasonally unemployed, or unemployable. Furthermore, Eva invented a lot of very humorous wheezes, as the current slang was, to embarrass us – some of them pretty close to the knuckle. But no tennis tournament took place; though a beautiful silver rose-bowl was waiting on the smoking-room mantelpiece to reward the winner.

Forgot to mention the Bishop of Bangalore, who had been invited in error. The fun never started until he had turned in, but fortunately the bish loved his pillow even more than his neighbour. On Monday evening then, about 12.15 a.m. in mellow lamp light, don't you know, when the ladies had retired to their rest and the Bishop had joined them – no allegation intended – Tom spoke up and said forthrightly: 'Gentlemen, I'm as deeply grieved by this tennis fiasco as you are, and I don't want that jerry knocking around the Castle for ever afterwards to remind me of it. Tell you what: I'll present same to the fellow who supplies the best answer to a question that Eva was too modest to propound with her own lips: "What were the most thrilling moments of your life?"'

We all drew numbers out of the Bishop's fascinatingly laced top hat, and spun our yarns in the order assigned by fate. Apart from Mungo and me, every personage present was a born raconteur. I assure you: to hear Charlie Batta, who tee'd off, tell us how he played *Hamlet* in dumb show to a cellarful of Corsican bandits who were holding him for ransom, and how, waiving the three thousand sov.s at which he had been priced, they afterwards escorted him in triumph to Ajaccio, firing *feux-de-joie* all the way in tribute to his art – that was worth a gross of silver bowls. And doughty Scrymgeour on safari in German East, when he bagged the hippo and the rhino with a right and left; my word, Scrymgeour held us! Next, the R.A. (told you his name, forgotten it again – had a small red imperial, eyes like ginger-ale, and claimed to have re-introduced the yellow hunting waistcoat, though that was an inexactitude). He recorded an encounter with a gipsy girl in a forest near Budapest – the exact physical type he had envisaged for his picture *The Sorceress* – whom he persuaded with coins and Hunnish endearments to pose in the nude; after which he painted those Junoesque curves and contours, those delicate flesh tints – and so forth, don't you know – with ecstatic inspiration and anatomic exactitude, careless though her jealous lover had by this time entered the grotto and was covering him with an inlaid fowling piece. At last the murderous weapon clattered to the ground and he heard a strangled voice exclaim: 'Gorgio, I cannot shoot you. I bow before your genius! Keep the girl – leave me the picture – go!'

Finally poor old Mungo, who had drawn No. 13, was prevailed upon to take the floor. My heart went out to him, me having made a damned mess of my own effort. These were Mungo's exact words: 'Gentlemen, I'm a simple chappy, never had any exciting adventures like you chappies. Sorry. However. If you want to know. The most thrilling moments of my life were when I married Doris – you all know Doris – and, well, when she and I... (Pause)... They still are, in fact.'

Mungo brought the house down. Tom thrust the rose-bowl into his unwilling hands, treated him to the stiffest whisky and soda on which I have ever clapped eyes, and sent him crookedly upstairs to the bedroom; where Doris was being kept awake, not by the sounds of revelry from the smoke-room, but by the frightful snores of the Bishop next door.

'What *have* you got there, Mungo?' she asked crossly.

'Rose-bowl,' Mungo mumbled. 'Tom offered it to the chappy who could best answer Eva's question about the most thrilling moments in his life. They all told such capital stories that, when it was my turn, I got into a mortal funk. But we had drawn lots from the Bishop's hat, and this inspired me. I said: "When Doris and I kneel side by side in church giving thanks to Heaven for all the blessings that have been showered on us." And they gave me the prize!'

'How *could* you, Mungo! You know that was a dreadful lie. Oh, now I feel so ashamed! It's not as though prayers and Church are anything to joke about.' She enlarged on this aspect of the case for quite a while, and Mungo resignedly hung his head. Whisky always made him melancholy; I can't say why.

The next morning the party broke up: one and all were catching the 10.45 express to Town. Doris Montserrat noticed a lot of admiring or curious glances flung in her direction, and conscience pricked. She stood on the hall staircase and made a startling little speech.

'Gentlemen, I'm afraid that Mungo won that rose-bowl on false pretences last night. He has only done... what he said he did... three times. The first was before we married; I made him. The second was when we married; he could hardly have avoided it. The third was after we married, and then he fell asleep in the middle...'

He Went Out to Buy a Rhine

'HE WAS A very quiet, very sensitive young gentleman,' concluded Mrs Tisser, 'and punctual to the hour with his rent. I am truly sorry that he took the coward's way out. My own opinion is that the balance of his mind was upset.'

'Witness is not being questioned for her medical opinion,' whispered the Coroner's clerk. 'She is being asked for facts.'

The Coroner said: 'Mrs Tisser, you are not being asked for your medical opinion. You are being questioned for facts. The jury wants to hear more about the demeanour of the late Angus Hamilton Tighe on the morning of his death.'

Mrs Tisser stuck to her guns: 'The young gentleman's demeanour, your Honour, suggested that the balance of his mind had been upset.'

'Enlarge on that, please,' ordered the Coroner, conceding the point.

'He behaved very strangely, your Honour. At breakfast he told me, as I set down the tray beside him on the sitting-room table: "Mrs Tisser, I've been doing it wrong all my life: I keep my mouth open instead of shut." Well, that was what I had been praying for weeks that he *would* say, because the poor gentleman snored as a pig grunts. So I said: "Well, Mr Tighe, I'm glad to hear you make that confession. You ought to get Dr Thome to operate on your nose, so that you'd never do it again." "Oh, but I enjoy the sensation," he said, with a wild look in his eye. "It invigorates the whole system. And it's a cheap pleasure, like sitting in the sun, or combing one's hair, don't you agree?"'

We glanced gravely at one another, as Mrs Tisser continued: 'I told him that I didn't agree, and that I'd dearly knock a shilling a week off his rent, if he could break himself of the habit. He laughed in what I can only call a fiendish manner, and I left the room without another word. He had never before made mock of me. Not that I felt vexed exactly. But his demeanour was certainly most alarming.'

'That took place shortly after 8 a.m., you say, Mrs Tisser? Did you see him again that morning, before the fatality occurred?'

'I did, your Honour; about five minutes later. We met on the stairs. He seemed to be in a state of suppressed excitement, and told me that he was going out to buy an "eternity" and do the job properly at last. "An eternity?" I asked, thinking that perhaps I had misheard. "A rhine, if you like, Mrs Tisser," he answered, grinning like a devil.'

'And then?'

'And then, your Honour, he was away between ten minutes and a quarter of an hour, and at last came rushing upstairs like a whirlwind. Half a minute went by, and then I heard an extraordinary sound: a sort of muffled explosion from the sitting-room. And I saw him dash through the open door, across the corridor, and into the bedroom where he flung himself headlong at the balcony beyond. I screamed, and hurried downstairs.'

'Thank you, Mrs Tisser, that will be enough. You need not repeat that part of your evidence; we have inspected the french windows and the shattered woodwork of the balcony which bear out your evidence. One more question. Do you know anything about the dead man's emotional life?'

'If you mean, did he ever try to bring a young woman home, he certainly did not, your Honour. He was a most exemplary young man in that respect; his medical studies seem to have been "both parent, child and wife" to him, as the saying goes. The only thing I recall...'

'Yes, Mrs Tisser?'

'One night he confided to me his love for a lady whom he had never met; someone who had taken complete possession of his heart. I thought at first that it must be a film actress, but he said that he didn't even know what she looked like, and he couldn't understand a word of what she said, either. It was then I first began to question his sanity. Well, about a week ago, as I was doing his room, I noticed a crumpled letter lying half-charred in the grate. My eye caught the first line: "O my wonderful Yma." But I was too honourable to read any further, and I hardly like to mention it even now. She seems to have been his dream-lady: because once he came back from a visit to London, and his eyes were shining as he said: "Oh, I am so happy, Mrs Tisser." I asked: "On account of the lady you mentioned?" and he answered: "I spent the whole afternoon with her, Mrs Tisser." "So you've met her at last?" I said. "I mean in spirit," he told me.'

More evidence was called as to the late Angus Hamilton Tighe's state of health, but it proved to be inconclusive. We could not even decide that he had been overworking, or had financial difficulties, or was being blackmailed. Dr Thorne had never treated him for anything more than a twisted ankle. He possessed no close friends among his fellow medical students, and no relatives nearer than Canada. So we retired.

Since it seemed unlikely that Mrs Tisser had pushed him over the balcony, we naturally wanted to spare the feelings of the Tighe family in Alberta, by adding 'while of unsound mind' to the obvious verdict of 'suicide'.

Only one juryman, Mr Pink, a retired chemist, dissented. He called for silence, and then spoke in grave, authoritative tones. 'I think, ladies and gentlemen, that we can improve on that verdict. To begin with, I cannot regard it as a symptom of insanity in myself that I too admire, nay adore, the celebrated Peruvian singer Yma Sumac, though I have never seen her, nor do I know one word of Spanish. Her voice, surely the most wonderful in the world, compasses five full octaves and is true as a bell in every register. Poor young Tighe! I own a rare set of Yma's early recordings which would doubtless have given him infinite pleasure, had I been aware that he shared my view of her genius.

'But I have another observation to make of even greater importance: it is that when we inspected the corpse I noticed a discoloured right nostril.'

We gaped at him as he went on: 'Which did not figure in the post-mortem report and was, in my view, caused by a "sternutatory", not an "eternity"; or by an "errhine", not "a rhine". In non-technical language, by tobacco snuff. If the Coroner permits us, we will send a policeman to visit the only tobacconist in this town who sells that old-fashioned commodity – Hackett of Cold Harbour Cottages. The officer will almost certainly find that the late Tighe visited Hackett at about 8.15 a.m. The fatal sternutatory is probably contained in the pencil-box on his desk. Moreover, I noticed a familiar medical work on elementary physiology lying on the breakfast table. Look up "sternutation" in the Index, turn to the relevant page, and you will find, I think, a sentence to this general effect:

STERNUTATION: an involuntary reflex respiratory act, caused by irritation of the nerve terminals of the nasal mucous membrane, or by severe luminary stimulation of the optic nerve. The sternutator, after drawing a deep breath, compresses his lips; whereupon the contents of the lungs are violently expelled through the nostrils.

'I remember well the impression that this passage made on me years ago, while I was studying for my pharmaceutical degree. I said to myself, in the very words of the deceased: "I have been doing it wrong all my life; I keep my mouth open, instead of shut." The next time that I felt a sneeze coming on, I duly compressed my lips and, hey presto! found myself hurtling across the room like a stone from a catapult; but fortunately did not make for the french windows. In fact, I knocked myself out on the corner of the mantelpiece. Let me therefore record my opinion that the late Angus Hamilton Tighe died a martyr to scientific experiment and was no more suicidal than I am.'

So we brought in 'Death by Misadventure', after all, with a rider against experimental use of sternutatories; which, I fear, didn't mean a thing to the general public.

Kill Them! Kill Them!

THE POTTERIES WERE by this time a distant smudge on the horizon behind us and the map showed us close to the Welsh border. Jenny drove.

Wales reminded us both of David, who had done his battle training in this region. So presently I said, knowing that this must be Jenny's line of thought too: 'They would have given him the award posthumously, of course, if the ground he won had been held. Not that it would have meant much to anyone, except the Regimental historian. Anyhow, the Japs infiltrated, the Indian battalions on the flanks rectified their line (as the saying is), and the Regiment had to fight its way back. It's a rule that a reverse cancels all citations.'

'An R.A.F. man who was giving the Brigade air-support – I met him last year in Trans-Jordania – says the attack was suicidal and criminal.'

'It wasn't the C.-in-C.'s fault. He had orders from London to secure a tactical success in that area before the monsoon broke. And felt awful about it.'

'How do you know that, Father?'

'Warell wrote to me as soon as the War ended and brought up the subject himself. His G.H.Q. was a thousand miles away, and though, when he'd seen the plan of attack submitted, he felt strongly tempted to fly up and run the show in person, a C.-in-C. couldn't very well take over from a brigade commander. It just wasn't done. Or so he said in his letter. I've kept it for you.'

'According to my R.A.F. man, everyone was hopping mad at having to assault a scientifically entrenched position without proper artillery support – and just before the rain bogged everything down for the season. That sense of victimization must have been what sent David berserk. As you know, he was a confirmed pacifist, and had nothing against the Japs.'

We kept silent for a mile or two. Then I said: 'One thing that he did has always puzzled me. At Oxford, when he was four years old, we were driving up the High and a great pack of black-coated, dog-collared parsons debouched from Queen's College and swarmed across the street, making for Oriel. An Ecclesiastical Congress was on. David shouted excitedly: "Kill them! Kill them!" Did he hate the colour of their clothes, do you think? Or was he simply anticlerical?'

'Neither,' Jenny answered. 'I should say that it was the *unnaturalness* of the sight. Probably he always thought of clergymen in the singular, as I do. The vicar on the altar steps: singular. Like the mother beside the cradle: singular. Or the headmistress in her study: singular. Each aloof, self-sufficient, all-powerful and, in fact, singular. Don't all Mothers' Meetings, Ecclesiastical Congresses, and Headmistresses' or Headmasters' Conferences seem terribly artificial and awkward and dismal to you – I mean because of the loss of singularity? Whereas soldiers or sailors, or undergraduates, or schoolchildren, who go naturally into the plural...'

'Clergymen do behave very awkwardly in a bunch, I agree, and David may have wanted to put them out of their misery by a sudden massacre. He had a kind heart.'

'Also,' said Jenny, 'Mothers' Meetings and Headmistresses' Conferences go with seed-cake. When David was twelve and I was thirteen and we got invited to parties, he used to wander round and inspect the food supply as soon as we arrived. If it passed muster, we stayed. Otherwise he'd nudge me and whisper: "Seed-cake, Jenny." And then we always sneaked out. He hated seed-cake. Seed-cake's impersonal, and David was a real person.'

Green Welsh hills and wild-eyed Welsh sheep and the syllable *Llan* appearing on every second fingerpost. Hereabouts David had commanded his platoon in aggressive tactical schemes; perhaps had sten-gunned the imaginary garrison of that farmhouse at the top of the slope. It was a splendid eighteenth-century building with a broad whitewashed front, generous windows and an irregular slate roof yellow with lichen; also a large midden, cocks and hens of an old-fashioned, handsome, uneconomical breed, black cows, and bracken litter at the entrance to the byres. A sign read: TEAS.

As we rounded a sharp corner we came on a glossy charabanc, which had just disgorged its load of excursionists by the farmhouse gate. They were all earnest, black-coated, dog-collared clergymen, and seemed profoundly ill at ease. Forty or fifty at least, and – this is a true story, not a joke, for neither Jenny nor I felt prepared for a joke – every one of them had a slice of impersonal seed-cake in his hand, out of which he had taken a single thoughtful bite.

I had a vision of a serious apple-cheeked little boy, sitting between Jenny and me and shaking his fist in a fury.

'Kill them, kill them!' I shouted involuntarily; but Jenny, scared as she was, had the presence of mind to swerve and drive on.

Harold Vesey at the Gates of Hell

THE DIM OLD 'Pelican' sign had been wittily repainted by a modern poster artist. The once foul stable yard, frequented by hordes of sooty sparrows, had been converted into a car park. White muslin curtains graced the windows. An adjoining network of howling, stinking, typhoidal slum, where in my childhood policemen dared enter only four by four – truncheons drawn and whistles in their mouths – had utterly vanished; garaged residences now occupying the site were already well matured, their elms almost overtopping the roofs. The road-crossing which pale-faced street-Arabs with ragged trousers, bare feet and scanty brooms used to sweep clear of mud and horse-dung for us gentry to cross – 'Don't forget the sweeper, lady!' – had become a gleaming asphalt roundabout, and the rain-water gurgling down the gutters looked positively potable.

'There are the gates of Hell!', I nevertheless reminded myself, as I pushed open the door marked 'Saloon Bar'. Amelia, my nurse, had told me so when I was four years old, pointing across the road through the bathroom window. 'A man goes in at that door sober, industrious and God-fearing; he comes out a fiend in human guise, whether it's the beer or whether it's the gin.' She then dabbed her eyes with a handkerchief. 'I had a good home and husband once,' she said. 'I never thought as I should be forced to earn my living in domestic service at twenty pound a year. And look what's happened to that poor foolish Annie! The Pelican has been her downfall, too.' She was referring to our parlour-maid's fatal love for Harold, the barrel-man, a big red-faced ex-soldier with shoulder-of-mutton fists, green baize apron, and shiny black corduroys. Annie had stolen two of our silver entrée dishes to buy Harold a watch-chain for Christmas; and been dismissed without a character.

Mr Gotobed, Junior, the plump-faced innkeeper – probably 'Brassy' Gotobed's grandson – lounged alone behind the bar. He was youngish, with side-burns, Savile Row tailoring and an Old Malthusian tie. I entered hesitantly and earned an easy though enigmatic smile.

On the walls hung three Baxter prints, two matched warming-pans, a cluster of knobkerries, an Indian Mutiny bundook, a dartboard, a large wooden spoon, a pair of indifferent French Impressionist paintings in art-gallery frames, and an iron hoop.

'With what may I have the pleasure of serving you, sir?'

'A double brandy,' I ordered, remembering the beer and the gin.

'Splash?'

'No, thanks; neat.' And I drank it at a blow.

'These were the gates of Hell, Mr Gotobed,' I remarked, putting down two half-crowns.

'Sir?'

'I used to live in that big house opposite.'

'You mean Rosemary Mansions?'

'I mean Rosemary House, before it became immansionized. That was when the Pelican's best beer still sold at twopence a pint; and was strong as the kick of a dray-horse. When tankards and curses flew along this ancient bar like bees on a summer's day. When soused lobsters went tumbling out into the inspissated muck, heels over busby, with almost boring regularity, propelled by the hobnailed boots of courageous Corporal Harold Vesey. These, I repeat, were the gates of Hell.'

'That will have been in what I might call pre-Reformation days, sir,' he said rather crossly. 'My clientele now consists almost entirely of City men. But we have a lot of quiet democratic fun here together. It amused us last year to form a Saloon Bar Darts Club and enter for the South-West London Championship. We won that wooden spoon fair and square; and my team treasure it like the apple of their corporate eye.'

But I refused to be sidetracked. 'It was the time,' I insisted, pointing to a handsome portrait of the Duke of Cornwall suspended behind the bar, 'of that boy's great-great-great-grandmother. I remember the old lady well, driving along High Street in an open barouche with a jingling escort of Lancers.'

He eyed me with awe. '*Three* greats?' he inquired, 'are you sure?'

'Rip van Winkle's the name,' I answered. 'I suppose it's no use asking you what happened to Corporal Harold Vesey? I'm sure of the surname because he sent our parlour-maid Annie a lace-Valentine inscribed: "Yours respectably, Harold Vesey, Corporal, 1900"; that was after he came back gloriously wounded from the South African war. Harold was barrel-man; and porter at the Gates of Hell.'

'Rings a bell,' said Mr Gotobed meditatively. 'Hell's bells, if you like, ha, ha! 1900? Time of my grandfather?'

'If your grandfather was the bold hero in the purple waistcoat whom the boys nicknamed "Brassy",' I said, and ordered another brandy.

He waved that one off. 'Funny,' he remarked, 'how we reckon time here in terms of war. South African. First World. Second World.'

'Harold Vesey had served at Tel-el-Kebir in 1882. He was a veteran when I knew him.'

'Indeed? Well, I never saw any service myself, and I'm not ashamed to tell you the story, now it's all over. If it had been a question of volunteering, I dare say I'd have gone along with all the other b. fools. But not under Conscription. We Malthusians have our pride. Between you and me I fooled the Board by a simple and quite ingenious wheeze. A fortnight beforehand I started eating sugar. Gradually worked up to two pounds a day. Ghastly treatment with ghastly symptoms. Ghastly expensive, too, with rationing in full blast. Naturally, just because of the rationing, the medicos never suspected a thing.'

'Naturally,' I agreed. 'Harold once fooled his M.O. too, to avoid being drafted somewhere on garrison duty. He chewed cordite, which sent up his temperature to 106. When duly crimed, he owned up; whereupon the Colonel drafted him to South Africa instead, which was what he wanted. And he subsequently had the pleasure of relieving Ladysmith. But that, of course, took place in the days before Conscription.'

'Good for him!' said Mr Gotobed without conviction and switched the topic again. 'By the way, see that iron hoop over there? It's a curious relic of my grandfather's days. I bought it at an antique shop for our Christmas celebration to use as a frame for the wreath of holly and ivy over the door. The old merchant told me that iron hoops were trundled here in the days of gaseous street-lighting and horse-drawn traffic.'

'Harold Vesey gave me an iron hoop once,' I said, 'but unfortunately I wasn't allowed to use it. I was a little gentleman and little gentlemen were supposed to use only wooden hoops. We were also forbidden to whistle on our fingers or turn cartwheels, because that was what the street-Arabs did. Thus you obscure the relentless evolution of modern society, Mr Gotobed. The street-Arab is forced by industrial progress to become a respectable citizen. His grandsons, if not his sons, are born little gentlemen; and therefore forbidden to whistle on their fingers or turn cartwheels on the bemuddied crossing. And iron hoops, like peg-tops with dangerous spikes (another ancient working-class distinction) are relegated to the antique shops. Harold Vesey would have been surprised.'

I kept on the Harold Vesey tack mercilessly, until the bell rang again in Mr Gotobed's mind.

'Vesey? I've got it now. Yes, my grandfather employed one H. Vesey at the Pelican. Comic story in its weird way. It seems that soon after he sent that Valentine to your parlour-maid, an aunt died and left him an Essex country cottage and a small legacy – in recognition of his patriotic services. However, just before Hitler's War, when he was in his late seventies, the County Council condemned the cottage and transplanted him to a brand-new Council-house: modern plumbing, well-equipped kitchen, built-in cupboards, everything laid on. But the obstinate old – well – basket didn't take to it. Sulked. Sat out on a bench in the garden, all weathers, "just to spite them," he said – until he was carried off by pneumonia. The joke was that they never got around to pulling down the cottage after all. Its timbers were still sound and the premises served during the War to accommodate evacuees. Recently my father bought the place – that's how I happen to know the story. He spent four or five thousand pounds on doing it up for a week-end hang-out. But the Council wouldn't let us alter the façade or build another storey, because by then – this is the real pay-off – the cottage had been scheduled as an ancient monument. What a country, eh?'

But at that moment jovial members of the City clientele came wandering in, and called for dry Martinis. I managed to retire without comment or attention.

Life of the Poet Gnaeus Robertulus Gravesa [1]

THOUGH SOME DETRACTORS are found who affirm that Gnaeus Robertulus Gravesa was born of mean stock, his father being a servile Irish pedlar of mussel-fish, and his mother a Teutonic freedwoman, daughter of an ambulant apothecary, yet his descendants, on the contrary, claim that the Gravesae were an ancient equestrian clan of Gallic origin and that the poet's paternal grand-father was both High Priest of Hibernian Limericum and a man very learned in the mathematic sciences.

This difference of opinion may be left unsettled. In any event, Gnaeus Robertulus Gravesa, whether of ancient stock or of parents and forefathers in whom he could take no just pride, was born in a suburban villa at the tenth milestone from Londinium, when L. Salisburius was sole Consul, in the year following the death of A. Tennisonianus Laureatus, whom the deified Victoria raised to patrician rank. It is handed down that the infant, being the eighth child of his father, did not cry at his birth, but wore only a beast-like scowl, which already gave assurance of a determination to overcome the cruel pricks of fate by a mute and cynical habit of mind. There was added another omen: a cauliflower plant growing in his father's garden began to sprout with unnatural and unwonted shoots, namely with such alien potherbs as leeks, onions, mallows, parsnips, marjoram, turnips and even samphire of the cliff, thus portending the excessive variety of the studies to which he would devote his stylus, and which subsequently earned him the title of Polyhistor. But on the crown of the cauliflower burgeoned Apollo's laurel.

He studied grammar and rhetoric at a school maintained by the Carthusian Guild, but interrupted them to march in the war against Gulielmus the German, being appointed centurion in the XXIII Legion. It is related that when, riddled with wounds at the battle of the Corvine Wood, his supine body was set aside by his comrades for cremation on the common pyre, lo! the god Mercury, distinguished by winged sandals and *caduceus* as well as by conspicuously divine grace, appeared to the military

---

[1] From Gaius Seutonius Tranquillus's Lives of the Britannic Poets. Translation by W. Wadlington Postchaise (Loeb Classics, 1955).

Tribune who was lamenting this premature death, and spoke as follows: 'Man: there remain yet the seeds of life in that gory and mutilated frame. Do not anger the gods by conveying to the flames that which they have themselves spared! My Robertulus, recovering his spent forces, will yet lead a life profitable to the Legion on account of his shining sword, and pleasing to his fatherland because of his well-tuned lyre and replete tablets.' So saying, the Herald of the Gods vanished, and the Tribune did not despise this message, for after binding up the wounds which had ceased to bleed, he wrapped his own military cloak about the seeming corpse, whereupon a she-weasel (or a witch in weasel's disguise) appeared on the right hand and blew life with her own mouth into those motionless nostrils.

He was above the usual stature and not over-fat, with curly hair ill-combed, a crooked nose broken in youth while he contended in the gymnasium, and the same physical disproportion noted by the divine Homer in Ulysses, namely that his legs were too short for his body. His skin was exceedingly white and did not vary its colour even in the hottest suns of Egypt and Spain; but, at the most, freckled only moderately, so that if ever two freckles joined together in one, he would exclaim: 'This is the nearest that you let me approach, O Phoebus, to a manly bronze.' He often suffered from affections of the stomach and lungs, but nursed no jealousy against the gods on this score, and is recorded to have said that, since his parents had left him a rich legacy of health, he alone must bear the blame if he frittered away this gift by insalubrious practices.

Upon being presented with the wooden foil and hanging up his arms and helmet in the temple of Mars, he resumed his rhetorical studies, inserting himself among the Oxonians, but determined thereafter to be beholden to no man as his patron but always remain to his own self a master; and this resolution, confirmed with an oath to Infernal Hecate, he obstinately maintained throughout his life.

In the fatal year that saw the universal ruin both of the moneylenders and of the grain merchants, an event which sowed widespread poverty in every part of the world, he went into voluntary banishment, choosing the Greater Balearic Island for his retreat. Some say that he departed in haste and a dark cloak to avoid the lictors, being accused of the capital crime of murder, and that he left word with his freedmen to forward his household goods by ship secretly, lest they be seized; certain it is that for the space of the next six years he kept himself close in the Balearic villa which he had built for himself, not even crossing over to the Hispanic mainland, and practising it is not known what strange and secret rites.

He married twice, each wife being a Briton of generous birth, and had four children by the first marriage and an equal number by the second. With several vernacular languages grown familiar, besides his own and the pure Latin and Greek tongues, he spoke all with greater fluency than accuracy or elegance. His vices were few, apart from an immoderate greed. He himself confesses, in a letter, to a peculiar relish for coarse bread rubbed with garlic and dipped in olive oil; and for the sausage of raw and greasy pork for which the island of his choice is notorious. To this failing must, however, be added a severe pride and a certain disregard not only of his personal appearance but – except in formal company – of befitting table manners. His eldest daughter, though she loved and honoured him, often complained in public that he would at times wear two *socci* of different colour, one on the left foot and one on the right; and that his hair was at times smeared with honey and sprinkled with dead leaves. Moreover, one of his ex-slaves has reported how once, lifting the cover from a particularly succulent dish of mushrooms at a birthday banquet, Gravesa asked eagerly: 'Are all of these for me?' His pride showed itself nowhere to worse advantage than in his refusal to do what all his more experienced friends-implored, *viz.* to write the same book often, changing merely the names and the scenes, since the crowd loves to be reminded of what it has once enjoyed and to which it has become accustomed. Indeed, when they voiced this plea with tears and torn white locks, he, being set upon a continuous change of theme, petulantly inquired: ' Sirs, would you have me grow rich by inventing a formula for limning comical rabbits?' This he confirmed with the following sharp improvisation, magisterially declaring that the awkward scansion of 'rabbits' (cŭnīcŭli) should not deny them the glory of entering his hexameters.

> *Pintori species comicorum cuniculorum*
> *Laetius occurrens mores mercede subegit,*
> *Heu! tragica at persona tegit nunc ora jocosi*
> *Insidiis capti comicorum cuniculorum.* [1]

At other times he composed both prose and verse with difficulty and many cancellations, so that often nothing was left to Felix, his friend and transcriber, but two or three scrawled words in the margin of the wax-tablets, these also being destined to cancellation before the work should be done.

It is said that, while Vinstonius the Dictator took his ease after the downfall of Hitlerus, this same Gravesa (to whom he had shown many distinguished marks of favour) read out to him from his poetical works for twelve days in succession, from breakfast-time until the supper-hour, seated on a bench in a retiring room of the Senate House; the Consul

---

[1] He found a formula for drawing comic rabbits
This formula for drawing comic rabbits paid,
Till at the end he could not change the tragic habits
This formula for drawing comic rabbits made.

Atlaeus taking a turn at the reading whenever the poet was interrupted by a certain weariness of his voice. But though, truly, Gravesa visited Londinium about this time, the story is hardly to be credited. For Vinstonius did not relax his taut mind even for a day after this great victory, being intent rather on restraining the victorious onset of his Scythian allies. Moreover, though Gravesa's verses are now praised by many urbane critics and learned grammarians for their tart flavour and curious quality, he himself always read in a hoarse voice, undramatically and with a glazed expression of the features, pouring forth the Muse in a flat and toneless mumble. Nor was Atlaeus's delivery of verse, if we may trust our authorities, so sweet and effective as to charm the grim soul of his powerful colleague.

The death of Gravesa was portended by evident signs. The house in which he was born collapsed suddenly because of dry rot creeping in upon the beams; furthermore an eel of prodigious size, lifting its head from the neighbouring lake called The Mere of Rushes, cried: 'Lament, Londiniensians, for the twilight of poesy is upon you.' A thunderbolt also struck the Athenaeum where his father and uncle had aforetime been priests (but he himself never enjoyed this honour); and a fire spontaneously sprang up and burned five hundred shelves of books in the Britannic Museum, though not a single one of his own works suffered so much as a light singeing.

The marvellous manner of his apotheosis is common knowledge. As he sat one evening beneath his Balearic mulberry-tree, about the Kalends of May, conversing with friends and grand-children who constantly felicitated him upon the active intelligence remaining to his mind, despite a decrepit body, on a sudden (strange to repeat) a woman of effulgent form and more than human vivacity appeared, cleaving the air with a car drawn by dragons, though some say by doves. This Goddess reined in her docile team and hovered near by at a height of some six cubits from the ground, therefrom offering the poet such customary allurements as a vitreous castle, apple orchards, and a vat of mead watched over by lovely virgins. Gravesa being beckoned to climb up and sit beside her, his companions averted their eyes from this unlawful sight; but presently, when they dared to look again, he had vanished without farewell, even as Romulus vanished from the company of the shepherds, his trusty associates, in the very middle of Rome. Thus it was said: ' Once it seemed Gravesa died, yet he returned from the dead; again, it seemed Gravesa did not die, yet he departed.'

Nevertheless, Ganymedus Turpis, a low comedian, has introduced a scene into his mime 'The Poetasters', portraying Gravesa as being hacked to death by enraged Palmesanian fishwives, in consequence of a bitter haggle about the market price of lampreys.

Explicit Vita Gn. Rob. Gravesae.

Ever Had a Guinea Worm?

HE SWUNG HIMSELF into the carriage just as we pulled out of Padding-ton, and sat down opposite me. 'Who says that losing your temper won't get you anywhere?' he asked bellicosely. He must have had an argument on the subject with the station staff, because loud shouts came from the platform. A porter was running alongside the train, shaking his fist and, behind, I could see another porter sprawled on the platform, bleeding violently from the nose. But the train was well under way and the next stop would be Rugby.

'There are occasions,' he went on, 'when not to lose your temper would be morally wrong. What did God give us tempers for, unless to lose them? Tell me that!'

We were four in the compartment, but none of us answered. Even if we had liked the look of him, it was far too early in the journey to get involved in a theological discussion. But I was the only one without a morning paper, so he tapped me on the knee.

'Take travelling in Egypt,' he persisted. 'Ever been in Egypt, by the way? Those Cairo guides cling to you like leeches. You're sunk if you don't lose your temper with them. Shifty-looking fellow comes up to you and says: "I show you tombs of all 'Gyptian kings, large and small, for tidy fee, fifty piastres." " No thanks," you answer politely. " I just want to see the Museum." "I take you to Sadoum, in desert," he says. " I know cheap taxi, take us for very little. Him English. Me English. We see long line ancient ministers and kings, now dead." "No," you say, weakening, "I only want to visit the Museum, really." "Museum bad: 'Gyptian," he says. "Me English. In my house Sadoum are many women: 'Talian, Grik, English. Also Book of Dead. Real ole Book of Dead given me Churchill. In 1920 Egypt ruled with good old stern English. Me: trusted servant Lawrence 'Rabia, also Churchill. Here is cutting: Lawrence say me the limit. Here, see, personal letter Churchill. Him, my brother. Me English. Me: good sport!" "No," you say, "it's very kind of you, but, please, I just want to see the Museum. And I can't afford fifty piastres." Then he fixes you with his beady black eye and grabs you by the sleeve: "I say, I take you to Sadoum, my private house? English! All 'Gyptians bad men. Me,

English: good! My name Brown. In London, me big Hotel. In my house I have Book of Dead. You give me fifty piastres now, we go fetch Book of Dead – after, we go Museum..."'

I glanced appealingly round the carriage, but nobody would meet my eye.

'I'm right, eh? Show them a spot of weakness and they'll burrow under your skin like guinea-worms. Any of you fellows ever had a guinea-worm, by the way? They're the plague of the Gold Coast. Get into your system *via* the toe – if you choose the wrong pool to bathe in – and wriggle merrily up your leg, growing bigger and bigger, battening on your blood-stream. The blighters insist on doing a complete tour of your body. They reach the thigh, ascend the hip, twine round your middle – then up the shoulders and neck, across the back of your eye-balls, that's the trickiest passage, pretty painful too, then down and round once more, and out by the same toe. When they begin to emerge, you wind them carefully round a match-stick, a little each day, until they're free. By that time they're a good yard long. If you pull too hard, they break in two, and then of course, you're in serious trouble. Have to rush along to the tropical medicine wallahs for treatment. But if you lose your temper, you're all right, they respect that, the blighters, and scamper off over the desert.'

I was puzzled for a moment; but probably he had reverted from guinea-worms and tropical medicine wallahs to the Cairo guides.

'And not only people, but *things*,' he went on. 'Things respect it too. Suppose you try to open a screw-top jar that's stuck, and can't manage it, not even with a damp cloth, because you can't get enough purchase. What do you do? Lose your temper, drop the cloth, and go homicidal. You seize the damned bottle and wring its ruddy neck. Off the screw-top comes, sweet as oil! But you feel like hell afterwards. Takes it out of you, that sort of thing.'

He stopped to gaze with surprise at his umbrella; he had just wrenched the plastic handle clean off. Stuffing it morosely into his overcoat pocket, he went on: 'Same with rugger. Ever play rugger, by the way? You're in the scrum now, and the enemy scrum is heavier and better trained and pushing you all over the place... Back into your own twenty-five you go, foot by foot, and there's no heart left in any of you – the side's as good as beaten. And then one of the enemy picks up the ball and starts running. You tackle him half-heartedly; he gets between you and the referee and fists you off, and catches you where it hurts.'

Here he dealt himself a vicious crack on the cheek-bone in illustration. 'Happened to me once, at Murrayfield in '37. What did I do? Lost my temper, what else? – turned and flung myself on him and brought him down with a diving tackle –'

'Steady on!' I said coldly, disengaging his huge hands from my ankles.

'– and a second later I had the leather under my arm and was running upfield like stink. Burst through a group of forwards, leaped clean over the head of a half, swerved and zigzagged at right angles, skittled down another row of forwards, handed off a wing-three, and was away down the middle of the field with nothing but the back between me and the try-line!'

We were now alone in the compartment. The stolid, red-faced ex-R.A.F. type, the correct bank-manager and the worthy headmaster in the clerical collar – all of whom had been involved, somewhat freely, in that Murrayfield run – were not, it seemed, rugger players, nor even anxious to learn the game. But, being English, they had made no protest. They merely folded their morning papers and trooped out into the corridor.

The tale crashed on: 'The back was a tall, vicious fellow fourteen stone if an ounce, J.J. Hamilton-Dewar, capped for Scotland that season. His speciality was a smothering tackle: he'd leap on you like a lion on a sheep, bear you down by sheer brute avoirdupois and rub your nose in the mud. So J.J. Hamilton-Dewar came charging up like an express-train, from just inside his twenty-five line and smother-tack...'

An express-train flashed past the open window with a sensationally dramatic roar, drowning the rest of the sentence.

'But believe it or not,' he shouted above the racket, 'I charged on, full butt, with the blighter twined around my neck, and touched down between the posts! Never so much as faltered. But I felt like hell when the whistle blew and I'd cooled down. Takes it out of you, that sort of thing.'

He sighed and mopped his face with a fold of his ruined umbrella.

'Ever been in action, by the way?' he resumed after a pause. 'Astonishing what one does in action. "Going berserk," the old Vikings called it. A man would take a spear right through his body, break off the haft because it got in his way, and lay out a dozen or so of the enemy with whatever weapon came handy, until he sobered up and suddenly realized that he was a goner. Chap I knew in Korea went berserk – scared the life out of the Chinks because he should have been dead ten minutes before. Half his head had gone, and one of his hands, but he just went on batting them over the heads with an entrenching tool. Killed a whole machine-gun section of 'em before he conked out.'

'Put that umbrella down, sir!' I said, controlling myself with difficulty.

He reluctantly lowered the weapon.

It was in a gentle, almost cooing voice, that he began again: 'Ever been stranded in Los Angeles, by the way? Happened to me once. Because of a girl called Louella. A lovely girl, a girl in a thousand; her one fault was an obsession about wanting to be dominated, and I didn't meet the bill. She kept on at me to lose my temper; but it's always been my trouble that I can't lose my temper with a woman. With a man, there's no trouble of course; but if ever a woman is unkind to me, I just want to sit down in a corner and cry. Curious, don't you agree? It seems that what Louella needed was some great, ill-tempered, husky pug, to take her by the hair, swing her around the apartment, and then make love to her among the smashed crockery and broken chairs. But I couldn't even begin to play that sort of game with her. I could only sit on the bed and cry. So one fine evening she scratched my face, grabbed my wallet, and kicked me out. I went off like a lost lamb.'

Would it never stop? Rugby was still a thousand miles off.

'A couple of days later,' he continued, with a catch in his voice, 'I found myself, hungry and red-eyed in the sun, sitting on the kerb of the Le Moyne sidewalk. Opposite was a big, pink building, something between a pagoda and a county-jail, with a notice-board over the portal: "All, All Are Welcome!" – but welcome to what it didn't say, and I didn't much care. I only needed some place to sit down and do a bit more crying. I crossed the street, went into the lobby, and listened. It sounded like a lecture. I'm good at sitting through lectures, looking interested and thinking my own thoughts. To have someone else talking and the audience listening helps in a way to isolate my mind... Ever go to lectures to think your own thoughts?'

'No,' I said, 'I prefer railway trains. But you don't give me a chance.'

He waved the interruption aside. 'I took a seat at the back and had a look around me. An enormous cool Gothic hall with great banks of flowers and coloured lanterns, and a smell of too much incense, and a screwy congregation – screwy even for California. I learned later that it was the temple of Simon Magus Redivivus. Ever read the *Acts of the Apostles*, by the way? Tells you a lot about Simon Magus. Well, on the side of the chancel there was a choir of women, dressed to look like doves, in white feather costumes – and a battery of African drums was being beaten to a tricky rhythm where the altar should have been. That was all right, but what I didn't like was the stained-glass windows with wide-open pairs of yellow eyes glaring at me, and the creepy-looking mosaics in blue, black and white on the walls. The boss of the show was a short, square, swarthy fellow, in evening dress and a gold crown, who stood bang upright on a low throne. And a bevy of chorus-girls, dressed in nylon and tinsel, squatted around him on little stools.

'Well, I had a good cry, and blew my nose and began thinking about whom to touch for money; I felt sure I must know someone in the city besides Louella. I was racking my brains for the name of the fellow with whom I'd been working when I was in the Security Police at Brussels. Nice city, Brussels. Ever been there, by the way? Said he was a Los Angeles garage proprietor. Irving Something-or-other – and it began with a *Sch* – big fellow with rimless glasses. I couldn't get it, but went on trying hard until, suddenly, I was aware of a great booming noise from the chancel. It sounded like the fellow in evening dress being angry with someone; but I didn't know him and he couldn't have known me, so I didn't take it personally. I went on thinking: "Wasn't it Schellingman or Schellinger or Schlaffinger, or something of the sort...? I must have a search through the phone-book." The voice grew angrier and angrier, until I realized at last that I was the goat. I looked up, and he accused me of being a hostile influence. Shouted that I was breaking the sacred communion of gnosis – he used that word, I remember – and I had better scram because he was the Standing One, immortal and invincible and unassailable...

'So I rose to my feet, feeling a little less like a lost lamb, and pointed out that the notice-board said "All, All are Welcome!" and that I wasn't used to being bawled out – and, what was more, I didn't believe he was any less mortal or vincible than the next man. This put my lord Simon on his mettle, and he roared again into the microphone: "I am the Standing One! He who stood, stands, and will ever stand! Step up here, worm, and make obeisance at my throne!" When I told him that I'd come up the aisle and punch his nose for him if he liked, he laughed in a god-like way and informed me that nobody could strike the Standing One. "You cannot reach me," he boomed, "your feet will stick to the floor."

'I didn't like this. I marched boldly up the aisle towards that ugly face at the other end, but each step was more difficult to take than the last. The congregation were silently and solidly behind him, willing me to get back to my seat. I felt as if I were lugging my legs through liquid clay. I struggled another inch or so, and then stuck dead. And I hadn't even got half-way.

'Simon Magus sneered at me: "You see, you are helpless! Come now, I make you free to move. Step up and make obeisance!" I could feel the united congregation willing me: "Make obeisance, make obeisance to the Standing One!" And I had to lean back and dig in my heels to stop being propelled forward.

'I still meant to punch his nose, mind you, but my fists hung down at my sides like hundred-pound weights at the end of strings. And then – then I happened to look at one of the chorus-girls – Simon's gnostic wives they were, I learned afterwards: and, lo and behold, there sat Louella, peering down at me pityingly, as much as to say: " Domination, what do you know about that, you sap? The Standing One, *he* certainly understands domination." And she got up and whispered in Simon Magus's ear.

'"I'm coming to hit you!" I shouted at Simon. This confused the congregation. Most of them were still trying to push me ahead. A few were doing their damnedest to hold me back. I know that, because I felt their wills like spiders' webs snapping across my face as I rushed forward and mounted the chancel steps. I was within two yards of the throne before the going got sticky again. Simon Magus had regained control of the situation – called up his spiritual reserves and was hitting at me with all the voodoo in his vocabulary. I was stuck again: stuck, bogged and pinioned.

'He said: "You see, helpless as an infant! Come now, make obeisance, you big blubbering Limey! Make obeisance to the Standing One." Blubbering Limey! – that saved me! It was an insult Louella had put into his mouth. I recognized it. Then I lost my temper as I'd never lost it before. I drew both feet from the gnostic bog. I hauled up both my fists. The congregation began to get scared, I could feel it – even the spiritual wives and the doves in the choir, even the Standing One himself...'

He slowly discarded his overcoat and jacket, and slowly rolled up his shirt-sleeves. ' A red fire of anger swept over me,' he said earnestly. 'I took a step forward, I braced my right arm; I measured the distance... Ever boxed, by the way?'

That was a question I was not sorry to answer.

'Yes!' I yelled, as I delivered a furious right hook to his jaw.

He slumped back in his seat and passed out.

Presently, the stolid, red-faced ex-R.A.F. type, the correct bank-manager and the worthy headmaster in the clerical collar trooped in again and resumed their seats as if nothing had happened, each with only a casual glance at the inert body, and not a word of thanks to me.

'Who says that losing your temper won't get you anywhere?' I shouted at them bellicosely. 'Ever been in Egypt? *Ever had a guinea-worm?* EVER GONE BERSERK?'

But I felt like hell afterwards. Takes it out of you, that sort of thing.

A Bicycle in Majorca

It was not always so. Majorca used to be the most crime-free island in Europe. When I came back here with my family shortly after World War II, one could still hang one's purse on a tree and return three months later to find its contents intact. Unless, of course, someone short of change had replaced the small bills with a larger bill of equal value.

I am wasting this morning in the draughty corridors of the Palma Law Courts, because of my son William's 'abstracted' bicycle. He lent it to his younger brother, Juan, a year ago, when Juan's own bicycle... But forget Juan's bicycle for the moment and focus on William's. We imported both of them from England. The Spaniards certainly know how to ride bicycles; they are heroic racing cyclists, and the mortality among leaders of the profession is a good deal higher than among bullfighters. A recess at the back of the Palma Cycling Club provides a shrine for one of its members killed on a mountain road during the Tour of Spain – his pedals and shoes hung up beneath a plaque of St Christopher, with candles perpetually burning. Other members, who have died in lesser contests, are not so commemorated. But we British at least know how to *make* bicycles. I hasten to say that I am not criticizing Spanish workmanship. The British just happen to be experts in this particular trade; they even export vast quantities of bicycles to the choosy United States. The Spanish government will not, of course, agree that anyone else in the world can make anything better than Spaniards do, and surely a government's business is to foster faith in the nation's industrial proficiency? This attitude, however, makes it difficult for a Spaniard or a foreign resident in Spain – here comes the point – to import a British bicycle, especially when Spanish sterling reserves are low. Such a person must fill out fifteen forms in quintuplicate, supplying all his own vital statistics, with those of his relations in at least the nearer degrees, and showing just cause why he should be allowed a British bicycle (despite the hundred-per-cent Spanish import duty) instead of a much better, locally manufactured machine, which can be bought at half the cost. When he has waited fifteen months for an answer, while sterling reserves continue to fall, the chances are that the answer will be: 'We lament to inform you that last year's bicycle import quota has already been satisfied; we therefore advise you to fill out the necessary forms in quintuplicate for the present year's quota' – the year which, as a matter of fact, ended three months before. The most painless, therefore, way to import a British bicycle, as I learned from a friendly clerk at the Town Hall, is to arrive with it at the frontier, prepared to pay the import duty in cash, and insist on entry.' ✦

'If you are accompanied by children,' said the friendly clerk, 'there should be no trouble. All Spaniards are sympathetic toward fatigued fathers of families who have taken long journeys by train.'

'And if, by ill luck, I hit on an exception?'

'Then try a frontier post farther up the Pyrenees. On occasion, the officials at remote posts have no information about the rate of payment due from residents of Spain for imported bicycles. If the traveller happens to be a fatigued father of a family, they may well advise him – this has, in fact, happened – to rub a little mud on the machine and so convert it into an old one. His son can then ride across the frontier as a summer tourist.'

It's a long story... At any rate, we got William's bicycle to Majorca legally enough. That was in 1949, and no immediate trouble ensued. The British bicycle was much admired, for the solidity of its frame and for being the only one on the island with stainless-steel wheel rims and spokes, brakes that really braked, and an efficient three-speed gearshift. Then, around 1951, British, French, and American travellers accepted the fantasy of Majorca as the Isle of Love, the Isle of Tranquillity, the Paradise where the sun always shines and where one can live like a fighting cock on a dollar a day, drinks included. A tidal wave of prosperity struck these shores, and though statistics show that a mere three per cent of the Paradise-seekers return, there are always millions more where they come from. Which means, of course, that thieves, beggars, dope peddlers, confidence tricksters, gigolos, adventuresses, perverts, inverts, deverts, and circumverts come crowding in, too, from all over the world – of whom no less than ninety-seven per cent stay. Their devious activities place unreasonable burdens on the shoulders of the gentle Civil Guards. Repeat 'gentle'. The Civil Guards are, by and large, gentle, noble, correct, courageous, courteous, incorruptible, and single-minded. They are probably the sole Spaniards without the national inferiority complex about not being bullfighters, which attacks even racing cyclists. You are earnestly advised to refrain from laughing at the Civil Guards' curiously shaped patent-leather helmets and calling them 'comic-opera'. This antique headgear usually covers real men.

A Civil Guard barracks stands just around the corner from our Palma apartment. Conditions inside are pretty austere, the living quarters being not unlike those in the prison recently demolished near Boston – what was it called? The one where they had so many mutinies? I know two or three of the Guards there, and my family has a standing invitation to their annual show on March 1st (the Day of the Angel of the Guard), which is really quite something. So when, one evening in 1952, William's bicycle was stolen from the entrance hall of our apartment house – we live on the second floor – I went straight to a Guard, whom I remembered as a fat and dirty baby back in 1929, and asked him for immediate action. He called a plainclothes colleague, whose children had been at school with mine, and sent him down to the gipsy camp by the gasworks. (One early sign of Majorcan prosperity was an influx of undisciplined and picturesquely filthy gipsies from the south of Spain.) The camp, consisting of low, unmortared, doorless stone shelters, roofed with driftwood, rags, and odd sheets of rusty metal, is where one would normally search for stolen bicycles. On this occasion a blank was drawn. But as the plainclothes Guard, trudging back, came within sight of the barracks – its entrance inscribed 'All for the Fatherland' – a bicycle shot across the road out of control, brushed past him, and piled up against a lightpole. Its rider, a half-witted young man from Minorca, was severely injured – and so was William's bicycle. Unaccustomed to a three-speed gear, the poor fellow had changed down as he passed the barracks, without ceasing to pedal, had broken a cog in the gearbox, and thus lost his head, his balance, his consciousness, and his freedom. I had to sign a long charge against the Minorcan and also swear to the bicycle before being allowed to take it back. 'Mind you,' said the lieutenant, 'this machine must be produced in evidence when the criminal comes up for trial. Since we know you well, you may keep it temporarily, but look after it with care!'

The wave of prosperity had caused such a fearful bottleneck in judicial activity that the case is still on the waiting list. Prisoners are allowed bail, but the Minorcan could not even afford to pay for the damage done to William's bicycle, so if he has not succumbed to his injuries, I imagine some prison or other holds him yet. All I can say is that the local press keeps silence on the subject. A young English acquaintance of mine saw the wrong side of a Palma jail not long ago; he was charged with being drunk and in possession of a lethal weapon. When the Captain General released him, in return for some obscure favour from the British Consul, I heard a lot about that jail. A prisoner could earn a day's remission of sentence for every full day of voluntary work (this meant plaiting the palm-leaf baskets, which have 'Souvenir of Majorca' and a few flowers stitched on in coloured raffia, for tourists), also two days' remission for overtime on Sundays and national holidays. The only other inmate, besides the Englishman, who refused to work was a Valencian pickpocket, found guilty of several delinquencies and sentenced to a stretch totalling a hundred and eighty years. From my friend's description, it seemed a very old-fashioned jail as regards bedding, plumbing, and social arrangements – 'pure eighteenth-century, a regular collectors' piece'. But card-playing, drink, unimproving (i.e., non-devotional) books, and American cigarettes were forbidden. No Majorcans figured among the eleven criminals with whom he shared the cell – they had to occupy the only three beds in four shifts – because Majorcans seldom commit crimes (unless smuggling be so regarded, which must remain an open question) and can always raise bail from near or distant relations.

Well, when the bicycle case comes up, perhaps even this year, and the Minorcan is given a ten-year sentence, he will already have cleared it off and be a free man again, with a trade at his fingers' tips, and money in his pocket – accumulated payment at one cent for each and every basket plaited, less deductions for an occasional coffee or shave. Meanwhile, we have repaired the bicycle, which had lost a pedal bar, and fitted it with a Spanish lamp and a Spanish front mudguard, the original ones having become casualties. The three-speed gear is hardly what it was, but the bicycle still runs, despite other accidents soon to be related.

Now, to speak of Juan's own bicycle, also legally imported – or very nearly so. We chose one of pillar-box red, for conspicuousness, because the wave of prosperity was mounting and we did not want it stolen. Being a perfectionist, Juan treasured that bicycle like the apple of his eye, treating it daily with oily rag, duster, and saddle soap. In an evil hour we entered him at – let us call it San Rococo – reputedly the best boys' school in Palma. Juan is a Protestant, and the worthy priests who run San Rococo hoped to steer him into the Catholic fold, as they had just steered in a little Dane, two little Germans, and another little Englishman. But Juan, who has inherited bitter black Protestant blood from both sides of his family, remained obdurate. The baffled priests withdrew their fatherly protection, and Juan was soon assaulted by a group of his classmates. It happened that England had just beaten Spain at association football, four goals to one, so these patriotic lads accused the English forwards, and Juan, of foul play. They kicked out two of his bicycle spokes, threw the top of his bell over a wall, wrecked his lighting dynamo, and made away with his pump. It should be explained that they were not Majorcans but sons of wave-of-prosperity Galicians, recently come to Palma, and that Spain's goalkeeper had been a Galician.

'Juvenile high spirits,' sighed Father Blas when I complained. 'It would be virtually impossible to discover the names of the culprits, because in San Rococo we do not encourage tale-bearing. Besides, your son's lack of co-operation in our Christian devotions...'

So Juan's bicycle was repaired at our expense, but it was stolen, early one Monday morning, from the school lockup inside the building while he was at his studies. I went to protest that same night. Father Blas beamed, and would not take the matter seriously. He had no doubt but that one of his sportive pupils was playing an innocent joke on my son. The solution – please God! – would appear the next day, and I need hardly disquiet myself, since the lockup was under the charge of a reliable seminarist. 'If it does not turn up tomorrow,' I said, 'please report the matter to the Civil Guard without delay. My wife and I are flying to Madrid tonight and cannot attend to it ourselves. Juan's is a distinctive bicycle, and even if it were repainted –'

'Not another word, my dear sir! What you say is perfectly logical,' cried Father Blas.

Juan's pillar-box-red bicycle was not returned by any sportive pupil. On the following Monday another bicycle was stolen, and on the Monday after that five more – all non-Protestant machines. On my return from Madrid, I went to see Father Blas again, and asked for news. Father Blas admitted to having taken no practical steps in the matter as yet, since the school had been engaged in a severe course of spiritual exercises (this was a sideswipe at the unco-operative Juan), but tomorrow, without fail, the reliable seminarist would advise the Civil Guard of the mysterious disappearances.

I said firmly that unless Juan got back his legally imported British bicycle within the next ten days, I should expect San Rococo College to repay me its value, which amounted to two thousand pesetas, including duty – or, say, fifty dollars. Father Blas shook hands warmly on my departure; he would write to me at once after a deliberation with his reverend colleagues. His answer came just before the end of term, enclosed with the school bill: a terse note to the effect that in the considered opinion of the lawyers retained by San Rococo College, the said college incurred no responsibility for the disappearance of bicycles from its lockup, since no particular charge had been made to scholars for the privilege of keeping them there during school hours.

One soon learns in Majorca never to sue for anything so unimportant as a bicycle. An action, I knew, would cost far more than the bicycle's value, and a year or two must elapse before the case would come to court; besides, as my barber pointed out when I discussed the matter with him, the Church always wins – always has won, except during the iniquitous Liberal regimes of the early nineteenth century and under the equally iniquitous Republic. So I simply took Juan away, wrote Father Blas a courteous letter thanking him for the care he had lavished on my son's education, and omitted to pay the school fees. It cuts both ways: San Rococo would never sue me – an action would cost them far more than the value of the school fees, and my counterclaim for the bicycle would do the college no good, especially if our lawyer cited the six other thefts as evidence of negligence.

Since then, Juan has taken most of his lessons at home, but attends French classes at the *Alliance Française*. And William, now being educated in England, has lent him his bicycle during term-time. 'And if you ever forget to fasten it with a chain and padlock while I'm away, I'll kill you!'

This brings us to February 1957, when I gave some lectures in the States. My Majorcan friends were anxious about my voyage to that land of gangsters, neurotics, Red Indians, and sheriffs' posses, so familiar to them from the cinema; the more pious of them, I believe, burned candles on my behalf to their favourite saints. I had a clamorous welcome when I returned home bearing my sheaves with me – candy, nylons, rock-'n'-roll records, Polaroid film, ballet slippers, a Panamanian shrunken head – and a respectful salutation in the local press. To my relief, I found William's bicycle safely chained and padlocked to the newel post at the bottom of our staircase.

At eight o'clock next morning, as I dressed unhurriedly for breakfast (to be followed by a revision of Juan's Latin exercises done in my absence), I was startled by a yell and a fearful crash. I assumed that Juan had been celebrating the shrunken head in a truly Indian orgy and had accidentally knocked over the crockery cupboard. 'Stop it!' I shouted.

Juan appeared, looking scared. 'It's outside,' he said. 'I think they must be fighting again.'

Two years ago, the staircase of our apartment house had been the scene of a sanguinary battle. A respectable Majorcan couple living on the fourth floor had objected to the constant flamenco singing of a servant girl employed by a non-Majorcan woman living below them. In Majorca, nobody sings or dances flamenco except gipsies and girls in the red-light district and occasional American lady tourists who buy castanets and attend (let us call it) Pascualita Pastís's School of Spanish Dancing to justify the shawls, tortoise-shell combs, and earrings they have bought in Seville. The Majorcan couple called the flamenco-singing girl by a bad name. She flew at them, bit the wife's hand to the bone, and broke the husband's ankle. Her employers, who hated the Majorcan couple – their old aunt's venerable sewing machine shook the ceiling above them far into the night, and their young child played at ninepins all day – did nothing by way of dissuasion. The incident gave our street quite a bad name.

But this can hardly be another fight, I thought, as I hurriedly put on my slippers. The flamenco singer and her mistress had moved away long ago, and the whole building was respectable again. We were the only non-Majorcans left, so far as I knew.

I ran out of the apartment and stood on the landing. As I touched the iron banisters, a drop of blood fell on my hand and I heard a gurgling noise overhead. I looked up. A young man with contorted features, glaring eyes, and a bleeding forehead stood poised on the banisters one floor above me. He was about to leap down the well for the second time. I shouted in Spanish: 'Get off from there, and behave in a Christian manner!' – but he screamed and jumped. I made a grab at him as he flashed past. His weight was too much; down he went to the bottom of the well, struck the bicycle with the same crashing noise that had startled me only a minute before, rolled over, and lay still.

This second attempt at suicide looked pretty successful; all I know about first aid is how to apply a tourniquet above a gun shot wound in a limb – I learned that during World War I – and how to administer morphia if anything worse has happened. So I ran downstairs, then out of the front hall and around the corner to the Civil Guard barracks. I reported, panting, to the Guard on duty: 'A man has just tried to kill himself outside my apartment door. Please fetch a doctor.'

'One moment, sir! Do you wish to make a charge? If so, you must wait until the office opens; the desk sergeant has not yet breakfasted.'

'No, no, man! He may be dying, and though I regret disturbing the sergeant's breakfast –'

'Is the individual personally known to you?'

'No.'

'Does he seem to be a foreigner?'

'I could not say. The important thing is to fetch a doctor.'

'I cannot take that upon myself. Who would pay him? Why not fetch a doctor yourself? Try the nursing home down the road. It would surely be quicker than waking the sergeant and asking him to wake the lieutenant.'

I saw the force of his argument, and hurried to the nursing home. By chance, a car labelled 'MEDICO' had just drawn up there. I buttonholed the driver as he got out: 'Please, Doctor, come at once to my house – no more than a hundred yards away. A man has jumped from the third floor and hit the paved floor.'

'Let me alarm the nuns,' he said. 'Myself, I am only an analyst. My surgical training lies many years behind me.'

I thanked him for his kindness. Well, I thought, we had better get the madman on a mattress and under a blanket, if he is still alive. Returning to the scene of the incident, I found a great crowd of jabbering neighbours – but no victim. It seems that he had recovered enough to crawl up two flights of stairs and start making a third gallant attempt at suicide from the landing, but that Juan had summoned the rest of my family, who held him until help arrived. Then the midwife who lives in our building, and has had no lack of experience with excitable husbands, took charge.

When all had quieted down again, a couple of Civil Guards turned up. Since the would-be suicide proved to be a respectable Majorcan grocer, who blamed his fall on a sudden blackout caused by an anti-catarrhal injection given him by a French doctor in Marseilles a few days previously, the sergeant was able to report the incident as a regrettable loss of balance overcoming Don Pedro Tal y Cual while he descended the stairs from a business visit to friends on the third floor. 'Any important damage done to your machine,' the sergeant said to me, 'will be paid, naturally, by the unfortunate man himself – against whom, it is hoped, you will bring no charge.'

'No, no,' I answered. 'After all, he is our neighbour and a Palma man – not by any means to be suspected of criminal intent.'

'They take a lot of punishment, these British bicycles,' said the black-smith admiringly as he straightened the fork. 'If it had been one of ours, that grocer would not have bounced off the frame. By the way, how is the poor fellow?'

'Suffering from a headache, I am told, and a grazed elbow.'

'A miracle!'

'This is a very historic bike,' Juan told the blacksmith. 'It has sent one man to prison and saved another's life.'

A week had not passed before the bicycle was stolen from the lockup at the *Alliance Française* during one of Juan's evening classes. He went at once to the Civil Guard barracks and reported the loss. 'Run away, boy, you are far too young to make a proper charge,' he was told. 'Besides, the charge office is closed until tomorrow morning. Ask your professor to come here at about ten o'clock.'

Juan trailed miserably home, late for supper. 'William's bike is stolen,' he managed to force out between sobs, 'and William said he'd kill me...'

'Wasn't it chained?'

'No, that's the worst of it. On the way to class, I remembered that I'd forgotten the chain and padlock, so I biked back, but then I couldn't remember what it was I'd forgotten, so I whizzed down to the class again and hoped it would be all right. But it wasn't!'

We gave Juan some sausage and coffee, and then hurried to the port. The night boat to Barcelona had not yet sailed. I asked the Civil Guard sergeant at the barrier whether an English-type bicycle had come through, by any chance. 'We have just had one stolen,' I explained. 'Sometimes, they say, thieves steal bicycles and hurry them aboard at the last minute, aware that official charges cannot be made at this late hour.'

'No, sir. No such bicycle has passed through this barrier. But you are misinformed. This being an era of prosperity, the Barcelona fences are now interested only in stolen motor bicycles.'

'We shall never see that historic bike again,' Juan mourned. 'I can't face William when he comes home at Easter.'

Since bicycles are occasionally borrowed for a joy ride and then aban-doned, we went to the Lost Property Office at the Town Hall, where municipal policemen bring them in. No luck.

The man in charge advised us against reporting the loss to the Civil Guard. 'If they do find your bicycle, you may never get it back. It will be held in evidence until the case comes up in court.'

'Better that than never, surely?' I asked.

'A distinction without a difference, I fear, sir,' he answered gloomily.

I regret not taking his advice. Although by this time the Civil Guard had forgotten about the Minorcan prisoner, and associated the bicycle only with an attempted suicide, they made me put the loss on record. And the very next day Juan's best friend at the *Alliance Française* happened to spot the bicycle in a disreputable alley, some distance away, propped unattended against a wall. We celebrated the discovery with a chicken dinner. But a Civil Guard called soon afterward to inquire whether the bicycle had been recovered. We reported that – God be praised! – it was in our possession once more.

'My friend Pepe found it in Oil Street,' said Juan.

'Who is this Pepe? What is his surname? Where does he live?'

Today I have been ordered to appear before the judge in the matter of 'a summary which instructs itself concerning the ninety-sixth bicycle abstraction of the current year; on the penalty of the prescribed fine.' It occurs to me that our new Captain-General may have started tightening things up and demanding vengeance on bicycle thieves, and that the lieutenant of the Civil Guard may suspect Juan's friend Pepe of abstracting the bicycle himself. I don't know whether the difference between abstraction and robbery is the same in the States as in Spain. Here, if the lockup had been really locked, or if Juan had remembered to chain the bicycle, and if the thief had then used force to possess himself of it, why, that would have been robbery, and worth several more years in jail.

I don't see Pepe anywhere around, nor do I expect to see him marched up presently between a couple of Civil Guards. Though not a respectable Majorcan (which would exempt him from all suspicion), he happens to be even better placed: his father is the new Civil Guard captain at the other barracks, a fire-eater from Estremadura.

Evidence of Affluence

IF I DO not know what degree of mutual confidence exists in the United States between income-tax official and private citizen, this is so because the question does not immediately concern me. I have never in my life been asked to fill out an American income-tax return; as a British non-resident I have all my American earnings painlessly taxed at source, and there the matter ends. In Great Britain, of which by an ingenious legal quirk I am 'deemed to be a resident, though permanently domiciled abroad', my earnings are also taxed at source; but I am at least allowed to employ an income-tax consultant, or rather a pair of them – Messrs Ribbons & Winder of Aquarium Road, Rhyl – in my defence. Every year they send me a form to fill in (we British fill in, not out, I don't know why) and discreetly advise me how, by clever albeit legal devices, to get a chunk of my forfeited earnings refunded. This year, however, they took twelve months to conclude their business, because the Bank of England ('Safe as the Bank of England!') admitted that it had lost certain documents relevant to my case – the Government meanwhile enjoying an interest-free loan of my money. Unfair, surely, to Graves, who left his country only for his country's good?

Nevertheless, Mr Bloodsucker, as we British affectionately call the income-tax collector, is a decent man at heart and, not being himself responsible for the Schedule he is called upon to implement, does his best to mitigate its cruelty. Long ago, while a struggling poet, still domiciled as well as resident in Great Britain, I used to visit Mr Bloodsucker once a year, and actually looked forward to our confabulations. He would beam at me through his horn-rims and say: 'Now, don't forget to claim for the upkeep of your bicycle, young man – or the heating of your work-room, not to mention library subscriptions. And, I suppose, you take in some learned journals? You can recover a bit from that source. By the bye, are you sure you are not contributing in part to the support of an aged relative? Oh, and look here! This claim for postal and telegraphic expenses is remarkably low. Why not add another couple of pounds for good measure? Doubtless you have left something out.'

You see: in Britain the theory is (or at any rate was in those halcyon

'Twenties) that since the simple blue-jeaned or fray-cuffed citizen, as opposed to the clever-clever natty-suited businessman, seldom, if ever, tries to cheat the government, he should be discouraged from cheating himself. And my Mr Bloodsucker possessed great moral rectitude: if he found an anonymous note on his desk informing on Mr Ananias Doe or Mrs Sapphira Roe as unlawfully concealing taxable income, he always (I was told) would blush and tear it into a thousand fragments. To be brief, the British system of income-tax collection was not then, and is not now, fraught – have I ever used that word before in my life? Never, but here goes! – *fraught* with so much drama as that of certain Latin countries, where it is tacitly understood that only a fool or a foreigner will disclose more than a bare tenth of his net earnings. And where, also, the authorities have no effective means of discovering what these earnings are, since many a – I hesitate to say 'every' – sensible businessman, besides keeping at least two sets of books, running at least two secret bank accounts, and forgetting to record cash payments, has the collusive support of a large family and of the political party or racket to which he belongs. Income-tax sleuths in those countries are therefore forced to rely on what is called 'evidence of affluence', meaning the worldly style in which a man lives, and make a preliminary assessment of ten times the amount they hope to recover. Then battle is joined and victory goes to whichever side has displayed the greater strength of character.

Since 1954 I have become liable to Spanish income-tax and, although an honest English fool, take care to offer the minimum evidence of affluence. Indeed, while I occupied that Palma apartment, I found income-tax a splendid excuse for wearing old clothes, shaving every other day, dining at the humble fonda round the corner rather than at the neon-lighted *El Patio* or *El Cantábrico*, and living an obscure, almost anti-social, life. For Señor Chupasangre (Mr Bloodsucker's Majorcan counterpart) lurked behind the cash-desk of every expensive restaurant in Town, and behind the curtains of every night club as well. Moreover, if I had joined the Tennis Club and bought a shiny new car, a motor launch, or even an electric gramophone, Señor Chupasangre would have heard of it the next day through his very efficient intelligence service.

Well, I must stop talking about myself – there is no more threadbare subject in the world than a writer's finances – and get on with my story about the Sánchez family, whose apartment adjoined ours. Since Majorcans always talk at the top of their voices (I once dared ask why? and was told: 'lest anyone should think us either ill or frightened') and since the party-walls of Palma apartment-houses are extraordinarily thin, for the sake alike of economy and of neighbourliness, I can describe in faithful detail a domestic scene which I did not actually witness. You think this impossible, and suggest that the french-windows of both apartments must have been wide open all the time? Permit me to sneer! Half an inch of sandstone, thickened to three-quarters by twin coats of plaster and white-wash does not provide adequate insulation even against a devoutly mumbled Sánchez rosary.

Don Cristóbal Sánchez, the smart young owner of a newly-established furniture factory, and his plump, brown-eyed, sallow-skinned young wife, Doña Aina, with incongruously beblonded hair and a heavy gold crucifix dangling on her bosom, always greeted us politely on the stairs, however often we might meet in the course of the day; they also borrowed from us with monotonous regularity methylated spirit, matches, bread, electric light bulbs, needles, thread, iodine, aspirins, and our step-ladder, and came calling at unreasonable hours, frequently when we were in bed, to ask whether they might use our telephone for a long-distance call to Barcelona. The family Sánchez owned a radio-set and a baby, both shockingly audible; but I persuaded Doña Aina not to turn on the radio during my work-hours, except on red-letter feast days (of which the Spanish calendar, to my Protestant way of thinking, contains far too many). The baby I could disregard: when other people's babies are teething, their wails are almost a pleasure to one who has suffered as much as I have from the sorrows of his own large family. Besides, teething babies do not cry in any tune, or use words intelligible enough to interrupt my inner voice and so destroy the rhythm of what I am writing.

Twelve years ago, before the Majorcan real-estate boom began, Aina's father, a scion of the Aragonese nobility who came over here in 1229 with King James the Conqueror and drove out the Moors, was forced to sell the family palace in Palma, and two heavily mortgaged country estates, to satisfy his deceased uncle's creditors. The prices which they realized were pitiful. Aina's father, however, managed to keep a row of fourteenth-century houses in the centre of Palma, which the Town Council subsequently commandeered and pulled down to make room for a new arcade lined with tourist shops. This brutal act did the poor fellow a lot of good, because under the Rent Restriction Law his tenants were paying him at a rate fixed in 1900, when the peseta was still a silver coin and a labourer's daily wage; it is now not worth two U.S. cents. The generous compensation awarded for the sites saved Aina's father from the poorhouse, and he even started speculating in new suburban building schemes; though not with much judgement, as will appear.

Aina, in the circumstances, was lucky to marry as well as she did. Don Cristóbal comes of respectable, if hardly resplendent, lineage; and has looks, industry, optimism and money to recommend him. Not that Aina had no previous offers; we heard from our maid's brother, who works in a fashionable El Terreno bar, that she was engaged for three years to her second cousin, Don Gregorio de la Torre Oscura y Parelada – whom we never met, but about whom Cristóbal teased Aina pretty often with loud guffaws of laughter. Cristóbal's major failing, it should be emphasized, was his self-satisfaction, complicated by an inability to keep his large, neatly-moustached mouth shut. We had overheard Doña Aina making some pretty caustic remarks on this trait. Our maid's brother described for us the precise means by which Cristóbal contrived to detach Aina from Don Gregorio. Briefly, it was as follows. Owing to the impossibility of forming new political parties under Franco's rule, Majorcan youth had found an alternative outlet for its intellectual energies: the ultra-religious group known as 'Mau-Mau'. Aina's parents were among its founders. Mau-Mau was ascetically ultra-Catholic, aghast at the present decadence of manners, and run somewhat on the catch-your-buddy principles of Moral Rearmament: with earnest parties called together amid delightful surroundings, and an active policy of infiltration into high society and the learned professions. Ordinary Catholics, such as our maid's brother, were offended by the Mau-Mau's custom of referring to the Deity as *Mi Amo*, 'my Master'; and the word 'Mau-Mau' stands, he told us, for *Mi Amo Unico, Mi Amo Universal*, 'My only Master, my Universal Master'.

Cristóbal Sánchez, it seems, joined the Mau-Mau and volunteered to act as the Group's secret watchman at the Club Náutico, our local yacht club, keeping tabs on not-too-trustworthy young Mau-Mau members there. His motive may only be guessed at, not roundly asserted. All we can say for sure is that though Don Gregorio had also joined the Group as a means of conciliating Aina's parents, his mind was not wholly bent on heavenly things. He used to get drunk at *Tito's* and *Larry's* and *Mam's*, kept disreputable company, preferred American jazz to the *Capella Clásica*, consorted at the *Granja Reus* with a Mexican divorcée, and in his cups used to sneer at Mau-Mau by making an irreverent single-letter change in one of the words that form its nickname – but our maid's brother would not disclose which. Cristóbal reported all this to Aina's father, as was his duty, and Don Gregorio found himself ignominiously expelled from the Group. Moreover, the Mau-Mau's *vigilante* squad, being authorized to take strong-arm action against such of their fellows as had fallen from Grace, waylaid him outside *Tito's* one night, pushed him into a taxi, drove him to a lonely building outside the town, and worked on him until dawn, with austere relish.

Aina, having already heard from a friend about the Mexican divorcée, shed no tears for Don Gregorio; he had nearly run through his inheritance, but refused to work and took her complaisance too much for granted – 'almost as if they had already married and put their honeymoon behind them.' She very sensibly switched to the more eligible Don Cristóbal. Having secured his law-degree, he was now embarking on a prosperous business career, kept an *esnipé* (or fourteen-foot sailing dinghy) at the Club Náutico, and also enjoyed conveying her on the pillion-seat of his motor-scooter to beauty spots not easily accessible by sea. After an apotheosistical scene in the Club Náutico – the sordid details of which I must withhold – Don Gregorio shook the dust of Palma (and very dusty it can be in the sirocco season) from his pointed shoes, and left for Madrid, where he had relatives. 'But listen to me well, you assassin, you pig,' he warned Cristóbal, 'the day will come when I shall return and settle accounts with you!'

And return he did. One hot morning in May, as I sat at my table patiently translating Lucan's *Pharsalia*, and begging my inner voice to disregard the gramophone across the street playing 'La Paloma', a very loud ring sounded through the wall of Cristóbal and Aina's unusually quiet apartment.

'A beggar,' I thought. 'Beggars always press the bell-push twice as hard as tradesmen or friends. In half-a-minute he'll be pushing at mine...'

I waited, but no beggar appeared. Instead, Doña Aina hurried out to the Sánchez terrace, which is separated from ours by an iron railing. My work-room mirror showed her flattened against the house wall, clasping and unclasping her hands in obvious anxiety. Cristóbal, I guessed, had looked through the grilled spy-hole of the front-door and signalled for her to vanish; so I laid down my pen and listened.

Cristóbal was greeting the visitor in his high tenor voice with every indication of pleasure: 'Why, Gregorio, what a magnificent surprise! I thought you were still in Madrid. Welcome home!'

To my relief, I could distinguish an answering warmth in Gregorio's resonant baritone: 'It is indeed delightful to shake you by the hand, Cristóbal, after so long a time. I have been thinking of you often, remembering the trotting track, and the pigeon-shooting, and our *esnipé-races* across the harbour, and all the high times we had before... in fact, before...'

In the mirror I watched Doña Aina's face, alert and troubled, as Cristóbal replied: 'Gregorio, I honour your nobility of mind. That you deign to visit my house after the painful threats you uttered at the Club Náutico on that sad day, suggests that you have at last forgiven me for my great felicity. Aina is now not only my wife but has given birth to a precious little boy.'

An anxious moment, but Gregorio, it seemed, took the blow stoically enough. 'Well,' he said, 'your behaviour was a trifle violent, I must confess – when Aina and I had been courting for three years and made all our wedding preparations; but, of course, now that your theft has been legalized, and crowned with the registered birth of a new citizen, what can I do but felicitate you in a truly Christian spirit? Not another word, man! Besides, Aina is by no means the only girl in Spain. In fact, though I do not mean to insult either of you by invidious comparisons, I have lately formed strong relations with (some might say) an even more intelligent and beautiful girl, of a better family also – if that were possible. We met at

Seville during the Fair. As it happens, she also is a native of this city, and loves me madly.'

Ice having thus been broken, the two former rivals grew still more affectionate.

'My heartiest congratulations, dear friend!'

'Accepted with enthusiasm... The only defect in this new situation is, however, the exaggerated wealth of my fiancée's family. It is a constant trouble to me.'

'Well, Aina's family do not suffer from *that* defect, at least. On the contrary, they come to me every second Monday, asking for material support.'

'Naturally! Aina was a prize that demanded handsome payment. But your furniture business flourishes, I understand?'

'Like a row of runner-beans: I am pretty well off now, thanks be to God and the tourist boom. Thirty-three new hotels, sixty new *residencias,* and eighty-four *pensiones* are building this winter! But, dear Gregorio, if your fiancée is so deeply attached to you, why should her family's wealth discommode you?'

'Don't pretend to be a fool, friend Cristóbal; clearly, they wish to assure themselves that their daughter will continue to live as she is accustomed to live – with servants, parties, visits, tennis, plentiful new clothes, an hour at the hairdresser's every day, and so forth. However, she's a match for that old egoist, her father. She threatens to enter a nunnery if she may not marry me. So he has given way, with bad grace. But first I must make a respectable quantity of money in my new job; that is his firm condition.'

'You really have a job, Gregorio? Love indeed works miracles!'

'Oh, not much of a job; hardly, indeed, one to boast about, or even mention in polite society. But it has certain possibilities.'

'Black market, I presume?'

'No, no: my future father-in-law, Don Mariano Colom y Bonapart, is so highly connected that he would never think of damaging his reputation by putting me into any dubious business.'

'No? I suppose that the fortune he made a few years ago, smuggling penicillin from Tangier to our hospitals – so-called penicillin that required an act of faith to make it work – has now been decently invested in those fantastic tourist novelties? He must be prospering.'

'Well, of course, nobody ever proved that he smuggled penicillin – a most charitable business, by the way – still less that it was ineffective when properly used. I have no doubt but that the doctors themselves adulterated their supplies to make them go further. At any rate, the case against him has been officially dropped... Oh, yes, the novelties you mention are doing well enough, especially among conducted groups of Germans – best of all, the diverting little dog that cocks its leg. Don Mariano is now considering more austere lines for the English; he has consulted an

English judge who is here on holiday.'

'But your job, Gregorio?'

'Forgive me, Cristóbal; I am ashamed. It is with one of the Ministries – too boring and distasteful to discuss.'

'Yet it carries its traditional perquisites?'

'Of course! Would Don Mariano have arranged it for me otherwise?'

'You seem a trifle gloomy, Gregorio. Will you drink a nipkin of brandy?'

'I don't drink, for the present. Don Mariano would not favour an alcoholic son-in-law. It will have to be an orangeade, I fear.'

'Why not a Coca-Cola? I'll fetch you one from our electric refrigerator.'

'So you own a refrigerator, Cristóbal?'

'Thanks be to the Virgin! We are not among those who cool their butter in a pail let down the well!'

'It is very pleasant to hear of your increased earnings and domestic amelioration, dear Cristóbal. This refreshing Coca-Cola is conclusive evidence of prosperity... Friends tell me that you gave a grand party the other day at the Hotel Nacional?'

'Ah, I wish you had been there! How the champagne corks popped! It was to celebrate the christening of our son.'

'That must have cost you a capital!'

'It did, and Aina's parents contributed not a single peseta of all the five thousand. I can speak freely to you – Aina is away at the moment, being fitted for an evening dress. By the bye, she still thinks very highly of you.'

To judge from the tightening of Doña Aina's lips, Cristóbal would pay for this remark as soon as Gregorio left. But she continued in hiding, though I could see that the sun's glare was bothering her. I quietly opened my french-windows, went out and, with a polite smile, handed her a pair of sun-glasses through the railing. Doña Aina looked startled at this unexpected loan, but gratefully slipped them on.

Gregorio was saying: 'Your wife's opinion flatters me. And you could hardly expect much help from those Mau-Mau simpletons, her parents. They have suffered several financial reverses of late, or so I hear from my lawyers: particularly their need to compensate the former tenants of that new apartment-house. What an unfortunate investment it proved!'

'You are altogether right!' Cristóbal agreed. 'Your prospective father-in-law palmed it off on my actual father-in-law only just in time. I trust Don Mariano will not be sent to jail when the Inquiry publishes its findings on the cause of the building's collapse.'

'Don Mariano in jail!' laughed Gregorio. 'What a ridiculous thought! No, no! The Inquiry has already been closed. You see, the plans were the City Architect's, and a City Architect is above suspicion; and if Don Dionisio Gómez, the building-contractor, economized in cement and used defective beams, how was Don Mariano to know? Don Dionisio emigrated to Venezuela, I understand, before Aina's father could sue him...'

'Of course, that was a great blow to us. But, by the mercy of God, no one perished in the disaster, except the Ibizan widow without relatives; all the other tenants were away, watching the Corpus Christi procession. As for the automobile in the garage below, which got smashed to pieces when the four apartments with their furniture fell on top of it – fortunately, that old museum-piece was Don Dionisio's own! In the circumstances, he will hardly dare claim compensation.'

'I agree, my dear Cristóbal. It is, as a matter of fact, about that automobile that I have heard an amusing story. You yourself sold it to Don Dionisio in 1953, as I recall?'

'Exactly; and very glad I was to rid myself of it, at so good a price, too. Not only were the brakes and the steering defective, but someone warned me just in time that, under the new income-tax system, possession of an automobile would be regarded as evidence of affluence. I acted at once...'

'That was smart! But, Cristóbal, what about your other signs of affluence – the 5000-peseta christening party, that electric refrigerator, this vacuum cleaner, your honoured wife's evening dresses, the English baby-carriage in the hall, the financial help you are known to give your father-in-law? Don't you realize that these must inevitably catch the attention of Señor Chupasangre, the Chief Inspector?'

'Aina and I laugh at him. We pass for poor folk; I am careful to keep no automobile.'

'But Cristóbal, you do!'

'*I* keep an automobile? What joke is this?'

'I mean the one which got crushed by the deciduous apartments.'

'Idiot, I sold that to Don Dionisio four years ago!'

Gregorio said slowly and clearly: 'Yes, you sold it, but Don Dionisio never registered that change of ownership at the Town Hall; consequently it remains in your name. As I see it, you are liable for income-tax during the whole of 1954, 1955, 1956 and 1957, at a high rate that is almost certain to be discussed between you and Señor Chupasangre.'

'The insect! How did you discover this trick?'

'I happened to consult the register at the Town Hall in the course of my business.'

'But, Gregorio, that is nonsense! The automobile has been Don Dionisio's, not mine, since 1953!'

'In the eyes of the Law it is still yours, pardon me. And Don Dionisio is not here to tell them otherwise.'

'Pooh!' blustered Cristóbal. 'Who says that I am liable to income-tax? I can show Señor Chupasangre my business accounts – the more pessimistic official ones, naturally – to prove that I do not qualify. If he asks me, I shall swear that the refrigerator and the vacuum cleaner were wedding presents, and that the English baby-carriage has been lent us by my sister. As for the party and Aina's evening dresses...'

'Do you take Señor Chupasangre and his colleagues for fools?'

'Why not?'

But Doña Aina had already scented danger. I saw her involuntarily clap a hand over her own mouth, since she could not clap it over her husband's.

Gregorio protested: 'Cristóbal, dear friend, as I have been trying to tell you throughout this pleasant conversation, Aina is no longer anything to me, except your faithful wife and the mother of your little son; yet I owe to myself, and to my Ministry, the performance of a sacred duty. For, granted that I may be the fool you call me, this new job of mine...'

'Gregorio! What are you saying, man?'

'... this new job, however distasteful it may be at times, carries with it (as you suggested) certain traditional perquisites. By your leave, I shall call again officially tomorrow. Meanwhile, my best regards to your distinguished wife! Tell her how enchanted I am that she still remembers my name.'

The door slammed. Gregorio's footsteps could be heard retreating unhurriedly down the stairs.

In the mirror, I saw Doña Aina stoop to pick up a sizeable pot of pink geraniums. Would she drop it, *¡catacrok!*, on Gregorio's head as he emerged into the street?

But I should have known that this would not be Doña Aina's way. Instead, she flung wide open the french-window of her own apartment and stood for a moment with one foot advanced, the flower-pot poised low on her right palm, the left hand raised as though in a Falangist salute.

'Animal! Imbecile!' she cried, and let fly at Cristóbal with all her strength.

I stuffed a finger into each ear to drown the crash.

The French Thing

'WHO THE DEUCE put this foul French thing on my surgery table?'

Bella Nightingale took the crumpled magazine from him and studied the photographs over her breakfast plate. 'Oh, Lord,' she giggled, delightedly. 'Aren't they *horrors?*'

'I didn't ask for your aesthetic criticism,' Dr Nightingale snapped. 'I just wanted to know how that foul thing got on my surgery table. It certainly wasn't there last night, and Nurse Parker hasn't arrived yet.'

'Even if Nurse Parker *had* arrived, darling, you surely don't think she'd have given you so highly unsuitable a present? I know she adores you, but I can't see her risking her professional reputation by trying to get your mind working along lines like these... Oh, Harry, *do* look at this anatomical monstrosity of a female – and taken from such a queer angle, too!'

Dr Nightingale snatched the magazine back. 'For Heaven's sake, Bella, get a grip on yourself and answer my question!'

'Mrs Jelkes came early today – I don't suppose you noticed – because she's got a funeral at eleven o'clock. She dusted your surgery after first doing out the spare room. That oafish nephew of yours left it in a fearful mess the other morning when he scrambled back to Camp. My theory is that Mrs Jelkes found the passion parade under his pillow and thought she ought to warn you what sort of a lad he really is.'

Dr Nightingale's anger passed. 'Oh, well,' he sighed, 'I suppose that must be the explanation. It's her way of saying: "Don't invite Master Nicholas here again, or I'll get another job and tell the neighbours why." A pity! I hate sacrificing Nicholas to Mrs Jelkes's non-conformist conscience; but she's irreplaceable, I'm afraid. Or, at least, she's in a position to make herself so by blackmailing us. It'll be a bit awkward when Nicholas comes for another flying visit; I'll have to send him off and explain why he's no longer *persona grata*.'

'It's his own stupid fault. I'm sorry for young soldiers as a rule, but your Nicholas is a lazy, careless young dog, and you know it.'

'Do I? I'm relieved, at any rate, to know that he's a healthy heterosexual – one never can tell these days, especially when they write verse. Now, please burn it in the stove.'

'Can't. Mrs Jelkes is in the kitchen, and I don't want to give her the satisfaction of sniffing contempt at me.'

'Well, then hide it somewhere until she goes.'

The door-bell rang loudly and insistently.

'Road accident, by the noise,' said Dr Nightingale.

He was right. A lorry-driver with a gashed head and a dangling arm stood on the porch, supported by his mate.

As Dr Nightingale beckoned the pair in, the lorry-driver's mate fainted dead away across the threshold. 'He could never stand the sight of blood,' said the lorry-driver scornfully, 'this silly mucker couldn't!'

Nurse Parker had not yet appeared, so Bella Nightingale gulped down her coffee, shoved the magazine among a pile of weeklies stacked on the radio, and hurried into action by her husband's side.

In the middle of the confusion Nurse Parker's aunt rang up. She was grieved to say that Nurse Parker couldn't come that morning. Her bus had been run smack into by a lorry, and she was back in bed. 'No, no bones broken, praise the Lord! Only shock.'

It was lunch-time before the air cleared. Bella had taken Nurse Parker's place and, besides the familiar Saturday patients, a stream of walking wounded came in from the Summer Camp – sardine-tin cuts, infected midge-bites, and badly grazed knees.

'Where's that French thing, Bella?'

'I shoved it in among the magazines.'

'Oh, you did, did you?... Well, *now* we're in the soup right up to our necks!'

'Oh Lord, you don't mean that the Reverend Mrs Vicar... ?'

'I darned well do mean it. I happened to see her through my window, tripping down the garden path with the whole stack of magazines under her arm. Had you forgotten Mrs Jelkes's orders to hand them over to her on the last Saturday of every month?'

Bella laughed hysterically and then began to cry. 'Darling, we're socially ruined, and it's all my stupid fault! Mrs Vicar can't fail to go through the pile and when she comes across Nicholas's Parisian popsies, God, how the teacups will rattle and the kettle hiss in this frightful village! Mrs Jelkes has a far stricter code of honour than Mrs Vicar. She won't breathe a word unless Nicholas comes to stay here again. But Mrs Vicar...'

'You must rush across and get the thing back. Explain that an important paper got mixed up with the magazines.'

'She'd insist on finding it for me. No, our only hope is that she'll bang the whole lot along to the Cottage Hospital unread. Let's cross our fingers... Once it gets to the Hospital, we're safe. The Lady Almoner will find it and carry it home as a cosy reminder of her dead past. According to Dr MacGillicuddy, she was a photographer's model herself once, and not for face and ankles only.'

'*That* old hag? It must have been a long time ago; and I wouldn't trust her an inch, anyhow.'

'Harry... about your French thing...'

'Don't call it *my* French thing! Any new developments?'

'None. I've met Mrs Vicar several times since Saturday, and her manner is absolutely unchanged...'

'That's really very odd. You see... Well, I knew MacGillicuddy was a sportsman; so I rang him up at once at the Hospital, told him the story in confidence, and asked would he please see that the magazines got sent to his office, unsorted, the moment they arrived – not to the Lady Almoner. And it wasn't there, he swears.'

'Maybe the Vicar...'

'The Vicar was away last week-end.'

'Maybe his locum, the sandy-haired youth with pince-nez...'

'Maybe. He certainly preached a very odd sermon the next day on Jezebel and the dogs...'

'Maybe Dr MacGillicuddy himself...'

'Maybe. He's a bachelor. Anyhow, let's forget the unpleasant subject.'

'Bella... talking of that French thing. It occurs to me that possibly...'

'And to me! You mean what Mrs Vicar was telling us about the sudden gratifying increase in Sunday School attendance?'

'Exactly. Not girls, only boys. Four in all, including Harold Jelkes – and our little Robin Lostwithiel, of all children. She said that the dear laddies are so keen on Sunday School that they turn up half-an-hour early and play with her lonely little Evangeline.'

'Never underestimate the power of a woman, even at six years old.'

'This is worse than ever. If we're right, Evangeline is sure to be caught with the foul thing before long, and then it'll be traced to us. She'll open her baby-blue eyes wide and say: "Oh, I didn't think there was any harm in it, Mummy! Mrs Nightingale sent it us with the *Picture Posts* and things." We simply *must* get it back somehow, by fair means or foul. It'll be somewhere hidden among her toys.'

'Harry, how on earth do you expect me to burgle Evangeline's play-room?'

'I don't know. But it was you who got us into this mess. So you'd better get us out again pretty quick. Or else...'

Barbie Lostwithiel, extravagantly dressed and perfumed as usual, strolled in unannounced through the french-windows and kissed both the

Nightingales on either cheek, Continental fashion. Dr Nightingale rather liked this unconventional salute, especially as Bella didn't grudge it him.

'Chums,' Barbie said in a husky whisper, 'I do want your advice so badly. You know how I am with Robin, ever since I got sole custody. No lies, no secrets, no half-truths, all absolutely above-board between us twain. I know you don't approve altogether, but there it is! Well, a tiny little rift in the lute occurred last Sunday after lunch, when Robin cancelled our old-time ceremonial game of draughts and wanted to hurry off early to the Rectory. Of course, I had thought it a bit odd when he said the week before that he wanted to try Sunday School; but I didn't care to oppose him if that was his idea of fun. So this time I asked: "Bobbie, are you in love with Evangeline by any chance?" "No, Barbie, of course not," he said with that engaging blush of his, "but she has some very interesting photographs of ladies in a magazine from Paris. Ladies don't wear any clothes in Paris, you see, and I feel sort of happy looking at them just as they really are underneath. But I'm not to tell anyone, not a soul – of course you don't count, Barbie darling – in case Evangeline gets in a row with the Vicar. She stole it from the Hospital magazine collection."'

The Nightingales said nothing, but their fingers clenched and unclenched nervously.

Barbie Lostwithiel went on: 'I've been wondering what to do about it all the week. I don't in the least mind Bobbie's admiring the undraped female figure, so long as it's not misbehaving itself too shockingly – as I gather it isn't in this case, apart from a bit of candid acrobatic posturing. But I *do* mind his getting involved in a dirty little, sniggering, hole-and-corner Rectory peep-show – that *Turn of the Screw* Evangeline's clever contribution to the Church's standing problem of how to fill empty pews. Unfortunately, I can't confide in Mrs Vicar. She hates my guts as it is, because I'm a *divorcée* – even if I'm billed as the innocent party. I mean: I couldn't tell her what's in the air without breaking Robin's confidence and spoiling his faith in my absolute discretion. Besides, I'd be getting him in bad with the Sunday School gang. Harry, can't you, as the local physician, have a man-to-man talk with the Vicar? Say that a boy's father has been complaining; which would let Robin out nicely. *Please!*'

'Barbie, dearly as I may be supposed to love you and yours, I can't and won't do anything of the kind! The Vicar would toss me through his study window if I accused his innocent little daughter of keeping a… a *salon des voyeurs*, I suppose the official phrase would be. The Vicar played "lock" in the English Rugger pack only six years ago.'

So Bella Nightingale and Barbie Lostwithiel put their heads together. Their main problem was how to administer the doped chocolate without suspicion. Barbie solved that one easily. She borrowed the Church key from the sexton, on the pretext of putting two vasefuls of Madonna lilies from her garden on the Communion table; and, as she went out, paused briefly at the Rectory pew. There she hid the chocolate under Evangeline's prayer book – wrapped in a small piece of grimy exercise paper marked: 'Love from Harold Jelkes XXX.'

Bella, a certified dispenser before she married, had calculated the dose nicely. Soon after Sunday lunch, Mrs Vicar rang up to say that Evangeline was down with a violent tummy-ache and would Dr Nightingale be good enough to come at once?

Dr Nightingale answered that surely a simple stomach-ache... ? He was just off with his wife for a picnic on the Downs. Still, since poor wee Evangeline...

'Now's your heaven-sent chance, Bella,' he said, when Mrs Vicar had rung off.

'Oh, very well, if I must, I must,' said Bella. She had carefully not told him about the chocolate, because such a bad actor as he would be sure to give the game away. Besides, it was notoriously unethical for a doctor to charge fees for curing an ailment in the causing of which he had connived. Harry would certainly prefer not to know of her device.

They collected the picnic things and drove to the Rectory. Bella went into the house, too, to express sympathy, but waited outside in the play-room, while Mrs Vicar was closeted with Dr Nightingale in Evangeline's bedroom.

Bella unearthed the magazine, after a rapid search, from under the snakes-and-ladders board, which lay under an illustrated *Child's Wonders of Nature*, which lay under a row of Teddy Bears. She shoved it down the neck of her blouse, buttoned her coat, replaced the Teddy Bears, and sat down placidly to read *Sunday at Home*.

Meanwhile, Dr Nightingale was puzzled. As Bella had foreseen, Evangeline did not own up to eating sweets in Church, especially love gifts from vulgar little boys.

'Odd,' he told Bella as they drove off. 'I don't think that stomach-ache is due to a bug. The action is far more like colocynth or some other vegetable alkaloid of the sort; yet she seems to have eaten her usual break-fast and lunch, with nothing in between but a glass of milk. Anyhow, I put her on a starvation diet for a day or two, the little basket! Did you find the French thing?'

'I did.'

'Good girl! Burn it!'

Bella showed the magazine to Barbie, as she had promised. Barbie gave a little yelp. 'Oh, my poor darling Robin!' she said, tragically throwing up her hands and eyes. 'To think that his first introduction to the female form divine should have been a set of five-franc cats like these!'

'Really, Barbie! Your language!'

'It's enough to upset his psychic balance for all time. I could *slap* your Mrs Jelkes for starting this lark.'

'She's already suffered quite a lot, I'm glad to report,' said Bella. 'Her poor Harold passed a terrible night with so-called "hives" – tossing, turning, screaming, scratching, and keeping the whole household awake until the small hours. Not a wink of sleep, did Mrs Jelkes get. When Harry called in the morning, he found nothing wrong with the brat – except itching-powder in his pyjamas. Evangeline's hit back for the stomach-ache, I suppose. I wonder how she worked it? Thank Goodness, she doesn't suspect *us*!'

Barbie was left to burn the French thing in her garden incinerator. When she got around to doing so, a week later, Robin strolled up unexpectedly and asked what the funny smell was.

Barbie got flustered, and told him her first lie. 'I'm just burning a few bills, darling. So much easier than paying them, as you'll find when you grow up.'

'I see... But, Barbie darling!'

'Yes, my love?'

'We met Evangeline in the wood. She says the Vicar found that Paris magazine and snatched it away from her. He was awfully cross, she says, and gave her a terrible beating with a knobbed stick – so bad that she had to be put to bed and Dr Nightingale was sent for, to cure her with bandages and iodine. And after that the Vicar nearly starved her to death. And she told us that our fathers will give us all terrible whippings, too, and starve us nearly to death, if they hear we've looked at the undressed Paris ladies. (Lucky I haven't a father now, isn't it?) But she's promised to watch for someone to send another copy. She doesn't know whose pile the first one came from. She *thinks* it was the Nightingales'. But there's sure to be another, she says. And she'll find a safer hiding place next time.'

A Toast to Ava Gardner

IN SPAIN, A married woman keeps her maiden name, but tacks on her husband's after a *de*. Thus, on marrying Wifredo Las Rocas, our Majorcan friend Rosa, born an Espinosa, became Rosa Espinosa de Las Rocas – a very happy combination. It means 'Lady Thorny Rose from the Rocks'. Rosa was much luckier than her maternal cousin Dolores Fuertes, who thoughtlessly married a lawyer named Tomás Barriga, and is now Dolores Fuertes de Barriga, or 'Violent Pains of the Stomach'. My wife and I first met Rosa at a Palma store. We were complaining bitterly, in English, of an age-old Majorcan superstition that the sun shines brightly throughout the year, and that consequently no trouble about drying clothes can ever imaginably arise. Majorcans provide no airing-closets in even their grandest houses, and scorn that old-fashioned English contrivance, the nursery towel-horse, which allows harassed mothers to keep abreast of their children's washing during long rainy spells. We had by now visited every furniture shop in Palma, searching for one, but been greeted only by shrugs and smiles.

Then Rosa piped up at my elbow, in beautiful clear English, with hardly a trace of a Spanish accent: 'Excuse me! I could not help over-hearing your conversation. My husband Wifredo Las Rocas will, I am sure, be delighted to make you a towel-horse. He knows all about towel-horses. My dear old English nurse, the late Nanny Parker, brought a towel-horse with her when she came to us from the British Embassy at Madrid; but I'm afraid my elder sister in Saragossa has it now. If you care to come along with me...'

Wifredo and his partner, Aníbal Tulipán, worked in a large furniture factory on the outskirts of Palma. Though originally they owned fifty per cent each of the factory shares, the building got badly damaged by fire; so the Central Bank rebuilt and restocked it for them at the price of a control-ling interest. Wifredo and Aníbal were, in fact, reduced to mere employees of the Bank, subject to dismissal if they failed to show a profit – an uncomfortable position in times as difficult as those, for men so proud.

Aníbal looked after supplies and sales; Wifredo, after design, production and personnel. They had been brothers-in-law, but the death of Wifredo's sister from an overdose of sleeping-pills, taken in protest against Aníbal's too serious liaison with a dentist's receptionist, snapped the family tie; and if ever two men were temperamentally more unsuited to become partners, these were they. Aníbal, who loved all things German, especially metaphysics, music and sauerkraut, closely resembled Goering in appearance, and had a truly Wagnerian ill-temper; often, when he felt cross, he would emulate Adolf Hitler by throwing himself on the floor and biting the carpet. Until the war ended victoriously for the Allies, Wifredo – tall, fair, and rangy – was careful to conceal his strongly anglophile tendencies. These had been excited some years previously when he first fell in love with Rosa and came under the posthumous spell of the celebrated Nanny Parker. Nanny Parker, on entering the Espinosa household, had brought with her a bound series of the *Illustrated London News,* dating from 1906 to 1925, and kept adding a fresh one every year. In 1936, the outbreak of the Spanish Civil War and Nanny Parker's death – under a fast car driven by a party of non-intervening Italian airmen, remember? – closed the series. But a constant study of these volumes had made Wifredo an expert in all things English for the thirty years that they covered.

When Rosa introduced us to Wifredo, and asked whether he could supply a nursery towel-horse, he agreed with enthusiasm, seeing in us a helpful source of information about all that had happened to the British race since the death of George V. The outcome was an almost breath-taking towel-horse, stout and capacious as a church, in solid mahogany, with fluted rails and brass knobs – and that at a period when mahogany was practically unobtainable on the island. Wifredo charged us only a nominal sum for this masterpiece, assuring us that the pleasure was entirely his.

Then Aníbal heard about the towel-horse from the factory foreman, flew into one of his infernal rages, called Wifredo all sorts of gross names, and accused him of cheating the business, wasting valuable materials, delaying the execution of other orders, and allying himself with certain ancient and inveterate enemies of Spain. He even threatened to bring the ridiculous towel-horse to the notice of the Central Bank. Wifredo replied passionately that Great Britain was Spain's best customer and, after Spain, the noblest country in Europe. He also commented on Aníbal's Teutonic lack of taste, humour and imagination, adding that he proposed to start immediate production, though on a rather less expensive model than the prototype, of no less than one hundred 'Nanniparkér' nursery towel-horses. Then followed some very pointed remarks, such as: 'The priest must have had a bad cold when he christened you "Aníbal". He surely meant "Animal". You are indeed a fat, brutish, sophistical, Germanic beast, save for whose degraded adventures in the lowest haunts of Santa Catalina, my poor sister would still be alive today!'

A rough-house ensued. Wifredo was the stronger of the two; but at some stage or other of the Civil War, Aníbal had attended a hard course in street-fighting, and learned all sorts of clever tricks from his SS volunteer-instructors. Both combatants were seriously injured.

The factory had not been running too well even before this. Worn-out but irreplaceable machinery; power cuts; timber shortages; new national fiestas commemorating the triumph of the Forces of Light, on each of which the management was obliged to reward the workmen with double pay for taking a patriotic vacation; trouble with the syndicates; decrees forbidding the dismissal of a single workman however inefficient, dishonest or redundant – all this had been bad enough; but a complete breach between the partners brought matters to a crisis. Wifredo and Aníbal now obstinately pursued their own unco-ordinated policies: Wifredo designing his furniture in a yet more provocative English style, Aníbal starving him of suitable timber and making no attempt to sell whatever he might manage to make.

Realizing that the factory would soon go bankrupt unless someone intervened decisively, Rosa did so. She had the good sense to phone a certain Cathedral Canon: elder brother and confessor of the man who stood with a whip above these warring partners – the Central Bank Director himself. After explaining her predicament, Rosa begged the Canon to impose peace by whatever means he thought best, short of ruining both households. 'Very reverend Father,' she said, 'although it is true that Don Aníbal began this disgraceful quarrel by calling Wifredo gross names which no man of honour could accept, I must admit that Wifredo's reply did nothing to ameliorate the situation. It is equally true that Don Aníbal struck the first blow; yet Wifredo failed to turn the other cheek. Now, however, he repents of his un-Catholic attitude. It is no joke that every day, on going to the factory, he must carefully remove his wristwatch and place it on a shelf, together with his spare reading-glasses, for fear that they may both be splintered in a fresh hand-to-hand encounter.'

The Canon listened with encouraging snorts, and finally gave his opinion. 'My daughter,' he said, 'I can see only one way out of the trouble which you have so clearly presented. It is that you and Don Aníbal's wife must form a realistic alliance for peace. Until your husbands can be persuaded to clasp hands in friendship, you must insist, at least, on their jointly asking the Bank to appoint a permanent arbiter who shall settle all disputes between them. Such an arrangement should involve no great expense: some retired military man of rectitude and discretion will, I have no doubt, be pleased to undertake the task. Not for a monetary remuneration but, let us say, for a daily allowance of refreshments. Thereafter, your two husbands need not meet except in this arbiter's presence; though the Bank will of course desire them to accept all his decisions without question – as football players accept those of the umpire, on pain of being ordered off the field. If you can answer for your husband's agreement, let us arrange a meeting between yourself and Don Aníbal's wife at my house tomorrow; there, with God's help, all will be decently settled.'

The name of Aníbal's new wife, the pretty ex-dental receptionist, was Gracia Joncosa de Tulipán. (Another floral combination of names: 'Reedy Grace of a Tulip'.) Gracia was a tough girl and also, like Aníbal, stubbornly anti-clerical. She attended the meeting, but warned the Canon straight out that, since the initiative had clearly come from Rosa, Aníbal would reject the plan of arbitration as energetically as if it had been proposed by the Kremlin itself.

This brought a frown to the Canon's roseate face. Yet he refrained from dredging up Gracia's reprehensible past, and merely begged her to imitate Rosa's truly Catholic spirit. 'Blessed are the peacemakers!' he intoned, wagging a fat finger.

'Blessed are they indeed!' Gracia echoed, impressed against her will by the huge, cigar-scented study: its dark, forbidding bookcases, its dark, forbidding pictures of saints being flayed alive, being grilled over hot coals, or merely kneeling in ecstasy on a mountain crag surrounded by winged demons. 'But my Aníbal,' she went on, 'will at once convince himself that such an arbiter was chosen by connivance between yourself and Don Wifredo as a means of ousting him from his post.'

The Canon replied smoothly: 'Dear daughter, your hot-tempered husband must have no fear. Assure him that I, a Canon of Palma Cathedral, solemnly guarantee to find an arbiter of such absolute rectitude and insight that he might well be a descendant of King Solomon himself. If, however, your husband refuses my assurances, I shall feel that the Church has been spurned, as well as the Bank, and will inform my brother of his obduracy.'

Gracia saw the red light. She cried: 'No, no, most reverend Father! Pray do not talk in that sense! Aníbal is, at bottom, a peace-loving man, and entertains the highest esteem both for yourself and for your distinguished brother. Let me try to make him see reason.'

'You will do well to try, my daughter,' the Canon answered grimly; and so the interview ended.

Aníbal threw another fit when Gracia delivered the Canon's message. 'It is a hold-up!' he is reported as exclaiming. 'Must I indeed hand over my wallet to these shameless gangsters with a truly Catholic smile?'

Yet there was no way out when the Bank Director offered as a possible arbiter the retired and much-decorated Colonel whom I shall call Don Hilario Tortugas. During the Rif War he had been shot on three separate occasions, through calf, knee and shoulder, finally losing all the fingers of his left hand in performing a deed of such terrific valour that it earned him the Grand Cross of San Fernando. For Aníbal to challenge the integrity of so outstanding a hero would have made him ridiculous. Moreover, Don Hilario, bored by inactivity, had readily accepted the task, asking a daily honorarium no larger than two cups of coffee, a salami sandwich, a bottle of beer, and a Canary Islands cigar. The coffee must be scalding hot; that was his one stipulation.

The arrangement worked well enough. True, Don Hilario could claim only the most meagre knowledge of how a factory was run – an educational fault displayed in Spanish history by a long sequence of gallant, honourable, high-ranking Army officers who have found themselves charged with their country's economic fate. Nevertheless, experience in the command of men had sharpened his natural intuition as to whether people were telling him lies, truths, or half-truths; and, when disputes arose on technical points he decided them by a careful study of the partners' voices, faces, and demeanour, rather than of the documents laid before him. Thus he settled the vexed question of the 'Nanniparkér' towel-horses by arguing that though Wifredo would doubtless turn out a superbly professional product, if given the required materials, Aníbal's lack of confidence in these novelties suggested the wisdom of postponing their manufacture. He also ruled: 'The factory should, however, bear the expense of creating the prototype, and of selling it at a minimal price to an influential foreign family by way of justifiable propaganda.'

Don Hilario's daily appearance at the factory did much to restore the morale of the workmen. They used to boast in the cafés: 'We have the famous Colonel Tortugas on our payroll – he who once ran his sword through seventeen Cabyls, one after the other, though wounded in a score of places. There's a fighter for you!' Yet Aníbal found it difficult to swallow his resentment: 'Only imagine! That ancient military relic set over me as supervisor and spy!' He continued to make things as difficult as he could for Wifredo, by misrepresenting both the supply situation and the sales prospects; at the same time complaining to Don Hilario that Wifredo spoiled the workmen and showed an utter ignorance of modern furniture trends.

On Rosa's advice, Wifredo kept cool and behaved as Englishly as possible, in the hope of provoking Aníbal to over-reach himself by some crude act that could not escape official censure. But he was secretly worried by Aníbal's attempts at ingratiating himself with Don Hilario. For instance, when he gave Don Hilario a box of a hundred *Romeo y Julieta* cigars on his Name Day. Don Hilario, needless to record, firmly declined the gift, swearing that much as he enjoyed a good smoke, he could never allow himself to deviate one hair's breadth from his more than Draconian code, and must avoid even the suspicion of venality. Nevertheless, Wifredo saw him eye the box with badly disguised wistfulness.

From time to time, Wifredo offered Don Hilario a lift back to the centre of town in his boat-shaped 1922 Renault two-seater – Majorca is where good cars go to die, and they take unconscionably long about it – but Don Hilario always insisted on walking, even on wet days when his wounds troubled him. He would accept no more and no less than the daily two cups of sweet, scalding coffee, the Canary Islands cigar, the salami sandwich, and the bottle of beer stipulated in the contract. Once only, his conscience permitted him to borrow from Wifredo a couple of cigarette papers with which to roll his own cigarettes; but paid them back the very next day.

So much for the situation at the factory. Now for that of the 'influential foreign family'. We had an unexpected visit from Ava Gardner, a close friend of our Maryland friend Betty Sicre. Betty suggested that Ava should take a short holiday from the exhausting social life of Madrid to visit soporific and truly rural Majorca. There she could catch up on sleep, study Spanish grammar, swim daily, and consult me about how to finish her random education by a crash-course in English poetry. We had met Ava at Betty's house a few months before and found her great fun; afterwards she sent us a huge bouquet of red roses, an attention which my wife and I appreciated all the more because, as we already knew, Ava is not one to distribute idle favours. She was feeling lonely at this time, her elder sister having just gone back to the States, and would borrow each of Betty's four small sons in turn to keep her company at night. 'The other boys at the American School will think me a sissy,' the youngest but one had tearfully complained, 'if they find out that I sleep twice a week with Ava!'

At Palma's Son Bonet airport, she came rushing towards us across the tarmac: a startled deer, pursued by a hungry-looking wolf. When the wolf saw her suddenly engulfed in our large family – the children had played truant from school by telling their monks and nuns that an aunt was arriving from London – he slunk off slavering. But word flew from end to end of the airport that the famous Ava Gardner had finally come to Majorca; and crowds went milling around in search of the red carpet, the bouquets, and the press photographers. Meanwhile, we hurried Ava into our Land-Rover, and hauled her baggage off the air-line truck. One film-struck enthusiast saw a woman who closely resembled his idol bandying nonsense with our children in the dusty car; he stopped, narrowed his eyes, and passed on – it could not, of course, be she. We made a clean get-away.

Ava explained that there had been two really troublesome Spanish wolves aboard the plane. The first, seated across the gangway, kept addressing her in an experimental sort of Italian, until she slammed shut the *Oxford Book of English Verse* (supplied by Betty for the poetry course) and said: 'If you must interrupt my reading, why don't you at least talk your own language?'

The wolf answered gallantly: 'Signorina, I decided to give myself the honour of employing your own musical tongue.'

Ava looked puzzled. 'You must have got things mixed,' she said. 'I happen to have married a Sicilian, but my Italian is even worse than yours.' The wolf leered at her craftily. 'Do not think to deceive me! All our papers assure us that you are a true daughter of Naples.'

'Then they're lying. I was born and raised in North Carolina.'

A horrid doubt overtook the wolf. 'Then I am mistaken? You are *not* Sofia Loren?'

With a cry of indignation Ava leaped up and took refuge in a vacant seat forward, but found Wolf No. 2 waiting there to pounce. So she read the *Oxford Book of English Verse* in the washroom, from which she emerged when the plane had landed; only to find the wolf waiting for her with amorous yelps at the foot of the landing-steps. Female film stars, it seems, are bound by a strict code: they must never insult journalists or press photographers, never refuse to sign autographs (unless desperately pressed for time), and never either slug wolves with overnight bags or poke out their eyes with parasols.

Ava's plans for improving her Spanish grammar and catching up on sleep did not come to much. There are too many places in Palma where gipsies strum at guitars and dance *flamenco* all night; and Ava can never resist *flamenco*. Besides, her first visit to Majorca attracted such immense attention that she was forced to change hotels four times in five days; but it fascinated us to bask for a while in the spotlight of her glory. Though far preferring, she said, a meal of shepherd's pie or sausages-and-mash at our Palma flat, she gallantly took us out once or twice to the lusher restaurants.

After dinner, in one of these, she asked me for her poetry lesson, and I told her that so few poems were worth reading, and so many were wrongly supposed to be worth reading, that she had better make sure she would not waste her time by this poetry course. Washing for gold could be very dull work. Then, changing the metaphor, I said that a clear, personal voice was better than all the technical skill and daring experimentation in the world – really good poetry always makes plain, immediate, personal sense, is never dull, and goes on making better sense the oftener one reads it. 'Poems are like people,' I said. 'There are not many authentic ones around.'

Questioned about the monstrous legendary self which towers above her, Ava told us that she does everything possible to get out from under, though the publicity-boys and the Press are always trying to clamp it even more tightly on her shoulders. Also, that she has never outgrown her early Hard-Shell Baptist conditioning on that North Carolina tobacco farm, with the eye of a wonderful father always on her; and still feels uncomfortably moral in most film-studios; it isn't what she does that has created her sultry reputation, but what she says. Sometimes she just can't control her tongue.

A photographer suddenly let off a flash-bulb at us, and Ava flashed back at him almost as startlingly in the fiercest language. But when he apologized at once, she half forgave him. The rest of our talk was punctuated by the waiter's handing a succession of autograph-books to Ava for signature; she obliged automatically with a fixed, sunny smile, not losing the thread of our conversation until one autograph-hunter, an overstuffed sofa of a woman, plumped herself down next to me, leant across me, and said: 'Oh, dear Miss Gardner, I have seen *every single one* of your films! Now I wonder whether you would be so good as to give me your *personal* autograph for my seven-year-old grandchild. Her name is Wendy Solgotch Wallinger.'

Ava frowned. 'Is the Solgotch Wallinger strictly necessary?' she asked. 'And what am I supposed to write on?'

'Oh, I thought film stars always supply the paper!'

Ava frowned more deeply. Her comments on that paper shortage had better stay off record. They were quite enough to account for her sultry reputation. Nevertheless, loth to infringe the code further, she tore a corner off the menu, scribbled 'Wendy, with best wishes from Ava Gardner,' and waved Mrs Wallinger away with it.

Having found my *Collected Poems* at our apartment, Ava asked which of them to read first. This question embarrassed me, after what I had already told her. However, there was one, I said, which she might perhaps like to take personally; though it had been written long before we met. I marked the page for study when she went to bed that night – if she ever did.

> *She speaks always in her own voice*
> *Even to strangers...*

and:

> *She is wild and innocent, pledged to love*
> *Through all disaster...*

That was Ava to the life.

Meanwhile, at the furniture factory, Aníbal had been consistently difficult. He accused Wifredo to Don Hilario of stirring up the workmen and alleging that the timber he supplied was so green, warped and knotted that it would serve only for making rustic seats and the like. Confronted with this charge, Wifredo informed Don Hilario that he had made a factual statement, not a complaint: indeed, far from stirring the workmen up, he had encouraged them to hope that something at least could be made from the eccentric lumps of raw tree which were all that his partner could now buy.

When Don Hilario looked at him quizzically, Wifredo went to the workshop and returned with a particularly unattractive section of local pine, consisting almost wholly of large knots. He asked: 'Am I seriously expected to fulfil a municipal order for eighty class-room desks with timber of this quality? And what about my saw-blades?'

Don Hilario eyed the exhibit and ventured cautiously: 'Well, you might hammer out these knots and use the holes for securing the scholars' ink-wells; but I shall make it plain to Don Aníbal that if you were to take this course, there would undoubtedly be many times more ink-wells than scholars.'

Seven o'clock struck, and Wifredo exclaimed: 'Pardon me, Don Hilario! The workmen have gone off, and so has my partner. I must lock up without delay. Since I am aware that any invitation to ride home in my battered car will be declined, let me wish you a respectful good night. There is a certain haste; my English friends, the intellectual Graves family, are honouring my house with a visit, and hope to bring Miss Ava Gardner.'

Don Hilario caught his breath and clutched at Wifredo's sleeve. 'Do you mean the veritable Ava Gardner?' he asked slowly. 'She... is here, in Majorca?'

'Yes, the one inimitable Ava,' Wifredo answered easily. 'The Señores Graves assure me that she is as gracious and intelligent as she is beautiful.'

'"Gracious and intelligent" indeed! "Gracious and intelligent" is petty praise! For me, Ava Gardner is the greatest artist alive!'

Ava did not, as it happened, come to Wifredo's with us that evening. She had made a trip to the fine sandy beach of Camp de Mar; but, the weather being bitterly cold – it was just before the fearful February freeze-up of 1956 – she alone was hardy enough to swim. Several carloads of admirers stood watching, and a roar of admiration rose as she tripped down the hotel steps in her bright Italian bathing costume and dived into the tempestuous waves. Yet no would-be life-saver, we were told, jumped in after her; if only because Spaniards, though incurably romantic, are not altogether Quixotic. Later, Ava was whisked on to the Binisalem vineyards, where she spent so agreeable a time sampling our sole Majorcan vintage wine that we did not catch up with her again until midnight.

The next morning, Don Hilario drew Wifredo aside and said urgently: 'Friend, tell me about her!'

Hating to disappoint the Colonel, Wifredo answered: 'A phenomenon! So gentle, so beautiful, so humorous.'

Don Hilario sighed. 'Ah, Don Wifredo, your experience fills me with the greenest envy!' He added in a sudden rush: 'I have never, you know, accepted a gift or a favour from you, ever since I came to this factory. Not a cigarette, not a match, not a ride in your crazy automobile! However, I will say that, unlike your boorish partner, you always show the utmost consideration for my feelings in this respect, never making any move which might be open to malicious misinterpretation; and for that I honour you. Indeed, I honour you so highly, and so commend your correctness, that I feel emboldened to make a surprising request: one that you will, I am sure, recognize as being on a quite different level from the mundane round of industry in the ambience of which we daily meet. Don Wifredo, I am a lonely old man; all winter long my wounds ache; I have few pleasures. Well... to be short, if you could, by any plea, prevail on your distinguished English friends to approach Miss Gardner...'

Wifredo answered: 'Not another word, Don Hilario! And if anyone else in all Palma were to ask this of me – even the Director of the Central Bank, upon whose good will my livelihood depends – I should say: "Impossible!" But when the most courageous soldier of our race makes such a request, how dare I rebuff him? I trust that the matter can be arranged before Miss Gardner leaves the island early this afternoon.'

A few minutes later our phone rang. 'Robert,' Wifredo said excitedly, 'will you meet me at noon in the Café Mecca on a matter of the gravest importance? I cannot explain over the telephone.'

To my relief, Ava had read the marked poem and decided to accept it as a personal tribute; in fact, begged me to copy it out in long-hand and sign it for her.

'With great pleasure,' I said, 'if you'll do a trade. Ava, I want a print of your most supremely glamorous photograph, inscribed: "To the heroic Colonel Don Hilario Tortugas y Postres, with the heartfelt admiration of Ava Gardner." Let me write it down for you.'

'Is "heartfelt admiration" strictly necessary?'

'It's essential!'

I wrote out the poem for Ava in a fair hand, and soon after she had flown back to Madrid (with four crates of Binisalem wine among her luggage) a splendidly large signed photograph arrived, duly inscribed for the Colonel: a portrait, I was half-glad to see, of her exotic legend rather than of herself.

Rosa and Wifredo invited us to the most English dinner we had eaten in years: mulligatawny soup; roast beef with roast potatoes, Yorkshire pudding, a boiled cabbage; apple dumplings with cream; and (as Edward Lear has put it) 'no end of Stilton cheese'. Wifredo even produced a bottle of vintage port – how he got hold of either the Stilton or the port, beats me – and solemnly toasted Ava Gardner.

We all drank.

Then, in a voice thick with emotion, he announced: 'Dear friends, in consequence of Don Hilario's report to the Bank, delivered two days ago, I now have sole charge of the factory, being answerable to the Bank Director alone. Aníbal has been bought out and dismissed; and I am empowered not only to arrange my own timber supplies, but to choose a new sales manager!'

We congratulated him riotously.

'That is not all,' he went on. 'The "Nanniparkér" Nursery Towel-horse now goes into immediate production, as well as a similar contrivance, suggested by dear Rosa, for hoisting wet linen to the kitchen ceiling by means of a cord and pulley. It will equally serve, in better weather, for hams, sausages, strings of red peppers, and ropes of onions. How original, and how very useful! I propose to name it "The Ava Gardner Drying Rack". Each example will bear a beautiful coloured miniature of my benefactress, taken from the authentic photograph of her plunge into the sea at Camp de Mar. Do you consider that I need write to ask her permission?'

'She would consider it strictly unnecessary,' I answered, sipping my port, cracking my walnuts, and thinking: 'Dear Ava!'

The Viscountess and the Short-haired Girl

TWENTY-FIVE YEARS ago, Master Toni, the squat, bald, dark-eyed, muscular, smiling proprietor of our village garage, invited me to dinner on his Saint's Day. The fiesta of San Antonio, which falls on January 17th, is always marked in Majorcan villages by the priest's rather hilarious aspersion with holy water of as many asses, mules, sheep-dogs and motor-cars as his parishioners may care to bring along to the Church door; and by a bonfire, lighted on the previous evening, which around midnight has usually died down low enough for *buñuelos* – a sort of doughnut – to be fried over the embers. On this occasion, the fire being still alive after morning mass, Master Toni's wife Doña Isabel sent her children with shovels to salvage lumps of glowing charcoal for the brazier under our dinner table. The main dish was missel-thrushes stewed in cabbage-leaves, with snails, octopus and saffron rice. We also ate smoked ham; slices of out-sized radish; the first pickled black olives of the season; Minorcan sheep-cheese; fig-bread; ordinary bread; and plenty of Binisalem red wine. I remember the missel-thrushes, because a German lady had been enraged to see a pile of them heaped on the garage floor that morning. 'How dare you massacre our beautiful German songbirds?' she screamed.

'Señora,' Master Toni answered, 'your German songbirds are ill-educated; they come to steal the olives. Olives are our main source of wealth: olives, and figs – figs such as I often watched you steal from my trees as you went down the path by our house this last September.'

Missel-thrushes are caught by a method once known as 'bat-fowling' in England, but now, I believe, extinct there. Two men station themselves a few paces apart, in one of the broad alleys down which the thrushes fly from their roosts among evergreen oaks near the mountain top. The bat-fowlers stretch across the alley a length of fishing-net lashed to two very long canes, held upright. At dawn, the first coveys of thrushes, known as *tords d'auba*, descend on the olive groves and find themselves entangled in the net. Both canes are simultaneously flung forward and downward, after which the bat-fowlers wring the necks of whatever birds have been caught underneath. At about eight o'clock down flies a smaller wave of thrushes, known as *tords de gran dia;* then no more can be expected until the *tords de vespre,* or evening thrushes. Bat-fowling is one of the few sports in which the villagers engage. A mountain terraced steeply all the way up from the sea provides no level space large enough for a football field, or even a tennis court; and since 1906, when a passing traveller had his eye knocked out by a sling-stone flung by young Mateo of the Painted House – he had mischievously aimed at the man's pipe – the ancient Balearic sling has been officially banned even for rabbit-hunting.

Anyhow, Master Toni, having made merry on the Eve of San Antonio, and eaten quantities of *buñuelos,* had returned home for a couple of hours' sleep, then started off at five o'clock to catch *tords d'auba* for our dinner. But along came the sexton, in overcoat and slippers, to say that his sister, María the Spaghetti-maker, was desperately ill again and that the Doctor must be fetched at once from Sóller. So Master Toni climbed into his antiquated Studebaker; and by the time the Doctor had attended to María (on her death-bed these past fifteen years) and been driven back to Sóller, only the despised *tords de gran dia* were left to hunt. Nevertheless, Master Toni and a certain Sentiá Dog-beadle, the village odd-job man, managed between them to bag two dozen – a remarkable catch that year. And very good they tasted.

Perhaps I should explain that María Spaghetti-maker had never made any spaghetti; it was her great-grandmother who plied the trade, but the nickname persisted in the female line. There is now a grown-up grand-daughter who holds it, though she only sews gloves. Similarly, the timo-rous and greedy Sentiá Dog-beadle inherited his nickname from an ancestor whose task had been to keep stray dogs from taking sanctuary on hot days in the cool of Palma Cathedral. 'Sentiá' is short for Sebastián. There are almost too many things which need explanation, once one begins to tell stories about our village.

After dinner, over the coffee and brandy, I found it easy to swear that I had never eaten so well, or so much, in all my life.

'Not even in Piccadilly, Don Roberto?' asked Master Toni shrewdly.

'Certainly not, I assure you!'

'Well, Damián the Coachman, Sentiá Dog-beadle and I ate pretty well there, during our famous stay at the Regent *Palacio* Hotel.'

'Why have you never told me of this visit to London?'

'I am a busy man, you are a busy man. I have saved up the long history of the Viscountess and the Short-haired Girl for this fiesta.'

Here then is Master Toni's story, as I wrote it down that same evening. Respecting his inability to manage an initial *St, Sc, Sp* or *Sm* without an anticipatory *e,* I prefixed one to all the proper names which demanded it. Let that *e* stay as a convenient reminder of the estory-teller's Espanishness.

THE VISCOUNTESS AND THE SHORT-HAIRED GIRL

It all began one day in August when two gentlemen, both wearing black coats and striped trousers – hardly suitable clothes for the weather, which was of a barbarous heat – drove up in a very fine taxi from Palma and stopped at my garage. The chauffeur, who knew me, asked whether they might have a private word in my ear. 'At the gentlemen's service,' I answered, 'unless they are trying to sell me something. I am excessively short of money this month.'

One of the gentlemen, who could speak Spanish, heard what I said. He was a little game-cock of a man, and had a habit of tilting his head on one side inquiringly, as poultry often do. From his black mushroom hat, I judged him to be less important than the other, who wore a black silk stove-pipe hat. 'Then let me congratulate you, Don Antonio,' he said. 'My friend here, Mr P.P. Jonés, will soon remedy your financial straits. If you listen to his proposal, he will fill your pockets with silver *duros*. My own name is Charley Estrutt, at your service.'

'He does not require me to violate the Law?' I asked.

Mr Estrutt translated this question to Mr Jonés, who resembled a large, well-cured ham. Mr Jonés shook his head violently, saying: 'On the contrary!' – a phrase which I understood, the word 'contrary' being identical in our Majorcan idiom, though we sound it differently.

I asked them both upstairs, to take a coffee. They accepted, and when we had emptied our cups I waited until they should come to the point, after all Mr Estrutt's compliments on the beauty and tranquillity of our village. When he continued silent, I said boldly: 'By your gold watch-chains and your reticence, gentlemen, I judge you to be lawyers; and your black clothes indicate that you are here on business, not on a vacation. The labels on your brief-cases say "London". Therefore, since this village has had the honour of welcoming only one compatriot of yours during the past twelve months, that is to say a certain young girl with hair cut short like a boy's, who stayed for a week in May at the Hotel Bonsol with a tall foreigner from God-knows where, may I conclude that your business somehow concerns her?'

Mr Estrutt's face lighted up. He said: 'You are very intelligent, Don Antonio! That is almost precisely the case, though Señor Jonés alone is a lawyer. In effect, he represents the short-haired girl's disconsolate mother, recently widowed.'

I asked: 'And your profession, Señor? Would it be inconvenient to divulge it?'

Mr Estrutt smiled. 'No inconvenience at all,' he said. 'I used to be an inspector in our Metropolitan Police force. I am now retired, and have become a private detective employed by rich people to conduct delicate inquiries. The remuneration is better.'

I went on: 'By the formality of Mr Jonés's appearance, he must be a lawyer of great importance?'

Mr Estrutt whistled. 'He never accepts less than fifty thousand pesetas a week for a case! The fact is that the disconsolate mother in question reeks of money. Her father was a multi-millionaire from Chile. I worked for the family once; an illegitimate son of his happened to be blackmailing him.'

I remarked: 'One recognizes your accent as South American.'

He blushed a little: 'Yes, yes,' he said, 'you Spaniards despise South Americans for their abuse of your ancient tongue.'

Since Mr Charley Estrutt seemed a pleasant enough man, for all the ridiculous black mushroom-hat balanced on his knee, I assured him that here in Majorca we speak an even coarser dialect of Spanish than the Chileans. Our talk proceeded in this inconclusive manner until Mr Jonés, who did not understand a word, looked at his big gold watch and made some observation to Mr Estrutt. Clearly, the moment had come to discuss business. I told myself: 'These people can pay well. I shall certainly not accept the first price they offer – for whatever it is that they require of me.'

Mr Estrutt now put forward his proposal. He explained that the short-haired girl, a minor, having run away from a French convent where she was being educated, had been brutally kidnapped by a Bulgarian artist. The pair had, with great difficulty, been traced to our village. The disconsolate Viscountess, her mother, wished to collect sufficient sworn evidence about the tragedy to incarcerate this Bulgarian heretic for life. Yet scandal must be avoided at all costs, and therefore the Spanish police had not been invited to assist. Well, if I and two friends of mine could testify before an English judge to the Bulgarian's having dragged the wretched girl to our Hotel Bonsol, and there committed an offence against her, the unfortunate entanglement could be legally proved, and the criminal punished.

Mr Jonés, so Mr Estrutt told me, knew that I had conveyed the couple in my taxi from the mole at Palma to the Hotel Bonsol; that a certain Sebastián Vivés (meaning Sentiá Dog-beadle) had carried their bags up to a bedroom at the said hotel; and that Damián Frau, meaning 'Damián the Coachman', the hotelkeeper, had brought them breakfast in bed, on a tray, the next morning. Mr Jonés hoped that we would kindly visit London in a month's time, to avenge the honour of a noble English house, more particularly because the disconsolate Viscountess was a very devout Catholic; he had heard of our Majorcan zeal for the sanctity of a Catholic home.

I replied: 'Speaking between ourselves, Mr Estrutt, the short-haired girl seemed to be in no way acting under duress; in fact, on our journey from Palma she was embracing and caressing the heretic – as I could not help seeing in my driving-mirror – with every appearance of genuine enjoyment.'

Imagine my surprise, when Mr Estrutt winked at me (but with the eye hidden from Mr Jonés) and answered: 'Don Antonio, in England our young girls have been completely demoralized by the excitements of the recent war. Moreover, the poor child may have feared that, unless she caressed him in public, he would ill-treat her most cruelly once they were alone.'

To be brief, the terms offered us three witnesses for a visit to London were twenty pesetas a day, besides travelling expenses, bed, board, laundry, wine, cigars, and anything else within reason that we might need, not omitting sight-seeing excursions; and another five hundred pesetas each, if we gave our evidence in a way that convinced the Judge. He also asked, would I be kind enough to repeat this offer to my friends, Don Sebastián and Don Damián?

I wanted to know how long we should be away, and Mr Estrutt estimated that we should be home again within three weeks. My reply was that we should answer yes or no after a night's reflection; but Mr Jonés urged us to sign a contract that same night. He intended to catch the Barcelona boat.

Well, I left the Englishmen at my house while I went to the Bonsol and took Damián for a little stroll. 'You are a knowledgeable man,' I said, 'and acquainted with the ways of the rich. I have been invited to visit London as witness in a kidnapping case. Now, for a commission of this sort, are twenty pesetas a day, all found, sufficient? I shall be away for about three weeks.'

Damián stopped, gazed at me in wonder, spat with emphasis, and said: 'Ka, man, you would be a fool to refuse! Myself, I would gladly go without pay – if only to escape from this dull hole and see grand civilization again.'

Damián, you must understand, had earned his nickname himself as coachman to the President of the Argentine Republic, and still remembered those days of glory. He added: 'But what, in the Devil's name, has the kidnapping case to do with you?'

'Patience, friend,' said I. 'First advise me whether the fee is correct in principle.'

He considered the matter. Then he spat again and said: 'In principle, Toni, you should insist upon thirty pesetas a day. The English, as a rule, allow fifty per cent for bargaining where Spaniards are concerned.'

'And five hundred pesetas on top of that!'

'A tidy sum, by God! I wish I had the chance to earn so much by a three weeks' holiday.'

'Then be joyful, Damián! You are invited too!'

He took this for a joke, but when he heard my story he threw his hat so high into the air that it sailed over the terrace, down the valley and into the torrent, and was not found again.

We went off together at once and acquainted Sentiá with his luck. As

Sentiá was earning hardly five pesetas a day, a casual labourer's wage at that time, his eyes truly bulged with greed. Yet we had to pour a deal of *coñac* down his throat before we could persuade him to join us. Never having left the island in his life, Sentiá cherished a tremendous fear of being drowned by a tempest at sea. Finally, however, he agreed; and after Damián and I had won the extra ten pesetas a day from Mr Jonés, without a struggle, we took Sentiá along to the Mayor, who was the local Justice of the Peace, and persuaded him to witness the amended contract. In effect, we all signed the document, which had been prepared by a Spanish notary. Sentiá scrawled his name and rubric with a trembling hand, saying: 'God grant that this be not my death warrant!'

Nobody from our village had ever seen the shores of England, and it seemed a great thing for us three to be the first. Naturally, our wives did not favour the adventure, unless they could come too; is that not so, Isabel? But Mr Estrutt declared that such an arrangement would be most unwise, even if we cared to pay those extra passages and expenses out of what we should earn. Then Sentiá's wife created a scandal. She called us fools for not asking fifty pesetas a day, and a thousand at the close, Mr Jonés having agreed to our demand so readily. She knew in her heart, she shrieked, that I had been bribed by the Englishmen to keep the payment low. But Isabel here, and Damián's wife, Angela, told her to be silent, since the offer was a handsome one and the document had now been securely signed.

Nothing more. After promising to write frequently, and making our wives promise to behave themselves during our absence and keep the children in good order, we declared, hands on heart, that we should never have dreamed of leaving the village even for three weeks, were the preservation of a Catholic home not at stake. Indeed, the women of this island are hardly less zealous in this matter than Mr Estrutt suggested; and I doubt whether any of the three concerned would have let us go for the money alone. I learned later that, while we were away, Isabel here spent half her days in church, praying for my safety and for the spiritual consolation of the unhappy widow.

Well, you have made that journey more than once, Don Roberto, so it is nothing new to you, but for me it was tremendous once we had crossed the frontier into France! It seemed a miracle that within half a mile of country the aspect of so many things could suddenly change: the clothes, the language, the uniforms, the telegraph-poles, the colour of the mailboxes, the very shape and taste of the bread!

Mr Estrutt had fetched us by taxi from the village in order to shepherd us through the customs, the passport inspections, and other troubles. He seemed a very different man, once he had emerged from the shadow of the serious Mr Jonés: being dressed now in a cream-coloured gaberdine suit, a hard straw-hat with a canary-yellow ribbon, and carrying a gold-headed cane. He also began to tell us jokes of the sort we call 'green'. He arrived at my house somewhat fatigued, having spent the previous night at the Bar Macarena. Perhaps you know the Macarena? If so, you will consider it no small feat that he escaped alive from those gipsies and even contrived to preserve his wallet, his pearl tie-pin, and his gold-headed cane. The Metropolitan Police must be a race of lions.

We embarked on the night-boat to Barcelona, and the tears streamed down our wives' faces as they waved us good-bye from the quay; and I confess that, for a moment, I wondered whether my decision had been a prudent one. As for Sentiá, he was in a lamentable condition, and Mr Estrutt made him swallow a tablet which rapidly put him to sleep.

As soon as we were clear of Palma harbour, Mr Estrutt invited Damián and me to join him in the Bar. Over a *coñac*, he said: 'Boys, presently I shall go to the cabin to restore my loss of sleep, but first let me be honest with you. That kidnapping story, you must understand, is a work of fantasy. The old Viscountess and I thought it out together as a means of convincing your wives that it was their duty to let you go. Moreover, we decided that we should say no word about it to Mr Jonés. Though an intelligent lawyer, he is insular and highly moral, and would never practise a little deception even to assist a good cause.'

'Well, then for God's sake tell us the truth at once!' Damián demanded fiercely.

'The truth,' he replied, 'is that this old witch of a Viscountess lost her husband, the Viscount, three months ago – he fell from the balcony of their bedroom at the Hotel Espléndido, Cannes, and perhaps it truly was an accident – who can say? But no matter! The widow is now enamoured of a retired officer in the King's Bodyguard; and this officer, whose profession is to direct a pack of foxhounds, possesses a large estate, but little money to maintain it – only a mountain of gambling debts. In fact, he is willing to marry the old trout, who is not bad-looking by candle light, if one places the candle well behind her and wears sunglasses. The sole bar to their union has been his young wife, an actress, who married him not long ago, thinking he was rich but, finding that he had cheated her, now considers herself free to take what consolation she can find in the company of others. Yet she carefully covers her tracks when she goes hunting – hunting men, not foxes, of course. She is good-looking, you agree?'

Since Mr Estrutt was clearly referring to the short-haired girl, Damián and I pronounced that, yes, she was a delicious morsel, though a little thin perhaps, and her eyes of too pallid a blue.

Mr Estrutt went on. 'So you see, boys, that your testimony will be most valuable to the Viscountess. If the fox-hunting officer wins his decree of divorce from the short-haired girl, the Viscountess can them marry him, having paid all the expenses of the trial. Now, this is how I enter the story. Last May, the short-haired girl was invited to stay with her elder sister at

Tossa on the Costa Brava; but when the Viscountess sent me there in July to make inquiries, I found that after only a single morning at Tossa the girl had crossed over to Majorca at the side of the Bulgarian artist, whom she had met on the Paris train. I discreetly followed their tracks and obtained your names, without visiting your village, from a friendly corporal of Coastguards. With such information I went back to London, where Mr Jonés resolved to make the Viscountess pay a capital sum for his corroboration of my story. I should add that other acts of adultery are charged against the short-haired girl; but this is the only one which Mr Jonés at present dares to bring into Court. Well, boys, do you forgive me for the lies I told you?'

I laughed. 'Ka, man, it is all the same to Damián and me,' I said, 'so long as we are paid according to our contract.'

Mr Estrutt slapped my back and cried: 'I like your spirit, Toni, if I may call you that? And you must call me Charley, as everyone else does who is anyone at all! Now, another thing. When you asked for those extra ten pesetas a day, I informed Mr Jonés that, being staunch Catholics, you were dead against the marriage of divorced persons, and must therefore obtain at least thirty pesetas in all before testifying in a matter that so little interested you. Now I have said enough; but I wager that we will enjoy a wonderful time in London. By the bye, you must not let my lovesick old baggage of a Viscountess know that I have given you the true story; and it would be well, surely, not to let the good Sentiá into our secret, either. It might unsettle his ideas about me.'

Then we refilled our glasses and toasted the Viscountess, the late Viscount, the short-haired girl, the fox-hunting officer, Mr P.P. Jonés and the Judge, together with many other persons more remotely connected with the affair, in a multitude of *coñacs*. Mr Estrutt did not restore his loss of sleep during that particular night.

Despite our excesses we reached port safely, and later ate a grand meal at the Hotel *Palacio* of Barcelona, with lobster mayonnaise, French wines, and everything of the best. Sentiá Dog-beadle, feeling much embarrassed by the elegant ambience, opened his mouth only a little when he introduced food and kept his enormous red hands under the table while not using them. But Damián gloried in this brief return to the high life he had enjoyed at the Presidential Palace of Buenos Aires, and recounted more about his past than I should ever have believed, though we had known each other twenty years or longer.

After a night spent on a train with very narrow beds, we came to Paris and were taken in a taxi to the Gare du Nord. At once Mr Estrutt said: 'Boys, will you do me a great favour? I am off into the city. Please wait for me in the restaurant yonder, order what food and drink may be convenient, but be careful to enter into conversation with no one at all! My orders from the Viscountess are never to leave you out of my sight. I shall be back in time to catch our train.'

Damián asked: 'What is this great favour worth to us, Don Charley?'

He answered: 'If you protect me, Damián, I shall protect you. Is that not sufficient?'

Since Mr Estrutt had all the money and our tickets, his answer could not fail to satisfy Damián. Yet it was embarrassing that two Palma businessmen whom I knew by sight should enter the Station Restaurant and greet me. I gazed blankly at them and pretended to be German. I even turned to Damián, saying: '*Heute ist Sonntag!*' which was all the German I knew. Damián, who is quick-witted enough, shook his head and answered: '*Donnerwetter!*' which was all the German *he* knew. The two Palma men sat down at a table in the far corner, and from there stared at us. We three dared not talk to one another in our own language until they had gone out again. The food, by the way, was not good.

This was two o'clock. Our train to Calais would depart at six o'clock; but four o'clock had passed, and five, and half past five, and a quarter to six, and still there we sat. At ten minutes to six, Damián said: 'I like this very little. What can have happened to Mr Estrutt?'

'Patience!' said I. 'He's a good fellow and will keep his word.'

But Sentiá grew more and more nervous. He cried out that we should never have come: we have been decoyed to Paris for some business of the Devil, he said – to be sold in slavery to the Moors, it might be. Had he no been plagued by a black foreboding on the day of the contract?

We made no reply. At last Damián stood up: 'Well,' he said, 'let us put on our overcoats and have everything ready. Mr Estrutt will, I have no doubt, appear mathematically at the last moment.'

Even as he spoke, Mr Estrutt burst into the restaurant, paid our small bill with a single large banknote, and rushed us off to the platform. We caught the Calais train with thirty seconds to spare.

'My God, that was close!' exclaimed Mr Estrutt, sinking into his seat. 'Nevertheless, I found what I went out to find!'

Damián asked: 'Was it a nice tender chicken?'

Mr Estrutt took the joke in good part. 'Alas, no,' he answered, 'this was serious business, not gastronomic pleasure. You shall hear about it one day. But I thank you very much for your great patience, boys! Now, what about a game of cards?' So we played *truc* until we reached Calais.

Contrary to all we had heard, the English Channel was as smooth as glass, and on the other side we found an altogether different country again, green and beautiful! Though it was already autumn, the sun shone without pause all the time we spent there. I cannot imagine why Spaniards call the English climate a bad one. At Dover, a huge Rolls-Royce limousine took us by road to London, in which we drove for hours, it seemed, through a wilderness of streets, and across the river *Támesis*. Finally we came to Piccadilly Circus with its fantastic coloured signs, and its hurrying crowds. Close by stood the Regent *Palacio* Hotel, where a private suite awaited us on the first floor, complete with two bathrooms, a dining-room, and every comfort in the world, including waiters to wait on us and a barber to shave us every day after breakfast!

Mr Estrutt was a humorous man. On the next morning he took Damián and me aside, and said: 'When the old hen enters to greet you, do not omit to condole with her on the fate of her poor daughter. The more profuse your condolences, the more it will disturb her conscience because of the kidnapping fiction; and the less carefully will she examine our expense account. Flatter her, too! I should have explained that we occupy this private suite owing to her fear of your making contact with the general public. I myself suggested that, were the short-haired girl's lawyer to hear of your presence here, he would surely try to impress the true story upon you; with the result that you might not wish to testify. It is a situation very useful for us. We shall play on these fears of hers, and enjoy a marvellous life together; and I shall never (in theory) let you stray from my sight.'

Scarcely had he spoken, when the Viscountess herself came through the door, wearing a fur-coat of black sable-skins, a black hat, and black gloves. She also kept a black-edged handkerchief pressed to her black eyes. After welcoming us in fluent Spanish, broken by many sobs, she thanked us from the bottom of a mother's heart for our readiness to rescue her daughter from that criminal Bulgarian heretic – whom the police, thanks be to the Virgin of Guadelupe! now held in safe custody. Sentiá wept too, and Damián assured her that he also had suffered a like tragic sorrow – his own daughter having once been decoyed away from home by an English Lord, ruined and cast aside like an old glove. Damián, as you know, is childless; and can lie without a tremor of his wicked face, which resembles carved mahogany. This tale impressed even Mr Estrutt, who patted Damián on the back and said in admiration: 'I wonder, Señor Frau, that your heart ever permitted you to forgive the English aristocracy. It must be ruled by a very pious spirit.'

A comedy, in short! For myself, I told the Viscountess that only so great a distress as hers could have persuaded me to abandon my island, my wife and my children, and venture to this unknown, this most terrifying city. The Viscountess, still occupied with her handkerchief, replied that only a Spaniard could have spoken so nobly. She was no less devout a Catholic than I, she declared, and God and the Virgin would bring the righteous cause to triumph.

I spoke what came into my mind. 'The Bulgarian heretic looked a veritable ruffian,' I said. 'Let us hope that they hang him high! Imagine any well-nurtured girl trusting herself to the beast! Yet that your poor daughter did so, must surely be a sign of her formidable innocence... But what surprises me in this painful affair is how you, Señora Viscountess, can be her mother – you do not look half old enough!'

'I married very young,' she explained, drying her eyes again.

When she went away, we opened the windows in order to drive out the strong perfume of violets and sandalwood which she had left behind.

The trial was postponed for a fortnight, because of some legal complication; we should now be absent for another three weeks at least, but none of us cared a tassel. On Mr Estrutt's advice, however, we told Mr Jonés that our business would surely go to ruin in our absence, and that we should need fifty pesetas a day, and one thousand at the close. The Viscountess was delighted to meet our demands, and we were delighted to sign a new contract. Never in my life had I earned so much money for nothing at all!

Mr Estrutt, I should tell you, had that same enormous Rolls-Royce limousine at his disposal whenever we wished to take an outing. He showed us the principal sights of London: the Tower and the Tower Bridge, and the Historical Waxworks, and the Museum of Animals and Birds, and the Docks, and the wonderful Botanical Gardens where one enters a tropical palm-house and nearly dies of the heat! Also the Law Courts, where we would soon give evidence, and many other places; with *cines* or music-halls nearly every evening.

Mr Estrutt also took us to visit his wives, first explaining to Sentiá that polygamy was customary among the Metropolitan Police force. Two of these wives lived in different parts of London – each occupying a small red brick house with a flower garden. We Majorcans sat in the sunny garden drinking beer and smoking cigarettes, while Mr Estrutt went upstairs to talk family affairs with his wife. Each wife also had a little boy, with whom we played, throwing a ball about on the lawn. We next met a third wife, who had a big house near Brighton. She seemed very rich, though not nearly so beautiful as the other two. The rich one gave us whisky and cigars, while we Majorcans sat on the lawn and played with a poodle-dog. Mr Estrutt afterwards showed us a new gold cigarette-lighter, his birthday present from this lady. The fourth wife, however, who lived many kilometres to the north of London, was old, ugly and ill-tempered. To judge from her curt greeting to Mr Estrutt, she must have been the head-wife. Or so Damián said, who had seen similar behaviour in Moorish families while doing his military service at Melilla; the head-wife was invariably jealous and spiteful.

One day Mr Estrutt took me aside and said: 'Toni, my friend, I think we need a little change. I have no complaint to make against the *Palacio*, but even the best hotel grows wearisome after three weeks. Nor should I wish my old clothes-rack of a Viscountess to think that I have forgotten the serious task that she has imposed on me. Be prepared, therefore, to move at midnight; but, as usual, not a word to Sentiá!'

That night, Sentiá retired at about eleven o'clock and was soon snoring. Then Mr Estrutt telephoned the Viscountess, speaking in tones of great seriousness. Damián and I heard her frightened voice ring high through the apparatus. Mr Estrutt answered: 'Yes, yes, yes, my lady!' several times. He told her, I believe, that though a Spanish-speaking waiter had been bribed by the short-haired girl's lawyer to provide us with the true story, his own prompt appearance fortunately interrupted the conversation as soon as it started. The Viscountess urgently begged Mr Estrutt to remove us to another hotel at once.

We packed our bags and woke Sentiá. Damián said: 'Lad, we are in great danger! The Bulgarian heretic has discovered us. Pack for your life!'

The Rolls-Royce limousine was waiting at the hotel door when we emerged. The Viscountess sat inside, very nervous, and wearing a purple scarf pulled over her face so that she might not be recognized. Mr Estrutt agreed that no time should be lost, and the chauffeur drove off without delay. We purred away at great velocity, but the Viscountess felt certain that we were being pursued. She ordered the chauffeur to dodge down side-streets at random, twisting and turning until we had shaken off the pursuit. The chauffeur obeyed but, however wild his course, she continued to peer through the rear-window and cry: 'There it is! The same car again!' Sentiá sweating with terror, kept crossing himself and asking: 'Do you think they will kill us?'

After an hour of this foolishness we reached open country. The chauffeur backed the Rolls-Royce down a lane, and turned off its lights. We sat in the darkness for another hour, while a stream of cars raced by. When at last the Viscountess was confident that she had cheated our pursuers, we turned back by devious ways, and at two o'clock in the morning found a new private suite awaiting us in the Estrand *Palacio* Hotel (hardly a kilometre distant from the Regent *Palacio*) where, for secrecy, we were admitted by the service door. Strange, was it not, that each of the hotels we visited on our journey was named the *Palacio*? But poor Sentiá had died a hundred deaths that night!

We wrote home once every week to say we were well, that business prospered, and that we trusted all would end normally; adding those graceful concluding phrases which one learns at school. Our families replied in the same manner, though more religiously. Nothing of importance had happened to the village during our absence, except that a great thunderstorm had torn many branches from my olive grove, and caused the walls of three terraces to collapse.

One day Mr Estrutt asked me: 'My friend, do you still enjoy this life?'

I answered: 'Enormously! Only think! under this new contract I shall soon have gained enough money for the purchase of a fine American car; giving my old Studebaker in partial payment. A just reward for all my hard labours! But, Don Charley, in one thing you have deceived us!'

'How deceived you?' he asked with surprise.

'Well,' I answered, 'you have fed us nobly, you have given us good beds, good drinks, and admirable Havana cigars, you have taken us often to the *cine* and the music-halls and once, even, to the Opera, besides showing us the famous sights of London... But you have not ministered to other pressing needs of ours! That is, as we say in Majorca, like asking children to view the confectioner's shop, but buying them no caramels. Though we are all good Catholics, none of us happens to be a monk.'

(How fortunate, Don Roberto, that at this particular stage of my story Isabel has gone off, to wash the dishes, I suppose, and feed the hens; otherwise I should have been forced to omit the subsequent incident. In any case, I must keep it short.)

Well, Mr Estrutt understood me before the words were well out of my mouth. 'If there is nothing else, my friend Toni, this can readily be arranged,' said he, 'but I had feared to make any suggestion that might offend your sensibilities. Not being members of the Metropolitan Police force, I thought you might consider yourselves less free in certain respects than I am. Very well, I shall at once telephone to an associate of mine who orders such matters. I promise that you will have no further cause to complain of having been deceived.'

He kept his word. That night after coffee, we heard a soft knocking at the door and in walked three beautiful smiling blondes, all wearing the tightest of silk dresses. Mr Estrutt at once made the necessary introductions, taking care to give us fictitious names. Then he uncorked a prodigiously large bottle of champagne and filled seven glasses. I quickly engaged the attention of the leading young lady; and Damián was not far behind me in securing the second. But Sentiá, who, as usual, had not been informed of the arrangement, sat perplexed and paralysed, goggling like a great moribund fish, when he saw the two young ladies perch on our knees. The third had addressed herself to Mr Estrutt, who explained, however, that the shy gentleman in the comer was her chosen sweetheart; he himself would merely be our interpreter. Although disappointed, she flung herself on Sentiá with a fine pretence of enthusiasm. Sentiá leaped up, knocking over his chair, and retreated to the bathroom; but the determined girl thrust her foot between the door and the jamb, calling on Mr Estrutt for help. Mr Estrutt pushed the door open, and when she had entered, locked it behind her.

I shall say no more than that Damián and I needed no interpreter... But, Lord, how ashamed of himself Sentiá was afterwards, and how we laughed! Of one thing we could be sure: once safely home again, he would never reveal one word of the proceedings, not even in the confessional!

The Viscountess came to visit us the next morning, with her usual tale of how God and the Virgin would uphold the right, and how greatly she appreciated our chivalrous defence of her Catholic home. Then, noticing suddenly how ill-at-ease Sentiá appeared to be, she laid a black-gloved hand on his shoulder to comfort him. 'My poor fellow,' she cried, 'you must miss your wife deeply!'

At that, Sentiá Dog-beadle wept like a little child. Fearful that he would make some foolish remark, I hastened to say: 'Yes, my lady, Sebastián here misses his Joana terribly, not having expected to be away so many weeks. Nor is he the only one of us who suffers. Don Damián and I are equally sensitive; but, for the sake of your unfortunate daughter, we try to suppress our misery.'

The Viscountess promised that we should never regret our visit, and charitably dabbed Sentiá's eyes with her scented black lace handkerchief. But even that did not console him!

Two days later, the divorce case began. Mr Estrutt sat with us in the Law Court and explained in a whisper who was who, and what was happening. The foxhunter had presented four or five charges of adultery in respect of the short-haired girl, but Mr Jonés and his squadron of lawyers chose from them only those two that seemed easiest to prove: namely, the affair with the Bulgarian artist at Damián's hotel, and an earlier affair in Paris with a rich Escottish manufacturer named Simon Macwilly. Mr Macwilly was married and, shocked to find himself cited as co-respondent in this case, had agreed to pay the short-haired girl's defence, so as to protect himself against the complaints of his wife.

It appears that an official of the British Embassy at Paris had lent Mr Macwilly his apartment during a temporary absence, and that the short-haired girl passed the night there with Mr Macwilly. This Embassy official, however, did not wish to be accused of pandering to his friend's vices, and when Mr Estrutt and Mr Jonés went to make inquiries of him, immediately sent his two servants away into the country, thus preventing them from becoming witnesses. The only relevant evidence could now come from a taxi-driver who had conducted the couple, with their bags, to the door of the apartment; and this would, perhaps, be found insufficient. Yet Mr Estrutt, by studying the calendar, reckoned that the short-haired girl must have spent another night somewhere in Paris, after vacating the Embassy official's apartment. Therefore, during our long wait at the Gare du Nord, he had persuaded his friends among the French Police to scrutinize the registers of certain hotels. Sure enough, they found a small hotel on the left bank of the *Sena* where Mr Macwilly had signed the register for himself and Mrs Macwilly on the night in question. The French hotel-keeper and his wife demanded an expense fee which Mr Jonés thought excessive, but which they refused to make less; to give the required evidence, they said, might injure their establishment's name for discretion. The Viscountess, however, would pay almost anything for this testimony, and an agreement was reached.

The charge of having committed adultery with Mr Macwilly was heard first. Now, on the previous afternoon the advocate, a King's Councillor, had explained to us just what questions he would ask, and how we should reply. This drama we rehearsed over and over again with the help of an interpreter; but Sentiá Dog-beadle proved so slow at learning his lesson that the advocate cried impatiently: 'Man, man, I hardly dare call you as a witness; for fear you may ruin our case! Your companions have far greater agility of mind.' We implored Sentiá to gather his wits, since three thousand pesetas hung on our satisfying the Judge; but he seemed like a lost man.

'You will be called next, boys!' Mr Estrutt warned us, as the first witness appeared and took the oath on a large Bible, which he kissed. Sentiá went whiter than a sheet at the warning, and began crossing himself like a madman. I felt uneasy myself, though with little cause, being now word-perfect in my lesson.

To be brief: the French hotelkeepers identified the short-haired girl, who was now wearing black in competition with the Viscountess, and swore to her presence at their establishment that night, in company with the fat, bald man who signed the register as Simon Macwilly. The couple had engaged two bedrooms with a communicating door, the key of which was on the short-haired girl's side.

When summoned to give evidence herself, the short-haired girl admitted having spent a night in that hotel, but strongly denied the charge of adultery. Mr Macwilly, she said, was liable to heart attacks and, as his only reliable friend in Paris, she had wished to be at hand to attend him if he were taken ill during the hours of darkness. Our advocate put it to her that misconduct had certainly taken place between them. She pretended to be outraged and cried: 'Misconduct, why, that is ridiculous! Mr Macwilly is an ancient man of sixty!'

It was a grave error in tactics. At once our advocate addressed the Judge (who was wearing an enormous wig, I did not ask why). Having observed the Judge's angry expression when the short-haired girl implied that, at sixty, a man is ancient and altogether spent, he said very shrewdly: 'My Lord, I shall call no more witnesses; but let my plea rest upon the evidence you have now heard.' For this Judge had not only just celebrated his sixtieth birthday: he had emphasized it by a third marriage!

Mr Estrutt had difficulty in repressing his joy when he heard these words spoken. He clapped Sentiá on the shoulder and whispered in his ear: 'My lad, you are saved!' Then he similarly told Damián and me: 'You also are saved. You will not be required to give evidence after all.'

Damián flew into a temper and asked in a loud voice: 'What of my thousand pesetas? I am being robbed. Why should I not give evidence?'

The Judge glared at Damián in great anger, calling for order in Court.

Mr Estrutt whispered: 'You madman, of course you will be paid!'

At that, Damián subsided, muttering.

We listened to the Judge's summing-up, and his decision that he could not believe the story told by this shameless young woman, and doubted whether anyone else present could believe it either. Then he praised our advocate for his great restraint in not pressing the second charge, and thus perhaps exposing the wretched woman as a common prostitute – since two proved charges of adultery, she must be aware, would under English Law earn her that disgraceful appellation!

In brief, he granted the divorce, and ordered the short-haired girl to pay all the legal costs of the case. Her advocate did not appeal from this decision, and so the case ended...

But that is not quite the end of my story. When the Judge and all the fashionable spectators had dispersed, there remained in Court only ourselves, the French hotelkeeper and his wife, several lawyers and their clerks, some ushers, the short-haired girl and the Viscountess. The costs of the case having been paid by Mr Macwilly's lawyers, the Viscountess came running up with eyes that shone like stars, and kissed us each in turn on both cheeks, including Mr Estrutt. She cried: 'God and the Virgin have listened to my prayers!'

It then amused me to say: 'Heartiest congratulations, my lady. Yet your poor daughter there seems quite overcome by distress. Perhaps she grieves for the fate of that Bulgarian heretic? Or could it be that she fears you will never forgive her?'

'Indeed, friend!' she cried. 'How stupid I am! I must make my peace with her at once.'

She hurried across to the short-haired girl, followed by Mr Estrutt, who was a most inquisitive man. He heard her say: 'My dear girl, you put up a very good fight, I must admit, and I do not wish to triumph over your misery, having suffered this sort of trouble myself once. What do you propose to do now?'

The short-haired girl smiled back at her faintly and replied: 'How can I tell? I have lost everything! Though Mr Macwilly has paid the costs of the case, his wife would never agree to a divorce, even if I consented to marry him, which I have no intention of doing. Boris is the man I love. Yet I have not a copper to call my own, and neither has Boris.'

The Viscountess kissed her on the forehead. 'My poor innocent,' she said, cooing like a pigeon. 'You should never have chosen an artist as your prospective husband, and really, were you not rather imprudent to tease the old Judge as you did? How much money would put you right with the world again?'

The short-haired girl thought for a moment. Then she said slowly: 'I fear I could hardly manage with less than ten thousand pounds. Boris and I might start some business with that, I suppose.'

'Let me make it twenty thousand!' cried the Viscountess in a burst of commiseration, producing her cheque-book and a gold fountain-pen. She signed the cheque then and there.

We Majorcans, too, profited from her generosity to the extent of still another thousand pesetas each; and six months later, we heard that she had married her foxhunter. On the very same day, but in a different city, the short-haired girl was united with the Bulgarian artist. They bought a *pensión* near San Sebastián, which is now very luxurious and always crowded; so Mr Estrutt recently informed me on a picture postcard. He wrote that his wife had accompanied him to San Sebastian for a holiday, and that he wished Damián Frau and I could have been present to share their fun. He did not specify which wife; but perhaps he had recently married a fifth, unknown to us, with the money that the Viscountess paid him.

You may wonder, as we all did, why the Viscountess, however fabulously rich, wasted so much money on the case when, by offering the short-haired girl twenty thousand pounds before the trial, she might have persuaded her not to defend the action. Well, the answer, supplied by Mr Estrutt, was that Mr P. P. Jonés advised against this course, which would have been a crime known as 'collusion', and therefore in conflict with his high moral principles. Besides, why should he deprive himself of an excessively profitable legal case? Again, the short-haired girl prided herself on having shown such prudence that no charge could possibly be proved against her; but she had not reckoned with a detective of the experience and perspicacity possessed by my friend, Mr Charley Estrutt!

She Landed Yesterday

AFTER COLLECTING THE family mail at five o'clock one Friday afternoon, in Majorca, where I live, I stopped by at the village café, and found
everyone disturbed and excited. I asked what was wrong. 'The Count of
Deià is dead,' Catalina told me, from behind the bar. She and her
husband, as proprietors of the café, know all the news. I could see that she
had been crying.

'But I met him only a few hours ago!' I exclaimed. 'He seemed in
perfect health and full of jokes, though perhaps rather sad ones.'

'Where was that, Don Roberto?'

'On the path near the Ass Rock.'

'At what time?'

'Just after the midday Angelus.'

'Then you must have been the last man to see him alive. What did he
say?'

'He asked me for a cigarette. I told him that I had no blond tobacco,
only black. "All the better," he said. "I do not enjoy smoking straw." I
handed him my old sealskin pouch and a packet of cigarette papers. We sat
down together on a rock. He rolled a cigarette, and I offered matches, but
he excused himself and used a small burning glass to light his cigarette. He
said that this was a more economical procedure, and besides the sun was
his friend.'

'Did he make any other remark?' Catalina asked.

'That the sun was indeed his only friend now.'

'The poor gentleman!'

'I had wine in my basket and gave him a drink. He took a sip, and then
considerately wiped the mouth of the flask with a clean handkerchief.
After discussing a Latin poet admired by both of us, we shook hands,
whereupon he went up the hill, hoping that I would soon pay him a visit.'

'He was found in the Ass Rock reservoir, at three o'clock – may his soul
find peace! Don Julián hurried there, followed by the doctor, who tried
artificial respiration. The Count had tied a heavy stone to his feet, but
Don Julián, who is a very good priest, always ready to give sinners the
benefit of every doubt, insisted that this had been an ill-advised means of

reaching the reservoir bottom in search of a fallen coin or some other small object. In effect, that the poor gentleman was the victim of an accident. He pointed out that the Count's gold watch and pocketbook had been placed for security on the wall. Then, although the doctor at last pronounced him dead, Don Julián would not believe it. He bent over the Count, asking him to make a sincere act of repentance. No reply came, but Don Julián says that the Count's face expressed humble assent, and that he therefore felt justified in giving him absolution. The deceased will be buried tomorrow, with the customary rites, the judge having now signed a certificate of accidental death.'

'A great solace for the Count's family,' I said.

'For what remains of it. He has a nonagenarian aunt in Madrid, and a second cousin, a nun, cloistered at Cartagena. The seven-hundred-year-old title is at last extinct.'

'There will be an all-night vigil at his house?'

'Yes, Don Roberto. My husband and I hope to see you there presently.'

How much did I know about the Count, after a casual acquaintance of four or five months? Not very much, really. He was what is called a character. My mother always warned me against becoming a character. I remember that when I once asked her the meaning of 'a character', she said, 'Like people who feed birds in public gardens, and usually have two or three perched on their heads.' But the Count would never have done anything so obvious and vulgar as that. Vultures, in a cemetery, perhaps. He was a neat, ugly little man of fifty, always dressed in the same grey fustian jacket and trousers, with a French hunting waistcoat, and his hirsute but well-manicured hands were, as a rule, fidgeting at the links of a thick gold watch chain. He never wore a hat, and his bald head was lavishly freckled. A humorous contempt for the world showed in the curl of his nostrils, and the anger smouldering behind his black eyes attracted me; most Majorcans are childishly stolid and complaisant. The Count talked a beautiful Castilian and a still more beautiful Majorcan. Our island aristocracy converse in *Mallorquí àulic*, a courtly dialect of their own, close to Provençal, and distinguished by numerous thirteenth-century forms that have disappeared from *Mallorquí plebeu*, the language of commoners. I gathered that the Count was recently widowed and had no children. I knew that he was an admirable Latin scholar, and an authority on the late-medieval Peasants' Revolt; he talked of publishing a monograph on Christopher Columbus, to prove him a Majorcan outlaw who had fled to Genoa after his family estates were confiscated at the collapse of the Revolt. The Count lived alone, attended by a valet, at Ca'n Deià – a tall sixteenth-century house, adjoining the church, which had his coat of arms carved above the lintel. Except for an occasional game of *truc* at the café, with the mayor, the schoolmaster, and the doctor, he took almost no part in village life. Women and children seemed to be scared of him, though I could not understand why, since he never raised his voice nor made a scene.

Every villager of consequence went to pay his last respects that evening. The Count ranked as a local man, because he owned Ca'n Deià; but the family seat was the Palacio Deià, at Palma, and until he settled among us, only six months before his death, Ca'n Deià had stood empty for generations, though it was opened and ritually whitewashed once a year, at Easter. The furniture, pictures, and china suggested the early 1830s as the period of its last tenancy. According to the sacristan, who preserved ancient village traditions, one of the Count's collateral ancestors – 'one afflicted with most informal habits' – was then guarded there by a couple of servants, to save his family the embarrassment of keeping him at home, or the disgrace of confining him in a madhouse. The sacristan explained that the unfortunate young fellow had had to be sewn into his clothes to prevent him from removing them in public, especially at Mass. 'He came here during the Carlist Wars,' he once told me, 'in the very year when a famine reduced the village to eating locust beans. It was he who contrived those silhouettes hanging on the passage walls. Are they not curious?' The silhouettes were intricate cut-outs, made of white paper: a palm tree, hunting scenes, pipe-smoking gallants in extravagant costume, heraldic designs, enormous doves, flowers, mermaids, and unicorns, all crazily juxtaposed on a background of blue sugar-loaf paper, but formalized by plain gilt frames.

The dead Count lay upstairs, among white roses and Madonna lilies, wearing court dress adorned with splendid orders. The flower scent nearly drowned the smell of camphor, and carefully placed rose petals hid, I discovered later, the more conspicuous holes (moths? mice?) in the black velvet of his suit – there had been no occasion for him to wear court dress since Alfonso XIII's abdication, more than twenty years before. The Count's face had been decently made up by the midwife, and everyone agreed that he looked as peaceful as a child; she had not disguised the characteristic half-smile at the corner of his mouth.

When I went in, a memory made my own mouth twitch sympathetically. '¡O Señor muerto!' I muttered. It was a joke that the Count had told me himself, about a village theatrical show he had once seen. A faithful page, discovering the murdered body of his liege lord, should have cried out, in desperation: '¡O Señor! ¡Muerto está! ¡Tarde llegamos!' ('O my lord! You are dead! We have come too late!') But the actor had learned his part from a prompt script without accents or punctuation, so he tripped onto the stage and gaily exclaimed, '¡O Señor muerto, esta tarde llegamos!' ('Oh, Mr Corpse, we are coming this evening!')

Downstairs, in the stone-flagged parlour, we mourners occupied a long line of low, corded chairs, such as almost every Majorcan family keeps for baptisms, funerals, weddings, and first communions. But these had been borrowed from the sacristan's house, next door; Ca'n Deià contained only huge seignorial armchairs in faded red velvet and tall black leather ones with octagonal brass studs. Black coffee and biscuits were served, and a box of cigars lay open on the two-inch-thick tabletop. As the last man to have seen the Count alive, I had to tell my story several times. For the sake of good manners, I embellished it by recalling his comments on the unstinted hospitality that the village worthies had shown him – the devout priest, the correct justice of the peace, the learned schoolmaster, the indefatigable doctor. But one genuine and most enigmatic remark of the Count's I kept to myself, for fear it might perhaps hurt someone's feelings. He had thrown the words over his shoulder as he turned toward the reservoir. 'She landed yesterday, you see. Not far from here. That is why I must leave you.'

Our solemn gathering grew somewhat cozier at eleven o'clock, when the electric light dimmed and recovered three times, as a sign that half an hour later it would be cut off for the night. At this signal, most of the villagers took their leave. Those of us who remained drew up our chairs in a circle around the table, and the Count's burly Majorcan valet, our host, lit long ecclesiastical tapers stuck in pewter candlesticks. Two bottles of brandy, and another of *anís* appeared on a tray, and we soon started talking freely. There were seven of us: Guillermo, the valet; the schoolmaster, who had literary pretensions; the emaciated sacristan; María, the midwife; Don Tomás Fons y Pons, the Count's family lawyer, whom I had not met before; Catalina's husband, who drives our village bus as well as owning the café; and myself.

'An ideally constituted party,' said the schoolmaster, beaming. 'More in number than the Graces, and less in number than the Muses.'

'But,' said the sacristan, 'precisely equal in number with those who sufficiently honour the memory of the deceased gentleman upstairs to keep an all-night vigil for him!'

'I have seen no member of the nobility about the village,' said Catalina's husband, 'though news of his accident must have reached the capital hours ago.'

The lawyer stroked his white moustache, hemmed, and explained: 'Many are out of town, the rest are attending the Italian opera. But we can expect representatives of all the great families at tomorrow's funeral service. They cannot well omit this act of courtesy to one who was not only the senior nobleman of Majorca but also hereditary pomander-bearer to His Majesty the King of Spain.'

'The hypocrites, how they disliked my master!' the valet burst out. 'His father fell in love with a beautiful peasant girl from Costitx at the

Martinmas pig-killing, and had the good sense to marry her, instead of seducing the poor innocent and flinging a hundred-peseta note in her lap, as any of them would have done. She was a woman of great character, was the old Countess, and pious to a fault. Those degenerates pretended to scorn our Count as the offspring of a misalliance, yet they envied him his learning, his courage, his independence of spirit! None of them but would have been the better for a few spoonfuls of wholesome peasant blood in his veins. The old Countess died when my master was five years old, and he adored her memory; indeed, some say that it was the unfortunate nobleman's ruin.'

'Come, man!' María, the midwife, challenged him. 'How can adoration for a mother's memory ruin anyone?'

Guillermo appealed to the lawyer. 'Don Tomás, correct me if I am wrong, but this is the story as told in the servants' quarters, and we are sticklers for accuracy.'

'Tell it your own way, Guillermo,' said the lawyer.

'Well,' the valet continued, 'Don Ignacio, the Count's only brother, two years his junior, drove a fast car down the La Puebla road. Rain had fallen, and the tarmac was slippery with mud from the potato carts. He had his wife beside him, and both were killed instantly when they skidded and hit a tree. Their graceful, green-eyed, thirteen-year-old daughter, Doña Acebo, came under my master's guardianship – she had no suitable aunts or other relatives on either side of the family – and since he was a bachelor, this embarrassed him a little. But he accepted his responsibility, and, finding the child sadly ignorant, though not lacking in intelligence or humour, removed her from the convent school where she had studied, and became her tutor. They lived in the Palacio Deià. He taught Doña Acebo history, heraldry, geography, botany, French, and Latin. She soon dropped her school friends, because none of them had the same interests or enjoyed the same liberty as herself, and my master kept her out of Palma society – "Lest she should turn into a profligate modern woman," as he said. Only three hours a day she studied, yet they were worth thirty hours at a convent, for he taught like an angel, and work was more like play to them. The family chaplain, of course, attended to her religious needs. My master took Doña Acebo everywhere with him – to theatres, concerts, bullfights, cockfights, freestyle wrestling matches – but both enjoyed far more the entertainments of their own devising. They were formidable jokesters, and would leave the palace at all hours, disguised as gipsies, or drunks, or pedlars, or peasants, and have a thousand droll adventures in the bystreets of Palma.'

'Give us an example,' said the schoolmaster. '"A thousand droll adventures" is no way to tell a story!'

'Well, they once competed as to who could first earn fifty pesetas from a stranger by barefaced fraud. I was the timekeeper. My master, wearing a cloth cap, a false beard, and spectacles, visited a second-hand bookstall, where he paid five pesetas for a volume on apiculture. He then added a zero to the figure on the flyleaf, wrapped the book in a sheet of brown paper, slipped into a café to find a newspaper, and went through the obituary notices on the second page of *La Ultima Hora*. Discovering that a certain Don Fulano de Tal, an importer of uralite piping, had died only two streets away, he took the book to his house, and inquired for Don Fulano. "Alas, he is dead!" sobbed the widow. "Alas, and doubly alas!" echoed the Count. "Don Fulano, a valued friend of mine, ordered this volume a week ago, and I have just managed to procure it in Barcelona." He was turning sorrowfully away when the widow asked leave to inspect the book. "Ah, a practical treatise on beekeeping," she said tenderly. "My poor angel must, after all, have contemplated the tranquil country life that I so often urged upon him, begging him to sell his business in good time. How right I was, for an overworked heart carried him off. I must buy this as a memento of his affection. How much did it cost you?" My master showed her the price on the flyleaf, and mentioned another five pesetas of postal charges. In the circumstances, he was prepared to forgo his commission, and the widow let him do so, thanking him for his nobility of heart. That game took less than half an hour, but Doña Acebo had already won the contest. She sold two out-of-date twenty-five-peseta raffle tickets for an automobile to some German tourists and was home before my watch marked five minutes.'

'Proceed with your story, man!' said María, the midwife. 'You mentioned the Count's ruinous love for his dead mother.'

'I am coming to that. The innocent comradeship between the Count and Doña Acebo could not last forever, because, as she grew older and plumper, she came to bear such a close resemblance to the portrait of her grandmother, the old Countess, whose Christian name she inherited, that they might have been twins. In short, when she reached the age of fifteen, my master fell in love with her, much to his alarm and confusion. What should he do? The two had become so deeply attached to each other, from living alone in the great palace, with only the chaplain and us servants as chorus to their prolonged comedy, that it seemed most cruel to send her away. But would it not be worse if she stayed? After much heart-searching, and with the chaplain's dubious approval, he decided to marry her. Of course, though marriage between uncle and niece can be sanctioned by the Church, out of respect for a well-known gospel precedent, such unions are extremely rare. Here in this village, if an uncle were to show a niece undue tenderness, conches would be blown all night around his house, and filth left on the doorstep. But to a Count of Deià all things within reason are permitted, for did not his ancestors play a distinguished part in restraining the Majorcan clergy from allegiance to the anti-popes at Avignon? Nevertheless, it was a costly and troublesome procedure, even for my master, to secure a dispensation from the Vatican; to begin with, the Bishop of Palma had to supply a covering letter, explaining the peculiar nature of the case, and the Bishop raised technical difficulties.'

'Enough, Guillermo!' interrupted the lawyer. 'Leave the intricacies of canon law to canons, and stick to the facts! The Count of Deià and Doña Acebo were married, and it proved no happy marriage.'

'That is the truth,' the valet agreed. 'At first, Doña Acebo, who was still only sixteen years old, treated the wedding as another of their wild, scandalous jokes, and one that would give her an enviable social status, so they went off on their honeymoon to San Sebastián in the highest spirits. Then, finding that she was seriously expected to become her uncle's wife, in fact as well as name, and to present him with an heir, she felt a certain distaste and even, it may be, moral scruples, though their union had been fully legitimized.'

'I heard some talk of that,' said the midwife, keeping a straight face. 'She rejected his caresses, but in a most affectionate manner.'

'"Affectionate" is right, Doña María,' the valet answered, no less gravely. 'The Count was very ticklish, and whenever he attempted any more than avuncular endearments, she would tickle him in the ribs until he nearly died from laughter and annoyance.'

The lawyer interrupted again. 'A tragic tale! The exasperated Count, aware that he had made a serious error, but determined to teach his Countess a lesson, sued for an annulment – which proved as troublesome and costly to obtain as the marriage licence – without her consent or knowledge. One fine morning, she awoke to find the wedding ring absent from her finger, and when she raised a hue and cry, Margalida the house-maid informed her, as she had been instructed, that she no longer had any need of the trinket.'

'Doña Acebo resented this joke so bitterly,' said the valet, nodding his head up and down for emphasis, 'that the couple never resumed their former carefree play, and soon she ran off with a young Colombian band leader, whom she had encountered at Tito's Bar. From every city they visited, to comply with his engagements, she would send the Count picture postcards of lovers – some sentimental, some grossly comic, and all in the lowest popular taste. The Count grew increasingly morose, and took to his bed, seeing nobody. When at last he regained his health, we found him altered and the prey to a compulsion for strange games. If we attended Mass in Santa Eulalia church, for instance, where patterns of alternate white and dark-red marble squares line the pavement, he would experience great difficulty in approaching the altar steps; there were always holy women kneeling in prayer on the red marble squares he felt he had to tread upon. "Excuse me, good woman," he would mutter. "Would you mind moving twenty centimetres to the right?" They would look up in great vexation, but he always got his way. The Mass priest would blanch when he saw him, because the Count, once he had gained the steps, would wring his hands and utter a low moan of "Oo-oo!" at the slightest mispronunciation or grammatic error in Latin.'

'I watched him once for a half an hour at the Palm Sunday Fair,' put in Catalina's husband, 'some three months after Doña Acebo's departure. He was leaning over the counter of the shooting gallery, and behind him waited a queue of little boys, whom he made stand to attention, like soldiers. Having fired a few preliminary shots to gauge the precise twist in his rifle barrel, he bought an enormous stack of counters and shot with monotonous insistence at the same iron plate. "Crack!" "Crack!" "Crack!" At each hit, a door would fly open, and out came a doll, dressed as a waitress, with a tray in her hands, and on it a miniature bottle of so-called *vermut*. He would beckon for the bottle, uncork it, pour the contents down the throat of the foremost boy, send him back to the end of the queue, and resume his marksmanship. The proprietor shouted curses at him, but could do nothing else.'

'Why did he leave the palace?' asked the sacristan. 'Was it to avoid unhappy memories of his marriage?'

'Perhaps,' said the valet. 'But he announced that he had taken refuge from the enemy, here in the mountains. When I inquired what enemy, he answered, "Those who smoke blond tobacco; those who strew our quiet Majorcan beaches with pink, peeling human flesh; those who roar round the island in foreign cars ten metres long; those who prefer aluminium to earthenware, and plastics to glass; those who demolish the old quarters of Palma and erect travel agencies, souvenir shops, and tall, barrack-like hotels on the ruins; those who keep their radios bawling incessantly along the street at siesta time; those who swill Caca-Loco and bottled beer!" The last straw came with the closing of the Café Fígaro, which everyone of character in Palma used to frequent, and the conversion of its premises into palatial offices for Messrs Thomas Cook & Son. He had sat there most mornings, at a corner table, playing dominoes with the Cat-stewer –'

'Who was that?' I asked.

Both the schoolmaster and Catalina's husband wanted to tell me about the Cat-stewer, but the sacristan held the floor. It appears that this well-known figure had been cook to the old Bishop of Palma, who died, and the new Bishop made the mistake of criticizing one of his sauces. Though he kept silent his pride was wounded, and at a banquet to which the new Bishop invited the Captain-General and his staff, he served up a delicious rabbit ragout. When called into the dining room to receive extravagant compliments, he said, 'Yes, beyond all doubt I am the best cook in Majorca! I can make stewed alley cat taste like the tenderest rabbit. And now, My Lord Bishop, I have finished, and wish you and your guests a very good night!' He threw his tall chef's hat on the floor, and marched out in glory. After that, he drifted around Palma picking up cigarette butts dropped by tourists, and accepting coffees from Palma folk who admired his spirit. He never cooked another meal. In the severe shortage of cooks caused by the building of too many hotels, the Cat-stewer was wooed with enormous offers – up to a hundred thousand pesetas a year – for his culinary services. He only spat for an answer.

'What did the Count do about his persecution by the ex-Countess's postcards?' I asked.

It was an embarrassing question. Three of my fellow-mourners stirred uncomfortably in their chairs, but kept silent, warned by the lawyer's frown.

María, the midwife, took pity on me. 'The Count had peasant blood, Don Roberto. It is known that, in his chagrin, he consulted a wise woman at Andraitx. Nothing can be said for certain as to the advice she gave him. At all events, the persecution ended when Doña Acebo died, early last year.'

'How did she die, Doña María?'

'By drowning, also. The new liner in which she and her young band leader were travelling from Brazil to the Argentine struck a rock and foundered.'

Don Tomás hastily changed the subject. 'The Count had the kindest heart,' he babbled. 'One day, plagued by his neurotic compulsion, he tried to pass from one end of San Miguel Street to the other while dodging alternately to the right and left of persons who approached. This made him perform a hazardous dance, because it was a busy Saturday morning, with the farmers, as usual, crowding the streets and the tables outside the Café Suiza. Along roared a Vespa motor scooter; the Count dashed across its path, trying to pass it on his right. The scooter struck his foot, the rider fell off, and the machine fell, though its engine continued to throb where it lay overturned by the sidewalk. A baker's boy astride a bicycle, balancing a huge tray of pastries on his head, ran into the Vespa, and all the pastries were spilled. "Young man," cried the Count to the Vespa rider, who was nursing a bruised elbow, "how dare you take your dangerous machine down San Miguel Street on a Saturday morning?" A blind woman lottery vendor, seated on the curb, felt her skirts lifted by the wind of the Vespa's exhaust, and let out a scream. The Count immediately paid the baker's boy, and then consoled the old creature, kissed her hand, bought five lottery tickets and tore them up – having a soul above money – and guided her into the Suiza, where she rapidly downed several brandies. The baker's boy collected the pastries, dusted them on his trousers, restacked them on the tray, and rode on, the richer by a hundred pesetas. The deceased had his faults, as who had not, but will we ever look upon his like again?'

We sat talking and drinking until five o'clock, and then prepared to depart. We went upstairs for a last farewell, before leaving the Count to the companionship of his best friend, who was already gilding the mountain-tops. 'The Spanish taste for black velvet,' observed the schoolmaster sententiously, eyeing the Count's court dress, 'is often thought to reflect the gloomy side of our national character. That is an error. Our ancestors gloried in the indigo plant, which alone afforded them a fast sable dye to contrast with the brilliant white of their linen cuffs and ruffs. Spanish black velvet never turned rusty or green. Guillermo did well in choosing those lilies and roses to set it off. Our friend's darkest moods were always enlivened by vivid flashes of the purest white.'

The funeral Masses for the Count took place at ten o'clock, and every noble house in Palma sent representatives. Our village square was crowded with their sleek American and Italian cars. The visitors kept together in a tight, silent bunch, and made me feel a peasant of peasants. Throughout the service, which the Bishop himself conducted, with the aid of several subsidiary priests, including Don Julián, I was puzzling to myself: 'She landed yesterday, you see. Not far from here. That is why I must leave you.' *Who* had landed that Thursday? Where? 'She' could not have been Doña Acebo, and it was generally agreed that no other woman had figured in the Count's adult life. María, the midwife, had hinted at a recourse to witchcraft, but since witchcraft is a subject that Majorcans never discuss with foreigners, I concluded that it would be wiser to let the problem lie.

The next day, as it happened, Jack and Gloria Stonegate – Jack is a shrewd North of England retired businessman, and Gloria is a genius at repairing antique china – had asked my wife and me to lunch with them at Paguera, which is a few miles from Andraitx. Paguera has the sunniest climate in Majorca, which means, of course, insufficient rain, and therefore a perpetual water shortage. But against that you may set a fine, sandy beach, pine forests, and swimming as early as March.

'Anything new happened here since last time?' I asked Jack, over drinks.

'Nothing much, old boy, except two motor-bike accidents, one death by drowning, a kerosene shortage, a fight between some Dutchmen in the grocery store, and a coffin washed up on the islet three days ago.'

'The coffin sounds the most interesting.'

'It certainly was! It contained a carved wooden doll, about three feet long – obviously a portrait of someone real – wearing a bridal robe and veil. What do you make of *that?* Round her shoulders she wore a miniature postbag, striped with the Spanish colours, and in the bag we found an assortment of rather stupid amatory picture postcards from all over the place – Tangier, Honolulu, Blackpool, Atlantic City, Copenhagen. The name and address of the person who had received them all had been care-

fully scraped away with a razor, and there was no message on any of them
– only the signature "A".'
'How big was the coffin?'
'Life-size. It must have been a long time in the water. I got a good look
at the cards. The latest one came from Rio de Janeiro, postmarked eighteen months ago. A yard or two of frayed rope hung from a handle of the
coffin. Evidently it had been weighted down by stones – the lead lining
wasn't quite heavy enough to keep it on the bottom – but it must have
broken loose in the big storm last week. The Guardias and the priest were
examining it as I wandered up. The priest seemed shocked to the core,
and even the Guardias were upset. What do you make of that story, old
boy?'
'Oh, just a practical joke,' I reassured Jack. 'Some Majorcans will go to
any length for a laugh – you'd be surprised!'
'I call it a damned macabre form of humour,' Jack grumbled. 'But then,
I'm English.'

Please do not ask whether, in my opinion, Doña Acebo's death by
drowning was just a coincidence. Be content with facts. The coffined doll
must be accepted as valid evidence that the Count, with a witch's assis-
tance, tried to procure Doña Acebo's death by magical means.
Unofficially, my fellow-villagers do not doubt that he succeeded. They
condemn his action as un-Catholic, of course, but the provocation was
enormous, and how else could a Count of Deià, with a peasant mother,
have been expected to act? Officially, they agree with the priest: it was a
sad coincidence. Officially, so do I.

The Lost Chinese

JAUME GELABERT WAS a heavily-built, ill-kempt, morose Majorcan lad of seventeen. His father had died in 1936 at the siege of Madrid, but on the losing side, and therefore without glory or a dependant's pension; his mother a few years later. He lived by himself in a dilapidated cottage near our village of Muleta, where he cultivated a few olive terraces and a lemon grove. On my way down for a swim from the rocks, three hundred feet below, I would cut through Jaume's land and, if we happened to meet, always offered him an American cigarette. He would then ask if I were taking a bathe, to which I answered either: 'You have divined my motive correctly,' or: 'Yes, doctors say it benefits the health.' Once I casually remarked that my blue jeans had grown too tight and, rather than throw them away, I wondered if they might come in handy for rough work. 'I could perhaps use them,' he answered, fingering the solid denim. To say 'thank you' would have been to accept charity and endanger our relationship; but next day he gave me a basket of cherries, with the excuse that his tree was loaded and that June cherries were not worth marketing. So we became good neighbours.

This was June 1952 – just before Willie Fedora appeared in Muleta and rented a cottage. The United States Government was paying Willie a modest disability grant, in recognition of 'an anxiety neurosis aggravated by war service in Korea', which supported him nicely until the tide of tourism sent prices rocketing. Brandy then cost a mere twelve pesetas a litre, not thirty-six as now; and brandy was his main expense.

Our small foreign colony, mostly painters, at first accepted Willie. But the tradition here is that instead of drinking, playing bridge, sun-bathing, and discussing one another's marital hazards, as at expensive resorts with more easily accessible beaches, foreigners *work*. We meet only in the evening around a café table, when our mail has arrived. Occasional parties are thrown, and sometimes we hire the village bus for a Sunday bullfight; otherwise we keep ourselves to ourselves. Willie disliked this unsociable way of life. He would come calling on trivial pretexts, after breakfast, just when we were about to start work, and always showed his independence by bringing along a four-litre straw-covered flask of cheap brandy – which he called 'my samovar' – slung from his shoulder. To shut the door in Willie's face would have been churlish; to encourage him, self-destructive. Usually, we slipped out by the back door and waited until he had gone off again.

Willie wrote plays; or, rather, he laboured at the same verse play for months and months, talking about it endlessly but making no progress. The hero of *Vercingetorix* (Willie himself disguised in a toga) was one of Julius Caesar's staff-captains in the Gallic War. Whenever Willie began his day's work on *Vercingetorix* he needed to down half a pint of brandy, because of the fearful load of guilt which he carried with him and which formed the theme of his Roman drama. Apparently towards the end of the Korean War, a senior officer had put Willie in charge of five hundred captured Chinese Communists but, when he later marched them to the pen, a bare three hundred were left. The remainder could neither have been murdered, nor committed suicide, nor escaped; yet they had disappeared. 'Disappeared into thin air!' he would repeat tragically, tilting the samovar. Any suggestion that these Chinamen had existed only on paper – a 3 scrawled in the heat of battle, we pointed out, might easily be read as a 5 – enraged Willie. 'Goddam it!' he would shout, pounding the table. 'I drew rations and blankets for five hundred. Laugh *that* off!'

Before long, we shut our doors against Willie. Let him finish his play, we said, rather than talk about it; and none of us felt responsible for his lost Chinese. Yet every night they haunted his dreams, and often he would catch glimpses of them skulking behind trees or barns even by day.

Now, it is an old custom at Muleta to support the Catholic China Missions, and on 'China Day' the school children paint their faces yellow, slant their eyebrows and dress themselves up in the Oriental clothes, of uncertain origin, which the Mother Superior of our Franciscan convent distributes from a long, deep, camphor-scented chest. They drive around in a tilt-cart and collect quite a lot of money; though who ultimately benefits from it remains a mystery, because (as I told the incredulous Mother Superior) no foreign missions have been tolerated in China for some years. Unfortunately, the young Chinese came tapping at Willie's cottage window one afternoon and scared him out of his wits. Accidentally smashing his samovar against a wine barrel as he stumbled into the café, Willie collapsed on the terrace. When he felt better, we recommended a Palma doctor. He groaned at us: 'You jump off a cliff! I'm through with you all. I'm going native.'

Willie did go native. To the surprise of Muleta, he and Jaume Gelabert struck up a friendship. Jaume, already branded as the son of a Red, had earned a reputation for violence at that year's *fiesta* of San Pedro, Muleta's patron saint. The Mayor's sharp-tongued son who owned a motorcycle and led the *atlots*, or village bucks, made Jaume his victim. 'Behold the Lord of La Coma!' Paco sneered. Jaume went pale. '"Lord of La Coma" comes badly from you, Paco, you loud-mouthed wencher! Your own uncle robbed my widowed mother of her share in the estate, and the whole village knew it, though they were too cowardly to protest.' Paco then extemporized a *copeo*, a satiric verse of the sort current on San Pedro's Day:

> *The Lord of La Coma he lives in disgrace:*
> *He never eats crayfish nor washes his face!*

A group of *atlots* took up the chorus, dancing in a ring around Jaume:

> *Ho, ho, that's how we go –*
> *He never eats crayfish nor washes his face!*

Jaume pulled a stake from the baker's fence and ran amok, felling Paco and a couple of other *atlots* before he was disarmed by Civil Guards and shoved without ceremony into the village lockup. The Justice of the Peace, Paco's father, bound Jaume over after a stern caution. At Muleta, no decent man ever uses force: all fighting is done either with the tongue or with money.

The two social outcasts became such close friends that it spared us further responsibility for Willie's health. He had decided to learn Majorcan from Jaume. This old language, not unlike Provençal, is in domestic use throughout the island, though discountenanced by the Government. Willie had a natural linguistic gift, and within three months could chatter fluent Majorcan – the sole foreigner in Muleta (except my children, who went to school there) who ever achieved the feat. Willie gratefully insisted on teaching Jaume how to write plays, having once majored in dramatic composition at a Midwestern university, and meanwhile laid *Vercingetorix* aside. By the spring, Jaume had finished *The Indulgent Mother*, a Majorcan comedy based on the life of his great-aunt Catalina. In return he had made Willie eat solid food, such as bean porridge and *pa amb oli*, and drink more red wine than brandy. Jaume did not question Willie's account of those lost Chinese, but argued that the command of five hundred prisoners must have been too great a burden for so young a soldier as Willie; and that omniscient God had doubtless performed a miracle and cut down their numbers. 'Suppose someone were to give me five hundred sheep!' he said. 'How would I manage them all single-handed? One hundred, yes; two hundred, yes; three hundred, perhaps; five hundred would be excessive.'

'But, if so, why do these yellow devils continue to haunt me?'

'Because they are heathen and blaspheme God! Pay no attention! And if they ever plague you, eat rather than drink!'

In 1953, Muleta suffered a financial crisis. Foul weather ruined the olive prospects, blighted the fruit blossom, and sent numerous terraces rumbling down. Moreover, Dom Enrique, our parish priest, had ordered a new altar and rebuilt the chancel at extravagant cost; while neglecting the church roof, part of which fell in after a stormy night. One consequence was that the village could not afford to hire the Palma Repertory Troupe for their usual San Pedro's Day performance. But Dom Enrique heard about Jaume's play, read it, and promised to raise a cast from the *Acción Católica* girls and their *novios*: if Willie would stage-manage the show, and Jaume devote its takings to the Roof Fund.

This plan naturally met with a good deal of opposition among the village elders: Willie, now nicknamed 'Don Coñac', and Jaume the violent Red, seemed most unsuitable playwrights. Dom Enrique, however, had felt a certain sympathy for Jaume's use of the stake, and also noted the happy improvement in Willie's health under Jaume's care. He preached a strong sermon against the self-righteous and the uncharitable and, having got his way, cleverly cast Paco as the juvenile lead. Nevertheless, to avoid any possible scandal, he laid it down that rehearsals must follow strict rules of propriety: the girls' mothers should either attend or send proxies. He himself would always be present.

The Indulgent Mother, which combined the ridiculous with the pathetic, in a style exploited by Menander, Terence, Plautus and other ancient masters, was an unqualified success. Although no effort of Willie's or Dom Enrique's, as joint stage-managers, could keep the cast from turning their backs on the audience, gagging, mumbling, hamming, missing their cues, and giggling helplessly at dramatic moments, the Roof Fund benefited by fifteen hundred pesetas; and a raffle for a German wrist-watch (left on the beach two years previously) brought in another eight hundred. The *Baleares* printed a paragraph on the remarkable young playwright, Don Jaime Gelabert, below the heading: 'Solemn Parochial Mass at Muleta; Grandiose Popular Events.' Paco and his *novia*, the heroine, also secured a niche in the news.

Meanwhile Willie, whom the *Baleares* unfortunately named 'Don Guillermo Coñac, the transatlantic theatrician,' had celebrated Jaume's debut a little too well, singing Negro spirituals in the village streets until long after midnight. When at last he fell insensible, Paco and the other *atlots* pulled off his clothes and laid him naked on a vault in the churchyard, with the samovar under his head. He was there discovered by a troop of black-veiled old *beatas*, or religious women, on the way to early Mass – an appalling scandal! Jaume had gone straight home, after the final curtain, to escape congratulations. In the morning, however, he pieced the story together from village gossip, caught Paco outside the café and threw him into the Torrent, where he broke an ankle. This time, Jaume would have been tried in the capital for attempted homicide, had Willie not intervened. 'Punish Jaume,' he warned the Mayor, 'and you will force me to sue your son. I have witnesses who can testify to his shameless behaviour, and the United States Government is behind me.'

Jaume and I remained on good terms. I told him: 'Jaume, in my view you acted correctly. No true friend could have done less under such provocation.'

Winter and spring went swiftly by, and another San Pedro's Day was on us. Willie visited Dom Enrique at the Rectory and offered to stage-manage a new play of Jaume's: *The Difficult Husband*. He did not arrive drunk but (as they say in Ireland) 'having drink taken', and when he announced that this comedy had merits which would one day make it world famous, Dom Enrique could hardly be blamed for excusing himself. A deceased widow, the Lady of La Coma, had just left the Church a small fortune, on the strength of which his parishioners trusted him to re-engage the Palma Repertory Troupe as in previous years.

Bad news further aggravated this setback. Jaume, due for the draft, had counted on being sent to an anti-aircraft battery, three miles away, from where he could get frequent leave; in fact, the Battery commander had promised to arrange the matter. But something went wrong – Paco's father may have spoken a word in the Captain's ear – and Jaume was ordered to Spanish Morocco.

Willie, with streaming eyes, promised to irrigate the lemon grove, plough around the olive trees, plant the beans when the weather broke, and wait patiently for Jaume's return. But two hundred phantom Chinese took advantage of his loneliness to prowl among the trees and tap at the kitchen window. Willie's samovar filled and emptied, filled and emptied four or five times a week; he neglected the lemon grove, seldom bothered with meals, and locked the cottage door against callers: at all costs he must finish an English translation of *The Difficult Husband*. I met him one morning in the postman's house, where he was mailing a package to the States. He looked so thin and lost that, on meeting the Mayor, I suggested he should take some action. 'But what would you have me do?' cried the Mayor. 'He is committing no crime. If he is ill, let him consult the Doctor!' That afternoon, Willie saw Toni Coll digging a refuse pit below the cottage: convinced that this was to be his own grave, he sought sanctuary in the church organ-loft, drank himself silly, and was not discovered for twenty-four hours. Dom Enrique and his mother carried him to the Rectory, where they nursed him until the American Embassy could arrange his transfer to the States. At New York, a veterans' reception committee met Willie, and he was sent to a Pittsburgh army hospital. On New Year's Day, 1955, he broke his neck falling out of a window, apparently pursued by Chinese oppressors. I felt bad about him.

If Muleta expected to hear no more about Jaume's comedy, Muleta erred. Just before the rockets soared up in honour of San Pedro two years later,

Mercurio the postman (who also acts as our telegraphist) tugged at my sleeve. 'Don Roberto,' he said, 'I have a telegram here from New York for a certain William Schenectady. Do you know the individual? It came here three days ago, and none of your friends recognize the name. Could he be some transitory tourist?'

'No: this is for our unfortunate Don Coñac,' I told him. In Spain only the middle name counts, being the patronymic, and Willie's passport had read 'William Schenectady Fedora.'

'A sad story,' sighed Mercurio. 'How can telegrams benefit the dead, who are unable even to sign a receipt? And there is no means of forwarding the message...'

'I'll sign, since that's what worries you,' I said. 'Probably it contains birthday greetings from some old aunt, who has remained ignorant of his fate. If so, I'll tear it up.'

After the fun was over, I remembered the cable. It ran:

WILLIAM SCHENECTADY FEDORA: MULETA: MAJORCA: SPAIN MAGNIFICENT BRAVO BRAVO BRAVO STOP DIFICTUL HUSBAN SENSACIONAL FUST THE PLOY NEEDED ON BIRDWAY WIT NEUMANN DIRECION HARPVICKE IN THE LED STOP AIRMALLING CONTRACT STOP PROPOSE FOLOV UP WIT PRESONAL VISIT SO ONEST KINDLY REPLAY STOP REGARDS EVERETT SAMSTAG EMPIRE STAT ENTERPRIXES NEW YORK

I frowned. My neighbour Len Simkin was always talking about Sammy Samstag, the Broadway impresario, and had even promised Willie to interest him in *Vercingetorix*; but somehow this cable did not seem like a joke. Who would waste ten dollars on kidding a dead man? Yet, if it wasn't a joke, why did Samstag send no prepaid reply coupon?

I tackled Mercurio, who admitted that such a form had, as it happened, come with the cable for Don Coñac; adding: 'But since Don Coñac is no more, perhaps some other foreigner may care to dispatch a telegram with its help.' So I cabled Samstag:

INTERESTED IN YOUR INTEREST STOP WILL ADVISE AUTHOR OF DIFFICULT HUSBAND CURRENTLY ON SAFARI TO GRANT OPTION IF FINANCIALLY COMMENSURATE WITH YOUR TRIPLE BRAVO STOP REGARDS

To explain that Willie was no longer available, and that the job of protecting Jaume fell to me, would have exceeded the prepaid allowance, so I signed 'Fedora'. 'Currently on safari' was cablese for 'at present trailing his rifle through North Africa, but will be back next week', and sounded far more opulent.

At the café, I met Len, a young-old fabricator of abstract mobiles. He had once briefly taken a very small part in an off-Broadway play, but was Muleta's sole contact with the Great White Way. 'A pity poor Willie's dead,' I said, when Len had finished his scathing comments on last night's performance by the Palma Repertory Troupe. 'He might have got you a speaking part in this new Broadway play. Willie always admired your delivery.'

'I don't get the joke,' Len grumbled. 'That wack gave me the creeps! One of those "creative artists" who create chaos. A few drinks from the old samovar, and I could *see* those goddamned Chinese! I bet they infiltrated into his coffin, and pulled the lid down after them.'

'If you take my front-page news like that, Len,' I told him, 'you'll not be offered even a walk-on!'

'Still, I don't get it...'

'Well, you will – as soon as Sammy Samstag turns up here toting an enormous box of Havanas, and you're left in a corner smoking your foul *Peninsulares.*'

'Neumann directing? Hardwicke in the lead as Vercingetorix?'

'No, the title isn't *Vercingetorix*. It's *The Difficult Husband*. Otherwise you've guessed right.'

'You're very fonny, don't you, Mister?' Len stalked away, then wheeled angrily, and came out with a splendid curtain line: 'In my opinion, jokes about dead Americans stink!'

When Jaume stepped from the Palma-Muleta bus, looking bigger and more morose than ever, no one rolled out the red carpet. That evening I found him alone in his cottage, cooking a bean and blood-pudding stew over the wood fire; and accepted an invitation to share it. Jaume asked for details on Willie's death, and wept to hear about the open window.

'He was a brother to me,' he choked. 'So magnanimous, so thoughtful! And since he could not manage this little property by himself, I had asked Toni Coll to tend the trees, and go half-shares in the lemons and oil. Toni has just paid me two thousand pesetas. We are not friends, but he would have lost face with the village by neglecting my land while I was doing my service. He even repaired the terrace that fell before my departure.'

I had brought along a bottle of red Binisalem wine, to celebrate Samstag's cable.

'Poor Willie, how wildly enthusiastic he would have been,' Jaume sighed, when I read it to him. 'And how he would have drunk and sung! This comes too late. Willie always wanted me to enjoy the success that his frailties prevented him from attaining.'

'May he rest in peace!'

'I had no great theatrical ambition,' Jaume continued, after a pause. 'Willie forced me to write first *The Indulgent Mother*, and then *The Difficult Husband.*'

'Did they take you long?'

'*The Indulgent Mother*, yes. Over the second I did not need to rack my brains. It was a gift.'

'Yet Señor Samstag, a most important person, finds the result magnificent. That is certainly a triumph. You have a copy of the play?'

'Only in Majorcan.'

'Do you realize, Jaume, what will happen if *The Difficult Husband* pleases Broadway?'

'Might they pay me?'

'Pay you, man? Of course! With perhaps five per cent of the gross takings, which might mean fifty thousand dollars a week. Say it ran for a couple of years, you'd amass... let me work it out – well, some two hundred and fifty thousand dollars.'

'That means nothing to me. What part of a peseta is a dollar?'

'Listen: if things go well, you may earn *twelve million pesetas*... And even if the play proved a dead failure, you'd get two hundred thousand, merely by selling Señor Samstag the right to stage it!'

'Your talk of millions confuses me. I would have accepted five hundred pesetas for the job.'

'But you would equally accept twelve million?'

'Are these people mad?'

'No, they are clever businessmen.'

'You make fun of me, Don Roberto!'

'I do not.'

'Then, at least, you exaggerate? What I want to know is whether this telegram will help me to buy a donkey and retile my roof.'

'I can promise you an avalanche of donkeys!'

Two days later the contract came, addressed to Willie. Its thirty pages covered all possible contingencies of mutual and reciprocal fraud on the part of author and producer, as foreseen by the vigilant Dramatists Guild of the Authors League of America; and dealt with such rich minor topics as Second Class Touring Rights, Tabloid Versions, Concert Tour Versions, Foreign Language Performances, and the sale of dolls or other toys based on characters in the play...

I was leafing through the document on the café terrace that afternoon, when Len entered. 'There's a man at my place,' he gasped excitedly, 'name of Bill Truscott, who says he's Willie's agent! Bill and I were at Columbia together. Nice guy. He seems sort of puzzled to find no Willie... See here: could it be that you weren't kidding me about his Broadway show the other day?'

'I never kid. Got no sense of humour.'

'Is that so? Well, anyhow, I told Bill you might be able to help him. Come along!'

Bill Truscott, a gaunt Bostonian, welcomed us effusively. 'I sent *The Difficult Husband* to Samstag's office ten days ago,' he said, 'and a spy I keep there sent word that the old s.o.b. was jumping my claim. Doesn't like agents, favours the direct approach. But let's get this straight: is Fedora really dead? My spy swears that he cabled Samstag from this place.'

'Correct. He's dead. Yet he promised to meet Samstag and discuss this document' – I tapped the contract – 'which maybe you'd better have a look at. Tell me, do you speak Spanish? Jaume Gelabert has no English or French.'

'Gelabert? Who's Gelabert? Never heard of him.'

'Author of *The Difficult Husband*. Fedora's only the translator.'

'Only the translator – are you sure? How extremely tense! That changes everything. I took it for Fedora's own work... What sort of a guy is this Gelabert? Any previous stage successes?'

'He made a hit with *The Indulgent Mother*,' I said, kicking Len under the table. 'He's a simple soul – you might call him a recluse.'

'Know of any arrangement between Fedora and Gelabert as to the translator's fee?'

'I can't think that they made one. Fedora drank, and did the job by way of a favour to Gelabert, who had been caring for him... Are you worried about your commission?'

'*Am* I worried? However, Gelabert will need an agent, and, after all, Fedora sent the play to my office. Len will vouch for me, won't you, Len?'

'I'm sure he will, Mr Truscott,' I said, 'and you'll vouch for him. Len needs some vouching for.'

'I'm on my knees, Don Roberto,' Len whined, grovelling gracefully.

I let him grovel awhile, and asked Truscott: 'But didn't Fedora acknowledge Gelabert's authorship in a covering letter?'

'He did, I remember, mention a local genius who had defended him against some Chinese and was now setting off to fight the Moors, while he himself guarded the lemon grove – and would I please try enclosed play on Samstag; but that's as far as it went, except for some passages in a crazy foreign language, full of x's and y's.'

'I gather the letter has disappeared?'

Truscott nodded gloomily.

'In fact, you can't prove yourself to be Fedora's agent, let alone Gelabert's?'

No reply. I pocketed the contract and rolled myself a cigarette, taking an unnecessarily long time about it. At last I said: 'Maybe Gelabert would appoint you his agent; but he's a difficult man to handle. Better leave all the talking to me.'

'That's very nice of you... I surely appreciate it. I suppose you've seen a copy of *The Difficult Husband*?'

'Not yet.'

'Which makes two of us! You see: after reading Fedora's crazy letter, I tossed the typescript, unexamined, to my secretary Ethel May, who, for all that she was the dumbest operator on Thirty-eighth Street, had beautiful legs and neat habits. Hated to throw away anything, though – even gift appeals. She filed it under "Try Mr Samstag." Ethel May got married and quit. Then, one day, I came down with the grippe, and that same evening Sam wanted a script in a hurry – some piece by a well-known author of mine. I called Ethel May's replacement from my sickbed and croaked: "Send off the Samstag script at once! Special messenger." The poor scared chick didn't want to confess that she'd no notion what the hell I was talking about. She chirped: "Certainly, Chief!" and went away to search the files. As a matter of fact, said script was still in my brief case – grippe plays hell with a guy's memory. Scratching around, the chick comes across *The Difficult Husband,* and sends Sam that. A stroke of genius! – I must give her a raise. But Sam is short on ethics. He bypassed my office and cabled the defunct Fedora, hoping he'd sign along the dotted line and remember too late that he should have got my expert advice on what's bound to be the trickiest of contracts. If ever there was a thieving dog!'

'Yes,' I said, '*if* Fedora had been the author, and *if* you'd been his agent, you'd have a right to complain. But, let's face it, you've no standing at all. So calm down! I suggest we call on Gelabert. He can probably supply supper.'

Night had fallen windily, after a day of unseasonable showers; and the path to Jaume's cottage is no easy one at the best of times. The ground was clayey and full of puddles; water cascaded from the trees. I lent Truscott a flashlight; but twice he tripped over an olive root and fell. He reached the cottage (kitchen, stable, well, single bedroom) in poor shape. I gave Jaume a brief outline of the situation, and we were soon sharing his *pa amb oli:* which means slices of bread dunked in unrefined olive oil, rubbed with a half tomato and sprinkled with salt. Raw onion, bitter olives, and a glass of red wine greatly improved the dish. *Pa amb oli* was something of a test for Truscott, but he passed it all right, apart from letting oil drip on his muddied trousers.

He asked me to compliment Jaume on 'this snug little shack. Say that I envy him. Say that we city folk often forget what real dyed-in-the-wool *natural* life can be!' Then he talked business. 'Please tell our host that he's been sent no more than a basic contract. I'm surprised at the size of the advance, though: three thousand on signature, and two thousand more on the first night! Sam must think he's on to a good thing. Nevertheless, my long experience as a dramatic agent tells me that we can easily improve these terms, besides demanding a number of special arrangements. Fedora is dead; or we could fiction him into the contract as the author.'

Unlike Gelabert, he was a non-resident American citizen, and therefore non-liable to any tax at all on the property. Maybe we can still fiction it that way...'

'What is he saying?' asked Jaume.

'He wants to act as your agent in dealing with Señor Samstag, whom he doesn't trust. The rest of his speech is of no interest.'

'Why should I trust this gentleman more than he trusts the other?' .

'Because Willie chose Señor Truscott as his agent, and Samstag got the play from him.'

Jaume solemnly held out his hand to Truscott.

'You were Willie's friend?' he asked. I translated.

'He was a very valued client of mine.' But when Truscott produced an agency agreement from his brief case, I gave Jaume a warning glance.

Jaume nodded. 'I sign only what I can read and understand,' he said. 'My poor mother lost her share of the La Coma inheritance by trusting a lawyer who threw long words at her. Let us find a reliable notary public in the capital.'

Truscott protested: 'I'm not representing Gelabert until I'm sure of my commission.'

'Quit that!' I said sharply. 'You're dealing with a peasant who can't be either bullied or coaxed.'

A cable came from Samstag: he was arriving by Swissair next day. Mercurio asked Len, who happened to be in the postman's house, why so many prodigal telegrams were flying to and fro. Len answered: 'They mean immense wealth for young Gelabert. His comedy, though rejected by Dom Enrique two years ago, is to be staged in New York.'

'That moral standards are higher here than in New York does not surprise me,' Mercurio observed. 'Yet dollars are dollars, and Jaume can now laugh at us all, whatever the demerits of his play.'

Len brought the cable to my house, where he embarrassed me by paying an old debt of two hundred pesetas (which I had forgotten), in the hope that I might deal him into the Broadway game. 'I don't need much... just an itty-bitty part,' he pleaded.

Why dash his hopes? Pocketing the two hundred pesetas, I said that his friend Bill would surely recommend him to Samstag.

News of Jaume's good fortune ran through the village two or three times, each time gaining in extravagance. The final version made Samstag a millionaire second cousin from Venezuela who, reading the *Baleares* account of *The Indulgent Mother*, had appointed him his heir. I asked Jaume to say no more than that he was considering the American offer: it might yet prove unacceptable.

Truscott and I met Samstag's plane at Palma airport. Spying Truscott among the crowd, he darted forward with scant respect for the Civil

Guard who was shepherding the new arrivals through Customs, and grabbed his hand. 'By all that's holy, Bill,' he cried, 'I'm glad to see you. This solves our great mystery! So that anonymous package emanated from you, did it?'

'Yes, it did, Sammy,' said Truscott, 'and, like all packages I've ever sent you, it was marked all over with my office stamp.'

'Why, yes, my secretary did guess it might be yours, and called you at once – but you were sick, and I couldn't get confirm –'

The Civil Guard then unslung his rifle and used the barrel-end to prod Samstag, a small, dark roly-poly of a man, back into line. Finally he emerged with his baggage and guessed that I was Mr William Fedora. When Truscott undeceived him, he grew noticeably colder towards me; but the two were soon as thick as thieves, and no less suspicious of each other. Climbing into our taxi, Samstag lighted a large cigar, and turned away from me; so I asserted myself as a principal in the business. 'I can use one of those,' I said, stretching out a finger and thumb.

Startled, Samstag offered me his case. 'Take a couple,' he begged.

I took five, smelt and pinched them all, rejected three. 'Don't mind me, boys!' I said through a fragrant cloud of smoke. 'You haggle about the special arrangements. I'll manage the rest.'

At this reminder of our compact, Truscott hastily enlarged on the strong hold I had on Señor Gelabert, assuring Samstag that without me he would get nowhere. Samstag gave him a noncommittal 'Oh yes?' and then back to his discussion of out-of-town performances prior to a possible London *première*. Just before we sighted the village round the bend of our road, I tapped Samstag on the arm: 'Look here, Sam, what told you that *The Difficult Husband* was God's gift to Broadway?'

'Not *what*, but *who*?' he answered cheerfully. 'It was Sharon, of course! Sharon always knows. She said: "Pappy, believe me, this is going to be the hottest ticket in town." So I cabled Fedora, and flew. She's only fourteen, my Sharon, and still studying at Saint Teresa's. You should see her grades: lousy isn't the word! And yet she always *knows*... Takes a script, sniffs it, reads three lines here, four there; spends a couple of minutes on Act Two; skips to the final curtain... Then' – Samstag lowered his voice and ended in a grave whisper – 'then she goddamwell *pronounces!*'

'So you haven't read the script either? That makes three of us. What about having a look at it after supper? Or, to save time and eyesight, we might have Len Simkin – another Thespian chum of yours, Sam – read it aloud to us?'

'If you insist. Perhaps Señor Gelabert has a copy. I haven't brought one myself – came here for business, not to hear a dramatic reading.'

In fact, nobody had a script. But that did not prevent Samstag and Truscott from arguing Special Arrangements together at the village inn all the rest of the day, until everything seemed sewed up. The meeting with

Señor Gelabert, they congratulated themselves, would be a mere formality.

Hair slicked, shoes well brushed, Jaume arrived at our rendezvous in his Sunday best, and showed impressive *sang-froid*. Early cares, ill luck, and the tough barrack life at Melilla had made a man of him. After profuse congratulations, which Jaume shrugged off, Samstag sent for the village taxi and invited us both to dinner in Palma. Len, to his disappointment, was left behind. We chose *Aquí Estamos*, Majorca's most select restaurant, where Samstag kept slapping Jaume's shoulders and crying '*¡Amigo!*', varied with '*¡Magnífico!*', and asking me to translate Sharon's appreciative comments on the play, one of which was: 'The name part couldn't be more like you, Pappy!' (*¡El papel titular corresponde precisamente contigo, Papaíto!*') At this Jaume, now full of crayfish, asparagus, roast turkey, wild strawberries and champagne, smiled for the first time that evening. We wound up around 3 a.m. drinking more and worse champagne to the sound of flamenco in a gipsy night club. Truscott and Samstag, who were flying back together at 8 a.m., had let themselves go properly; their good-byes could not have been warmer.

However, Jaume had stood by his guns: declining to commit himself until he could read the amended contract and get it approved by a reliable notary. Nor would he anticipate his good fortune by the purchase of so much as a pig, let alone an ass.

When Truscott finally sent me the document, Len offered his expert advice gratis – he knew all about Broadway contracts, and could tell at a glance whether anything were wrong. 'Maybe Bill and Sammy did a crooked deal together,' he suggested. 'Of course, he's an old friend of mine, but in show business...'

Shaking Len off, I took the contract to Jaume's cottage. 'A letter from Señor Samstag is attached,' I told him. 'Shall I read it first, or shall I first translate this document?'

'The document first, if you please.'

I read: 'Whereas the Author, a member of the Dramatists Guild of the Authors League of America Inc. (hereinafter called the "Guild") has been preparing the book of a certain play or other literary property now entitled *The Difficult Husband*. And whereas the Producer etc., etc., desires to produce the said play in the United States and Canada, etc., etc... Now therefore, in consideration of the premises and the mutual promises and covenants herein contained and other good and valuable considerations, it is agreed:

'FIRST: The Author hereby a) warrants that he is the author of the said play and has a right to enter into this agreement –'

Jaume interrupted: 'But I am not a member of this Guild!'

'Never mind, you can apply for membership.'

'And if they won't accept a foreigner?'

'Don't worry! Señor Truscott will fix you up. Let's get on: "The Author b) agrees that on compliance with this contract –"'
'Maybe, Don Roberto, you should translate the letter first.'
'Very well, then… It says here that Señor Samstag greatly enjoyed his visit to Majorca, and is delighted that we all see eye to eye, and that it only remains for you to sign the attached instrument, your agent, Señor Truscott, having agreed with him on the terms.
'Then, wait a bit… then the tone of the letter changes. While still considering the play to be superb, Señor Samstag suggests certain radical changes in the treatment. It is by no means good theatre yet, he writes. The Difficult Husband, for instance, remains too static a character; his actions are predictable, and so is the eventual victory of his wife. In a sophisticated play, the leading man's character must develop; and this development must be substantiated by brisk dialogue. Here, the Husband should grow gradually less difficult, more *human*, as the action advances. Also, he should be granted an occasional small victory over his wife…'
Jaume's eyes were smouldering. 'He says that, does he, the imbecile?'
I tried to smooth him down. 'After all, show-business people are apt to understand the market. They study it year in, year out.'
'Read on!'
'He insists that the scene where the couple quarrel about household accounts must be changed. Let the husband, instead, teach his wife how to manage something else, something *visible* – say, a television set or a garbage disposer. "In the theatre we want to *see* things," he writes. "Then, when the wife wins his permission to take a long cruise and pretends that she has gone, but stays ashore to save household money – this is most unconvincing! Let her go for her health, really go, and fall in love with a handsome adventurer on the ship! Her husband can get comically jealous at the beginning of the Third Act –"'
'Stop!' Jaume roared. 'Why does this fellow first telegraph that my play is magnificent, and now want to change it altogether, though offering me the same immense sum of money?'
'Patience, Jaume! He cabled "Bravo!" because he hadn't read your play. Now he writes the reverse because he still hasn't read it. Knowing you to be inexperienced, he naturally entrusts The Difficult Husband to his assistants, who are expert play-doctors. The suggestions you so dislike emanate from these play-doctors. If you will not rewrite the play, that task necessarily falls to them, or to someone working under their direction.'
'Then it will no longer be mine?'
'Oh yes, it will be! You're protected by the contract. Your name will flash out in red, green, and yellow neon lights from the front of the theatre, and you will get the big money. Play-doctors get no more than their salaries. They can't *write* plays; they can only rewrite them.'
'Willie would never have agreed!'

'Are you sure?'

'Willie would not have changed a single word! He had a stubborn nature.'

'Well, I admit that this letter sounds nonsense – not that I've read *The Difficult Husband*... But you are faced by a clear choice. Either fight for every word of your play, and be lucky if you keep one in ten; or else refuse to sign the contract.'

'Enough, enough, Don Roberto! My mind is made up. The devil take this contract! If Señor Samstag's assistants care to rewrite my play, very good! Let them spin a coin to decide who shall be the author. I will sell *The Difficult Husband* outright, making no conditions whatsoever, except that Señor Samstag must pay me a sum down, in pesetas, and – *pff!* – that's it!... What might he pay?'

I told him: 'Fortunately it's not a case of buying your *name:* he's only buying your story. Since the Señorita Samstag believes in it so strongly, he might be good for ten thousand dollars – around half a million pesetas. That's nothing for a producer like Samstag.'

Jaume said slowly: 'Not having yet signed my agreement with Señor Truscott, I am still my own master. Let us telegraph Señor Samstag that, if he flies here again, a new one-page contract will be awaiting him at the notary's.'

'And Señor Truscott?'

'For three hundred thousand I can become the Lord of La Coma, which is in the market now; so, since Señor Truscott envies me this cottage, he may have it and welcome. I will add a terrace or two, to round off the property. As for the lemon grove and olives, which are worth far more, they are yours, Don Roberto.'

'Many thanks, Jaume; but I want nothing but your friendship. We should dispatch your message at once.'

Three days later Samstag flew in, delighted not to find Bill Truscott about. 'Agents create unnecessary complications between friends, don't you think?' he asked us. A one-page contract in legal Spanish was easily agreed upon, and Samstag had arranged for the necessary pesetas. They went straight into an account which Jaume opened at the Bank of Spain.

As we drove home from Palma, Jaume said the last word on the subject: 'What can be done with a man who complains that a play is dramatically bad before he even reads it? *The Difficult Husband,* as many Majorcans know, though perhaps few Americans, enjoyed a remarkable success at the *Cine Moderno* some years ago. My poor mother took me there. The film ran for three whole weeks. Only an imbecile would wish to change its plot. It was called – what was it called? – ah, now I remember: "*La Vida con Papá*". How does one say that in English, Don Roberto?'

You Win, Houdini!

Jenkins, Howell & Edwards,
Solicitors,
3, Victory Chambers,
Pontypool,
S. Wales.

July 24th, 1959

Dear Captain Graves,

You're unlikely to recall my name after so long a lapse, though we coincided at the Royal Welsh Depôt a couple of times in 1916; but you can't have forgotten 'Houdini' Cashman. I had a mind to write you about him when I first read your autobiography, and there came across a mention of his abrupt departure from the regiment two or three months after the Armistice. You say:

> ... next day the senior lieutenant of the company which I was to have taken over went off with the cash-box, and I should have been legally responsible for the loss of £200. Before the war he used to give displays on Blackpool Pier as 'The Handcuff King'. He got away safely to the United States.

The subject nagged at me again when you reissued the book last year and, to cap it all, I had a letter from young Bob Stack – the bigger, taller brother of Dick Stack, who was in the 2nd Battalion with you; I don't think you knew Bob. He was one of the best, and did pretty well for himself when he emigrated to Australia and made a fortune in wool. He now has nine grandchildren, one of whom is named Daniel in my honour. We still write each other every so often and regularly exchange cards at Christmas. Anyhow, he sent me a Melbourne newspaper cutting about the death in prison of one Victor Cashman, formerly a professional conjuror. There can't be more than one Victor Cashman in the conjuring world: besides, the story makes good sense to anyone who knew Houdini. So, before it's too late, I'm going to get the whole saga off my chest, and apologize in advance for its inordinate length, hoping that you won't be bored.

I recall Houdini's arrival at the Depôt in June 1917, when the Military Service Act was flooding the regiment with swarms of skrim-shankers who had been winkled out of non-essential jobs – scrapings from the bottom of a pretty foul barrel. Of course, along with them came some red-hot lads just old enough to qualify for the sausage-machine. As for the new officers, they were – you remember – a thoroughly mixed lot, and caused Colonel Jones-Williams a deal of trouble, what with affiliation orders, bringing women into the Camp, complaints of dud cheques from tradesmen, etc.

Houdini came wearing two Boer War ribbons. The Adjutant didn't question them, but they made some of us very suspicious. He claimed to have served in South Africa with the City Imperial Volunteers, but when Jock Wilson, who won a D.C.M. with the same corps in 1900, cross-examined him about the various engagements in which they'd taken part, and about their officers, Houdini could remember nothing. He'd been kicked on the head by a mule, he said, just before the Cease-Fire sounded, and his war memories had faded completely from his mind. We began to wonder how the hell Houdini had got a commission, because he knew no more drill than he could have picked up in the Boys' Brigade. And with what regiment, if any, had he served since the war started? He claimed to have been a despatch rider during the Retreat, and carried his left arm as though he'd been wounded in the shoulder. I reckon that Houdini Cashman, with his cissy manner, simpering through his ingrowing moustache, and sitting cross-legged like a Buddha on the floor of his hut, was the queerest fish in the entire British Army.

Most of us felt some sympathy for true-blue Bible-punching Conchies, who quoted the Sixth Commandment at the tribunals, and damn well meant it – what we couldn't stand were dirty yellow-bellied column-dodgers of the Cashman type, who banked on being safer *in* the Army than *out*, if they played their cards properly – and Houdini Cashman had his tunic sleeves stuffed with aces. Literally, as well as in a manner of speaking, because a deck of fake cards was his principal stock-in-trade. He'd nearly dug himself in at the Depôt as Assistant Musketry Officer, on the strength of his ribbons, having ingratiated himself with old Major Floods by his usual thimble-rigging tricks, when Jock Wilson called on the Adjutant. 'Willie,' he said, 'that Cashman fellow's a wrong 'un. You'd be wise to put him on the next draft before worse befalls us. And in case the stinker goes sick, as I think he will, be sure to warn the M.O. beforehand.'

So Houdini found himself at Rouen Base Camp soon afterwards, on the same draft as myself – ten officers and two hundred men. You'll remember Captain Sassoon's lines:

> *When I am old and bald and short of breath*
> *I'll live with scarlet Majors at the Base*

And speed glum heroes up the Line to Death:
You'll see me with my puffy, petulant face
Gulping and guzzling at the best hotels...

In my opinion, Houdini must have inspired that poem! At Rouen, he followed much the same procedure as had nearly proved successful at the Depôt. He gave a conjuring gaff in the Y.M.C.A. hut – Magic Circle stuff, almost up to Maskelyne's show at the Egyptian Hall, though he hadn't the requisite mirrors and gear. Then he sucked up to the Commandant, Major Charlie Short (Sir Wm. Short's brother) by letting him spot the right card every time where everyone else failed – and by making a fool of Captain Hotson of the South Wales Borderers, whom he knew Major Short disliked. In a mind-reading and fortune-telling turn, Houdini told the audience: 'I've lost a photograph of Gigi, my French fiancée. The cards inform me that someone present has it in his wallet.' Major Short smilingly inquired whom the cards suspected. Houdini tapped the knave of hearts. 'It's that Captain sitting in the corner,' he said. So the Major asked Hotson if he would produce his wallet and open it. Hotson said: 'Of course!' and pulled it out. There he found a postcard of a great buxom French nude with 'From Gigi to her darling Monsieur Victor!' scrawled across the back in violet ink. You should have seen Hotson's face when Houdini displayed the card to the front rows!

Invited to dine that night at H.Q. Mess, Houdini brought the conversation round to a party of deserters, said to be ensconced in a wood near the Camp, and living by armed raids on our transport. Four thousand of our chaps would be beating the wood next day, strung out at a few paces' interval, with Major Short in charge. Houdini remarked: 'I've no doubt that you'll catch those toughs, sir; but be careful with them afterwards. They're all old lags, so they'll probably be able to slide out of a pair of Army handcuffs in just one minute.'

'Nothing wrong with our handcuffs,' barked the Major. '*You* try and get out of a pair, my friend! I'll bet a hundred francs you can't do it in five minutes, let alone one.'

'If they're ordinary Army handcuffs, I'm willing to risk the bet,' says Houdini.

I happened to be invited too that night, having known Major Short, J.P., all my life. As the squire of Llanfihangel, my native village, he recommended me for my commission in September 1914. Let me confess that Houdini was using me as his confederate. One of my tasks had been to hold Hotson in conversation at the shower baths, just before dinner, while Houdini planted the postcard in his wallet. Half Houdini's tricks depended on a confederate, and I was the last person anyone would suspect of associating with such a crummy character. It beats me, in fact, why I ever took on the job!

When the port came round, Major Short sent for the Provost-sergeant, and said: 'A pair of handcuffs, Sergeant! I'm about to put one of the officers here under close arrest.' The Provost-sergeant saluted smartly and marched out again. I was watching whether he would let his eye stray for a moment in Houdini's direction, but since he didn't, I don't know to this day whether he was in the know: I mean, whether what he brought back – perhaps just a little too promptly – were a pair of trick handcuffs, or the real thing.

Major Short led Houdini into the middle of the mess-room and announced: 'Gentlemen, this officer has cast grave doubts on the efficiency of our handcuffs. We've agreed that if he can't release himself within five minutes from this regulation pair, he'll wear them until reveille tomorrow.'

Houdini answered in his prissiest tones: 'Fair's fair, sir. But if I succeed, everyone here will see how it's done, and the news will soon get around. For the sake of good order and discipline, I suggest you put a screen around me.'

Major Short agreed and sent for the screen. Then he snapped the bracelets on Houdini's wrists from behind. 'Ready, now?'

'Ready, sir!'

I noticed a skylight above the screen, and quietly slipped out of the mess, set a handy fire-ladder against the wall, climbed on the roof and peeped down. Houdini was shaping to wriggle his fat bottom through his arms when he spotted me. 'Stop!' he squealed. 'There's a Peeping Tom up there!' I shinned down the ladder in double-quick time and stowed it back where I'd found it, before returning. 'That makes one minute, Mr Cashman,' said Major Short, as he studied his gold half-hunter, 'but I'll let you have an extra ten seconds because of the interruption.'

'Thank you, sir, but I don't need it,' simpered Houdini, as he emerged smiling from behind the screen and presented the handcuffs to the Major.

'A hundred francs, wasn't it?' asked the Major glumly, taking out his wallet. Then his face went purple at finding the same nude lurking among the larger notes.

'No need to settle at once, sir. What about a double or quits? I'll handcuff Captain Hotson, or anyone else you care to name, and if he can slip the bracelets in five minutes no money changes hands.' Houdini didn't refer even obscurely to the postcard; which was tact, and not far short of blackmail.

Hotson declined the honour: 'I never did time in Parkhurst or Princetown, where one learns these things.'

To show he was a good sport, Houdini joined in the laughter against him and – would you believe it? – the next morning he came on parade mounted! The Commandant had made him Assistant Adjutant. And I'm damned if that same evening Houdini didn't read out the roll of officers and men due to entrain for the Line!

You win, Houdini! A very fine performance! No blood sports on Pilckem Ridge for you, no free-for-all tussles with Jerry in salubrious Langemarck, no mudlarking in the airy shell-craters of Passchendaele. Your job from now on is to 'speed glum heroes up the Line to Death.' *'Bonjour et bonne chance, cher Monsieur Victor!'*

When Winnie Churchill lost his job at Whitehall as a result of the Dardanelles mess, he volunteered for the trenches and for a while commanded the 6th Royal Scots Fusiliers. We relieved them once on the Somme. Then his friends at the War House, afraid that he might collect too much glory, broke up the battalion. Winnie reappeared in Parliament, and you may remember that debate on combing out more civilians from jobs which could be held by women and disabled ex-servicemen, because the Army needed cannon-fodder. Winnie made a speech saying that hundreds of thousands of able-bodied men already in the Forces were being kept behind the lines on useless jobs. He turned the Gospel verse 'Physician, heal thyself!' into 'Physician, comb thyself!' This had some effect. A few young, red-tabbed pimps from Army H.Q., for example, were moved up as far as Divisional H.Q.; also A.1 men were taken off road repair and replaced by B.1's; but that was about all. At Rouen, Houdini kept his charger and increased his hold on Major Charlie Short.

I got hit twice more, once at Langemarck in September 1917; and again in February 1918, while marching up the *pavé* towards Messines. Each time, when I rejoined the Battalion by way of Rouen, there was Houdini as large as life and a great deal uglier. He now wore a wound stripe, also three stars, which were more than I ever collected. Though several times in temporary command of a company – and once of the Battalion, when everyone else got knocked out – I was always superseded just before reaching acting rank. A subaltern I would die, that was clear! Nor did I collect any decorations.

Came the summer of 1918. It was 'Backs to the Wall!' Old Ludendorff had driven our gallant allies, the Pork-and-Beans, out of the Neuve-Chapelle sector, bust the line wide open, and forced Butcher Haig to evacuate the whole Ypres salient. Then he pushed the French off the Chemin des Dames, and if the Yanks hadn't come up just in time, and held him at Château-Thierry, he'd have goose-stepped into Paris, and that would have been that!

At home, they raised the military age, and combed away for dear life. Down by the Somme, we waited at Stand-to every morning for the biggest, bloodiest Boche barrage ever, that would blast Ludendorff's way clear to Amiens. The wind was up, vertically, with a whiff of panic even in the bumph that the brass-hats circulated from their cosy *châteaux*. In fact, things must have looked pretty desperate down at Rouen because, one evening, who should stumble into our Company dug-out at Beaumont-

Hamel, but Captain V. Cashman!

Jock Wilson was commanding 'B' Company; he'd lost three lunch-hooks and was full of odd pieces of metal, but still ticking. The dour old bird, by the way, had been engineer at the Blaenau-Ffestiniog slate quarries before the war, and spoke a glorious Merionethshire Welsh, which endeared him to the troops. He picked up the field telephone and at once rang Battalion, insisting that Houdini should take down two of his three stars (acting rank only). The Colonel saw the point. If Jock got scuppered, Houdini would be left in charge of the company, though not having hitherto muddied his boots in shell-hole or sump-pit, and knowing *cooch nay* about trench warfare.

Jock's own military value had sunk by this time. Scots are pretty good drinkers, born with two livers and a spare set of kidneys; but this one had reached the three-bottles-a-day stage. In point of fact, he was almost a passenger, and left the running of the company to me and young Stack. Jock needed a spot of leave to set him up again. He'd been sweating on that for months, but to no avail. His only hope now was another wound, preferably not either in the head or stomach.

A sequence of barrages had played hell with the Beaumont-Hamel trench system. But at least it wasn't yet a row of shell-craters sketchily joined together with a few hurried scrapes of an entrenching tool, as at Passchendaele and elsewhere. We 'B' officers even sat down to dinner that night at a small table, in an at least pip-squeak-proof dug-out, and each had a solid ammunition box under him. Young Stack was on duty, which left Jock, Houdini and me to eat our stew together.

Well, you know how it is with beasts when they're scared: most species have only one way of facing danger. Cats enhance themselves into great spitting furies; rabbits scud off; bulls lower their horns and charge; some insects and reptiles sham dead. Houdini was properly scared, but neither enhanced himself, nor scudded off, nor charged, nor shammed dead. Instead, he started on his usual stunts, in the pathetic hope, I suppose, of softening Jock's heart and wrangling himself a cushy job as Company Entertainments Officer. Psychologically very interesting, I suppose, if I'd happened to be a psychologist, which I wasn't.

He put a fist into his mouth and planked down on the table beside me a complete set of dentures, joined by a spring. As he removed his hand, they sprang open. Jock's face was as red as the side of a Cuinchy brick-stack, and his eyes bloodshot and unwinking. He'd seemed almost unaware of Houdini's presence, except that his jowls hung heavy with dislike; but now they stirred slightly. 'Take that damned animal away!' he growled.

Houdini pushed the set in his pocket, smiling feebly.

'Keep it there!' said Jock. 'And button up the flap!'

Since, a few seconds later, Houdini was munching away at ration-biscuit, I conclude either that the comic dentures had not originally come from his mouth, or that he hadn't really put them back in his pocket. Between mouthfuls, he palmed my knife and fork; produced an egg from my gas-mask case; wrapped a tumbler in a piece of newspaper and smashed it with a blow of his revolver – but the tumbler wasn't inside after all; and kept up the fun for about twenty minutes. Neither Jock nor I made a single comment. Maybe Houdini took this for a respectful hush of awe, but pausing at last and looking expectantly at Jock's face, he found it as impassive as a Jubilee statue of Queen Victoria. No flicker of interest. Suddenly Jock turned to me and said in Welsh: 'Dan bach, take this toad away before he does something clever with his bloody navel!' So I took Houdini along to relieve young Stack, whom we found at Left Post.

Left Post hung in the air; the Borderers had abandoned their suicidal front-line trenches and were holding a position parallel to us, fifty yards back. Young Stack gave Houdini his orders. 'You're to stay here until relieved. Keep the troops on their toes. Take an occasional tour of the company frontage. And don't use the telephone except in an emergency. "Emergency" means when Jerry's barrage drops.'

'You can forget about the telephone,' I interrupted. 'When the barrage drops, there'll be no need to announce the fact – it'll be audible in Calais, Dover and Whitehall. Besides, in two minutes we'll all be wiped out. Dead men don't phone.'

I couldn't see in the darkness how Houdini had reacted to this information. It was a quiet night. 'Suspiciously quiet,' said young Stack, taking his cue from me. 'That's typical of Ludendorff. He doesn't want to give his hand away, so he orders quiet. But these Jerries are too damned thorough. There should at least be normal activity if they want to pretend that this is a normal night, and not *the* night.'

Sergeant Foster, commanding No. 1 platoon, winked at me, and contributed his bit. 'Not a Verey Light for hours, sir. It's coming, for sure!'

Houdini had already squeezed into the Post cubby-hole, but we went on chatting outside.

'Good night, Sergeant,' I said. 'Look after Mr Cashman. He's an old soldier, but he's seen no action since Mafeking, and this isn't the sunny South African veldt.'

'Not "good night," sir! It's "good-bye"!'

On getting back to Company H.Q., I found myself in command. Jock hadn't been killed, wounded or even carried off by an attack of D.T.'s. His leave had miraculously come through, and off he'd buzzed, in too much of a hurry even to finish his third bottle of whisky, which he's just opened when the news arrived.

Twenty-four hours went by before I revisited Left Post. I had to keep close to the phone, and trips to either flank were pretty dangerous by daylight. Also, I'd lost young Stack – lent to 'C' Company, two of whose

officers had been killed by the same shell. But he came home to us that
night, when someone was sent to relieve him.

Dinnertime, and no Houdini. 'I'm disappointed, Dan,' says young
Stack. 'My batman tells me you had a buckshee conjuring show last
night.'

'We can command a repeat performance,' I suggested.

Still no Houdini. Then a runner arrives with a verbal message from
Sergeant Foster. 'Rum shortage: will the Company Commander be good
enough to inspect Left Post as soon as convenient?'

I asked Ought-Three Davies, the runner: 'Where's the new officer, my
lad?'

'Haven't seen a sign of the gentleman, sir.'

Young Stack took over the phone, while I went up to reconnoitre. 'If
the C.O. wants to know where I am, say I'm investigating a report of
trouble near Left Post.'

Sergeant Foster wore a grim look as he jerked his head towards the
cubby-hole. 'The new officer's been out but once, sir, since you left; and
then only for a certain purpose.'

'Right, Sergeant. Let's dislodge him!'

I squeezed in, and shone a pocket torch around. A two gallon rum jar
lay on its side in the middle of the floor. I handed it back to the Sergeant.
'Not a drop left, sir.'

Houdini huddled on some sandbags in the far corner, watching me.
How queer he looked! Ingrowing moustache meeting two days of blue
stubble, and his eyes like currants in a half-cooked suet pudding.

I could get nothing into Houdini, or out of him. He crouched there,
making whining noises, for all the world like a puppy that's been caught
misbehaving in the best parlour.

'Goddam that fellow! Turn your back, please, Sergeant, while I give
him the pasting of his life. I don't want witnesses.' But when I came
closer, Houdini squealed. It was a terrible noise that ran down my spine
and churned my bowels.

I came out again, regretting that the rum jar was empty. 'He'll not get
away with this lot,' I said. 'I'm going down to Battalion H.Q. Set a sentry
on him; Sergeant!'

So I pushed off, stopping only to put young Stack in charge of the telephone. But soon I barged into Barney, our new Medical Officer, who had
graduated from Trinity College, Dublin, two months before, and still
found the war a great joke.

'Begob! Ye look as though yer heart's throubled and sore,' he said in the
exaggerated stage-Irish he used for our amusement.

I unloaded on him. 'Ah, so 'tis like that, is it?' says Barney. 'Let's be
taking a sly peep at the poor divil.'

Back with Barney to Left Post. Barney put his head into the cubby-hole, then slowly shook it in wonder and admiration: 'Holy Mother of God, 'tis powerful drunk he is!'

But when I let myself go on the subject of Houdini in plain English, Welsh, and other languages, Barney got the point. 'Very well, Dan,' he said soberly, 'I'll go down to Battalion myself. Trust me to save awkward questions. It won't do anybody any good if you bring a charge against the bastard.'

Barney was right. The C.O. would appreciate my silence, and keep the case dark. What with young Howland, who had deserted off leave and barely escaped the firing squad, and Lance-corporal Peters, the one who murdered an estaminet-keeper, and the Sergeant Phillips scandal, we'd had more than our plateful of notoriety in recent months.

I let Barney have his way, and that was the last I ever saw of Houdini; for the Adjutant smuggled him down the line in an ambulance, without even informing me that he'd gone.

'You win, Houdini!' But the magnitude of his victory did not appear until Jock returned off leave. Jock had stopped at Rouen to replenish his whisky store, and whom should he meet in the main square but Houdini! Once more a captain, and in the saddle again. Houdini explained that he'd been invalided back as a food-poisoning case, and written to Major Short from No. 2 Red Cross Hospital. The Major, it seems, was delighted, because Houdini had been giving him lessons in trick shuffling and trick dealing – guaranteed to fascinate an indefatigable bridge-player who had once lost a packet to some sharpers on an Atlantic voyage.

Jock didn't know the facts of the story until he got them from Barney and me. And even if he'd known, what could he have done to upset Houdini's apple-cart? Officially, it *was* food-poisoning!

More posh dinners for you, Houdini, at the *Couronne* and the *Fleur de Lys;* but for Jock and young Stack and me the glories of the wading of the Ancre, and the hundred days from Albert to Maubeuge. Ludendorff had shot his bolt, and it was our turn again. Near Maubeuge, Jock succumbed at last to a spent machine-gun bullet that entered his temple – not very deeply, but deep enough – as we bivouacked in a plum orchard. He was asleep, and nobody knew a thing about it until next morning.

In November came the eerie Armistice; then a lot of square-pushing and shining up of brasses, and education courses, and other morale-raising employment.

The day after I got demobbed, I picked up the *Daily Mail*, and read:

OFFICER ABSCONDS WITH COMPANY CASH. ARRESTED AT LIVERPOOL.
AWARDED TWO YEARS' HARD LABOUR.

But you write that Houdini got clear away to the States. He must have slipped his handcuffs; which makes me think that those he used at Rouen weren't trick ones.

I don't know how or when he went to Australia, or what his activities were in the long gap between 1919 and 1958; but I can tell you how he ended. While serving a ten-year stretch for fraud, he was made a 'trusty', and endeared himself to the Prison Governor 'by his remarkable talents as a conjurer'. The Governor, in fact, managed to get the last four years of his sentence remitted for good conduct. You win again, Houdini!

But this time his victory was short-lived. The day before he should have been freed, they found him in the Prison Library with his throat cut by the jagged edge of a dinner plate. R.I.P.!

With good wishes and more apologies
for the length of this screed,
very sincerely yours,
DANIEL EDWARDS
(late R.W.F.)

The Tenement: A Vision of Imperial Rome

'GREETINGS, MY LORD! Red dawn and a clear sky,' says Sophron, as he gently opens the shutters of an unglazed window. I can see climbing plants on my balcony, and the similar balcony of a tenement house opposite. Throwing off blanket and quilt, I look about me at the familiar square room, unfurnished except for my bed, a bedside table, and a wooden chest painted with a spirited scene of cupids mounted on hares and hunting a weasel.

We Romans sleep in loincloth and tunic, so the old Syrian slave merely hands me my shoes and lifts the toga (a huge semi-circle of thick white woollen material) from its peg. He shakes his head sadly at last night's wine stain. 'Arrange the folds carefully, Sophron, and it won't show,' I say.

He drapes one toga-end over my left shoulder, letting it fall to the thigh; next, winds the straight edge round the back of my neck and under the right arm, then grabs the mass of material low down and throws the other toga-end past the first, so that it hangs behind me. Finally, he fixes the 'navel boss' at my midriff. That leaves me warmly swathed, except for the right shoulder, and provides a capacious pocket at chest level. Whenever possible, one wears only a tunic, supplemented by a rough, hooded poncho if the weather is bad; because togas are clumsy, burdensome, and difficult to keep clean in this filthy city, though required dress on all formal occasions. Into the pocket go my wax tablets and stilus, my handkerchief, and a small heap of money from the table. The coins are mainly those of the Emperors Augustus, Tiberius and Caligula; but here's the latest issue – a bright bronze piece with Claudius' head on one side, on the other an oak-wreath, commemorating his recent fantastic conquest of Britain.

'Hand me the goblet, Sophron!'

I rinse my mouth with water, spit out into the street, drink the rest. 'Send Alexander for the mule! And, while you are waiting, empty the chamber pot.'

I married three years ago. My maternal uncle arranged the match when he paid my debts. I did not love Arruntia, nor she me, but the creditors were savage as wolves, and her substantial dowry, inherited from a great-

aunt, was tempting. Arruntius, my father-in-law, is armourer to the
Imperial School of Gladiators on the Via Labicana, which this uncle runs.
He lets me live, rent-free, in a first-storey apartment above his armoury,
so long as I help him with the business. A terrible man, though! Sentenced
to death ten years ago for the brutal murder of Arruntia's mother,
pardoned on condition that he became a gladiator – gladiators are public
slaves – took up the net-and-trident style of fighting and killed or maimed
twenty-five opponents in his first two years. When he had brought the
score to fifty, a vociferous Amphitheatre crowd demanded his release, and
Caligula sent him the customary wooden foil; but also an insulting
message: *'Rude rite donatur ignavus'* – 'The coward is duly granted
freedom.' Arruntius angrily snapped the foil in two, and re-engaged. His
score had crept up to seventy by the time of Caligula's assassination.
When the crowd again demanded his release, Claudius, the new Emperor,
sent him another wooden foil with the characteristic message: *'Desine:
tridens tibi nimium placet'* – 'Fight no more; you take too much pleasure in
your trident!' So he obeyed, was given back his forfeited possessions plus
ten years' interest, and bought this six-storey tenement house near the
Subura.

At Rome almost everyone lives in tenements like ours; the whole city of
a million people can't contain more than a thousand private houses.
Apartments are excessively hard to find; besides, Arruntius' ground floor
has real running water, piped from a reservoir, which he puts at our
disposal – the other tenants depend on the dirty goatskins of thievish
water carriers. He also has an oven heated by the forge, and we may use
this in the afternoons; otherwise we should have to get our joints and
poultry roasted at the baker's two streets off.

Since I collect Arruntius' rents, I know that he makes a profit of over
twenty per cent on his investment. The rooms are more and more
crowded, the higher one climbs. Fifty-five poor wretches jammed in the
attic – Cilicians, Syrians, Moors – jointly pay almost the same rent as we
first-floor tenants. They buy space by the square yard – just enough to put
down a mattress and a small cooking stove – and dispute possession with
fleas, bedbugs and mice. Nor do they dare ask Arruntius to mend the
hazardous roof.

'Any message for the Lady Arruntia, my lord, if she rises before your
return?'

'Say that I'll ride straight home after my duty call.'

Sharp words, a blow and a whimper from next door indicate that the
new slave girl is at work on Arruntia's tedious toilet. Arruntia always
keeps up with the fashions. She has discarded the simple Republican coif-
fure (hair parted down the middle and coiled into a bun at the nape) for
the latest style which piles her tresses high in curls and braids, supported
by a good deal of false hair from the Orient, and held by gold pins and

combs until it suggests the wall of a fortress. But first the slave girl slaps lotions and pomades on Arruntia's face and neck; applies chalk and white lead to her arms, eye-black to her eyes, rouges her cheeks with ochre, reddens her lips with wine-lees, dabs scent behind her ears... Not being vulgarians, Arruntia and I occupy separate bedrooms, and I am forbidden to see her until she is wearing a load of rings, ear-rings, necklace, brooches, pendants, bangles, bracelets, and that long violet silk tunic, gathered at the waist by an embroidered belt, not to mention the Tyrian shawl.

'Allow me to pass a comb through your lordship's hair,' says Sophron. Meanwhile Alexander, my younger slave, mutters a surly 'Good day!', unbars the apartment door, and pads out. Soon I follow him down the stairs and step inside the armoury. The master-smith has no time for chat. 'My lord Egnatius, excuse me! We're sadly short-handed since that prize-fool Hylas insulted his master.'

Sophron carries the chamber pot past me to the street corner. Tenement houses have no plumbing at all. Night soil is dumped on a midden at the dead end of the nearest alley. Chamber pots are emptied into a big tank outside the laundry; the laundrymen use its contents to clean woollens, with the help of potash and fuller's earth. They pay a City tax for this privilege.

I cross the street, and glance up. A bulge in the wall of our second storey worries me; so does the wide crack near our front window. It may be my imagination, but both seem more pronounced than in September when I last looked. Most modern houses in Rome are jerry-built, because the building contractor need not submit his plans to a municipal architect, and because only temples are erected for eternity. Still, Arruntius swears that the fabric is sound, and continues to live underneath us.

By now the last straggling cart has left the city. To end traffic jams once and for all, Julius Caesar prohibited all wheeled vehicles – with the exception of ceremonial chariots and wagons engaged in the building trade – from using the streets between sunrise and dusk. As a result, our nightly sleep is forever broken by rumbles, creaks, bumps, shouts and oaths as the carts pass. Rome's streets and alleys, none of them lit or marked with its name, run higgledy-piggledy in every direction. Carters often lose their bearings, and when two lines of traffic meet in an alley, argue half an hour as to which of them must back out again. Carts caught by police patrols after sunrise must stay empty and immobilized for the next twelve hours; so traffic quarrels grow more violent at first cock-crow.

Several stores have opened, and their stock is being piled on either side of the street, leaving only a narrow passage between – and a foul one at that. Near me, under an awning, a boys' school is already at work. No history, geography, literature, religion, or rhetoric taught here! It's reading, writing, arithmetic all the year round, from dawn to noon, without a break; except summer holidays, and one day off in eight. The schoolmaster, a ferocious wretch in a rickety chair, sits waggling his birch rod. Frightened pupils huddle together on benches. He distributes bead-frames among them, one to every group of three and, while I am waiting, sets them a problem. 'Add seventeen, two thousand, and one hundred and fifty-four. Hurry, villains! And no prompting!' Each boy moves beads along the wires for his third-share of the problem, and when everyone has finished, the tyrant checks results. There follow heavy blows of the rod, dealt out by groups – he never bothers to find out which boy has miscalculated.

Alexander leads up Bucephalus, harnessed. As I mount him from a handy barrel, he backs into a pyramid of earthenware pots. Several break. The shopkeeper explodes with rage, schoolchildren shout and cheer; the master rains blows on them indiscriminately. 'Two sesterces will cover the damage,' I tell Alexander, dipping into my pocket for the coins. 'Street vendors display breakable goods at their own risk.'

My beard is so fair that I can get by with a shave every other day. Oh, what a bore shaving can be, even though my rank allows me to jump the queue! Our street barber happens to be a patient, painless operator, who softens one's whiskers with warm water, hones his iron razor frequently, and takes at least half an hour over the job; but I'd rather be bored by his gossip than trust myself to the assistant – a slapdash fellow who shaves four customers to his one, and never apologizes for a gash as he stanches the blood with spiders' webs and vinegar.

I clatter off to pay my morning duty call on Lucius Vitellius. Some years ago, I served as commissariat officer in Northern Italy under his eldest son, recently Consul. Old Vitellius, a close friend of the Emperor's, is a model patron. When Sophron got wrongfully arrested this summer, after a brawl in the Fish Market, Vitellius sprung him at once and had the charge withdrawn. At New Year, he always gives me a handsome present of table silver, or a toga. Last time it was Bucephalus. I try to be a model client, and frequently perform delicate missions for him – sometimes with the help of two ex-gladiators, Arruntius' cronies.

Having tethered Bucephalus outside Vitellius' mansion on the Quirinal Hill, I enter the marble-walled lobby. Clients by the hundred are assembled here, among them a dozen senators. We are admitted in strict order of precedence to the hall, which is flanked by ancestral statues. Old Vitellius has a nod or a joke for each of us. He asks me: 'How's the mule, Spaniard?' 'Magnificently frisky, my lord.' 'Kicked anyone of importance today?' 'No, my lord, we met none of your enemies. He merely pulverized a display of Sicilian glassware. The merchant is claiming fifty denarii damages.' 'Then he'll accept twenty? Very well, my lad. Collect them and, in future, give your steed less food and more exercise.'

Noble Bucephalus! He's earned me nineteen denarii. I collect from the steward, who stands behind his master's ivory chair, and will soon be dealing out the daily food allowance – six sesterces per man – to all the poorer clients.

Back again. Since Arruntia is still inaccessible, I remove my toga and set off for the Fish Market with Sophron, who shoulders the baskets. Our women are not trusted to do the shopping; in theory, they sit at home and spin. (Imagine Arruntia handling a spindle!) I try Zeno's stall, and my luck is in: he offers large red mullets at only half a denarius the pound! We shall be six to dinner; no, seven with Arruntius. I buy accordingly. Thence to the poultry and vegetable markets. A sauce for grilled red mullet, Sophron says, demands rue, mint, green coriander, basil, lovage, fennel – all fresh; also Indian pepper, honey, oil and stock, which we have in the larder. Agreed. And after the fish, chicken? I insist on Fronto's recipe: pullets first browned and then braised with stock, oil, dill, leeks, savory and coriander. One each will be enough. I buy seven large pullets at the price of six. The dessert? Let us say pomegranates, quinces stewed in honey, and a couple of melons. At Oppian's fruit and vegetable stall I pick out all I need, bargain loudly for a while, and beat Oppian down to nine sesterces – he has asked twelve. 'Put these in the other basket, away from the fish, Sophron!'

I find Arruntia looking like Messalina, Caesar's naughty wife, or like some ruinously expensive Greek courtesan from Baiae; and tell her my morning's adventures. When she grows restless, wondering whether I have forgotten her birthday, I produce a square silver cosmetic-box engraved with the Judgement of Paris, and underneath: 'Formosissimae adjudicatur' – 'The verdict goes to the most beautiful.' She kisses me tenderly. The fact is, I can't yet afford to divorce Arruntia, and her latest lover happens to be an aedile – one of the City magistrates responsible, among other things, for prosecuting breaches of the civil decencies, such as flagrant immorality, or betting (except on chariot races), or throwing filth into the street from windows. If I cross her, she may easily get him to frame me.

We breakfast together on bread, cheese and grapes. The bread is a tough, flat, wholemeal cake baked in a mould. We rub garlic on our slices and dip them in oil. Arruntia asks after the investments which I manage for her. 'Remind me about them in a month's time, and I'll have good news,' I smile. She need not know that I bought the silver box with a bribe given me by the owner of a tile factory: not to foreclose on her mortgage, but let him have another month to find the interest.

'What are you doing this morning, my beloved?' 'Oh,' she says, 'I have to attend a coming-of-age ceremony across the Tiber. Later, my friend Pyrrha will be taking me... I forget the street – somewhere in the same district – at any rate, it's a recital of poems by that boring Marcus What's-his-name...' She invites me to join her there. I excuse myself: Arruntius needs me to examine the shields and weapons for tomorrow's gladiatorial fight, and make sure that they'll pass muster. Owing to the shortage of smiths he's including some second-hand stuff from the provinces. Arruntia sends her slave girl round the corner to hire a 'senatorial' litter. Evidently she means to create an impression on someone. On whom? That Indian scent she's wearing was not intended merely to please me, and her aedile lover will be busy in Court all morning. Still, what do I care?

After checking the weapons with Arruntius, who is in a jovial temper, I stroll along the Subura towards the Forum; and have reached the Temple of Castor and Pollux when sudden shouts go up. 'Clear the way! Clear the way!' Lictors come swaggering down the street, six abreast, followed by the Imperial sedan and an escort of Praetorian Guards. Old Claudius reclines inside, head jerking, fingers trembling. The crowd cheer, and laugh. A young Gaul tosses Claudius a petition, which hits him in the face. He protests angrily: 'Is this the way to treat a fellow-citizen, my lord? You'll be throwing paving stones next, I shouldn't wonder!' 'Roses, only roses, never paving stones for the Conqueror of Britain!', the embarrassed Gaul cries. Claudius smiles indulgently, unrolls the petition, reads a few lines, and hands it to Secretary of State Pallas, who is riding beside him. 'Petition granted,' Claudius says. 'The man looks honest and can write a good clean Latin.'

I visit Sosius' publishing house, close by in the Forum, at the corner of the Tuscan quarter. The open patio holds some eighty desks, at each of which a scribe sits, bent over a long parchment scroll. A clear-voiced reader delivers the text which these slaves are copying: Claudius' own learned *History of the Etruscans*. He spells it out, letter by letter, warning them beforehand where each line ends; so that all copies will be uniform and mistakes easily checked. The book is to consist of twenty scrolls, at five denarii a scroll. [1]

At Sosius' I meet the very man I have been looking for: Afer, just up from Herculaneum, near Naples. 'Is it true, Afer, that you have a red-headed British slave named Utherus for sale?' 'Well, maybe... if the price is right.' 'Then I'll be frank. One Glabrio, who wants to marry my sister, bought another of your Britons recently, but can't get him to work. The fellow spends most of his time weeping, and won't eat; and all because he's been separated from his brother Utherus. Glabrio is my neighbour, and I happen to need a porter. It would be a charity...'

Afer considers. 'What would you pay?'

'Twelve hundred. The slave's strong and healthy?'

'I'll guarantee that.'

An hour later we settle for fourteen hundred denarii, and strike hands

---

[1] About $30 for 150,000 words.

on the bargain before witnesses. Glabrio's slave, let me confess, is not really pining; but has casually told Sophron that Utherus was one of King Caractacus' most experienced sword-smiths, and that if I could find him a job... I'm pretty sure I can sell Utherus to my father-in-law, and make a couple of thousand on the deal. Or, failing him, then to his rivals in the Via Impudica. This is a lucky day! I shall buy my pretty mistress Clyme a blue silk scarf.

Home to luncheon a little late. Arruntia is even later. Nobody excuses himself for not being on time in Rome, where only millionaires own water-clocks. We guess at the hours from sunrise to noon, and then the official timekeeper at the Law Courts shouts: 'Midday, my lords!', and his cry is joyfully taken up and carried along all the streets and alleys. Tools are downed, shops shut, pleadings end: for no Romans work in the afternoon, apart from tavern keepers, barbers, policemen and public entertainers. And almost every other day, on one excuse or another, is a public holiday.

Questioned about Marcus What's-his-name's recital, Arruntia returns the vaguest possible answers; but I know where she's been, because I sent Alexander to tail her. Not content with the aedile, she's started a serious affair with Ascalus, the famous pantomime actor!

Luncheon consists of cold left-overs from last night: spiced Lucanian sausages and mock-anchovy pâté. For want of anchovies, Sophron took fillets of sea-perch, grilled and minced them, simmered them in stock with eggs, added pepper and a little rue, laid a fresh jellyfish on top to cook in the steam. None of us guessed the ingredients.

While Arruntia takes her siesta, I slip out to give Clyme the new silk scarf. How generously she shows her gratitude!

Later in the afternoon I escort Arruntia to the Hot Baths of Agrippa, beyond the Forum; her slave girl carrying the silver cosmetic-box, Alexander carrying my gear in a leather satchel. Mixed bathing is the rule there. Only shy young virgins and sour matrons who have lost their figures attend the private establishments reserved for women. At Agrippa's, neither sex wears a stitch while in the water, but the aediles' police are present in force to discourage loose behaviour. Arruntia undresses in the women's quarters; I in the men's. Then, clad in short tunics, we skip off to the enormous exercise room. Arruntia and two girl cousins play triangle-catch; she has brought three small balls of kidskin stuffed with feathers. The object is not to drop any of them, while gradually increasing the pace. Experts use both hands and six balls instead of three. The most popular sports is bladder-ball: anyone may join in and try to keep the bladder off the floor. Personally, I prefer *harpastum:* you grab the heavy pigskin ball, full of sand, and carry it hither and thither until robbed – dodging, feinting, leaping, handing off. But first you oil yourself all over to get slippery. Tripping and low tackling are against the rules.

Today I am in splendid form and twice break through a group of twenty players, running from wall to wall and back again, before someone jumps on my shoulders, and down I go. By an extraordinary coincidence, both of Arruntia's lovers have joined the party. I flash Licianus the aedile a pleasant smile, and rob Ascalus of the ball after a long run. Licianus congratulates me on my play; so does Ascalus.

Presently we remove our tunics and go naked into a duck-boarded sweat-bath, which lies above the main furnace. Sweat flows in rivers, and soon we totter to the warm bathroom. There our slaves sponge us with hot water from the central cauldron, scrape us with silver *strigils,* and rub us down with towels. Clean as cupids, and some five pounds lighter, we make for the cool swimming pool, where we frisk about like dolphins.

Arruntia, mother-naked, swims up to the rope which divides the sexes. 'What shall we do?' she wails. 'Neither of my brothers can come to dinner, only my dreadful sisters-in-law!' 'They're not too bad,' I say, 'when on their own.' Then one of the gods – perhaps Vulcan the Cuckold – prompts me to add maliciously: 'I'll persuade two distinguished friends of mine to fill the vacant couches.'

'Do you know my wife Arruntia?' I ask the aedile as he swims by. 'This, my dear, is Licianus the Aedile, who has been playing a tough game of *harpastum* with me. May I invite him to dinner?' Ah, I do it all so innocently; and the aedile accepts so innocently; and Arruntia beams so innocently! To point the joke, my other guest must be Ascalus!

The day approaches its climax. Arruntia hurries away to get her face fixed up again – she has kept the elaborate tresses well out of the water – and then I take her home. She is unusually silent; and I unusually talkative. At nightfall the guests arrive. We recline around our expensive citrus-wood table. The red mullets are beautifully served, and Sophron has excelled himself with the braised pullets.

At first, Licianus and Ascalus address most of their conversation to the sisters-in-law or Arruntius, afraid of treating Arruntia too familiarly by mistake. And Arruntia is at pains to flatter me. Soon I produce a jar of the best Falernian. Licianus, our Master of Ceremonies, wearing his purple-bordered toga, insists on mixing it with as little water as is decently allowed – none but thieves and gladiators drink neat wine – and when the usual toping match begins, at dessert, shows his hand more boldly. He proposes toast after toast, always increasing the number of cups that must be downed for each: hoping, I suspect, to make us all dead drunk, keep a clear head himself, and end up in Arruntia's arms.

But the old Falernian is mischievous. I heave myself up from the couch and call for silence. 'Arruntia, dearest wife, listen to me! On my birthday gift which you admire so much, is engraved a Judgement of Paris. Prince Paris, Homer says, was ordered to present the loveliest of three goddesses with an apple – a choice that needed remarkable tact. Paris chose the

Goddess of Love, and thereby won the favours of Helen. Now, here's a "Judgement of Helen" for you! Give this pomegranate to the handsomest of us three young men... Pray, my dear, do not yield to self-interest as Paris did, but make an honest judgement. Consider neither the rank and eminence of Licianus, nor the fame of Ascalus, nor the wifely duty you owe Egnatius, your humble husband. Speak straight from the bottom of your truthful breast! I can count upon my equitable father-in-law to see fair play.'

Through her chalk and rouge Arruntia blushes a deep red. Licianus hides his aquiline nose in an agate wine-cup. Ascalus assumes a theatrical posture, like Ajax defying the lightning. But Arruntius bursts into a roar of drunken laughter and thumps me on the back. 'Egnatius,' he yells, 'you're a man after my own heart! Go on! Roast that she-ass for us on the public spit!' Both sisters-in-law giggle nervously. They hate Arruntia, but are scared of scenes, especially when Arruntius has been drinking. He never knows his own strength; and this, indeed, was his plea long ago when, suspecting Arruntia's mother of infidelity...

'Choose, then, most beautiful of women, Rome's own Helen!' I insist, perfectly master of the situation. 'Choose!'

Arruntia cups her chin in deep thought. Will she? Won't she?

The dramatic hush is broken by a loud crash and horrified shrieks from somewhere high above us, followed almost immediately by an echoing boom and a still louder shriek. Fascinated, I watch the street wall slowly buckle and give... Then everything falls at once!

Did any of us survive? I doubt it. My next distinct memory is of being a child once more. Martial music sounds. Mother lifts me up to watch, through a well-glazed English nursery window, the decorated carriages and red-coated soldiers of Queen Victoria's Diamond Jubilee procession.

The Myconian

I

OUTSIDE THE WINESHOP everyone was teasing the mild-mannered stranger who wore the grey cloak of a Greek philosopher. The usual run of philosophers are much-travelled, sharp as needles, knowing as vultures; but this one seemed ignorant and artless, a regular hick.

'In Hell's name, where do you spring from?' Scorpus asked. 'Anyone would think you'd been asleep a thousand years and just woken up!'

'From Myconos, the Aegean island. It's not very big, but quite famous. Why, the Giants who attacked Heaven are buried beneath our granite rocks, which the God Hercules threw at them. And we show the Tomb of Ajax, too – a Trojan War hero.'

The philosopher then began to quote Homer, but Scorpus cut him short. 'You're not a real Myconian,' he teased.

The philosopher blushed. 'How did you guess?'

'Look at your thatch! *"Myconi calva omnis juventas!"* – All Myconians are bald as pumpkins, even boys.'

'Yes,' he mumbled. 'My family, I confess, originated in Athens. Political refugees. This thick hair does make me somewhat conspicuous at home. But I have the most beautifully bald wife and children.'

He spoke in such earnest tones that we took to him in a big way. 'Ever travelled before?' I asked, when the laughter had subsided.

'Some years ago I attended a course in philosophy at Athens. From there I went to the Olympic Games: an unforgettable experience! As Homer says...'

'Forget Homer! We're not buying Homer. Did you see good sport at Olympia?'

'Sir, it was fabulous! A score of events crammed into five days! First, the sacrifices and the classification of athletes; then a contest between trumpeters. Great Heavens, you should have watched them puff out their cheeks until they looked like pigs' bladders – veins swelling on foreheads, eyes bulging. A little fellow from Sicily ought to have won, but the judges disqualified him after an objection; it seems he had once served a prison

term at Syracuse for striking a priest. Only freeborn Greeks of good character may compete at Olympia. But, by Jove, how he blew – what sweet
thunder! Next, to whet our appetite, the boys' races! So two days glided
by in the horseshoe Stadium. No less than forty thousand visitors must
have gathered there from all over the Greek world! We put up tents and
picnicked beside the river. The third day, the day of champions... Two-
hundred-yard sprint, quarter-mile and two-mile footraces. Classical
wrestling. A race between armed soldiers carrying shields and spears; our
Myconian champion came in third. Hard-glove boxing. Free-style
wrestling. Magnificent! The competitors had trained for years.'

'*Footraces*!' scoffed Bufotilla, Scorpus' green-eyed girl friend, blowing
her nose daintily with thumb and fore-finger, and wiping them on my
cloak. 'Left, right; left, right; left, right – elbows jogging, lungs whistling,
eyes glazed – round and round and round... I can't imagine a drearier
spectacle.'

'Ah, dear women!' sighed the philosopher, 'you're all alike –
pretending to despise the Games which you are forbidden, on pain of
death, to witness!'

Bufotilla stared at him. 'Forbidden – on pain of death? And why, pray?'

'Because Olympic athletes wear no clothes, young lady,' replied the
philosopher.

'By the Girdle of Venus, what's wrong with that? Don't you have nude
mixed bathing at public baths in Greece?'

This time it was the philosopher who stared at Bufotilla.

'Well, don't you?' she insisted, sharply.

Scorpus had heard vague talk, some place or other, about the Olympic
Games, and broke in: 'Big prizes, eh? Heavy bonuses?'

'No, Sir. The same award serves all events: an olive-wreath, cut with a
golden sickle from the sacred tree.'

'Yes, yes, that's the token award, I don't doubt. But how much cash
does it mean? You can't tell me that these fellows train for years, then
flock to Olympia from all over the Greek world, in the hope of winning
only a wretched wreath, such as they could cut anywhere themselves?'

The philosopher smiled reprovingly. 'We are Greeks, not barbarians,'
he said.

'So what? Doesn't anyone ever sell a race or match at Olympia?'

'They swear a solemn oath beforehand that they won't. At the altar of
Olympian Zeus, in front of all the judges.'

'And if an athlete breaks his oath?'

'The judges fine him severely, and the city he represents is shamed. At
Olympia, you can see rows of bronze images flanking the Temple steps.
They were paid for with fines imposed on men who bribed their oppo-
nents to lose: long rows of images, worth I don't know how much.'

'Thanks, I knew that money came into it somehow,' said Scorpus. 'It always does.'

We burst out laughing, but the philosopher saw no joke. 'It's true,' he said, 'and on each image is engraved a warning that the Olympic Games were founded by Hercules as a contest in manliness, not in money; and that the Gods always discover cheats.'

'Oh, get on with your tale! Bufotilla's growing nervous; aren't you, my honey? We want to hear about the chariot race. That's the main draw at any Games.'

'Not at Olympia. When we talk of bygone Olympics, we always identify them by the name of whichever athlete won the sprint – our earliest and most important athletic event. The chariot-race winner may be a moribund old prince from Cadiz, or the Black Sea provinces, who never saw Greece before but happens to own a good stable. In the sprint, it is the *man* who wins, the *man* whom poets celebrate – not a team of dumb horses. Therefore we philosophers despise the chariot race: it infringes the Olympic rule that money is no substitute for manliness.'

'Haven't you forgotten the charioteer?' asked Scorpus gently, stroking his large nose. Any other member of Scorpus' profession would have knocked the philosopher down, instead, and jumped on him. But Scorpus could afford to be forbearing.

'Oh, yes,' the philosopher answered. 'Charioteers get the best out of their teams, I suppose; but at Olympia nobody pays them much attention. It is not a dangerous race: a driver who deliberately fouled an opponent's chariot, why, he would be disgraced for life!'

This drew fresh guffaws from our party, and Bufotilla cried: 'By all the Gods in Heaven and Hell, what a nation of sissies! No wonder our Roman legions went through you like string through cheese!'

Scorpus, controlling his mirth with a great effort, said: 'Go on about this most ethical chariot race. How many laps are run?'

'Laps? Just one – as in Homer's day.'

'Mention Homer again, and I'll *scream*!' screamed Bufotilla.

'And the length of the run?' Scorpus asked.

'Five hundred yards.'

'You call that *sport*?'

'Certainly!'

'Then you'd better watch a Roman race this afternoon, and improve your education. Take charge of him, Glabrio, will you? See he gets a seat with the Family.'

I said I would. Then along came a crowd of young noblemen, all wearing blue favours, caught sight of Scorpus, lifted him on their shoulders, cheering madly, and bore him off.

'With what paragon of men have I had the honour to converse?' exclaimed the philosopher.

'With Scorpus: our greatest charioteer for generations. He's turned the

tide of fortune from the Green faction to the Blue – won us over eleven
hundred victories since the Emperor's accession. Worth nearly two
million in gold! If he'd slit your throat just now, when you talked of charioteers as though they were country carters, would any Roman have dared
inform against him? Not one! So far as he's concerned, police and magistrates can go to Hell. He hobnobs with the Emperor Domitian himself.
Senators' wives and daughters pant for him, but he brushes them off like
flies.'

'This Scorpus comes of noble stock?'

'Noble? His father was a slave from York, employed in the Imperial
stables. And if you want to know why he despises the Olympic chariot race
no less than you philosophers do, it's because *his* course is seven times
round the Great Circus, with bloody murder lurking at each post. Few
charioteers escape a broken leg or arm for long. Ten races; twenty
perhaps, if they're lucky: then, crash!... Scorpus' luck has been phenom-
enal; only three serious accidents in five years. Everyone wonders why he
doesn't retire on the winnings.'

'Why doesn't he?'

'Says he mustn't fail his public. But I don't think it's quite that. In his
heart he despises the public; all experienced charioteers do. I guess he just
gets a kick out of playing with death. Besides, if he retired, tell me some
other job he could take and still feel a man – short of turning gladiator?'

A poster on the wineshop wall announced that one of Menander's
comedies would be playing that afternoon in Pompey's Theatre. The
philosopher wanted to see it. 'No,' I said, 'you're not going!'

'Why not?' he asked, rebelliously.

'For three good reasons. First, because it's in Latin translation; and
you're short on Latin.'

'I'll risk that.'

'Second, because you'll find the Theatre's altogether too big. I've been
around in Greece; I've seen plays acted there... Audiences of two thousand at the most. Here, they're nearer sixty thousand! Against all that
talking and coughing and shuffling, how can dialogue be followed, even
with a wind blowing from the right quarter? And the back rows can't
easily distinguish between the players. So prostitutes always wear yellow;
old men wear white; the hero wears mixed colours; merchants, purple;
beggars, red; etcetera... And all you get of the comedy, besides madly
expensive sets, are fragments of shouted dialogue, and theme songs.
Theme songs played by the orchestra, sung by the choir, and danced by
Paris.'

'Who may Paris be?'

'The leading man, whom our women dote on. As he cavorts across the
stage he registers terror, anguish, obscene passion, filial tenderness, corny
humour, bestial cunning – the whole works! Does it all with gestures.

Menander would turn in his grave to see what's happened to his lines; and I gather you respect Menander? Our actresses strip to the buff in aid of greater realism. And no holds barred. It's a liberal education, some-times... Why, recently the Emperor let a convict be substituted for the brigand chief in the last act of *Laureolus*, and actually be crucified on-stage!'

'What is your third reason?'

'The most important one! It's that Scorpus expects you to watch the chariot-racing in the Great Circus. See?'

We ate lunch – bread and black puddings – at another wineshop, near the Citadel. The big race wouldn't be run for another two hours; which left us plenty of time to visit the late Emperor Titus' Amphitheatre, commonly called The Colosseum. I own a couple of good seats there, on the shady side; and even if I forget my tickets, I can always get in as a member of Scorpus' 'family'. I'm his saddle-master: the man solely responsible for his reins, traces and harness...

We strolled past the Forum. A pretty girl in a violet silk gown, wearing half a pound of bangles and necklaces, linked the philosopher's arm endearingly in hers. 'Coming for a walk, Socrates?' she inquired. 'I could ask you some tough questions.'

I firmly unhooked them, and shooed her away.

'Why did you do that?' he bleated.

'I'd hate my friends to find me arm in arm with a philosopher *and* a prostitute...'

'But I thought prostitutes always wore yellow?' he sighed. What superb innocence! I must remember to tell Scorpus!

This being the noon interval, we found the Colosseum less than half-full: a mere thirty thousand spectators. During the interval, second-class entertainment is the rule – animal turns or acrobatics; but I'm glad we went, because a 'No-reprieve' show was put on. 'No-reprieve' is an amusing alternative to crucifixion – and the criminals appreciate it: death comes quick, and most of them get the pleasure of killing as well as the misfortune of getting killed. Ten criminals were announced that day: among them bandits, men convicted of incest or arson, and parricides. A villainous lot, except for one fine-looking Sicilian bandit, by name Julius Ferox. Every woman in the audience waved her scarf at him on hearing that, before his capture, he'd flattened three soldiers and their sergeant. Julius would appear third.

A roll of kettle-drums, and the parricide was led in, naked. He glanced wildly about: gates shut and barriers too high to scramble over. Then in strutted another criminal in full armour, with shield and sword – a mad Moor from Tangiers, who had burned down an apartment house, causing considerable loss of life. He caught his man after a long chase which ended rather tamely, because the desperate parricide took a leap at the barrier and knocked himself out. Then the Moor was himself disarmed by two guards, who gave his gear to Julius Ferox. The Moor had not run three paces before Julius thrust him through the lungs.

Poor sport; but now came Julius' turn to be disarmed, and a ruffian from the Sabine Hills had the chance to murder him. Julius showed no dismay. Though mother-naked, he met the rush, flung back his head and dealt a violent kick at the Sabine's wrist. Away flew the sword; Julius tackled low, got hold of the shield, and drove its sharp boss through his enemy's temple. He rose, walked up to the guards, and remarking carelessly: 'I'll fight without these,' handed over the arms. 'Next customer!'

The crowd cheered his bravado. He now confronted a tough cut-throat from Naples, cleverly working him round to face the midday sun; then, stooping, he threw a handful of sand in his eyes and took a running kick at his genitals. In no time at all he'd won a third victory.

'Next customer!'

Terrific applause; and the lady below me screamed at her husband: 'Oh, Tullius, if only you had that bandit's physique, what a happy woman I should be!'

'And if only I had his kick,' growled Tullius, 'I'd soon cure your itch!'

Julius had little trouble with the miserable Tuscan dandy, convicted of raping his niece. No gladiator, this one! Julius went up, saying: 'Your sword, lad!', calmly borrowed it and cut off his head at a stroke.

'Next customer!'

His new opponent was a fellow-bandit, formerly his lieutenant, who'd betrayed him to the authorities in the vain hope of winning a pardon. While tussling for the sword, Julius was gashed and stabbed in three places; but then used it mercilessly, lopping off the traitor's ears, nose and hands before dispatching him. The crowd stood up, roaring delightedly, and appealed for pardon; but this was a 'No-reprieve' show. So Julius committed suicide. He didn't seem to mind, now that suitable vengeance had been taken.

'Congratulations!' I said to the philosopher. 'Beginner's luck. Best show this year; and in the Interval, too! The regular fights will seem flat after this... Of course, if Hermes were on, that would be another kettle of fish! A wonderful gladiator; but he's in hospital just now – jabbed in the thigh by a net-and-trident expert. An all-round man is Hermes: trident, spear, sword, on horseback, or on foot. Fills all the tiers. Well, what about getting along? The next numbers will only be a negro tight-rope walker, a dwarf riding a goat over a row of obstacles, and a duel between two delinquent housewives armed with cleavers.'

The philosopher's face had turned green, and he'd shut his eyes tight so as not to see the remaining criminals done in.

I nudged him again: 'Coming?'

'Where can I vomit?' he gasped.

'You talk of manliness,' I said, leading him out, 'and yet you want to vomit! How was that for a display of manliness? If a bandit can prove himself a hero, what do you think the rest of us are like?'

He kept silent until we'd left the Colosseum and his nausea had passed. Then he answered: 'The heroism of a Sicilian bandit gives me no clue to the spirit of ordinary Roman citizens – wine sellers, actors, or saddle-masters. Have you yourself taken part in a war? No? Or faced a storm at sea? No? Do you box, even with soft gloves?'

I shook my head.

'What are your sports?'

'None, now. At the Baths, I sometimes raise a sweat by joining in an aimless medicine-ball scrimmage. I used to wrestle, but not after I put my thumb out. And no self-respecting Roman boxes; we leave that to gladiators – cauliflower ears and broken noses have no attraction for pretty ladies. Gladiators don't care; they cheerfully use spiked knuckledusters. The other day I saw Hermes taking on an enormous black bear – killed it, too, with a left to the muzzle and a right to the jaw.'

'Then you expect slaves, criminals, and the desperately poor to display courage on your behalf?'

'Put it that way, if you like. I won't argue against a philosopher.'

'Is it true,' he asked, 'that at the Colosseum batches of Jewish mystics are daily thrown to hungry lions?'

'Yes, I believe so: in the early morning when the gates first open. They're let down in cages, by a crane. Few people attend, because there's nothing to bet on. And it's a pretty tame spectacle. These Christians, as they're called, show no fight when released from the cage; just kneel down, pray and sing. Curious, isn't it? But they can't be altogether Jewish: I hear they eat pork freely.'

As we mixed with the crowd streaming towards the Great Circus, a couple of policemen frog-marched a bedraggled fellow to the lock-up.

'Betting?' I asked.

They nodded and went on.

The philosopher exclaimed: 'Yet at the wineshop I heard one of those young noblemen openly backing Scorpus for ten thousand gold pieces to six! Is there one law for the poor, and another for the rich?'

'You've missed the point. The law forbids casual betting. If caught, you're fined four times the value of your stake, or else go to gaol. But everyone's encouraged to bet on the chariots and the gladiators. I'm sorry now that you missed seeing a Colosseum fight. We should have stayed. It can be great fun – if it's not rigged... Say you bet on a targeteer who's meeting a gladiator with a large shield. Say you stake a month's wages; say they fight good and hard – without any need for the whipper to warm them up by lashing their legs. The crowd yells: "At him, the Blue!", "Murder him, the Green!" (We have Blue and Green factions here, too.)

Soon it's: "Burn him, roast him, flay him, gut him, pickle him!" Or: "Hey, mind out, Green!" Then at last: "Good lad, that got him!" – and you watch the targeteer's sword sink up to the hilt in Green's belly... You feel fine, see? It's as though you'd killed him yourself. The Blue targeteer's brought home your bacon. A grand instance of Roman sport – manliness and money, hand in hand.'

'Well,' said the philosopher, irritably twitching his grey cloak, 'you Romans have indeed mastered the art of making poor wretches commit mutual murder for your sakes! And do you have even one native Roman out of every ten soldiers enrolled in your legions – apart from senior officers?'

'I doubt it. That's what the poet Virgil, or maybe it was Cicero, calls being a master race,' I answered cheerfully.

II

As we walked towards the Great Circus, I pointed up at a gilt statuary group on a massive marble pedestal.

'The Sun-god?' The philosopher asked.

I grinned. 'Don't his nose and chin remind you of some one?'

'Yes, indeed! What a strange resemblance to your friend Scorpus!'

'It *is* Scorpus!'

The philosopher stopped dead. 'Once,' he said severely, 'it was considered a sin to honour even kings with statues. Yet today one may mistake the gilded statue of an ex-slave for a divine image!'

'Why not? The Blue faction set up that group to celebrate Scorpus' thousandth victory. If every god treated his worshippers as generously as Scorpus has treated the Blues, religion wouldn't be in such a poor way.'

He asked me to explain the factions in easy language. A difficult task for a professional like me...

'Well,' I said, 'each faction is known by a colour, one of those that everyone's wearing – Green, Blue, White and Red. The four racing stables are managed by millionaire syndicates. Green has White as its partner; Blue has Red. You'll have noticed that Green and Blue favours predominate. But don't despise the minor colours: White and Red charioteers come in handy by opening up for their partners, or baulking the enemy.'

'Do these colours mean anything in particular?'

'Not that I've ever heard.'

'Yet I seem to be the only person here not wearing a favour!'

'It's quite a story,' I told him. 'A few generations back, we Romans fought one Civil War after another: all for political reasons. They lasted till the Republic broke down and Augustus made himself Emperor. Since then, discounting a spot of trouble at Nero's death, we've had continuous peace – and no politics! So Rome's grown incredibly rich. Rich in slaves, rich in trade. This is the "Good Life" of our ancestors' dreams. Free citizens need to work only till noon. What's more, they can take every other day off, buy all they need, and still have money to jingle... Here's a novel problem: How to spend their leisure time? Every blessed afternoon, every other morning as well! I'm fortunate to be in show business; keeps me occupied.'

'*I* should buy books,' said the philosopher eagerly.

'Books? But then you're Greek. We Romans don't read unless we're sick. Elsewhere, idle men finding themselves without jobs or money nurse political grievances; here they're denied even that comfort. And the Emperor can't set them all to work raising colossal pyramids – which, for all I know, may have been how the Pharaohs solved Egypt's leisure problem. He'd run a risk of assassination. Instead, he subsidizes free gladiator shows and chariot races, and lets faction politics replace party politics. Only a fool would want a change in government when the factions supply a simple means of turning his spare cash into a fortune.'

'How so?'

'By betting, of course! Anyone can join either the Blues or the Greens; and though both factions are equally crooked, the betting works well enough.'

'I should find it demoralizing to be a perpetual spectator!'

'There the Emperor agrees with you. He's just proclaimed a four-yearly "Roman Games" on the Olympic model; doubtless hoping that we'll all turn enthusiastic athletes. But even if the factions take over, which seems improbable, I can't see a future in athletics. Apart from popular music and dancing at the Theatre, Rome cares for little except sex, gladiators, racing and betting: we don't pretend to be Greek idealists.'

A cockfight announcement, posted on a building, caught the philosopher's eye – one of the entries was a Myconian bird. He insisted on going inside. Look-outs stood by the door of this miniature Colosseum, where one may bet only in hazel-nuts. The audience wore patched and dirty cloaks; yet the stakes were heavy. Neither the stink and vermin of the cockpit, nor its obscene wall-paintings troubled the philosopher. He forced me to sit through three fights until the Myconian cock was put in, for the main, by a bald compatriot of his.

Though a small bird, ye Gods!, what a game one... The tall Tanagran, matched against him, mauled his head to a gory mess; but he kept his stubby crest erect and fought like Jove's eagle. Pretty soon he had the Tanagran guessing, and took his revenge. Up in the air he flew and, with a single backward thrust, too quick to follow, drove a sharp spur clean through his opponent's skull. 'Great Heavens, what timing!' exulted the philosopher. He made as much fuss of that cock as if it had saved all Greece from disaster!

I teased him: 'So you're a convert to the Roman view of sport? Just now you griped because we like watching gladiators commit mutual murder for our amusement.'

He had his answer ready: 'Who needs to train cocks at a gladiatorial school? Who forces them to fight desperately, like your doomed ruffians, by way of avoiding jail or the galleys? Who stands behind them with a whip? Cocks battle to the death of their own free will, because such is their nature – and in the barnyard as readily as in the pit.'

'Don't under-estimate our gladiators,' said I. 'Hermes, for instance, leader of the Blue troop at the Colosseum: he's a born killer. Enjoys every minute of life, except when he's in hospital.'

We pushed our way into the Great Circus through Titus' Arch, and found Opimus, the stout Blue faction-chief, fuming outside his office. 'You're late, Glabrio!' he bellowed. 'Hurry off and check the harness. Hurry! There's only a quarter of an hour left.'

'Checked it before lunch, Sir. Scorpus was with me. Ask him! Zeno's been keeping an eye on it meanwhile.'

'Zeno! What do I care about *him*?' Opimus stormed. 'How can I tell he's not been got at? Zeno's a Red, and no employee of mine. Don't you know that a million in gold hangs on this race? Check everything again! And hurry, I say!'

I went to the Harness Room, a stable-guard at my side, unlocked the door, and checked again. The gold-plated chariot, inlaid with lapis lazuli and turquoise, was not my concern – not even the harness rings. But the traces, yes! I paid them out slowly – thirty flawless yards of new bull's hide, tough and supple, every inch of it; the splices sewn and oversewn with fox-gut! Then the reins: also brand-new. Harness: sound, though too lavishly decorated. I hate seeing good leather spoiled by plaques and jewels and amulets; however, if the crowd admires that sort of nonsense... Finally, the bronze bits. I'm expected to wash these before each race, for fear someone may have doped them, and to use water from a sealed jar. The stable-guard keeps a beady eye on me.

'All correct, Sir!' I told Opimus.

The grooms wheeled out Scorpus' chariot, fastened the yoke, and threw the harness over the waiting stallions. First the team, a matched pair of Thessalian duns, on either side of the shaft. Then the two bay tracers: this course is always taken counter-sunwise, so the tracers are made fast to rail-rings on the off-side. A posse of stable-guards watched sullenly. No one in the Circus trusts anyone.

Now cock your ear for a stable secret! We Blues pamper our stallions on barley mash doctored with raw, chopped horseflesh – which makes canni-bals of them! Remember how King Diomedes, whom Hercules slew, fed his mares on human flesh? I once laughed at that as a poetic fable; now I know that horses are gluttons for meat. The Greens haven't yet discovered why Scorpus, apart from his wonderful driving, gets an extra half-length out of his team in every lap. They've tried most known stimulants on their beasts, even peppered oysters! But raw meat's the answer, either beef or horseflesh.

Scorpus emerges from his dressing-room – in a sky-blue silk tunic, with long strips of buckskin swathed around his legs, crash-helmet, dagger and whip. His nose and chin jut magisterially. 'All set?' he asks Opimus.

'All set, champion. How do you feel?'

'As I look.'

I prod the philosopher out of his dreams. 'Aren't you betting?'

'I never laid a bet in my life – not even on the cocks.'

'What? You're still a virgin? Lend me your luck, in Heaven's name: lay a maiden bet for me! I'll give you half the winnings, I swear.'

'It goes against my principles.'

'To the crows with your principles! Take this purse: there should be ninety-six gold pieces in it. Run across to the Greens at once, and put the lot on Scorpus! Lodge your bet at the corner bookmaker's. The Greens somehow fancy Thallus to win; so don't accept less than evens! A maiden bet, ye Gods! I've never once known a maiden bet go astray. If you won't help me, Myconian, I'll beat you till you sneeze!'

Most reluctantly, he took the purse and placed the bet, getting evens all right. I could have done better, probably, because Thallus and Scorpus were almost equally fancied, and five to one was being quoted against the field. Five to one may seem short odds, but think how many eager punters back the field!

There we sat, in marble seats, up front, beside the rest of Scorpus' 'family' – his trainer, chariot-master, head stable-lad, veterinary, and his green-eyed girl friend Bufotilla. It's 'First come, first get' here with all seats except the Imperial Enclosure and the rows reserved for Senators, Knights, and faction officials like ourselves. That's why thousands of sportsmen queue up, the evening before, to grab good seats when the gates open at daybreak. An hour later they'd find standing-room only. You never know whom you'll be next to; I first met my Syrian wife in a Circus queue...

Thallus' 'family' sat near us, across a gangway. The philosopher's grey cloak puzzled them. 'What business has Scorpus with philosophy?' they wondered. 'Philosophy's something that generals and statesmen take up in retirement. Can Scorpus be retiring?'

We let them wonder. Jokes and insults flew between the rival families.

The philosopher had been enormously impressed by the Colosseum audience; but at the Great Circus he doubted his eyes. 'How many! How many!' he groaned, gazing around him.

'Almost a full house,' I said. 'Above a quarter of a million people. Including the Emperor Domitian himself – over there in scarlet! With the purple cloak, the golden wreath, and his favourite dwarf.'

I remember the veterinary saying he felt worried. Something he'd
heard in the crowd suggested that Blue had been got at.
We took him up on this at once. 'What do you mean "got at"? By
whom? Let's have it! Together, we five are responsible for the whole turn-
out – except for Scorpus. And that's Bufotilla's job. Got anything against
Bufotilla?'
'He better hadn't!' said Bufotilla fiercely.
'No, no, don't talk that way,' protested the veterinary. 'It's just something in the air. Those Greens look so damnably cocksure.'
Trumpets blew and, amid tempestuous cheers, the four teams entered
at a trot and lined up behind the starting-rope. The draw for places had
been unfortunate. Scorpus got the outer berth; his Red partner got the
inner; and between them Green and White – so that from inside to outside
the colours ran Red, White, Green, Blue.
A beautiful, warm, windless day; the vast, tight-packed Circus; the fine
yellow sand; the charioteers poised like gods, leaning back a little, with the
reins wound fast about their waists; the horses pawing, snorting, and
flaunting coloured favours. Above them, on the long, narrow embankment around which the course ran, towered the immense obelisk brought
by Augustus from Egypt; and on either side of it stood marble images of
Neptune, Hercules and the Heavenly Twins. Also bronzes of deified
Caesars: Augustus, Claudius and Vespasian – each of whom in his lifetime
had generously patronized this Circus.
The Emperor waved his napkin to signal 'Begin!' Another trumpet
flourish: the taut rope fell, four whips cracked as one, and the chariots
were off, scattering clouds of sand.
Blue's partner, Red, having drawn the best berth, should have gone hell
for leather to reach the turning-post first, then rounded it in a wide
enough sweep to hold White and Green securely on his flank, while
letting his partner, Blue, nip in behind and steal the turn. I've watched
that manoeuvre often; but it needs judgement. On this occasion Red got
away to a slow start, let White crowd him into the embankment, four
lengths before the post, and thus open the inner berth for Thallus.
Scorpus, counting on Red to reach the post unchallenged, hadn't let his
team go full out; by the time he'd whisked around White at the turn,
Green was well ahead. (These two posts, at either end of the embankment,
are pillars of gilt bronze; seven huge wooden eggs rest on a frame above
them. An Imperial slave takes one egg down as soon as the leading chariot
has gone past; and another at each lap, until all seven eggs have disappeared. It saves charioteers and spectators the trouble of keeping count.)
A bad beginning. Thallus kept his lead of three lengths, and completed
the first lap with so sharp a turn that I'd swear his wheel shaved the gilt off
both sides of the bronze! After him shot Scorpus, now far enough away
from White not to be worried by him; though plainly worried by the

Green tunic in front. Later we heard that our near team-horse had not been in top condition.

Three very fast laps, no change in position, and towards the end of the fourth lap Scorpus challenged; he ran neck to neck with Green for a while, but failed to make that inner berth at the turn.

Four eggs down! Five eggs down!

Scorpus didn't challenge again; he waited, despite jeers, protests, whistles and encouraging yells. He waited patiently, until Red had lost a whole lap and was hugging the embankment, some lengths in the rear of White, with Green threatening to pass him at the post. *'Ag'ut primā debebas!'* Scorpus shouted – he lay a little behind and beyond Green – 'Do what you should have done at the first post!'

Red understood; he flogged blood and sweat out of his nags, and this time rounded the turn wide enough to carry Green with him. Scorpus, wheeling almost at right angles, nipped in behind so neatly that his off-tracer's shoulder grazed the Red chariot-tail: he'd beaten Green to the inner berth and won three lengths.

'Successit et vicet!' the Blues roared – 'He's gained the lead, and he'll keep it!'

Six eggs down!

Now White, just ahead of Scorpus, though still in the fifth lap, was weaving in and out to hamper him; Green ran a close third. Caught between his two rivals, Scorpus made a bold decision. He forced his tracers to take the last turn wide; whereupon White lost his whip, as well as his head. Mistaking Thallus' team for Scorpus' – the Green tracers being also bays – he baulked him at the critical moment. Thallus' wheel struck the post, square, the chariot broke up. In the nick of time he used his dagger to cut himself free from the reins. On rushed the horses, hauling the wreckage after them.

A thunderstorm of cheers and curses. It was Blue's race all right – Scorpus could have finished at a walk. But as he walloped his triumphant Thessalians at high speed down the stretch, a small, ragged-shirted figure leaped the barrier and ran across the sand, shaking his puny fists. There he stood – directly in the chariot's path! Expecting him to lose his nerve and dart back, Scorpus neither reined in nor swerved. The intruder sprang at the duns' heads, then fell with a scream under their iron hooves. The tracers, meanwhile, had shied and plunged, slewing the chariot around. Scorpus was thrown, and his helmet struck sickeningly against the marble embankment. He was dragged past the winning-post – one lap and five lengths ahead of White.

An indescribable hubbub. I heard the chariot-master's gasp of horror. In a nightmare, I heard my own groans, as if heaved from some other man's guts. Scorpus, our great Scorpus! Down at last with a smashed skull and broken neck! The long play had ended. We wept like orphan children.

Bufotilla fainted; the veterinary took charge of her. I was glad she'd fainted. We all thought the world of her. She and Scorpus were to have married in the New Year. One can find no words of comfort on such occasions...

Further hubbub. The judges were signalling a Blue victory. Someone tugged at my sleeve. 'You've won your ninety-six gold pieces!' said the philosopher. 'I renounce my share. It would be disgraceful to profit from a man's death.'

He was being illogical. Dead men don't win races, and the judges' decision clearly showed that Scorpus had been dragged alive past the mark. But why argue?

'What pain! What misery!' I mourned. 'Scorpus is gone! Those murderous Greens must have been counting on Ragged Shirt to save their bets. A suicidal wretch, who'd bet against Scorpus once too often? But I won't believe a man could have scrambled over that barrier without help!'

Just then the Imperial catapults opened up: a volley of metal vouchers scattering in showers among the seats. Some were for money, anything from a single gold piece to a hundred; some had even higher value, gifts of farms, houses, shops – properties confiscated by the Emperor from banished noblemen, or left him in wills.

'I can stand no more!' the philosopher exclaimed shrilly. 'Tomorrow I shall return to Myconos, if the kind Gods will arrange my passage.' And that the Gods were kind, and very kind, a most curious coincidence proved. A voucher struck the head of some woman sitting behind us and bounced into the philosopher's lap. It entitled him to 'a fifty-ton merchant vessel, the *Good Fortune*, at present lying off Naples; warranted sound and well found.' How's that for maiden luck? And only five days later an Imperial Edict banished all philosophers from Rome!

Not since the Emperor Titus died have I seen a better attended funeral. The Spanish poet Martial wrote a graceful dirge: 'Let Victory sadly break her palm, *etcetera, etcetera*...' Also an epitaph: to the effect that an envious Fate having counted Scorpus' victories, decided that at twenty-seven years he'd won enough for a lifetime; then took up her shears and snipped his vital thread. I'm no judge of verse, but I admired the sentiment.

Thallus has succeeded to Scorpus' throne; and we Blues seldom win these days. Besides, racing isn't what it was: the Emperor, for inscrutable reasons of State, has formed two new factions – Purple and Gold. Our harassed bookmakers never know how to figure the odds.

And I'm sick of the Colosseum as well. Hermes, my favourite gladiator, left hospital too soon and got chopped in his first show. Talk of the Good Life! If things don't improve soon, and if I get any balder from worry, I'm half inclined to sail for Myconos myself and open a quiet little cockpit there.

Christmas Truce

YOUNG STAN COMES around yesterday about tea-time – you know my grandson Stan? He's a Polytechnic student, just turned twenty, as smart as his dad was at the same age. Stan's all out to be a commercial artist and do them big coloured posters for the hoardings. Doesn't answer to 'Stan', though – says it's 'common'; says he's either 'Stanley' or he's nothing.

Stan's got a bagful of big, noble ideas; all schemed out carefully, with what he calls 'captions' attached.

Well, I can't say nothing against big, noble ideas. I was a red-hot Labour-man myself for a time, forty years ago now, when the Kayser's war ended and the war-profiteers began treading us ex-heroes into the mud. But that's all over long ago – in fact, Labour's got a damn sight too respectable for my taste! Worse than Tories, most of their leaders is now – especially them that used to be the loudest in rendering 'We'll Keep the Red Flag Flying Still'. They're all Churchwardens now, or country gents, if they're not in the House of Lords.

Anyhow, yesterday Stan came around, about a big Ban-the-Bomb march all the way across England to Trafalgar Square. And couldn't I persuade a few of my old comrades to form a special squad with a banner marked 'First World War Veterans Protest Against the Bomb'? He wanted us to head the parade, ribbons, crutches, wheel-chairs and all.

I put my foot down pretty hard. 'No, Mr Stanley,' I said politely, 'I regret as I can't accept your kind invitation.'

'But why?' says he. 'You don't want another war, Grandfather, do you? You don't want mankind to be annihilated? This time it won't be just a few unlucky chaps killed, like Uncle Arthur in the First War, and Dad in the Second... It will be all mankind.'

'Listen, young 'un,' I said. 'I don't trust nobody who talks about mankind – not parsons, not politicians, nor anyone else. There ain't no such thing as "mankind", not practically speaking there ain't.'

'Practically speaking, Grandfather,' says young Stan, 'there *is*. Mankind means all the different nations lumped together – us, the Russians, the Americans, the Germans, the French, and all the rest of them. If the bomb goes off, everyone's finished.'

'It's not going off,' I says.

'But it's gone off twice already – at Hiroshima and Nagasaki,' he argues, 'so why not again? The damage will be definitely final when it *does* go off.'

I wouldn't let Stan have the last word. 'In the crazy, old-fashioned war in which I lost my foot,' I said, a bit sternly, 'the Fritzes used poison gas. They thought it would help 'em to break through at Wipers. But somehow the line held, and soon our factories were churning out the same stinking stuff for us to use on them. All right, and now what about Hitler's war?'

'What about it?' Stan asks.

'Well,' I says, 'everyone in England was issued an expensive mask in a smart-looking case against poison-gas bombs dropped from the air – me, your Dad, your Ma, and yourself as a tiny tot. But how many poison-gas bombs were dropped on London, or on Berlin? Not a damned one! Both sides were scared stiff. Poison-gas had got too deadly. No mask in the market could keep the new sorts out. So there's not going to be no atom bombs dropped neither, I tell you, Stanley my lad; not this side of the Hereafter! Everyone's scared stiff again.'

'Then why do both sides manufacture quantities of atom bombs and pile them up?' he asks.

'Search me,' I said, 'unless it's a clever way of keeping up full employment by making believe there's a war on. What with bombs and fall-out shelters, and radar equipment, and unsinkable aircraft-carriers, and satellites, and shooting rockets at the moon, and keeping up big armies – takes two thousand quid nowadays to maintain a soldier in the field, I read the other day – what with all that play-acting, there's full employment assured for everyone, and businessmen are rubbing their hands.'

'Your argument has a bad flaw, Grandfather. The Russians don't need to worry about full employment.'

'No,' said I, 'perhaps they don't. But their politicians and commissars have to keep up the notion of a wicked Capitalist plot to wipe out the poor workers. And they have to show that they're well ahead in the Arms Race. · Forget it, lad, forget it! Mankind, which is a term used by maiden ladies and bun-punchers, ain't going to be annihilated by no atom bomb.'

Stan changed his tactics. 'Nevertheless, Grandfather,' he says, 'we British want to show the Russians that we're not engaged in any such Capitalist plot. All men are brothers, and I for one have nothing against my opposite number in Moscow, Ivan Whoever-he-may-be... This protest march is the only logical way I can show him my dislike of organized propaganda.'

'But Ivan Orfalitch ain't here to watch you march; nor the Russian telly ain't going to show him no picture of it. If Ivan thinks you're a bleeding Capitalist, then he'll go on thinking you're a bleeding Capitalist; and he

won't be so far out, neither, in my opinion. No, Stan, you can't fight organized propaganda with amachoor propaganda.'

'Oh, can it, Grandfather!' says Stan. 'You're a professional pessimist.
And *you* didn't hate the Germans even when you were fighting them – in
spite of the newspapers. What about that Christmas Truce?'

Well, I'd mentioned it to him one day, I own; but it seems he'd drawn
the wrong conclusions and didn't want to be put straight. However, I'm a
lucky bloke – always being saved by what other blokes call 'coincidences',
but which I don't; because they always happen when I need 'em most. In
the trenches we used to call that 'being in God's pocket'. So, of course, we
hear a knock at the door and a shout, and in steps my old mucking-in
chum Dodger Green, formerly 301691, Pte. Edward Green of the 1st
Batt., North Wessex Regiment – come to town by bus for a Saturday night
booze with me, every bit of twenty miles.

'You're here in the exact nick, Dodger,' says I, 'as once before.' He'd
nappooed a Fritz officer one day when I was lying with one foot missing
outside Delville Wood, and the Fritz was kindly putting us wounded out
of our misery with an automatic pistol.

'What's new, Fiddler?' he asks.

'Tell this lad about the *two* Christmas truces,' I said. 'He's trying to
enlist us for a march to Moscow, or somewhere.'

'Well,' says Dodger, 'I don't see no connection, not yet. And marching
to Moscow ain't no worse nor marching to Berlin, same as you and me did
– and never got more nor a few hundred yards forward in the three years
we were at it. But, all right, I'll give him the facts, since you particularly
ask me.'

Stan listened quietly while Dodger told his tale. I'd heard it often
enough before, but Dodger's yarns improve with the telling. You see, I
missed most of that first Christmas Truce, as I'll explain later. But I came
in for the second; and saw a part of it what Dodger didn't. And the moral
I wanted to impress on young Stan depended on there being *two* truces,
not one: them two were a lot different from one another.

I brings a quart bottle of wallop from the kitchen, along with a couple
of glasses – not three, because young Stan don't drink anything so
'common' as beer – and Dodger held forth. Got a golden tongue, has
Dodger – I've seen him hold an audience spellbound at 'The Three
Feathers' from opening-time to stop-tap, and his glass filled every ten
minutes, free.

'Well,' he says, 'the first truce was in 1914, about four months after the
Kayser's war began. They say that the old Pope suggested it, and that the
Kayser agreed, but that Joffre, the French C.-in-C. wouldn't allow it.
However, the Bavarians were sweating on a short spell of peace and good
will, being Catholics, and sent word around that the Pope was going to get
his way. Consequently, though we didn't have the Bavarians in front of

us, there at Boy Greneer, not a shot was fired on our sector all Christmas Eve. In those days we hadn't been issued with Mills bombs, or trench-mortars, or Verey pistols, or steel helmets, or sand bags, or any of them later luxuries; and only two machine-guns to a battalion. The trenches were shallow and knee-deep in water, so that most of the time we had to crouch on the fire-step. God knows how we kept alive and smiling... It wasn't no picnic, was it, Fiddler? – and the ground half-frozen, too!

'Christmas Eve, at 7.30 p.m., the enemy trenches suddenly lit up with a row of coloured Chinese lanterns, and a bonfire started in the village behind. We stood to arms, prepared for whatever happened. Ten minutes later the Fritzes began singing a Christmas carol called "Stilly Nucked". Our boys answered with "Good King Wencelas", which they'd learned the first verse of as Waits, collecting coppers from door to door. Unfortunately no one knew more than two verses, because Waits always either get a curse or a copper before they reach the third verse.

'Then a Fritz with a megaphone shouts "Merry Christmas, Wessex!"

'Captain Pomeroy was commanding us. Colonel Baggie had gone sick, second-in-command still on leave, and most of the other officers were young second-lieutenants straight from Sandhurst – we'd taken such a knock, end of October. The Captain was a real gentleman: father, grand-father, and great-grandfather all served in the Wessex. He shouts back: "Who are you?" And they say that they're Saxons, same as us, from a town called Hully in West Saxony.

'"Will your commanding officer meet me in No-man's land to arrange a Christmas truce?" the Captain shouts again. "We'll respect a white flag," he says.

'That was arranged, so Captain Pomeroy and the Fritz officer, whose name was Lieutenant Coburg, climbed out from their trenches and met half-way. They didn't shake hands, but they saluted, and each gave the other word of honour that his troops wouldn't fire a shot for another twenty-four hours. Lieutenant Coburg explained that his Colonel and all the senior officers were back taking it easy at Regimental H.Q. It seems they liked to keep their boots clean, and their hands warm: not like our officers.

'Captain Pomeroy came back pleased as Punch, and said: "The truce starts at dawn, Wessex; but meanwhile we stay in trenches. And if any man of you dares break the truce tomorrow," he says, "I'll shoot him myself, because I've given that German officer my word. All the same, watch out, and don't let go of your bundooks."

'That suited us; we'd be glad to get up from them damned fire-steps and stretch our legs. So that night we serenaded the Fritzes with all manner of songs, such as "I want to go Home!" and "The Top of the Dixie Lid", and the one about "Old Von Kluck, He Had a Lot of Men"; and they serenaded us with *Deutschland Uber Alles,* and songs to the concertina.

'We scraped the mud off our puttees and shined our brasses, to look a bit more regimental next morning. Captain Pomeroy, meanwhile, goes out again with a flashlight and arranges a Christmas football match – kick-off at 10.30 – to be followed at two o'clock by a burial service for all the corpses what hadn't been taken in because of lying too close to the other side's trenches.

'"Over the top with the best of luck!" shouts the Captain at 8 a.m., the same as if he was leading an attack. And over we went, a bit shy of course, and stood there waiting for the Fritzes. They advanced to meet us, shouting, and five minutes later, there we were...

'Christmas was a peculiar sort of day, if ever I spent one. Hobnobbing with the Hun, so to speak: swapping fags and rum and buttons and badges for brandy, cigars and souvenirs. Lieutenant Coburg and several of the Fritzes talked English, but none of our blokes could sling a word of their bat.

'No-man's land had seemed ten miles across when we were crawling out on a night patrol; but now we found it no wider than the width of two football pitches. We provided the football, and set up stretchers as goal posts; and the Rev. Jolly, our Padre, acted as ref. They beat us 3-2, but the Padre had showed a bit too much Christian charity – their outside-left shot the deciding goal, but he was miles offside and admitted it soon as the whistle went. And we spectators were spread nearly two deep along the touch-lines with loaded rifles slung on our shoulders.

'We had Christmas dinner in our own trenches, and a German bugler obliged with the mess call – same tune as ours. Captain Pomeroy was invited across, but didn't think it proper to accept. Then one of our sentries, a farmer's son, sees a hare loping down the line between us. He gives a view halloo, and everyone rushes to the parapet and clambers out and runs forward to cut it off. So do the Fritzes. There ain't no such thing as harriers in Germany; they always use shot-guns on hares. But they weren't allowed to shoot this one, not with the truce; so they turned harriers same as us.

'Young Totty Fahy and a Saxon corporal both made a grab for the hare as it doubled back in their direction. Totty catches it by the forelegs and the Corporal catches it by the hindlegs, and they fall on top of it simultaneous.

'Captain Pomeroy looked a bit worried for fear of a shindy about who caught that hare; but you'd have laughed your head off to see young Totty and the Fritz both politely trying to force the carcase on each other! So the Lieutenant and the Captain gets together, and the Captain says: "Let them toss a coin for it." But the Lieutenant says: "I regret that our men will not perhaps understand. With us, we draw straws." So they picked some withered stems of grass, and Totty drew the long one. He was in our section, and we cooked the hare with spuds that night in a big iron pot borrowed from Duck Farm; but Totty gave the Fritz a couple of bully beef tins, and the skin. Best stoo I ever ate!

'We called 'em "Fritzes" at that time. Afterwards they were "Jerries", on account of their tin hats. Them helmets with spikes called *Pickelhaubes* was still the issue in 1914, but only for parade use. In the trenches caps were worn; like ours, but grey, and no stiffening in the top. Our blokes wanted pickelhaubes badly to take their fiancées when they went home on leave; but Lieutenant Coburg says, sorry, all pickelhaubes was in store behind the lines. They had to be content with belt-buckles.

'General French commanded the B.E.F at the time – decent old stick. Said afterwards that if he'd been consulted about the truce, he'd have agreed for chivalrous reasons. He must have reckoned that whichever side beat, us or the Germans, a Christmas truce would help considerably in signing a decent peace at the finish. But the Kayser's High Command were mostly Prussians, and Lieutenant Coburg told us that the Prussians were against the Truce, which didn't agree with their "frightfulness" notions; and though other battalions were fraternizing with the Fritzes up and down the line that day – but we didn't know it – the Prussians weren't having any. Nor were some English regiments: such as the East Lancs on our right flank and the Sherwood Foresters on the left – when the Fritzes came out with white flags, they fired over their heads and waved 'em back. But they didn't interfere with our party. It was worse in the French line: them Frogs machine-gunned all the "Merry Christmas" parties... Of course, the French go in for New Year celebrations more than Christmas.

'One surprise was the two barrels of beer that the Fritzes rolled over to us from the brewery just behind their lines. I don't fancy French beer; but at least this wasn't watered like what they sold us English troops in the estaminets. We broached them out in the open, and the Fritzes broached another two of their own.

'When it came to the toasts, the Captain said he wanted to keep politics out of it. So he offered them "Wives and Sweethearts!" which the Lieutenant accepted. Then the Lieutenant proposed "The King!" which the Captain accepted. There was a King of Saxony too, you see, in them days, besides a King of England; and no names were mentioned. The third toast was "A Speedy Peace!" and each side could take it to mean victory for themselves.

'After dinner came the burial service – the Fritzes buried their corpses on their side of the line; we buried ours on ours. But we dug the pits so close together that one service did for both. The Saxons had no Padre with them; but they were Protestants, so the Rev. Jolly read the Service, and a German Divinity Student translated for them. Captain Pomeroy sent for the Drummers and put us through that parade in proper regimental fashion: slow march, arms reversed, muffled drums, a union jack and all.

'An hour before dark, a funny-faced Fritz called Putzi came up with a trestle table. He talked English like a Yank. Said he'd been in Ringling's Circus over in the United States. Called us "youse guys", and put on a hell of a good gaff with conjuring tricks and juggling – had his face made up like a proper clown. Never heard such applause as we gave Herr Putzi!

'Then, of course, our bastard of a Brigadier, full of turkey and plum pudding and mince pies, decides to come and visit the trenches to wish us Merry Christmas! Captain Pomeroy got the warning from Fiddler here, who was away down on light duty at Battalion H.Q. Fiddler arrived in the nick, running split-arse across the open, and gasping out: "Captain, Sir, the Brigadier's here; but none of us hasn't let on about the Truce."

'Captain Pomeroy recalled us at once. "Imshi, Wessex!" he shouted. Five minutes later the Brigadier came sloshing up the communication trench, keeping his head well down. The Captain tried to let Lieutenant Coburg know what was happening; but the Lieutenant had gone back to fetch him some warm gloves as a souvenir. The Captain couldn't speak German; what's more, the Fritzes were so busy watching Putzi that they wouldn't listen. So Captain Pomeroy shouts to me: "Private Green, run along the line and order the platoon commanders from me to fire three rounds rapid over the enemies' heads." Which I did; and by the time the Brigadier turns up, there wasn't a Fritz in sight.

'The Brigadier, whom we called "Old Horseflesh", shows a lot of Christmas jollity. "I was very glad," he says, "to hear that Wessex fusillade, Pomeroy. Rumours have come in of fraternization elsewhere along the line. Bad show! Disgraceful! Can't interrupt the war for freedom just because of Christmas! Have you anything to report?"

'Captain Pomeroy kept a straight face. He says: "Our sentries report that the enemy have put up a trestle table in No-man's land, Sir. A bit of a puzzle, Sir. Seems to have a bowl of goldfish on it." He kicked the Padre, and the Padre kept his mouth shut.

'Old Horseflesh removes his brass hat, takes his binoculars, and cautiously peeps over the parapet. "They *are* goldfish, by Gad!" he shouts. "I wonder what new devilish trick the Hun will invent next. Send out a patrol tonight to investigate." "Very good, Sir," says the Captain.

'Then Old Horseflesh spots something else: it's Lieutenant Coburg strolling across the open between his reserve and front lines; and he's carrying the warm gloves. "What impudence! Look at that swaggering German officer! Quick, here's your rifle, my lad! Shoot him down point-blank!" It seems Lieutenant Coburg must have thought that the fusillade came from the Foresters on our flank; but now he suddenly stopped short and looked at No-man's land, and wondered where everyone was gone.

'Old Horseflesh shoves the rifle into my hand. "Take a steady aim," he says. "Squeeze the trigger, don't pull!" I aimed well above the Lieutenant's head and fired three rounds rapid. He staggered and dived head-first into a handy shell-hole.

'"Congratulations," said Old Horseflesh, belching brandy in my face. "You can cut another notch in your rifle butt. But what effrontery! Thought himself safe on Christmas Day, I suppose! Ha, ha!" He hadn't brought Captain Pomeroy no gift of whisky or cigars, nor nothing else; stingy bastard, he was. At any rate, the Fritzes caught on, and their machine-guns began traversing tock–tock–tock, about three feet above our trenches. That sent the Brigadier hurrying home in such a hurry that he caught his foot in a loop of telephone wire and went face forward into the mud. It was his first and last visit to the front line.

'Half an hour later we put up an ALL CLEAR board. This time us and the Fritzes became a good deal chummier than before. But Lieutenant Coburg suggests it would be wise to keep quiet about the lark. The General Staff might get wind of it and kick up a row, he says. Captain Pomeroy agrees. Then the Lieutenant warns us that the Prussian Guards are due to relieve his Saxons the day after Boxing Day. "I suggest that we continue the Truce until then, but with no more fraternization," he says. Captain Pomeroy agrees again. He accepts the warm gloves and in return gives the Lieutenant a Shetland wool scarf. Then he asks whether, as a great favour, the Wessex might be permitted to capture the bowl of gold-fish, for the Brigadier's sake. Herr Putzi wasn't too pleased, but Captain Pomeroy paid him for it with a gold sovereign and Putzi says: "Please, for Chrissake, don't forget to change their water!"

'God knows what the Intelligence made of them goldfish when they were sent back to Corps H.Q., which was a French luxury *shadow*... I expect someone decided the goldfish have some sort of use in trenches, like the canaries we take down the coal pits.

'Then Captain Pomeroy says to the Lieutenant: "From what I can see, Coburg, there'll be a stalemate on this front for a year or more. You can't crack our line, even with massed machine-guns; and we can't crack yours. Mark my words: our Wessex and your West Saxons will still be rotting here next Christmas – what's left of them."

'The Lieutenant didn't agree, but he didn't argue. He answered: "In that case, Pomeroy, I hope we both survive to meet again on that festive occasion; and that our troops show the same gentlemanly spirit as today."

'"I'll be very glad to do so," says the Captain, "if I'm not scuppered meanwhile." They shook hands on that, and the truce continued all Boxing Day. But nobody went out into No-man's land, except at night to strengthen the wire where it had got trampled by the festivities. And of course we couldn't prevent our gunners from shooting; and neither could the Saxons prevent theirs. When the Prussian Guards moved in, the war started again; fifty casualties we had in three days, including young Totty who lost an arm.

'In the meantime a funny thing had happened: the sparrows got wind of the truce and came flying into our trenches for biscuit crumbs. I counted more than fifty in a flock on Boxing Day.

'The only people who objected strongly to the truce, apart from the Brigadier and a few more like him, was the French girls. Wouldn't have nothing more to do with us for a time when we got back to billets. Said we were *no bon* and *boko camarade* with the *Allemans.*'

Stan had been listening to this tale with eyes like stars. 'Exactly,' he said. 'There wasn't any feeling of hate between the individuals composing the opposite armies. The hate was all whipped up by the newspapers. Last year, you remember, I attended the Nürnberg Youth Rally. Two other fellows whose fathers had been killed in the last war, like mine, shared the same tent with four German war-orphans. They weren't at all bad fellows.'

'Well, lad,' I said, taking up the yarn where Dodger left off, 'I didn't see much of that first Christmas Truce owing to a spent bullet what went into my shoulder and lodged under the skin: the Medico cut it out and kept me off duty until the wound healed. I couldn't wear a pack for a month, so, as Dodger told you, I got Light Duty down at Battalion H.Q., and missed the fun. But the second Christmas Truce, now that was another matter. By then I was Platoon Sergeant to about twenty men signed on for the Duration of the War – some of them good, some of 'em His Majesty's bad bargains.

'We'd learned a lot about trench life that year; such as how to drain trenches and build dug-outs. We had barbed wire entanglements in front of us, five yards thick, and periscopes, and listening-posts out at sap-heads; also trench-mortars and rifle-grenades, and bombs, and steel-plates with loop-holes for sniping through.

'Now I'll tell you what happened, and Dodger here will tell you the same. Battalion orders went round to company H.Q. every night in trenches, and the C.O. was now Lieut.-Colonel Pomeroy – D.S.O. with bar. He'd won brevet rank for the job he did rallying the battalion when the big German mine blew C-company to bits and the Fritzes followed up with bombs and bayonets. However, when he sent round Orders two days before Christmas 1915, Colonel Pomeroy (accidentally on purpose) didn't tell the Adjutant to include the "Official Warning to All Troops" from General Sir Douglas Haig. Haig was our new Commander-in-Chief. You hear about him on Poppy Day – the poppies he sowed himself, most of 'em! He'd used his influence with King George, to get General French booted out and himself shoved into the job. His "Warning" was to the effect that any man attempting to fraternize with His Majesty's enemies on the poor excuse of Christmas would be court-martialled and shot. But Colonel Pomeroy never broke his word, not even if he swung for it; and here he was alongside the La Bassée Canal, and opposite us were none other than the same West Saxons from Hully!

'The Colonel knew who they were because we'd coshed and caught a prisoner in a patrol scrap two nights before, and after the Medico plastered his head, the bloke was brought to Battalion H.Q. under escort (which was me and another man). The Colonel questioned him through an interpreter about the geography of the German trenches: where they kept that damned minny-werfer, how and when the ration parties came up, and so on. But this Fritz wouldn't give away a thing; said he'd lost his memory when he'd got coshed. So at last the Colonel remarked in English: "Very well, that's all. By the way, is Lieutenant Coburg still alive?"

'"Oh, yeah," says the Fritz, surprised into talking English. "He's back again after a coupla wounds. He's a Major now, commanding our outfit."

'Then a sudden thought struck him. "For Chrissake," he says, "ain't you the Wessex officer who played Santa Claus last year and fixed that truce?"

'"I am," says the Colonel, "and you're Putzi Cohen the Conjurer, from whom I once bought a bowl of goldfish! It's a small war!"

'That's why, you see, the Colonel hadn't issued Haig's warning. About eighty or so of us old hands were still left, mostly snobs, bobbajers, drummers, transport men, or wounded blokes rejoined. The news went the rounds, and they all rushed Putzi and shook his hand and asked couldn't he put on another conjuring gaff for them? He says: "Ask Colonel Santa Claus! He's still feeding my goldfish."

'I was Putzi's escort, before I happened to have coshed him and brought him in; but I never recognized him without his grease paint – not until he started talking his funny Yank English.

'The Colonel sends for Putzi again, and says: "I don't think you're quite well enough to travel. I'm keeping you here as a hospital case until after Christmas."

'Putzi lived like a prize pig the next two days, and put on a show every evening – card tricks mostly, because he hadn't his accessories. Then came Christmas Eve, and a sergeant of the Holy Boys who lay on our right flank again, remarked to me it was a pity that "Stern-Endeavour" Haig had washed out our Christmas fun. "First I've heard about," says I, "and what's more, chum, I don't want to hear about it, see? Not officially, I don't."

'I'd hardly shut my mouth before them Saxons put out Chinese lanterns again and started singing "Stilly Nucked". They hadn't fired a shot, neither, all day.

'Soon word comes down the trench: "Colonel's orders: no firing as from now, without officer's permission."

'After stand-to next morning, soon as it was light, Colonel Pomeroy he climbed out of the trench with a white handkerchief in his hand, picked his way through our wire entanglements and stopped half-way across No-

man's land. "Merry Christmas, Saxons!" he shouted. But Major Coburg
had already advanced towards him. They saluted each other and shook
hands. The cheers that went up! "Keep in your trenches, Wessex!" the
Colonel shouted over his shoulder. And the Major gave the same orders to
his lot.

'After jabbering a bit they agreed that any bloke who'd attended the
1914 party would be allowed out of trenches, but not the rest – they could
trust only us regular soldiers. Regulars, you see, know the rules of war and
don't worry their heads about politics nor propaganda; them Duration
blokes sickened us sometimes with their patriotism and their lofty skiting,
and their hatred of "the Teuton foe" as one of 'em called the Fritzes.

'Twice more Saxons than Wessex came trooping out. We'd strict
orders to discuss no military matters – not that any of our blokes had been
studying German since the last party. Football was off, because of the
overlapping shell holes and the barbed wire, but we got along again with
signs and a bit of café French, and swapped fags and booze and buttons.
But the Colonel wouldn't have us give away no badges. Can't say we were
so chummy as before. Too many of ours and theirs had gone west that
year and, besides, the trenches weren't flooded like the first time.

'We put on three boxing bouts: middle, welter and light; won the
welter and light with k.o.'s, lost the middle on points. Colonel Pomeroy
took Putzi up on parole, and Putzi gave an even prettier show than before,
because Major Coburg had sent back for his grease paints and accessories.
He used a parrokeet this time instead of goldfish.

'After dinner we found we hadn't much more to tell the Fritzes or swap
with them, and the officers decided to pack up before we all got into
trouble. The Holy Boys had promised not to shoot, and the left flank was
screened by the Canal bank. As them two was busy discussing how long
the no-shooting truce should last, all of a sudden the Christmas spirit
flared up again. We and the Fritzes found ourselves grabbing hands and
forming a ring around the pair of them – Wessex and West Saxons all
mixed anyhow and dancing from right to left to the tune of "Here We Go
Round the Mulberry Bush", in and out of shell holes. Then our R.S.M.
pointed to Major Coburg, and some of our blokes hoisted him on their
shoulders and we all sang "For He's a Jolly Good Fellow". And the
Fritzes hoisted our Colonel up on their shoulders too, and sang *Hock Solla
Leeben*, or something… Our Provost-sergeant took a photo of that; pity he
got his before it was developed.

'Now here's something I heard from Lightning Collins, an old soldier
in my platoon. He'd come close enough to overhear the Colonel and the
Major's conversation during the middle-weight fight when they thought
nobody was listening. The Colonel says: "I prophesied last year, Major,
that we'd still be here this Christmas, what was left of us. And now I tell
you again that we'll still be here *next* Christmas, *and* the Christmas after.

If we're not scuppered; and that's a ten to one chance. What's more, next Christmas there won't be any more fun and games and fraternization. I'm doubtful whether I'll get away with this present act of insubordination; but I'm a man of my word, as you are, and we've both kept our engagement."

"'Oh, yes, Colonel," says the Major. "I too will be lucky if I am not court-martialled. Our orders were as severe as yours." So they laughed like crows together.

'Putzi was the most envied man in France that day: going back under safe escort to a prison camp in Blighty. And the Colonel told the Major: "I congratulate you on that soldier. He wouldn't give away a thing!"

'At four o'clock sharp we broke it off; but the two officers waited a bit longer to see that everyone got back. But no, young Stan, that's not the end of the story! I had a bloke in my platoon called Gipsy Smith, a dark-faced, dirty soldier, and a killer. He'd been watching the fun from the nearest sap-head, and no sooner had the Major turned his back than Gipsy aimed at his head and tumbled him over.

'The first I knew of it was a yell of rage from everyone all round me. I see Colonel Pomeroy run up to the Major, shouting for stretcher-bearers. Them Fritzes must have thought the job was premeditated, because when our stretcher-bearers popped out of the trench, they let 'em have it and hit one bloke in the leg. His pal popped back again.

'That left the Colonel alone in No-man's land. He strolled calmly towards the German trenches, his hands in his pockets – being too proud to raise them over his head. A couple of Fritzes fired at him, but both missed. He stopped at their wire and shouted: "West Saxons, my men had strict orders not to fire. Some coward has disobeyed. Please help me carry the Major's body back to your trenches! Then you can shoot me, if you like; because I pledged my word that there'd be no fighting."

'The Fritzes understood, and sent stretcher-bearers out. They took the Major's body back through a crooked lane in their wire, and Colonel Pomeroy followed them. A German officer bandaged the Colonel's eyes as soon as he got into the trench, and we waited without firing a shot to see what would happen next. That was about four o'clock, and nothing did happen until second watch. Then we see a flashlight signalling, and presently the Colonel comes back, quite his usual self.

'He tells us that, much to his relief, Gipsy's shot hadn't killed the Major but only furrowed his scalp and knocked him senseless. He'd come to after six hours, and when he saw the Colonel waiting there, he'd ordered his immediate release. They'd shaken hands again, and said: "Until after the war!", and the Major gives the Colonel his flashlight.

'Now the yarn's nearly over, Stan, but not quite. News of the truce got round, and General Haig ordered first an Inquiry and then a Court Martial on Colonel Pomeroy. He wasn't shot, of course; but he got a severe reprimand and lost five years' seniority. Not that it mattered, because he got shot between the eyes in the 1916 Delville Wood show where I lost my foot.

'As for Gipsy Smith, he said he'd been obeying Haig's strict orders not to fraternize, and also he'd felt bound to avenge a brother killed at Loos. "Blood for blood," he said, "is our gipsy motto." So we couldn't do nothing but show what we thought by treating him like the dirt he was. And he didn't last long. I sent Gipsy back with the ration party on Boxing Night. We were still keeping up our armed truce with the Saxons, but again their gunners weren't a party to it, and outside the Quartermaster's hut Gipsy got his backside removed by a piece of howitzer shell. Died on the hospital train, he did.

'Oh, I was forgetting to tell you that no sparrows came for biscuit crumbs that Christmas. The birds had all cleared off months before.

'Every year that war got worse and worse. Before it ended, nearly three years later, we'd have ten thousand officers and men pass through that one battalion, which was never at more than the strength of five hundred rifles. I'd had three wounds by 1916; some fellows got up to six before it finished. Only Dodger here came through without a scratch. That's how he got his name, dodging the bullet that had his name and number on it. The Armistice found us at Mons, where we started. There was talk of "Hanging the Kayser"; but they left him to chop wood in Holland instead. The rest of the Fritzes had their noses properly rubbed in the dirt by the Peace Treaty. But we let them re-arm in time for a second war, Hitler's war, which is how your Dad got killed. And after Hitler's war there'd have been a third war, just about now, which would have caught you, Stanley my lad, if it weren't for that blessed bomb you're asking me to march against.

'Now, listen, lad: if two real old fashioned gentlemen like Colonel Pomeroy and Major Coburg – never heard of him again, but I doubt if he survived, having the guts he had – if two real men like them two couldn't hope for a third Christmas Truce in the days when "mankind", as you call 'em was still a little bit civilized, tell me, what can you hope for now?'

'Only fear can keep the peace,' I said. 'The United nations are a laugh, and you know it. So thank your lucky stars that the Russians have H-bombs and that the Yanks have H-bombs, stacks of 'em, enough to blow your "mankind" up a thousand times over; and that everyone's equally respectful of everyone else, though not on regular visiting terms.'

I stopped, out of breath, and Dodger takes Stan by the hand. 'You know what's right for *you*, lad?' he says. 'So don't listen to your Grand-dad. Don't be talked out of your beliefs! He's one of the Old and Bold, but maybe he's no wiser nor you and I.'

My Best Christmas

'QUEEN VICTORIA WAS still alive that Christmas, and I was four and a half years old.'

'Who was she exactly? Queen Elizabeth's grandmother?'

'No: great-great-grandmother.'

'Wow! Do you remember her?'

'Yes: a fat little lady in black riding through the Park with an escort of Lifeguardsmen – her open barouche drawn by two splendid high-stepping grey horses, and the band playing: "Make way, make way, for the rowdy-dowdy boys".'

'Barouche?'

'Yes: no cars in those days. The streets cobbled, and so filthy with horse-droppings and mud that everyone wore boots. Ragged boys with dirty faces used to sweep the crossings with brooms, and beg for halfpennies. Sometimes they turned cartwheels to attract attention.'

'Wow! How ancient you are! Where did you spend that Christmas?'

'At home, near Wimbledon Common. A big house with twenty-five rooms and a coal cellar. But no electric light or lift, or vacuum cleaner, or refrigerator, or radio, or telly. Only rather dim gas-lamps, and coal fires, and a grand piano.'

'Were Christmas trees invented then?'

'Yes, Queen Victoria's husband, Prince Albert the Good, brought them in from Germany... We always had a big one in the drawing room. The same coloured glass decorations lasted year after year – never got broken. Things were made to last in those days and people treated them more carefully... We children always waited outside in the dark, cold hall for an hour or so, telling ghost stories, while Mother and Father dressed the tree and sorted out the presents.'

'Were they hung on the tree?'

'No: each of us had a chair or a sofa or small table, covered with a white linen cloth, and the presents laid out on it. But when at last the door opened and we rushed in and the tree blazed out at us like the Jewelled Garden of Paradise, we had to join hands first and sing: "O Come All Ye Faithful". Mother accompanied us on the piano with the loud pedal pressed hard down. At the foot of the tree was a Crypt – with St Joseph and the Virgin and the Christ Child and the ox and ass, and the Three Wise Men. Then Father Christmas knocked at the french window leading to the garden, and came in. He waved his hand at us and told us his reindeer were stabled at the "Swan" just across the road and wished us a happy Christmas. He complained of the cold so much that my father poured him a glass of cherry brandy. He drank it noisily and went out again into the thick fog, shouting: "See you again next century!" That's how I can fix the date: 1899!'

'Tell me about your presents.'

'I got a musical box that played "Home Sweet Home", and two boxes of soldiers – the Royal Fusiliers and the Egyptian Camel Corps – and a toy helmet and a toy drum, and a prayer-book in red morocco leather, and a painting book, and a clockwork horse.'

'You're making it up, aren't you?'

'No; I remember the list because soon afterwards I was taken away to a scarlet-fever hospital and my mother had most of my toys burned. The doctor said they were infectious for the baby. But my favourite sister hid the helmet and drum in the tool shed, and used to play with them sadly when her nurse wasn't about.'

'Did you believe in Father Christmas?'

'Yes, until the Mix-up Christmas (I'll tell you about that later), although he wore the same boots as Uncle Charles. But he hadn't such importance in those days as the advertisements have built up now. Christmas wasn't just fun and games. It was *Jesus's Birthday*, on which we gave one another birthday presents – a day of thanking God and being especially kind to everyone. We emptied out our money-boxes for the presents. I remember we always used to give the cook and the parlour-maid scented soap, at 2d. a cake... We got a penny a week in those days, and occasional tips from uncles and aunts.'

'A penny a *week*; sounds sort of stingy... Did you hang up your stockings?'

'We did, and anyone who had been naughty that winter got coal instead of almonds, raisins, apples, tangerines, a negro-teeth puzzle, and white sugar mice with pink eyes and string tails.'

'Wow! Did you often get coal?'

'Never. I was always as good as Prince Albert.'

'Ha, ha! What happened on Christmas Day?'

'We dressed up and went to church, which was decorated with chrysanthemums and holly. But the vicar wouldn't allow mistletoe; he said it was frivolous. Then back to Christmas dinner. The whole family was there: five boys (counting the baby), four girls, and Uncle Charles who couldn't spend Christmas at home because Aunt Alice had left him. Yes, turkey, plum-pudding and mince pies *had* been invented. In fact our cook had once been cook to General Gordon and used a plum-pudding recipe in his own hand-writing.'

'Who was General Gordon?'

'The Dervishes killed him at Khartoum. I once showed you the scene at Madame Tussaud's.'

'Did you? I don't remember. Go on with the story.'

'Then we pulled crackers, and put on coloured caps and asked one another riddles...'

'Such as?'

'Such as: "Why did Kruger wear thick boots?"'

'Who was Kruger?'

'President of the South African Republic. The Boer War had been on for two years that Christmas and every streetboy was whistling the song:

> Good bye, Dolly, I must leave you
> Though it breaks my heart to go –
> Something tells me I am needed,
> At the Front to fight the foe.

But nobody got called up; and it wasn't much of a war. Life went on as usual. Bombs and tanks and planes hadn't been invented yet.'

'But why *did* Kruger wear thick boots?'

'To keep De Wet off defeat.'

'I don't dig you.'

'De Wet was one of Kruger's generals.'

'Anyhow, what did you do that evening?'

'We went to a special children's service at the Parish Church: cinemas hadn't been invented, you see.'

'Then why was it your *best* Christmas?'

'Because it was the reallest.'

'Oh!... What's happened to the Wimbledon house?'

'Sold and cut up into six flats... I suppose six small families live in them now, and on Christmas Eve there'll be six tiny Christmas trees lighted – probably the artificial wire- and grocer's-grass sort that fold up, with a little string of coloured electric light bulbs tied on... And a couple of elderly baby-sitters will be drinking sherry there and listening to the carol-singers on TV, while the young folk go off somewhere to dance.'

'Well, I daresay that's a bit more fun than singing hymns to a grand piano and asking riddles. By the way: if I'm still on your Santa list what I *want* is a really good set of bongo-drums... Oh, and you had something to say about a Mix-up?'

'Yes, two years later – when Uncle Charles came in by one door and said he was Father Christmas, and Uncle Bob came in by the other, just after Uncle Charles had gone, and said he was Santa Claus.'

'Wow!'

No, Mac, It Just Wouldn't Work

A WILD CHARACTER, obviously high and wearing a Mexican hat, though he wasn't Mexican but, in fact, Boston Irish (which can be just as wild), edged up to me at the Green Hornet the other night and said abruptly:

'Speaking out, I mean, Professor... it's quite simple really... millions of poor devils starving in India and Africa and China and such places. Millions of them! Grant me that for the sake of the argument.'

'Granted, Mex. What's your problem?'

'And all the thousands of gangsters and delinquents and violent no-gooders in our big cities, grant me them?'

'Granted, Mex, for the sake of your argument. Go ahead!'

'And hundreds of Federal ships tied up empty in the Hudson, waiting for God only knows what. Grant me –'

'I'm a stranger here,' I said cautiously. 'English. But you may be right. There's always marginal tonnage lying around the ports, except in war-time. When freight rates rise, it can amount to a lot.'

'And all the farm surplus that we either hoard or destroy because nobody here can eat it all, and because the poor starving devils abroad can't pay for it! And all the criminal waste here in New York and the other big cities – enough to feed and clothe millions!'

'I've read of that, Mex. Speak on!'

'And all those philanthropic Christian and Jewish do-gooders and Peace Corps characters who want to prevent crime, starvation, idleness – the lot?'

'I seem to have met most of them,' I agreed.

The barman said: 'All granted, mac, but what the hell? All this doesn't hurt *you* none, surely?'

Mex said: 'Sure, it hurts me as a human being. I've got a Mexican conscience or something and I ask myself: Why can't we put the Christian and Jewish do-gooders in charge of the delinquent no-gooders? Why not give the no-gooders a grand job, which would be to load those idle boats – or marginal tonnage, as the Prof calls them – with surplus food and clothing and city waste, and make *men* of the no-gooders and send them sailing over the wide ocean with gifts for the poor starving devils abroad?

Sure, then everyone would feel good? What's amiss with that for a solution?'

'No, mac,' said the barman. 'It just wouldn't work. The Longshoreman's union and the Seafarer's union and the Teamster's union would raise hell. And you've got to respect big business. Big business wouldn't stand for any of that, even to save the world from communism – no more than the unions wouldn't. Free gifts destroy markets, don't you see?'

'But there's no market there, anyway. Those poor devils have no cash, so they have to starve. Only pump them up and they'll start producing again and have money to throw around.'

'And put us Americans out of jobs by undercutting prices?' sneered the barman. 'No, mac, it just wouldn't work. Forget it! What do you think, Professor?'

'I'm with you,' I said. 'Nothing sensible and simple ever works: because nobody *thinks* sensibly or simply. In the end, of course, something snaps and then you have a recession or a war, which changes the problem.'

Mex grinned: 'Then, Prof, why can't you university guys teach our Government and big business how to *think* that way?'

That was easy to answer. 'Because the university guys here, and everywhere else, depend for their easy life on money grants from the Government and big business. So they teach students not to think out of the ordinary rut. Any teacher who gets out of step has to think stupid or be fired.'

'You, too, Prof?'

I changed the subject. 'What's your job these days, Mex?'

'Selling encyclopedias. But I don't wear this hat on duty.'

'Good encyclopedias?'

'I wouldn't call them good, Prof. Every time I look up a subject I know something about – haven't we all our own little private pools of knowledge? – by God, it's always wrong. Like news reports about suicides in your own street: all slanted.'

'How do you account for that, Mex?'

'I guess the editors don't pay the writers enough.'

'Might be. I don't know about the States, but nowadays in England the editors expect learned men to feel honoured by contributing, and offer them around five dollars a thousand words. That was all right fifty years ago, but now learned men are too busy teaching or researching or advising the government to accept the honour. So the editors hire hacks for the job, and the encyclopedias go downhill, and the honour is every year less of an honour.'

'Why don't they raise their fees?'

'That would make the encyclopedia too expensive.'

'Too bad,' said the barman frowning.

'Well,' I said grimly, ordering three whiskey sours – the third one for an old Negro with a flattened nose and cauliflower ears, an ex-fighter who had joined us. 'Speaking out, it's quite simple, really. There's thousands of clever, industrious graduate students at hundreds of universities, all in need of doctorates in history or philosophy or literature or medicine or something – to give them a higher academic grade and raise their income level. Grant me them for the sake of my argument.'

'Granted, Prof. What's your problem?'

'Well, they have to choose theses for their doctorates and usually publish them. Offbeat theses: "Outbreaks of Thrush in Kansas State During the Late 19th Century"; "Walt Whitman's Use of the Past Indefinite Tense"; "Flaws in the Maternal Genealogy of Christian Seltzer". Or more complicated still: "Outbreaks of Indefinite Thrush in Walt Seltzer's Kansas Genealogy". Granted?'

'Granted, Prof, for the sake of your argument,' said Mex. 'My poor nephew Terence did one last year on that very subject – in law school.'

'And he got no pay for his job, now, did he, Mex?'

'Not a cent. And nobody alive or out of the funny farm wanted to read it afterward.'

'Exactly. And he'd worked like hell getting his facts together?'

'He sure had.'

'Well, now. About those encyclopedias getting their stuff wrong. You've already granted me that –'

'All right, Prof,' said the barman. 'What the hell? It don't hurt *you* none, surely? You can go back to the college library and get all the information from the real books.'

'Sure, but others can't. Why not collect the supervisors of these doctorates and make them draw lots for encyclopedia subjects – each college to get its fair share. Make the candidates mug up their facts and, if they do the job well, give them their doctorates *and* the honour of contributing to the *Intercollegiate Encyclopedia*, and everyone is happy.'

'No, Prof, it just wouldn't work,' said the barman. 'I'm not saying a word against Senator Benton's encyclopedia. It's said to be unique and marvellous – and for all I know he pays his contributors a dollar a word. But how could the universities compete with a man that big? Or with any other publishers of dictionaries and encyclopedias? There'd be a great howl against blackleg labour and robbing graduates of their copyrights. And Mex here would be out of a job. That *Intercollegiate Encyclopedia* wouldn't need to be bummed around from door to door. You'd find it on sale everywhere at a quarter the price – the doctorate guys would pay for the printing, same as for their theses.'

A pause.

'To get back to those delinquents,' said the barman doggedly. 'Even if the unions and big business allowed the do-gooders to load up those ships and dump free food among starving aliens, suppose the no-gooders refused to play – suppose they preferred to stick around and be violent?'

The old ex-fighter came to life. 'Speaking out,' he said, 'it's quite simple, really. Just *let* 'em be violent. If they have a yen for switchblade knives and loaded stockings and James Bond steel-toed shoes, just *let* 'em! In public, with a big crowd to watch. They'd not chicken out, those boys wouldn't, grant me that!'

We nodded, for the sake of the argument.

'No threat to business. You could make a crazy big gladiatorial show of it, like in the movies about ancient Rome. Stage a twice-weekly gang fight; sell the TV rights for millions. Those kids would soon become high society. And, man, that show would be better to watch than any ball game. Or any fist fight – where the damage don't show so much, but goes deeper. Grant me that!'

We granted it.

'And once you give the gladiators a good social rating, they themselves is going to clean up all the no-good amateur gang warfare, because that's just delinquency – gives their profession a bad name. OK, so the football and baseball and boxing interests might squeal? But they'd come over in the end. Blood sports are the best draw.'

'And the Churches?' I asked.

'The preachers'd have something to preach against. Maybe they'd win another martyr like who was it, long ago, rushed out into the arena and held out his arms and got clobbered. Anyhow, nowadays preachers can't even stop wars, if big business needs a hot or cold war to jack up economy.'

The barman said: 'No, fella, it just wouldn't work. There's Federal laws against duelling, and your gladiators might lobby like hell, but they would never get them repealed – not with the whole Middle West solid against bloodshed. You can't even stage a Spanish bullfight around here.'

Mex said: 'Guess not, as yet. But it's bound to come, someday. Like the licensed sale of pornography, and a lot of other things. Because of the shorter week, and what to do with your leisure time. TV isn't the answer, nor window-shopping isn't, nor raising bigger families for the population explosion. Nor a hot war, neither, even if it sends the no-gooders and the do-gooders into the Armed Forces and cuts down waste and sends up the value of marginal tonnage.'

'Speaking freely,' I said, 'it's quite simple, really. Another round of whiskey sours and we'll soon make it work.'

Miss Briton's Lady-Companion

NOT EVERY MAN remembers his mother with deep affection. A good many have had little cause to do so. Yet of this unfortunate minority some take one road, some another. Weaklings blame their moral lapses or their ill success in life on neglectful, selfish or tyrannical mothers. Others, the noble hearted, learn to bear them no rancour, to stand on their own feet and find love elsewhere. I remember being puzzled as a child by a verse in *Hymns Ancient and Modern.*

> Can a woman's tender care
> Cease towards the child she bare?
> Yea, she may forgetful be –
> Yet will I remember Thee.

The idea that any mother could possibly behave unkindly to her own child surprised me – I was one of the luckier ones.

My respect for Winston Churchill, whom I first met in 1915 and with whom I exchanged occasional letters until the 'Forties, rose enormously after his death. I then read for the first time of the almost brutal contempt shown him, as a mentally retarded boy with a cleft palate, by his beautiful Jerome mother. And the *Encyclopaedia* supplied the reason both for his physical abnormality and for her unmaternal attitude. His father, Lord Randolph Churchill, had died from general paralysis of the insane. Every doctor now knows what disease causes this fearful condition, and what effect it often has on the patient's children; one can feel only the utmost sympathy with an innocent wife and mother who suffered so much. And although Winston had many faults and, when younger, often acted with great irresponsibility, who can fail to admire the strength of his resolve never to brood revengefully, always to champion the deprived and oppressed? It was not, indeed, until his middle thirties that a chance medical discovery cleared his blood of the inherited taint, and set him at last on an even keel.

One can never tell. Who has not seen splendid talented children born from base soulless stock, and splendid parents cursed with worthless and evil children? Psychologists are baffled by the paradox. In the case of evil children, they usually accuse the mothers either of weaning them too early, or of weaning them too late, or of bottle-feeding them, or of beating them for their faults, or of not beating them at all. Or even of pre-natal misconduct. But it is never quite so simple. Heredity, which is as powerful a factor as environment, has become far too complex a subject for even a gifted psychologist to lay down the law about. I prefer to think that a child is born either with or without nobility of heart; and that although a mother may either foster or discourage this gift, she cannot be held responsible for its absence. And that goes for fathers as well. I write as a father of eight wholly dissimilar children. And as the eighth of a family of ten, also wholly dissimilar. But I give my mother full marks for nobility of heart and although, being extremely puritanical, she often disapproved deeply of my actions, I never resented her attitude in the least – nor, for that matter, felt that I deserved it.

This is her story. In 1848, a year of revolution throughout Europe, which sent independent-minded citizens, especially Germans, flocking for refuge to the United States, my grandfather, a Bavarian medical student, was expelled from his Prussian university for protesting against the trial for high treason of a young Jewish socialist named Karl Marx who had married into the Prussian aristocracy. My grandfather thereupon left Germany and travelled all around the Mediterranean. According to my mother, he bathed on one occasion in the Dead Sea where the salty slime on his skin so disgusted him that he mounted his horse and rode fifty miles north to the Jordan valley where he washed himself clean. In Spain he was one of the first passengers in the newly-constructed railway from Madrid to Toledo; it had caused great resentment among the muleteers. Finding their livelihood threatened they would lay tree trunks across the track by night and having forced the train to stop, would rob and terrorize the passengers.

My grandfather was seated in a compartment opposite an English colonel come to visit the battlefields of the Peninsular War, throughout which he had fought as a young subaltern. Suddenly the train stopped with a bump, shots rang out, followed by curses, screams, prayers and a general hullabaloo. The colonel slowly laid down his copy of *The Times*, reached for his pistol, primed and cocked it and then returned impassively to his reading. My grandfather, much impressed, thought: 'What a wonderful race! I must go to England and complete my medical education there.'

This he did, I believe at St Thomas's Hospital, and presently volunteered as a surgeon for the Crimean War, where he worked for some months with Florence Nightingale in a nightmare hospital at Scutari.

Just before sailing he had married a Danish girl, the orphan daughter of Tiarks, the Greenwich astronomer, but my mother, his first child, was not born until the war had ended. They returned together to Germany, where he presently became Professor of Medicine at Munich University and, so far as I know, the first doctor in Europe to supply his hospital with tubercle-free milk; which he did by buying a farm and personally testing his herd of sixty cows. He had learned about infected food and drink at Scutari.

My mother, born in London at the house of a Miss Briton, my grandmother's guardian, was soon the most responsible member of a huge family of boys and girls, and appointed by her father to keep them clean and in good order – which the scared, gentle little Dane, her mother, was incapable of doing. She took the job seriously and soon earned the nickname of 'Scrubbing-brush'. My uncles and aunts all turned out good citizens but, though later expressing their gratitude to her, were not altogether sorry when she was suddenly whisked off to London. That was the year 1873.

The reason given was that Miss Briton, now decrepit and lonely, needed a cheerful lady-companion; but in effect my mother had been banished from Munich for her own good. The then Bavarian Prime Minister – or so I later heard from an aunt – had fallen in love with her at a ball. Though rich, handsome, noble, virtuous and popular, he had two great disadvantages: he was far too old for her, and he was a Roman Catholic. My impression is that her heart responded, but that the match could not possibly be accepted by so Protestant a family as hers. Marriage would mean Catholic grandchildren, which in turn would mean that the religious unity of the family would be broken. The Prime Minister could not very well pursue her to London; nor would Miss Briton have admitted him across her threshold had he done so.

Here the story grows rather grim. My mother knew where her duty lay and always followed it, by however thorny a path. She felt bound to obey her experienced and powerful father, and at the same time to pay the debt of love that her mother owed Miss Briton. So she became not only lady-companion but cook-housekeeper, secretary and nurse to an old recluse living in a tall, cold, inconvenient late-Georgian house in Kensington. Miss Briton, of whose family I know nothing except that they manufactured lead soldiers, suffered from a delusion of extreme poverty. My mother had to sleep on a straw mattress in an iron bed next door to her, and all other rooms but kitchen, toilet, cellar and living room were kept locked up. She was given so minute a house-keeping allowance that she always had to buy the poorest cuts of meat and the cheapest fruit and vegetables; and to practise the most rigid economy with coal. She learned never to throw away a crust, always to scrub potatoes rather than peel them, to deny herself all finery and never even indulge in scented soap. Nor had she any friends of her own age, if only because she could not offer a fair exchange of hospitality with them. Her one solace was a piano.

Her brothers and sisters in Bavaria grew up, ate well, drank well, made scores of friends, were taken on tours to the picture galleries of Italy, and to Vienna for the Opera, attended the best concerts, married, had children. But she missed everything and spent her evenings playing bezique with Miss Briton, who got so upset when she lost that my mother had to bend her conscience, just a little, by cheating herself and allowing Miss Briton the victory. Apart from reading 'improving' books from a library – I don't think she ever read a novel in her life, except in old age to please my father – and occasionally visiting the museums in the neighbourhood, she had no real life at all. She soon lost all traces of her German accent, though Miss Briton, who had been born in the reign of George III taught her a very old-fashioned form of English; so that she used, I remember, to pronounce 'gas' as 'gahs' and 'soot' as 'sutt'.

If she had been sacrificed in this way at the age of twenty-five or so, when she knew more about the world, she would doubtless have taken a more independent line, asking to be relieved at her post, occasionally at least, by one of her four sisters. She would also have insisted on more help in the house and a higher standard of living. But no friend appeared to fight her battles for her, and at least she was not a nun. So she prayed, suffered, hoped and did her duty cheerfully.

One morning, many years later, in the 1880s, Miss Briton, who liked to be called 'Granny', sighed: 'Dear Amy, I fear that I may have no more money left in the bank after this grievous expense of mending the broken water-pipes. Pray, my dear, set my mind at rest! I do not, as you know, like to trouble you with money matters but today, I beg you, go to my room – here is the key of my writing desk – for I wish you to see what money we have left, if any. It would be a great inconvenience if we had to dismiss the scrubbing-woman.'

Half an hour later, after going through piles of quarterly and annual bank-statements, my mother came down in a daze, saying: 'Granny, only imagine! You are RICH! Read these!'

Yes, she was worth over one hundred thousand pounds, which today would have the purchasing value of perhaps five million dollars.

'This is indeed most welcome news, Amy. If the bank has made no error, we can now retain the scrubbing-woman. And, as you know, you are my sole heiress when I come to die.'

So my mother bought herself another blanket and no longer lived wholly on porridge, parsnips and scrag-end of mutton as heretofore, and a year later Miss Briton died in her sleep. That was the year 1890, when a woman was reckoned a 'wall-flower' at the age of twenty-seven and an 'old maid' by thirty-two. Being now nearly thirty-six, my mother decided to go to India as a medical missionary. She did her training and was on the point of booking a one-way passage by the P & O when –

I should have mentioned that as inheritrix of this huge fortune my mother had decided that she might prove a better missionary if she disburdened herself a little – like the loaded camel in the Gospel parable which could not be led through the Needle's Eye gate at Jerusalem without removal of its panniers. But she was not altogether imprudent. Though dividing her inheritance in five equal parts, one of which she gave to each of her four married sisters, she kept one for an emergency.

The emergency came almost at once. My mother's family, the von Rankes, were already connected with the Anglo-Irish Graves family. Her learned grand-uncle, Leopold von Ranke, since famous as the 'Father of Modern History' because the first historian to insist 'on what had actually happened, rather than what he would have liked to have happened' – as my mother put it to me very clearly – had to the surprise of both nations married the beautiful Clarissa Graves, a Reigning Toast of Dublin. So it was natural enough for my mother to meet Clarissa's nephew, Alfred Perceval Graves, already well known as a song writer. He had written 'Father O'Flynn', 'Trotting to the Fair', 'The Jug of Punch' and many other late Victorian favourites – now too often regarded as folk-songs, though the copyright will remain in our family until the year 1985 – but, being a bad business man, made no money from them. His wife had recently died and he was now a struggling Government Inspector of Schools in the West of England.

I do not know whether her family and his arranged the marriage in contemporary style, but certainly both my mother and my father agreed to its convenience. He was active, sprightly, good-looking and the son of an Irish bishop. She was tall, strong, beautiful, with an unlined face and black hair that did not turn grey for another half-century. And had a great many wifely talents. So she consulted her conscience, which told her that God had protected her against a previous unwise and irreligious marriage, and that the Indians were less deserving than this sad, charming, talented *Protestant* widower – only nine years older than herself – with five high-spirited quarrelsome children in need of a new mother's care. So the wedding took place soon afterwards.

At first, to judge from a diary which has survived, life was astonishing and difficult. Too many things happened, too many people came calling. My mother who did not expect at so advanced an age – she was now thirty-six – to have children, had never in her life shared a double bed with anyone or even, it seems, been taught the facts of life. The five orphans naturally resented her taking the place of their wonderful, joking Irish mother, and her German Scrubbing-brush methods were far from suitable for Irish children, two of them red-haired. Moreover my father, for all his respect and affection for my mother, was still in love with Janey Cooper, his first wife about whom he used to talk in his sleep Which gave my mother nightmare dreams about meeting Janey in Heaven where although there is 'no marrying or giving in marriage' such encounters could not help being awkward for wives unable to forget earthly monogamic principles.

And Janey had always kept him in order by constant playful teasing, which was a technique wholly beyond my mother's knowledge or powers. She had been trained to obey the Head of the House, without question or evasion; which was not the best thing for his character. They never bickered but mainly because, though my father was a hot-tempered man, it takes two to make a quarrel and at worst she looked pained and disappointed.

For awhile she still had nothing of her own, except responsibilities and the small fortune which she now allowed him to draw on for his children's education. She soon won their gratitude by helping them with homework and inviting their friends to stay. And then at the age of thirty-seven she had a child! A girl.

I am sorry to say that my mother did not greatly value daughters, having been one herself. Her view was: 'girl babies are quite useful to practise on' as her mother had told her. Boys were all that really counted in God's eyes – could she hope for another child? She could. But it was another girl – to practise on!

And then the most wonderful possible thing happened to her. She had a boy. Which incidentally was the most wonderful thing that ever happened to me. I unashamedly adore life. Nor was this the end of her triumphs. She seemed to get younger and younger, happier and happier, and bore my father two more sons, the last when she was forty-nine. And no more daughters, since practice had by now made her perfect.

They built a big house near London, where my father was now working, and another in North Wales where he had once taken her for a holiday by the sea. Stumbling on a peculiarly romantic spot near Harlech Castle she told my father: 'Alfred, this is beautiful beyond expression. I should like to die here.'

'Why not live here instead?' he countered impulsively in her own practical language.

So they bought the site and built a big house on it, and when my father retired, sold the London house and went to live there. It was our holiday heaven, with a sandy beach, wild hills, blackberries, raspberries, blueberries, flowers, mushrooms, adventures. For as we grew older, she allowed us more liberty, though continuing as religious as ever and pleading with us to take no risks in rock-climbing. 'I do not like broken children any more than you like broken toys.'

On a picnic one day she began singing a German song, to the effect that the person whom God wishes especially to bless He sends out into the wide, wide world. And afterwards, looking around us in pure joy, she said, 'You can't think how *fortunate* I feel, my darling children... There was a man once, a Frenchman, who died of grief because he could never become a mother.'

We had family prayers every morning, and as a rule went to church twice every Sunday, which was the day when we were forbidden to play cards or other games of chance. I remember persuading her to let us play charades on Sunday evenings provided that the scenes were wholly Biblical. None of us drank or smoked or had friends of the opposite sex until we were grown up. Yet somehow we never felt deprived, which is surprising when I look around me today. She trusted that eventually we should all meet together in God's glorious heaven, long after her own death. As an equally sincere salvationist, I asked her innocently once: 'Mother, when you die, will you leave me any money?' 'Yes, of course, darling.' 'Enough to buy a bicycle?' 'Yes, I hope so, but surely you would prefer having me to having a bicycle?' 'Well, but you'll be having a marvellous time in God's glorious Heaven, and I could ride the bicycle to put flowers on your grave.'

My mother (and this is no criticism of her) did not know how to dress, having been warned as a girl never to indulge female vanity and as a young woman having been unable, under Miss Briton, to experiment in fancy clothes. I only once remember her buying herself a present, and that was when I was about twelve and she showed me an antique shop where I could spend some birthday money on coins for my coin collection. There she found a gold Irish 'Tara' brooch, which she bought 'to please your father'. It was a bargain at only a trifle more than its intrinsic value in metal, and she wore it for the rest of her life almost every day. In those years only royalty, actresses or prostitutes 'made up their faces'; 'rouge' was a dirty word; and my mother actually spoilt her complexion by constant washing with carbolic soap. She also lacked any sense of humour except the simplest and most innocuous kind; but again this is no criticism of her. True humour is based on multiple meanings, and on a recognition that often only a hair's breadth of truth separates complete opposites. To her white was white, black was black and every word, except parables and metaphors, must be taken literally. She did not understand irony, sarcasm, or jokes about other people's misfortunes.

She was, however, a heroine in times of emergency. One day when we asked her whether she had ever ridden in a railway truck, she admitted that, yes, once after a severe railway accident she had helped in the rescue work, had administered first-aid, and taken the injured to hospital in a coal-truck. But our most splendid recollection was when we were very young, in the days before domestic electric light. At supper one evening, the kerosene table-lamp suddenly flared up. The screw that worked the wick had failed and a black pillar of smoke soon clouded the room. My father and elder brothers watched aghast, but my mother rose and said simply to my half-sister Susan: 'Susan, open that door if you please, and then the door into the drawing-room, and then the drawing-room door into the garden. Make haste!' She took up the flaming lamp, protecting her hands with a table napkin, and followed Susan through the hall, through the drawing-room, and into the garden where she set the lamp down on a path. Five seconds later it exploded. Not long afterwards she went to stay with a sister at Zurich, but in fact for a newly-invented throat operation there, with old-fashioned anaesthetics, insufficient analgesics, and only one chance in four of recovery. Yet she did not allow us to guess her anguish when she cheerfully kissed us goodbye. Later we learned that she had sustained herself with the hymn:

> Faint not nor fear; His arms are near,
> He faileth not, and thou art dear.

After that, all went well with her and us until, soon after my nineteenth birthday, the First World War broke out. The news dismayed my mother. She could not at first believe that the Germans could really have invaded Belgium in breach of a sacred treaty. 'My people must have gone mad,' she cried. I had just left school and would have gone on to Oxford University that autumn, but instead volunteered for the Royal Welch Fusiliers, our local regiment. Within a few months I found myself a young officer in trenches that faced Bavarian troops; Were my uncles and cousins among them? This fratricidal situation was so horrible that for a while my mother broke down and lost her faith in God. How could He allow her to suffer so? For which, a year later, her punishment was a letter from my Colonel, after our battalion had lost over two-thirds of its strength at High Wood, to the effect that I had fought very gallantly but had died of wounds, and that the doctor believed me to have suffered very little pain.

So she opened her heart to God with the Biblical: 'The Lord hath given, the Lord hath taken away. Blessed be the name of the Lord.' And the next thing was a letter from my Aunt Susan – Janey's sister, who lived in France and had noticed my name on a list pinned to a hospital ward door; she was visiting her son who had lost a leg in the same battle. I had been left for dead and escaped burial only because everyone was too busy fighting, or looking after the wounded, to spare the time. My mother's faith returned, and after another spell in the trenches, I got pneumonia, was forbidden further active service, married and had a child – 'a daughter to practise on' as she told my wife. Eventually the war ended and all again was well. But my mother's four sisters, with whom she had shared her inheritance, had been ruined by patriotically investing it in German Defence Bonds. So of course she helped them as far as she could, all but one of her own brood being by now more or less independent. And when my father died at eighty-six, she became the most respected woman at Harlech, with nobody to obey except God: meaning her noble conscience.

At the age of eighty-eight she was found to have cancer, but since at that age it is seldom fatal, she continued unperturbed to practise her good works, which were many.

Her death was sad. One of her many descendants – though married at thirty-six, she was already a great-grandmother – got involved in a libel action which threatened crippling damages, and came to her for help. The worry caused a nervous breakdown, the local doctor could not deal with the case, and my once 'practised-on' elder sister, who had become a very good doctor, happened to be holidaying in Austria and got back too late to save her life.

What lessons I learned from my mother can be told in very few words. She taught me to despise fame and riches, not to be deceived by appearances, to tell the truth on all possible occasions – I regret having taken her too literally at times – and to keep my head in time of danger. I have inherited her conscience, her disinterest in sartorial fashions, her joy in making marmalades and jams, and her frugality (I hate throwing away crusts) though it often conflicts with a spendthrift extravagance learned from my father. I have not inherited her dogma, which was the cause of her sadly cutting me from her will when my wife and I separated – but she remembered the children instead, and eventually welcomed my remarriage. One word of wisdom, which she whispered to me when I was seven years old, has always stuck in my mind, and I pass it on to my children and grandchildren – by the way I became a great-grandparent last year.

'Robert,' she said, 'this is a great secret, never forget it! *Work is far more interesting than play.*'

Hence my obsession with work, which is also my play.

After her death I was sent that gold Tara brooch, which arrived in the mail with its pin missing. I took it to a Spanish jeweller to have a new gold pin fitted, but he assured me that a gold one would be unnecessary, since the brooch itself was not gold but pinchbeck. That surprised me. My mother had always worn it for gold, we had always accepted it as gold, and so gold it had remained until her death. It would have distressed her to know that she had not merely been cheated by the dealer but made party to a fraud on the public... Or would she have taken this as an instance of God's just punishment on her for indulging female vanity?

There are, I find, variant traditions in our large family about my mother's life with Miss Briton. Some say that the old lady got justly scared about money when defrauded of £5,000 by a wicked solicitor, but that life with her was by no means so dreary as in my account. There is even talk of musical evenings: my mother, at the piano, delighting a wide circle of friends with her powerful contralto singing. It is said, too, that my mother cancelled her voyage to India not for my father's sake, but because of a peremptory letter from my grandfather at Munich: 'If you take this foolish step, my dear Amalia, we, your loving family, are resolved to forget you.' And that Miss Briton herself, though perhaps at my mother's insistence, divided her inheritance among all five sisters. They even give the house a different address and disregarding the evidence of a photograph dated 1857, which shows her at the age of two, knock a couple of years off her age.

Let them say what they like! She was my mother as well as theirs, and every legend of this sort has many variants.

My First Amorous Adventure

'MY FIRST AMOROUS adventure?' repeated Lord Godolphin thoughtfully. 'Well, in our family the tradition never varied much. There was always Miss Crewe, who had inducted my father and probably also my younger granduncle, Charles Martello, into the mysteries of sex. She had kept her little figure astonishingly well. That was due to her fruit diet, someone told me. In a sense, the tradition was, I agree, somewhat incestuous.'

'Did Miss Crewe attend to many families?'

'Not more than a dozen or so, and all in this county. Families like ours. Miss Crewe despised the lesser landed gentry to which she belonged.'

'May I ask what was her procedure?'

'It was no secret and, as far as I know, never varied. It began with general theory. The next lesson was sexual anatomy. The third was amatory practice. The fourth was deportment, or bed manners. The fifth, sixth and seventh were variety, based – I have since discovered – on Sir Richard Burton's translation of *The Perfumed Garden*, but omitting the chapter on homosexuality.'

'Did you ever meet Miss Crewe afterward?'

'Of course. She was a frequent guest at the castle, exceedingly witty and with perfect manners.'

'Did she educate the girls, too?'

'Heavens, no! In those remote days a girl had to be *virgo intacta* and innocent as a mountain primrose. But I gather that, just before the wedding night, the bride would manage to extract at least the general sexual theory from her favourite and least discreet brother. I don't know – we had only boys in our family. By the way, I have often wondered whether Miss Crewe's name derived from the act, or vice versa?'

'What became of her in the end?'

'She died in harness, so to speak, and – they say – with a saintly smile on her face.'

'Tell me, though, Godolphin: What was the tradition among your tenantry?'

'The tradition of first amorous adventure? I found it a trifle ambiguous.

I mean that the women were, or pretended to be, not quite so *practical* as the men. Take Jock Miller, for example; he was our head cowman and a Scot. One Sunday his wife approached him shyly: "Husband, dinna ye conseeder it high time that oor Duncan should be *instructed?*"

"'What do ye mean by 'instructed', wife?"

"'I mean instructed into God's holy mysteries o' natural reproduction. Hoo bairns are made... Ye maun begin wi' the pollination o' flowers."

"'Och, aye, wife! Mebbe I maun do as ye advise me."

'A week later, she asked him: "Husband, hae ye done as I asked wi' oor Duncan? Or did it slip your memory?"

"'Aye, wife, it did sae. But I'll gae to him the noo wi' the instruction."

'He found Duncan: "Duncan, laddie" he said, "ye mind what we did wi' they twa bonny lassies ahint the kirk wall last Sabbath eve?"

"'Aye, father!"

"'Weel, Duncan, your mither would hae ye ken that that was *preecisely* what the bees do wi' they bonny primroses on the mountain.'"

At this point, everyone in turn began detailing his own first amorous adventure – some comic, some sad, some horrific, few reprintable in a decent family journal. One poor fellow had found himself in bed with an ancient prostitute – brought there, while he was drunk and fast asleep, by witty Cambridge friends – and got a bad dose from her. Another unfortunate, a clergyman's son, had been raped by a little flaxen-haired monster for the bet of a box of chocolates. Another had been lured by nuns into a nunnery, very early one morning, at the back of a famous surfing beach at Sydney: apparently that was common practice.

Then, because I had kept silent and was clearly more than a little embarrassed, they mobbed me: and Lord Godolphin insisted on hearing the very worst.

'Very well, gentlemen,' I said. 'I don't want to be a spoilsport...' And this is what I told them:

'I apologize for being the odd man out, but, as my mother used to say, "Tell the truth and shame the Devil." I was born in July 1895 of what was then called "good family" – meaning a coat of arms and no recent surrounding scandal. As Godolphin will tell you, before World War One, only cads slept with unmarried girls of good family, and divorces in good families were all but unthinkable. When the war broke out and death was soon heavy in the air, such old-established conventions often broke down. Indeed, the phenomenon of "war babies" engendered by lovers just off the trenches – with three-to-one odds against their unmaimed survival – won almost universal sympathy in the not-so-good families.

'One day, when I was a nineteen-year-old lieutenant, at our fusiliers' mess near the ruined village of Laventie in France, our caddish colonel announced that he was ashamed to hear that he still had cock-virgin warts – warts meant lieutenants – under his command. All such had to parade under the assistant adjuntant that evening to be duly deflowered at the red-light establishment at Armentières reserved for officers. I did not admit to my cock-virginity. That was because I held a strong superstition that its loss would prejudice the magical power of survival that had so far taken me through five months of trench warfare – the average life of a wart was six weeks at that time. This parade order had been given shortly before the battle of Loos, where all our four company commanders were killed, with hundreds of other ranks, and the caddish colonel himself got wounded, not to return. I escaped with a slight cut on the hand from a shell splinter and was left to command a much reduced company without even a second lieutenant to help me.

'I remained a resolute C.V. for the next year. In July 1916, at High Wood, I got five wounds from an eight-inch shell, including one through my right lung, half an inch from my heart. I was left bleeding to death but knew I would survive; and did, though officially reported "died of wounds". They patched me up for another return to the trenches in 1917: and, now a captain but still a C.V., I found myself temporarily commanding the battalion, everyone else having been killed or wounded. Then I got bronchitis and pneumonia and was soon reported medically unfit for further service overseas. So I fell in love with an eighteen-year-old girl – of good family and therefore also a virgin – and married her. It would be embarrassing to recall our embarrassment and amorous gropings when we found ourselves naked in bed together at Brown's Hotel on January 23, 1918. But at least we were not persuaded by the warning hoots of sirens and the crash of bombs – during one of the zeppelin raids on London – to take refuge in the hotel cellars.'

Lord Godolphin cast me a baleful glance in the silence that followed. Then he said slowly: 'In *our* family, we considered it bad taste to discuss marital intercourse... Still, my dear fellow, I suppose it was my own fault for insisting.'

Notes

The Shout

'"The Shout" had been written in 1926, but I could not find a publisher until 1929, when it appeared in a signed limited edition as one of *The Woburn Books*. Unfortunately, the publisher insisted that it should be reduced from eight thousand to five thousand words, which was too drastic a condensation, and I have since lost the original version.' – R.G., introduction to *Occupation: Writer*. This 'drastic condensation' would account for Graves's erroneous reference to 'Friday' in the original text, when Richard speaks to the cobbler, and which I have amended to 'Monday'.

The following handwritten comment appears in the proof copy of the original edition in R.G.'s library: '1927. Written at Hammersmith. First draft at Cairo; March 1926.' Thus the 1924 date given in the *Collected Short Stories* is most probably a misprint.

The following text was eliminated from 'The Shout' when it appeared in *Occupation: Writer* (1950). It had previously preceded the present opening lines:

> Leave off now, I pray you, and speak no more for I
> cannot abear to hear such incredible lies.
> > M Apuleius, *The Golden Ass*
> > (tr. W. Adlington)

[This story occurred to me one day while I was walking in the desert near Heliopolis in Egypt and came upon a stony stretch where I stooped to pick up a few misshapen pebbles; what virtue was in them I do not know, but I somehow had the story from them, and three years later found it coming true to me. (True in an undistorted way, of course, with a most important character added, and with the macabre strangeness illuminated.) It is not just literature or an Ufa film-scenario. The asylum cricket-match was played at Littlemore, near Oxford, the sand-hills are those just beyond the Royal St David's Golf Links at Harlech, though with an added Egyptian cruelty. It will be found that Crossley, when he tells the story, admits that he has varied it each time he has told it; thus, in a way, apologising for the distortions of actual event.]

Avocado Pears

'"Avocado Pears" is also a true story. The narrator was T.W. Harries of Balliol College Oxford, who died soon afterwards while on a visit to India.' R.G., ibid.

Old Papa Johnson

'"Old Papa Johnson" is a true story; I omitted it from *Goodbye to All That* partly because it was too long for in incidental anecdote and partly because "Papa Johnson" himself might have objected. "Desolation Island" was South Georgia.' – R.G., introduction to *Occupation: Writer.*

Está en su Casa

'"Está en su Casa", "founded on fact", as the Victorians used to say in the days before writers had to worry about libel actions, records my happy return to Majorca in 1946.' – R.G., ibid.

Bins K to T

'"Bins K to T" is written in self-criticism of my absent-minded habit of pocketing pencils and match-boxes.' – R.G., ibid.

An Appointment for Candlemas

'"An Appointment for Candlemas" brought members of the revived British witch cult to my door in search of information about flying ointments and such like.' R.G., introduction to *Collected Short Stories.*

She Landed Yesterday

'Nor can I claim to have invented the factual details even of "She Landed Yesterday" [...] In fact, a correspondent who read "She Landed Yesterday" reproached me for not mentioning the two French copper coins found in the coffin-doll's pocket.' – R.G., ibid.

Sources

Abbreviations:

C   *¡Catacrok!* London: Cassell & Co. Ltd., 1956

CSS *Collected Short Stories* New York: Doubleday & Co. Inc., 1964; London: Cassell & Co. Ltd., 1965

MO   *Majorca Observed* London: Cassell & Co. Ltd.; New York: Doubleday & Co. Inc., 1965

OW   *Occupation: Writer* New York: Creative Age Press, 1950; London: Cassell & Co. Ltd., 1951

Honey and Flowers: *The Green Chartreuse*, July 1913.

My New-Bug's Exam: *The Green Chartreuse*, July 1913; *Goodbye to All That* (revised edition) London: Cassell & Co. Ltd.; New York: Doubleday & Co. Inc., 1957.

Thames-side Reverie: As 'By a Thames Window', *Evening News*, 26 February 1929; *OW*.

The Shout: *The Shout* London: Elkin Matthews & Marot, 1929; *CSS*.

Avocado Pears: *But It Still Goes On*, London & Toronto: Jonathan Cape, 1930; *OW*.

Old Papa Johnson: *But It Still Goes On*; *CSS*.

Interview With a Dead Man: As part of 'A Journal of Curiosities' in *But It Still Goes On*; *OW*.

Está en su Casa: As 'The Feud of St. Peter and St. Paul' in *Tomorrow*, August 1947; *OW*.

Bins K to T: As 'Dead Man's Bottles' in *OW*; became 'Bins K to T' in first English edition of *OW*.

School Life in Majorca 1955: As 'School Life in Majorca' in *Punch*, 6 January 1954; *MO*.

Bulletin of the College of St Modesto of Bobbio: As 'Bulletin of the College of St Francis of Assisi' *C*; *MO*.

Treacle Tart: *Punch*, 17 February 1954; *CSS*.

Week-End at Cwm Tatws: *Punch*, 31 March 1954; *CSS*.

The Full Length: *Punch*, 31 March 1954; *CSS*.

God Grant Your Honour Many Years: *Punch*, 31 May 1954; *CSS*.

6 Valiant Bulls 6: As 'Six Valiant Bulls' in *Punch*, 23 June 1954; *CSS*.

Flesh-coloured Net Tights: *Punch*, 4 August 1954; *C*.

Thy Servant and God's: *Punch*, 18 August 1954; *MO*.

A Man May Not Marry His…: *New Statesman*, 2 October 1954; *CSS*.

An Appointment for Candlemas: *Punch*, 1 December 1954; *CSS*.

The Five Godfathers: *Punch*, 29 December 1954; *CSS*.

The White Horse or 'The Great Southern Ghost Story': As 'The White Horse' in *Punch*, 12 January 1955; *Five Pens in Hand*, New York: Doubleday & Co. Inc., 1958.

Epics Are Out of Fashion: *Punch*, 16 February 1955; *CSS*.

Earth to Earth: *New Statesman*, 19 February 1955; *CSS*.

They Say… They Say: *Punch*, 20 April 1955; *CSS*.

The Abominable Mr Gunn: *Punch*, 29 June 1955; *CSS*.

The Whitaker Negroes: *Encounter*, 21-29 July 1955; *CSS*.

Trín-trín-trín: *Punch*, 5 October 1955; *MO*.

Cambridge Upstairs: *Punch*, 14 March 1956; *C*.

'Ha, Ha!' Chort-led Nig-ger: *Punch*, 21 March 1956; *C*.

Ditching in a Fishless Sea: *Punch*, 5 September 1956; *MO*.

Period Piece: *C*; *CSS*.

He Went Out to Buy a Rhine: *C*; *CSS*.

Kill Them! Kill Them!: *C*; *CSS*.

Harold Vesey at the Gates of Hell: *C*; *CSS*.

Life of the Poet Gnaeus Robertulus Gravesa: *C*; *Life of the Poet Gnaeus Robertulus Gravesa*, Deià, Mallorca: The New Seizin Press, 1990.

Ever Had a Guinea Worm?: *C*.

A Bicycle in Majorca: *New Yorker*, 22 June 1957; *CSS*.

Evidence of Affluence: *New Yorker*, 12 October 1957; *CSS*.

The French Thing: *5 Pens in Hand*, New York: Doubleday & Co. 1958; *CSS*.

A Toast to Ava Gardner: *New Yorker*, 26 April 1958; *CSS*.

The Viscountess and the Short-haired Girl: *Gentleman's Quarterly*, October 1958; *CSS*.

She Landed Yesterday: *New Yorker*, 7 March 1959; *CSS*.

The Lost Chinese: *Lilliput*, December 1959; as 'The Case of the Difficult Husband' in *Playboy*, January 1960; *CSS*.

You Win, Houdini!: *London Magazine*, February 1960; *CSS*.

The Tenement: As 'An Imperial Tale' in *Holiday*, April 1960; as 'The Apartment House' in the American edition of *CSS*; English edition of *CSS*.

The Myconian: As 'The Gaudy Games' in *Sports Illustrated*, 1 August 1960; *CSS*.

Christmas Truce: As 'Wave No Banners' in the *Saturday Evening Post*, 15 December 1962; *CSS*.

My Best Christmas: *Sunday Telegraph*, 23 December 1962; *The Crane Bag*, London: Cassell & Co. Ltd., 1969.

No, Mac, It Just Wouldn't Work: *Playboy*, January 1967.

Miss Briton's Lady Companion: *Family Circle*, 24 September 1967; *The Crane Bag*, 1969.

My First Amorous Adventure: *Playboy*, January 1972.